THE SUN AT NIGHT

by

Roger Williamson

ISBN 1-57353-113-8

EPB-AW-113
an
ESCHATON BOOK
from

ESCHATON™
PRODUCTIONS, INC.
60 East Chestnut Street, #236
Chicago, IL 60611

Send an S.A.S.E. for our current catalog!

Visit Eschaton on the Web:
http://www.eschatonbooks.com

CONTENTS

AUTHOR'S NOTE iv

DEDICATION v

INTRODUCTION vi

PREFACE vii

PART ONE - THE BUTTERFLY 1

THE MOON AND THE LAKE 1
SAMHAIN 6
SAMHAIN II 8
THE BOOK 10
MORRIGAN 18

PART TWO - THE WEB 25

VIVIAN 25
VIVIAN II 38
ARGOS 41
ARGOS II 48
ARGOS III 59
CROSSING THE RUBICON 61
INITIATION 68

PART THREE - THE KILL 75

RHIANNON 75
RHIANNON II 82
BELTAINE 84

EPILOGUE 87

AUTHOR'S NOTE

The Sun at Night was written within the coils of an induced atmosphere partly created by the following musical collections:

1. Celtic Symphony	Alan Stivell
2. Renaissance of the Celtic Harp	Alan Stivell
3. Gone to Earth	David Sylvian
4. Underwater Sunlight	Tangerine Dream
6. Quiet Life	Japan
7. Sacred Cities	Gary Hughes
8. Ancient Dreams	Patrick O'Hearn

It is recommended that the aforementioned sounds be used to invoke the spirit of the document's creation to derive full enjoyment.

DEDICATION

TO ALL THOSE WHO EACH DAY RISE
AND DO BATTLE WITH THE DRAGON.

Special thanks to:

Joan Utter, without whose efforts and patience this work would have remained a dream.

Andy and Karla, for their printer, paper and friendship across two continents.

And especially to Suzanne for being Suzanne.

Also to a multitude of others who would rather remain anonymous because of the manuscript's content.

INTRODUCTION

Beware of not being god, for the opposite of God spells dog.

PREFACE

The concept that Lucifer was thrown out of heaven by God is absolutely ridiculous to any intelligent thinking man when you consider that God loved and trusted Lucifer above all other Angels. He didn't throw his beloved Lucifer out of Heaven, he sent him on a mission that he knew only Lucifer could accomplish.

He sent Lucifer into matter to purify it.

Christianity, not wanting Man to rise in knowledge and become wise, individual, and free, has bastardized God's message for its own ends. It doesn't want to save Man, it wants to imprison and control him. It has, in fact, created Satan out of God's messenger. As it is said, one usually judges others by one's own standards.

Christianity is the true agent of ignorance. It represents the unpurified matter, inertia, which God sent his most beloved Lucifer to purge. In other words, Christianity is the base element of alchemy: Eve, Guinevere, and the mother of Christ. Christ is an image of the enlightened adept, the son of Lucifer. It was God's agent who impregnated the base matter.

But surely Lucifer was driven out of heaven before the start of Christianity, you may respond. True, but the Christian fathers were the descendants of those pagans who sought power through ignorance. They took old beliefs and bent them to their own ends, then they calculatingly destroyed the old religions in the hope that truth would be lost.

There is nothing acutely wrong with the fabric and props of Christianity because it is intrinsically pagan; observe the dates of its festivals. What Christians fear is knowledge and truth, the primary attributes of Lucifer. He gives us the ability to search and confront our true selves so that we can work to become closer to God and perfection.

Lucifer is on a mission from God, an agent of God, alive within the hearts of all men and awaiting discovery.

He is the hero figure and this figure is always perceived by the established order as entering the social circle by apparent violence; each new generation revolts against the established order. That is why Christianity lives in fear of the hero, he is the figure the old beliefs sought to destroy. The hero fights what is corrupt.

Remember in the Arthurian legend? How the hero Lancelot is discredited for manifesting Guinevere's true self? She was in reality the base matter, like Eve, from a similar book of legends called the Bible. He tore away the shroud and showed her for what she was, he demolished the pedestal of lies, Lancelot was the Lightbringer, Lucifer.

But remember, at the time of the Last Battle he returns and wins the day. They forgot to twist that, a grave error, for this Last Battle is a representation of Armageddon.

Cain is yet another example. Didn't he have to kill Abel, the conditioned man, the old order?

Abel was here the base matter, Cain was the hero, one in whom the energy of Lucifer had manifested.

The seven punishments put upon Cain were in fact the knowledge of the seven planets, each one representing an inner process of man. His punishment, if one can call it that, was the knowledge that he was not perfect until he had understood and harmonized these seven energies. The sign upon his brow, the five-pointed star point uppermost, the symbol of human intelligence, the faculty required to achieve this process.

The descendants of Cain live and work within the structure of society, ensuring that they do not make themselves conspicuous, either by dress or life-style, from the people that they live among. Through the course of centuries they have endeavored to change humanity's outlook by the power of example. They are the gardeners!

Always Lucifer is the drive forward of evolution. All who thwart this drive are an abomination and perversion. Lucifer will always be the rebel to each new generation until the time man reaches perfection. It is the task of the elect, those who are one with Lucifer and the descendants of Cain, to purge this black dragon and by degree raise it up through sublimation.

PART ONE - THE BUTTERFLY

On the bank of the river he saw a tall tree: from roots to crown one half was a flame and the other green with leaves.

'Peredur': The Mabinogion

THE MOON AND THE LAKE

The moon: the twilight of the place, that which encourages reflection.

The lake: a magic-mirror. In gazing into the mirror, one experiences the past, sees oneself as one truly is. If one faces one's self in truth, the future becomes a matter of consequence. Therefore, one knows the future.

....

It's over, and what has been gained? The knowledge that the fate of the meek is to inherit the earth? Well, they are bloody welcome to it! It's all they deserve.

For me the world is just a passive material, a clay. I am the creative fire that will mold it into whatever I choose. For days I have walked the earth, removed, alone, back to where I began. No, that's not entirely true. I have the experience, the education.

When did it all begin?

In retrospect, it is so hard to tell. Memories come and go and pin-pointing events is like trying to nail water to a wall. The more I delve into the lake of the past, the more the mist thickens and clouds the surface.

My mother appears to me now, mysterious and elusive like the orient. Strange in that she was the only child of her family to be born in England, her two sisters the ones born in the East. The only time I heard her boast was when she spoke of being "born in Albion". I try to focus on her image but it's like walking into a room filled with unknown people; you detect a perfume you are sure that you have encountered before, but the memory eludes you. It's as though one had tossed a stone into a silent lake beneath the dim glow of a spectral moon. In the silence one is left perplexed as to what leviathan may have been awakened in the dark murky depths beneath that deceptively placid surface. What denizen of the past may be summoned to the fore by the power of recall?

She it was who would relate strange stories: the enchantment of "the green eye of the little yellow god," the romance of the "willow pattern," and the times of the "Morning Star."

Oh yes, the magical order of the Morning Star whose members used the colors of the spectrum and the symbols of geometry to walk the rainbow bridge to communicate with the gods. Individuals who, although of this world, were also part of another. And it was from this other that they gained the powers which filled my mother's tales. Color and shapes that were the manifestations of gods upon the earth . . . manipulated by the descendants of Merlin who were the magicians of the Morning Star.

These stories continue to haunt me down the corridors of time from the dim vaults of the past. In dreams, images created will descend as doves of fire upon the humble sleeping herdsmen of my reason, attempting to smash their guardianship with the lightening of imagination.

My father was also a story teller, but far more mundane. His tales were set around what the family cat was doing in his nocturnal pursuits and were probably more fanciful than my mother's, he never mentioned that Old Billy was probably out fucking every lady pussy in the area. Instead, according to my father he was having daring adventures of the boys' comic book variety.

He was a very conservative man, a true product of his time. Correct and proud, a true blue.

The extreme of these two characters was truly the foundation of my being, not just physically but psychologically. My mother would become the image of my inner self, my father the icon of how one was expected to present one's self to the outer world. He the walls and armies of the city, she the inner and beautiful garden to be tended and protected with loving care.

Yes, it is difficult to remember.

I fire flaming arrows into an abyss of night, a sacrament to the memories that have died at the hands of time. Time, the false ally which would convince us that truth is a horror to be sidestepped . . . out of sight out of mind. Confrontation, though painful, is learning and with it comes growth. Fear, on the other hand, is a disease and therefore corrosive.

I am an archaeologist attempting to piece together an urn, each memory a broken fragment. I try to fill the gaps, re-construct my past.

Will the final recreation of this urn be the container of my funeral ashes? But then all things find completion in death. Will it find completion at the point of my demise?

I don't know if I was ever close to my parents. In retrospect, I see myself as a baby cuckoo that grew in the protected environment of its surrogate parents.

I was always fanciful, living adventures, anxiously willing adventure, looking and anticipating adventure that never came. Only later would I realize that the adventure was in fact my life.

But back then I would invent my own adventures; steal mother's jewelry, bury it, and make a map composed of clues and signs. The true meaning was occulted by symbols. This map I also buried, but far more elaborately. In a dark recess of the cool pantry I found an aged wine bottle with a faded mold- spotted label, which peeled at the corners. I thought it antique but in reality it was probably only a couple of years old. Then, carefully rolling up my document, I squeezed it into the narrow neck.

That evening after dark, under the pretense of going to a friend's house, I made a clandestine visit with my bottle and map, the latter which waited like a genie for release, to a local graveyard. Here it was that the dead were reborn as worms.

I had previously noticed amongst a group of yew trees a shaded stone sepulchre well away from inquisitive observation. Whoever the occupant was, he had obviously been long forgotten, for weeds grew in great profusion all around the dull grey granite sides.

The tomb was approximately ten feet long, four feet wide, and four feet tall. Across the top lay a slab of dressed stone with eroded script which once gave details of the deceased and those he'd left behind.

I discovered, on closer scrutiny that one corner of this topping stone had been broken off. Unfortunately, not enough for me to squeeze in the bottle, and there would be no easy way to slide the stone to one side.

At this point, probably triggered by the hooting of a passing owl, I began to feel uneasy. Previously I had been too occupied with my endeavors to think about the denizens of the night. Now, as I looked around, each shadow became a lurking beast and the wind through the trees the maidens of the Valkyrie. Wherever my back was turned, I felt that there was some obscene creature moving in upon me and taking advantage of my blind side.

The urge to run was overwhelming. Under this suffocating blanket of night, my skin prickled with impending doom and I stared wide-eyed at nothing.

I shook myself with the intent to invoke a rational state of mind to combat my rising panic. I was an adventurer and adventurers don't panic. This did the trick, for I placed the bottle on the grass, and with much effort, applied myself to the task of sliding the slab to one side.

The sound of its scraping in this secluded spot seemed to split the night asunder. Surely somebody must have heard. I waited silently for approaching footsteps upon the gravel path in answer to the scraping of the stone, but none came.

Expectantly, I peered into the yawning orifice. Alas, all that was visible in the soft moonlight was a mass of loam and a few aged dried leaves. I had expected the remains of a skeleton; to be confronted by its grinning lipless skull. Well, it was too late for a change of plan. I picked up the bottle and thrust it into the loam, ensuring it was well covered. Then, moving to the other side of the stone enclosure, I pushed the stone slab into its original situation.

Nobody ever found the map as far as I'm aware, but my father did find the jewelry while digging the garden one serene summer's afternoon. My adventure on this occasion was to spend the remainder of that dream-shattered day cleaning up this desecrated treasure trove which I thought, until that moment, would be discovered in centuries to come.

My dreams smashed, I came down to earth and spent the next few weeks occupied in gathering rather than storing . . . I went on shoplifting expeditions.

These excursions into the criminal domain were most exciting. It wasn't that I wanted what I stole, on most occasions I dumped the booty, it was the thrill! The adventure! The challenge!

I would spend hours planning my moves and tactics. Hours, that spent on other subjects, would have been intolerable and impatiently suffered. In contrast, the time spent devising the maneuvers of my dark deeds were electrifying and stimulating; a ray of brightness in an otherwise dark world. The world of the so called real.

These visits into "Hades," however, were brought to a sudden and quite unexpected end. I had noticed that a certain department store used bags without their name on them, a plain brown paper bag. Well, here was a gift indeed. What knowledge.

For several hours one morning I foraged through the house turning it over from top to bottom for plain brown paper bags. These accumulated I set off on my quest.

With the tools of my trade stuffed up the front of my shirt, I must have cut a weird sight. I made straight for the counter of my choice and hovered, waiting for the assistant to be occupied with one of the many customers clamoring for attention. The seconds passed so slowly that it seemed to take forever. While the crowds pressed ever more suffocatingly around me, the masses of people gave me more confidence. Perhaps because I felt insignificant in the presence of all these adults, there seemed less chance of detection. Inside of myself I experienced a great energy building, a fire of daring, a rolling of dice.

Finally, the back was turned towards me. Like an illusionist pulling rabbits from a hat, I withdrew the keys of my brilliant scheme.

While in the midst of discreetly filling my bag, there came a tap from behind upon my shoulder. "I'd put that back if I were you." The voice was resonant and quietly confident, possessing that indefinable quality of authority. I shot a glance backward and was confronted by a grey haired man wearing a dark charcoal overcoat.

It was difficult to put an age to the face for the youthful expression of the features was corroded by a crosshatching of wrinkles around the eyes. It was these eyes which were the most striking feature. They were the sharp blue of steel and maintained that steady penetration which only comes with the experience of life.

The energy which had been building within me suddenly erupted as blind panic. I dropped everything and raced from the store, pushing between the throngs of bodies, all of whom represented hounds in anxious pursuit of the fox.

All I wanted then was the security of my home, to be in the bosom of my family and the smiling clean world that was my mother and father.

I raced home taking a round-about route, constantly looking behind me. Having exercised my right of free will, I now feared I would have to face the consequences.

All evening I attempted to put from my mind my earlier episode. All the while waiting for that fateful knock at the door which would destroy the image of innocence with which I was beheld by my parents' eyes.

Where do I find the root of the blood which flows in my veins: in a family I know nothing about, in imagining beings from beyond the veneer of our atmosphere, from the sun whose energy is the foundation of our world? Is that the path to travel to be in search of "RA," the seed of all we are?

In searching for one's root, one has come to the root of all. At least to the root of what we know. Is this also the root of what we don't know? A fulcrum at the point of balance between two extremes?

But I digress from those early years and the search for the source of where the magic began. Like Lakme in the secret garden, I must quest for the spring of the mystical stream. There are minds which would consider these early pursuits trivial and a waste of time, but one can draw knowledge and experience from all one does or does not do.

I must admit though I did fritter away much valuable time in that I didn't direct my vivid imagination.

SAMHAIN

The end of summer. The Celtic Lord of the dead.

....

Was I upset at my mother's death?

No. Yes, I pretended to be, I felt it was expected, but I don't remember feeling any remorse.

Did I detect freedom?

England, oh Albion. Home of the druid stone and the relentless pounding of the sea; of roots and berries and things alive in the cold moist earth; of fog knotted tight on country lanes; the sound of a thrush warbling the "all clear" at the ending of a rain shower; the intimacy of moss-covered dry stone walls, which checker-board this pagan isle, the diamond-studded web of the common garden arachnid, a gift to the astute eye, a realm of ruins, of vanished kingdoms, long overgrown beneath twisted tendrils of vine and time passages.

The subtle forces are so close here that with fingers of fire they can reach out to touch, drawing the unsuspecting into the web and fibre of their world. Like the heroes of the old ballads, "Tam-Linn" and "Childe Roland", we are easily devoured by the energies of celtic thunder.

Ancient standing stones suddenly loom out of the mist like colossal giants, tense with the magnitude of their power. Are they portals which lead to the old ones, or are they the remains of once hostile armies turned to stone by Merlin's magick (magick, the medieval spelling) in his search for peace in a violent time?

The act of placing a hand upon these monoliths gives license to the powers within, a claim upon the energies of your imagination. Once touched you are lost forever in the reverie of expectancy, locked into the celtic twilight.

This was my world, the realm of my mother's stories. It was in the discovery of forgotten stone, deep within the far dark reaches of elder forests that I experienced harmony. What ceremonies must have taken place in these sanctuaries of the old gods!

Simple stained stones became the blood-soaked altars of Gwyn, the almighty one, to the innocence of my virgin imagination. They represented the image of my escaping.

Within these far reaches of forest, where no foot but nature's had trodden before me, the sky became a vaulted emerald green, and the sun a myriad of flashing stars invoking kaleidoscopic images. The spirits of the air supported the vision with a canticle of nature's symphony as they passed through the foliage in the guise of subtle breezes. The whole of nature was a cathedral where man and the gods became one. Here I was at peace, a disciple of Pan. All my pursuits and imaginings were a sacrament and ritual to the god of life.

While in these environs, I would desire to tear off my clothes and run naked and painted through the moist dew-spangled forest until, with my energy completely exhausted, I would collapse and hope to die; being at last, complete in death.

I was aware these were not the proper workings of a young lad's mind. My dream world therefore, was a double-edged sword. On the one hand, it evoked ecstasy, on the other, knowing that these were not accepted thoughts, it gouged deep and poisoned my system with guilt. I was chained with darkness in the dungeons of despair. I felt myself to be some kind of freak.

My mother gone, I was alone. There was no refuge. The world was now a hostile place, a void. I stood as an alien, marooned on a hostile planet far from home.

I have previously stated that I wasn't upset by my mother's death, and this was true. However, whether this was because I didn't know what death was or because of the gap I felt between us due to my parents love for each other, I can't answer, but I very soon missed her.

The world I now entered was a dark region. I was a school boy in hell. Long periods would be spent away from home with my grandmother, the "wing clipper". I was a victim to the talons of aged ignorance. Like a dried fruit hanging from a dead tree of Victoriana, she would hold court surrounded by the dumb obedience of her family. She devoured all self- expression and scoffed at individuality, ridiculing imagination with a tongue manipulated by a dull mind, the badge of her generation and class.

I'm sure she must have hated my mother and probably never forgave my father for marrying such a dream-weaver. I, being the result of this union, was therefore a constant reminder to her of how her son had been stolen by a Circe.

I would stand in the late evening watching my father's car as he drove away, abandoning me to the pit. Forever after, evenings would be a time of foreboding and dread.

She was a shadow figure, a black widow lurking with intent at the center of her web. I secretly hated my grandmother but was tormented by the thought that I was evil because of it. What I hadn't realized, was that everybody else felt the same. Unfortunately, this awareness of the true nature of the situation wasn't to manifest itself until years later.

There was one friend, however, during this period, a huge elm tree in the rear garden of the family home. In times of crisis I would seek sanctuary perched in the highest branches I could reach. Here it was that my solitude was breached by my conversations with the whispers of the wind, translated by the creaking of gnarled bow and veined leaf through the fragile senses of the infant. The feel of the bark was reassuring to the touch, positive and permanent. In the highest-most regions I was free, held in the protecting bosom of this giant. From the topmost arms which reached up in adoration to the sky, I could survey what I thought at the time was the whole world.

This tree was a true friend. No matter how I abused the bark with the thoughtlessness of clambering foot, or penetrating nail for supporting dream-castles in the sky, no matter what the pain, I was always offered refuge.

On reflection however, maybe it wasn't the tree itself which offered reassurance; maybe the tree was but the messenger of the gods. My climbing of the tree perhaps was an urge on my part to return to my father Myrddin the sky god.

SAMHAIN II

CATAPULT MY WILL TO MY STAR
RIP IT FROM THE SKY, HANG IT IN MY HEART,
NOW I SEE MORE BEYOND,
ENDLESS STARS, ENDLESS BEYOND.

....

Was it the glamor, the fire of ego, or was it the notion that I'd be more attractive to the opposite sex if I was to play Rock and Roll in a band? I knew it was of paramount importance to me that I lose my virginity and as soon as possible.

My generation focused all its attention on the emerging voices of the new religion: Rock and Roll. We were acolytes and paid homage by emulation. We made sacrifice to its continuance by purchasing the black vinyl ambrosia and the assorted trinkets which issued from the volcanic eruption of this new dawn.

I had, until this point, found it extremely difficult to speak with girls. It wasn't that girls didn't want to be with me, they did. Unfortunately, they weren't the ones that I necessarily wanted to be with. As for those I did aspire to, I had no clue as to how to make my opening move. What I lacked was the ability of choice, I was not free. I was devoid of an identity. Whatever individuality I had possessed had been trampled like a delicate flower under a harsh boot of insensitivity. I was a victim of the old order, of my father and aged relatives who believed that the only correct course to follow in life was in their footsteps. I was different and it was only a matter of time before I was to throw myself to safety from the path of the onrushing wheels of the family death chariot.

My school work was abysmal and every day spent within the institution's environs was a torment. But it was during my last days there that the rebel of my soul was born.

It was a religious studies class, the last lesson of the day, and in bored obedience I listened to the droning tones of the master who appeared equally bored in his relating of the Cain and Abel story. His interpretation was the generally accepted version that Cain was the usurper, the deceiver, and, generally, the bad guy. It was during the unfolding of this tale, however, that a different interpretation manifested itself through the weave and fibre of its meanderings.

Abel and the father represented to me the continuance of the old order. Cain, on the other hand, represented one of the elect, the hero in a myth. He was the energy of the evolutionary cycle, a symbol of those who took society forward. It was the old tale of Zeus deceiving his father; Cronus, bringing on the era of the Olympians at the expense of the Titans. It struck me that the story had been bastardized and misinterpreted to protect those in power, because any move forward necessitates the destruction of what is. The ancients, who we now find so convenient to consider primitive, were far closer to nature and the flow of life. I'm sure the story, when first created, was a simple observation of the rhythm of life. Only later, when certain factions had something to lose, did it become occluded by sentimentality, to withhold and cloud the truth.

Here was the answer. In playing the devil's music, I would be as Cain. I would be destroying the old values of my family and also opening the door to the garden of feminine pursuits.

It did take a couple of years for the key to loosen the lock which would give privy to the fruit of this exotic garden, and launch me into a voyage of romance and discovery. Of course, this was not the key to the problem, just a way around it. The answer was within myself if only I'd cared to look for it. I was really no more in control than before; it was just that I would now have more choice. The problem still remained, at best a little eroded by discovered confidence. Time would show, however, that this so-called confidence had little or no foundation, and that the slightest challenge would open up a hole for it to plummet into.

For the next fifteen or so years I rode a roller coaster of drink, drugs, and self-indulgence. There was nothing which I didn't expect to pay obeisance to my dream. I was Orpheus in the underworld, an underworld of my own making. The flower that I sought so desperately I trampled on every day. I went along unaware of its presence in the dim light which surrounded me, a light produced by the blaze of my own ego.

At thirty, Nemesis struck, the balance having reached an extreme, lurched in recoil. Lamed, Maat the goddess of the scale manifested. For thirty years, I'd subconsciously evoked her appearance, and now, in her dark mode she drew me into the jaws of the devourer. Blindfolded and bound, the seeker enters the realm of darkness; the setting sun in the coils of the dragon.

THE BOOK

The fire of heaven is imagination, that faculty which created the universe.

Uncontrolled, it is a raging demon.

Harnessed, it bestows the crown of the "godman".

....

It was a sunny spring day, a beautiful time to amble the labyrinth of London's Charing Cross Road.

In serpentine coils with scales of brick, these streets and alleys become the Dragon of London. The pedestrians enmeshed within these coils have no perception of the beast, but when separated and distanced, well, then the form of the being becomes apparent to the observer. One has to be removed from a situation to be objective, sad but true.

In this maze of twisting topsy-turvy streets lies a court which links St. Martin's Lane with the Charing Cross Road. On entering one immediately leaves the thunder of traffic and people behind. A quiet descends and one enters a realm suspended in time from the turn of the century. There is a feeling that all is covered by dust: the black timber of the shop fronts, books, knick-knacks, and relics from by-gone ages. Each entrance offers an adventure and beckons with intrigue and promise. Ill-lit interiors seem hearth and home to ones who seek answers outside those of technology.

Here for the dancer, the artist, and those lost in dreams is their Shangri-La; each step offers expectancy and quest.

As I ventured along this lane, idly gazing into grime-covered glass with an eye to what lay within, I came upon The Halcyon Days bookstore. Painted green with a display window on either side of the door, it impressed one by its appearance of freshness. After earlier displays of dust and rags, this was like the emergence of the sun.

On an aged wooden stand outside, were piles of ill-arranged discarded books. Some new and some which threatened to fall apart at the slightest touch. The right hand window displayed an array of titles on subjects brought to popularity in the 60's: Eastern philosophy, diet, geomancy, herbs, yoga.

I've never felt comfortable with Eastern mysteries. It somehow jars on my nerves, possibly because I see it as a left-over from those cool people of the dream who desired to live in squalor in the brokendown ruins of inner cities. Communities perceived by the inhabitants to be realms of kings and queens of the fairy world, a return to the golden age as depicted by Tolkien and Arthur Rackham.

This attitude was, perhaps, defensive. These were people who desired comfort and pleasure, educated by a do-gooder society into laziness, implying that every-day labor was for those with a less developed mind. The world of fantasy eased these troubled souls and supported their idleness. It was the realm of second-rate art and drug-induced egotism. Praise came for the obscure, irrespective of the quality. A one hundred and eighty degree turn around from what Tolkien and Rackham intended.

I turned and bounded into an exiting shopper. "Sorry," I said in a slightly off-hand manner. He didn't offer a reply which in another would have appeared rude, but there was something about his demeanor which didn't necessitate communication.

I watched this black-overcoated figure as he walked away. There was something disturbingly familiar about him which made me continue to follow his progress along the alley until finally he turned north out of sight into St. Martin's Lane. I had failed to catch sight of his face so I concluded that it must have been his poise which induced recall.

Putting the encounter behind me I turned my attention to the second window. It was quite bare compared to its companion. A display of aged worm-eaten first editions lay scattered in an off-hand manner on a piece of equally aged purple cloth.

My eyes swept half-heartedly across the array, eventually drawn to the center where there lay such a noticeable contrast.

In the midst of these aged tomes was a fresh and glaring light. My mother's voice echoed from the past. I heard her crystal tones reverberate from the title, "The Morning Star."

It kissed my soul. This was not chance; I had been summoned.

My whole life had been channeled towards this moment. The pain and laughter, the false turns, all were a part of the path to this moment. Her stories came alive, and for a split second all life became whole and complete. The meaning of my life was here in three words, "The Morning Star."

I stood as a man who, only an instant before, has experienced a bolt of lightning discharging itself along-side him. Awe! It's the realization that one has been granted a second chance at life.

The next day, I lay in the twilight of dawn remembering my dream of the previous night. In it I was again outside of the bookstore which I had visited the previous day. Before me stood the man I had blundered into with his black-coated back turned towards me.

Slowly he turned and faced me. I was confronted by a tanned face crowned by a shock of grey hair and, blazing from the midst, a pair of sharp blue eyes like glass orbs. I knew him immediately as the man from the department store of my youth.

He spoke without movement of lips.

"You've finally arrived then."

"Yes," I replied. I seemed to know what he was talking about.

He pointed to what appeared to be a ruined abbey. All that remained was a huge arch, supported by ornate pillars on either side of which were the remnants of a broken wall.

"This is the long sought after gate," he said.

"So many have searched and yet failed. Strange don't you think since it's so obvious?"

I stood in silence but he read my thoughts.

"It is the gate of tears, the gate of death, and the gate of the garden of Eden. It is the virgin daughter awaiting to become the mother at the hands of the hero. She is waiting to be stolen away, but remember, those who steal the fire of heaven must expect to suffer. Go rebuild those devastated walls and raise the roof upon the holy house, prepare the hearth for the flame of generation."

As in most dreams, the fine details and ending had already drifted off into oblivion before I had the opportunity to capture them with the net of my reason. But, irrespective of this, I was extremely disturbed by the dream and its association of the previous day's encounter. The emergence of a figure, which all those years ago had manifested my first knowledge of true fear, was extremely curious.

Yesterday there had been the vague knowledge of recognition when I bumped into the figure. Were the walls which separated sleep and the waking mind being broken down so that it would become impossible to tell where one ended and the other began? Was the man yesterday also the man from my youth, and if so . . . if so, what?

Perhaps my subconscious had found some similarity and used it to emphasize a point. There was no way that, after all these years, he wouldn't have physically changed in some way. Yes, that's far more logical. It is all too easy to get carried away and believe all kinds of hokus-pokus. Still, deep down I have this agonizing sensation that he is one and the same man.

As I lay in bed thinking about the whole encounter, the old sensation of adventure returns. Maybe I'm being drawn into some occult web, netted by aged sages. I leaned out of bed and reached down to the floor for the copy of the Morning Star which I had purchased the previous day. I still couldn't believe I had spent 25 pounds on a book.

The volume contained everything I could possibly want to know about the magical arts: rituals, weapons, in all a composite treasure house of arcane knowledge. There was so much, in fact, that after all my hours of reading I had only scratched the surface and understood even less. Finally, taking the author's advice in the introduction, I returned to the beginning with the good intent of plodding through the hundred or so pages thereof.

As the story of the history unfolds, my mother enters my mind in the garb and regalia of a Morning Star initiate assuming a strange god form in the temple of light. Was she really a member or did her tales come from what she had read and fantasized? Then there was my father. What part had he played in all this, if any? It was hard to perceive him, underneath the folds of his conservatism, gesticulating symbols in the air with which to control invisible forces.

Possibly my mother's sacrifice was to leave the order and, by example, spread the word into the world at large. Or, maybe I was the object of her sacrifice, to create a creature that was a union of the magical and mundane; an entity which embodied both imagination and perseverance.

Was it possible that my mother had used my unsuspecting father as a vehicle for her ideal? Had she loved him or had she used him as an element in her experiment? This, of course, would never have occurred to him, as he considered himself the all-knowing dominant partner.

Following this line of thought, I now asked myself is my mother really dead?

At the time I had never questioned. Not being allowed at the funeral, I had assumed that my father had not wanted to upset me more than necessary. What if she hadn't died but run off, and to save embarrassment, the story of her death was concocted for me? This may in part have accounted for my grandmother's hostile attitude towards me.

It was a possibility. Once she had witnessed that the result of her experiment had taken root she felt it timely to leave and allow the being to develop. But to what purpose? Did it really make sense to abandon me unprotected to the ruthlessness of the world, or was there something in her stories which she trusted me to remember as protection or guidance? If so, what?

This was just speculation, but it did account for a lot of loose ends. It was certainly something to think about.

The history of the order was bizarre, to say the least, but certainly no more bizarre than its array of richly colorful members. These individuals spanned the whole spectrum of society but were uniform in their quest for the intangible.

The order was purported to have existed from time immemorial in the far distant past of Egypt and Chaldea. Through the following centuries it had survived to the present because of the efforts made by its adepts, both material and ethereal. One of the dictates was that members were not to make themselves conspicuous either by dress or life style from the people that they lived among. Obviously, if the history was true, this was one of the reasons why it had survived.

From what I could gather, the order, which originated in England, had been founded upon information supplied by a female German adept from Nuremberg using the magical motto of Rhiannon. None of the members of the English order had ever met this woman. All communication had been by correspondence to the founding fathers who had initially contacted her by way of a mysterious document.

The correspondence was short-lived, however. Once the initial information had been supplied a letter arrived to say that Rhiannon had died and that no further information would be forthcoming. Enough had been given for the order to continue on its own and form its own link with the true order which is beyond this earthly plain.

From what I was reading it was apparent that, unbeknownst to the world at large, there were groups of individuals supposedly changing the unsuspecting populace by example. A living being composed of countless individuals coexisting within the structure of society, subtly changing its outlook, destroying the old order, driving humanity towards some far unforeseen goal.

The problem which now aggravates me is, whether it is possible to successfully work the system described in the book without being a member of the order?

Much of the doctrine appeared to depend upon the use of elaborate initiation ceremonies performed by affiliating officers of one degree or another, playing out the roles of gods creating a new universe.

It certainly wasn't the type of society that you applied to join. You were invited. But who decided who would be invited and what were the qualifications necessary?

I suppose one could always run an advertisement in the personal column:

33 year old male, 6', dark hair, single, wishes to join magical fraternity.

My mother, of course, may have possessed information but her belongings had long since been destroyed. Then again, the original founders of the English order had never come into physical contact with the German Rhiannon of the history, so perhaps one can assume that initiation is possible through one's own endeavors. Reading further, it does become apparent that the system can be utilized by a solitary student, but that it's a far longer process and one requiring far more care if the neophyte isn't to be devoured by the freshly-released energies of his/her own being. When a certain degree of initiation has been achieved, or survived, then the order will find the student.

Just reading the book filled me with enthusiasm, but at the same time the warnings were quite foreboding so I was anxious to take my time and not start off on the wrong foot.

My mind moved to thoughts of my mother and her stories, again searching for that key, which would open up the river of memories to quench the thirst of my searching. If only I could remember those stories of my mother. I'm positive there were keys within their banal simplicity for practicing that most demanding of arts, 'high magick'.

My ears popped and I detected a faint ringing much like tinnitus, then I remembered the sound of my mother's voice as it related the story of 'the curse of reason'.

It was of a mother narrating a story to her young son, of "the curse of reason and the secret of the stone."

Long long ago, before memorable time, my mother would begin, there lived a beautiful young woman who was rearing her young son, Randolph. It was obvious from her poise and use of words that she was of noble and well-educated birth even if her humble surroundings reflected little evidence of this upbringing, surrounded as she was by such poverty.

Long long ago, when men had only just risen from out of the earth and were only just beginning to congregate in cities, the mother began, the gods would communicate to man through a messenger who was called Reason.

Now this messenger was extremely swift and sharp-witted and also most comely to look upon and was well loved by the gods because of the keenness with which he delivered their Will to Man. Equally, whenever he appeared, men were always happy to see him and receive the gifts and messages of the gods; so in return they showered Reason with the fruits of the earth as a return offering to the gods for their kindness.

After many centuries, man came to regard Reason as god and the divine beings he represented became forgotten and lost in the cold tombs of mans ancestors. Reason, realizing how man looked upon him, began changing the messages of the gods to better his own interests, encouraging man to build temples and make offerings to him.

At first when man began thinking of Reason as god, the true gods hadn't been too worried. But the distortion of their words for his own ends was too much, however much they loved him; and so they decided on a plan to put an end to his deceitful ways.

On his next visit to earth, the gods directed Reason to say to man that the fox was to be a symbol of deceit and lying and that wherever the animal was found, he was to be hunted out and chased by the hounds, who were to represent truth and the elimination of falsehood. Reason, on this occasion seeing little profit to be gained, delivered the message truthfully but then immediately became transformed into a fox at the will of the gods. Man at once understood the message, and saw Reason for what he really was. So they destroyed the temples of Reason and chased him into the undergrowth and wilderness, exiling him from their company and warm hearth.

Now the gods still loved Reason and missed his sparkling personality in heaven. So they left a pathway open for his return, should he ever mend his ways. This is why the fox can so often be seen wending his way close to lonely roads and thoroughfares. He's searching for his way back to the gods. So if you ever see a fox padding along a path, it may be that that is the path to heaven.

That night the son went to bed and almost immediately fell asleep with the story still ringing in his ears. In the middle of the night he awoke. At first he thought it was the light of the full moon beaming through his window that had awakened him, but then he heard the sound of a fox and realized that this was probably what had aroused him.

He leaped from bed, remembering his mother's tale, and after quietly dressing, he padded from the house and sought the source of the sound.

Outside, by the light of the full moon, it was extremely easy to see, and a little way ahead of him on the path, which entered the wood, he saw a fox standing as though waiting for him, much as one would expect from a faithful hound. He walked towards the animal and as he did so, the fox moved away from him following the path into the wood.

Even in the shadows beneath the trees he could see the creature he followed quite clearly but was then disappointed when it seemed to disappear. He quickened his step to arrive at where he imagined he had last seen it and there discovered an almost invisible track leading off into the undergrowth.

Randolph hesitated a moment and looked over his shoulder towards his home, wondering if he shouldn't return to the safety of what he knew, but then in the undergrowth he dimly caught sight of the fox again standing as if waiting for him. This was too much, he pushed the world of security behind him and followed the fox.

After several yards the trees thinned out and the undergrowth cleared revealing a small hill covered with lush green grass. On top of the hill was a small circle of standing stones and standing in the middle a beautiful woman clothed completely in white. Swathed as she was in soft moonlight, which abounded in the clearing, it was possible to discern that around her head circled a crown of silver and about her feet a pair of silver shoes.

Randolph looked around for his guide, the fox, but it was nowhere to be seen. There was only the priestess, for this is how he imagined her. Without realizing he had moved, he now found himself in the arms of the woman, where he felt completely at peace. He was a sailor returning to a safe port after an arduous and testing voyage.

While in her embrace, she imparted a strange message to Randolph about a wondrous secret which could never be tarnished and which would give the possessor many extended lifetimes to live upon this earth, if he so wished.

It was this secret which was the power behind the gods. It was the ultimate magick. Its ownership bestowed the owner with nefter, the ability to recreate oneself at will and so make him the godman. This was the message that the gods had asked Reason to deliver to man but which he had so dreadfully corrupted for his own ends. He saw that this was the gift which would raise man above himself and unite man with the gods.

In the centuries to come, men would sacrifice and suffer much for their belief and quest of this secret, she continued, that's why it was essential that Randolph speak to no-one about it in case it should unwittingly fall into corrupt hands before he had the strength and wit to defend it. Knowledge of the secret's existence was imparted to every man in his subconscious at birth. Life was for the quest of this exquisite jewel, although life would not necessarily impart the wisdom of its use.

Randolph woke early and felt extremely tired. He slid his legs out of the bed and stood up but almost toppled because the soles of his feet were so sore. He returned to the bed and sat down to examine his feet, which were severely scratched and muddy. It was then that the night's escapades returned to him as he recalled the experience with the fox and the woman.

If it wasn't for the condition of his feet, he would have shrugged off the whole episode as a dream but the pain of standing gave credence to the memory which, if nothing else, should be explored.

He followed the path into the wood and without much difficulty, found the little track which led into the undergrowth. The tangled fauna and trees didn't clear but the ground did perceptibly rise until Randolph stood on the top of a small hillock. The whole area was completely overgrown, but on closer scrutiny, one could discern in the undergrowth the undeniable evidence of eroded broken stones circumscribing the brow of the hill.

Idly, Randolph kicked the ground halfheartedly and in so doing, turned up a lump of turf beneath which he could make out something sparkling. He bent down to explore the area and there, to his amazement, he discovered the most beautiful jewel that one could ever imagine.

MORRIGAN

> *Morrigan, Queen of Phantoms. Wherever the Morrigan appears, it is always by some mystical influence or by an act of sorcery.*
>
> *It's a known fact that as soon as one consciously begins on the path, the first effects are quite the opposite of what one expects. The student, in his naivete, believes that life will suddenly become simple and easy without the slightest effort on his part. Of course, quite the opposite occurs.*

....

The initial enthusiasm soon burns itself out with the repeated exercise of the art. What at first was exhilarating and exciting, rapidly becomes laborious and boring. The color soon fades; the rainbow of promise becomes a black hole.

At first I thought the incantations and movements would produce physical manifestation. This was not the case. Such manifestation, if any, takes place on so called "inner planes." With repeated practice, the student builds up inner mental images with which to effect the physical object. So faith is the only weapon with which to combat skepticism.

My present preoccupation with the arcane studies largely removed me from my usual social pursuits, namely evenings spent in the George and Dragon public house.

The hole left by my abandonment of music had been filled largely by the intake of large quantities of alcohol, which on most evenings, left me in an alcoholic twilight zone. At closing time, in dazed confusion, I would endeavor to stagger home, hoping it was still where I imagined I had left it.

My sudden disappearance from the scene had obviously caused some speculation, and it wasn't too long before I was visited by one of my old compatriots, Mark, a frustrated artist. Mark earned large amounts of money at his work in the computer industry but aspired to be a keyboard player. Thus he sought out the company of musicians in the hope of working with them by promising financial assistance. Actually, he wasn't a bad musician, but he lacked that quality which lifted one from the mundane to the talented.

It is said that owners tend to look like their pets. In Mark's case he thought like his work and this was the problem. He was a mechanical thinker, he had the mind of a scientist and not an artist. The former analyzes, the latter creates. He would lock onto a subject with a passion but would only see it from the point of view that he was presently programmed into. For all this, there was the undercurrent of a romantic within him but it would manifest in moods of frustration. It was something intangible that his reasoning mind couldn't understand and therefore threatened its superiority. In defense, the reason would ridicule the notions and friction was the outcome.

In me, he saw the potential of his dream. He imagined me disillusioned by lack of financial reward. This, of course, was not the case. I was simply bored.

His visit took me by surprise and when I opened the door, I was in something of a disarray, having just completed a small ritual which left me feeling somewhat dazed. I invited him in and nervously picked up the incriminating pieces of evidence which were clues to my present preoccupation. I was secretive in my pursuits out of fear of ridicule. I lacked the knowledge of the subject which would have armed me for its defense.

"Hi, good to see you Mark," I lied. "Care for some coffee?" He slumped himself down at the kitchen table. I must note that Mark's attempts at dressing casual were something of a joke. A loosened tie with an unintentionally crumpled suit were about as close as he got. He was one of those men who always wore a suit and tie but never looked smart. "Yeah, fine, love one. Haven't seen you for a while," he replied distractedly as he picked up and carelessly flicked through the pages of "Rock Dreams."

Although I was apprehensive about discussing my pursuits, I simultaneously wanted to let out what I was doing and share it.

"I've decided to cut down drinking," which was true. It had been a habit created to fill a vacuum which, although not out of control, had threatened to be. I came to the table and sat down, resting my head between my hands; I felt awkward and nervous, brittle I suppose would be a good description.

"You thought any more about what we were talking about?" Mark asked. Several weeks previously, the subject of forming a band had been a topic of conversation while drinking at the George. It was late in the evening, so enthusiasm was high. The following day I regretted the whole conversation.

"I'm sorry Mark I 'm really not interested."

He shifted in his seat, crossing and then uncrossing his legs, obviously agitated. "But it's such a waste. There's all this talent available and it's going down the drain." His words were coming with more speed now, the higher pitch of his voice evidence of his frustration.

"Yes, well I'm sorry, but I told you at the beginning I wasn't prepared to make any promises." He turned slightly, breathing heavily. "I've thought a lot about it and I really feel that it's best to say 'no' now." Thankfully, I heard the kettle boil and so was given a reprieve to go and make the coffee.

I returned and he was once more facing the table and appeared more calm as he fiddled with a piece of paper on which I had been jotting some notes earlier.

"You know, with the talent we have available we could get the work." It was as though he hadn't heard a word that I had said. I let him continue, hoping that he would talk it out of his system but I found the line of his argument annoying as he preached about all the money he had or was prepared to invest, of how he had loaned money to people and never been paid back. He was going off on tangents and using the present crisis as a release for all his pent-up aggressions.

"I'm afraid I'm different from you. If I lend something to somebody then I don't expect to see it back; if it is returned, then that's a bonus," I responded.

He raised his hands gesticulating a scramble of arcs in the air with negative results. Such a sharp contrast to my own earlier ritual positive hand movements which carved clean geometric figures in the aether to positive ends.

He sipped at his coffee and I followed his lead thankful for the silence. I wanted to tell him what I was doing but didn't know where to begin.

"Give me a good reason," he asked. Had he read my thoughts? Whatever the cause of the question, here was the opening.

"I've found what I have been looking for for years and I really don't have the time to do anything else for the time being. You ever heard of the Morning Star?"

He looked up. "No, what's that?"

Where was I to start? "It was a secret magical organization that existed at the turn of the century."

I then proceeded to give it credence by name-dropping, citing some of its more supposed worldly accepted members who had achieved prominence outside the confines of the order.

"Um, and what's the point?"

"Well, to find out more about yourself and the world at large, to be more in control of the self. At present it takes a lot of time and to me this is most important."

"You're just wasting your life. That's something you do when you're old, not now." I regretted now that I had ever begun this line of conversation, I should have listened to my earlier feelings and kept quiet. Against Mark's reasoning I possessed no ammunition, sense and feeling are no argument against logic.

I picked up my coffee cup, wanting to crawl within it. Instead I sipped casually and then with both hands returned it to the table top.

"I thought you were into this sort of thing."

"Yes, but life comes first. Success, we could have success and you would rather fiddle about with all this mumbo-jumbo. It's bloody ridiculous."

I stood up suddenly and threw up my arms theatrically and repeated a line I had recently read: "There is no part of me which is not of the gods."

Mark, thankfully, loosened up a little which meant he loosened his tie and smiled.

"You've cracked," was his only reply.

We spent the next half hour or so with small talk and then he rose to leave saying, "Well why don't you just come down to the pub tonight and have a drink, if it's allowed. You know they have this new girl behind the bar, a blond, she's really beautiful."

"OK, maybe. What time you going down?"

"Oh, about nine , nine-thirty"

With that I showed him out and returned to my cold coffee.

God, it tasted awful!

I sat and pondered on what he had said, doubt rose and I began to question what I was doing. I retrieved my diary where I kept a record of all my exercises and results from the place I had secreted it on Mark's arrival. I leafed through it. I hoped to glean reassurance from the pages but it read like a pathetic piece of third-rate childish ramblings. All the time and effort of the previous weeks appeared as a complete waste of time, a futile exercise in escapism. Line after line read of moods and frustrations with others, promises made and broken, at the end there was nothing to show.

From out of the ashes of my frustration rose the Phoenix of new endeavor. Mark's words and logic were ideas from my past and deserved no license to exist. The obvious weakness of my endeavors, clear in the reading of the journal, gave me the impetus I needed to drive myself forward toward a new horizon. I would make a concerted effort and damn the consequences.

Enough of the preparatory exercises. It was time to manufacture the weapons of the art and evoke the gods of the universe, my inner self. I opened a fresh notebook as a symbol of my new endeavor and began to write.

I've just completed the reading of my previous diary. It is very easy for me to pull it to pieces but I do not believe that this would be very beneficial. Most of the record comes across as being written by an immature, frustrated person.

Over all, it seems to concern itself with either self-congratulation or reproach at inadequacies of character. The frustration seems to derive itself from the failure of achievement. It's a shame I failed to realize my mistake was not putting those wasted energies into the work at hand.

When I began the previous record, I saw it as a great beginning which, by the time I'd finished, would bear fruit. I think it probably has, but not in the way I had imagined. I feel I have just said farewell to an old friend.

I turned the page and wrote the title of my new challenge.

CONVERSATIONS WITH THE SPHINX
(Or how I came to understand myself)

The presumption of the piece hit me immediately but it sounded impressive, so I left it.

I've overslept and have a splitting headache. What is more frustrating is the fact that I have missed the morning adoration. I pledged myself yesterday to make a concerted effort toward the work, and then within the first few hours I fail the promise.

Nine o'clock had come around last night and the feelings which Mark evoked with his visit returned. I felt the need for human contact. So, in good spirits, I took up his suggestion and headed out for the George and human companionship.

The bar was packed when I arrived and I really had to squeeze myself forward to get a drink. As I pushed through the throngs of drinking masses, I nodded to acquaintances as I scrutinized the smoke-filled atmosphere for Mark. Unfortunately, he was a little short, so seeing him had its problems.

Finally, reaching and leaning on the bar, I was able to survey the room more accurately.

"Are you being served?"

I turned towards the voice and was confronted by a tall, long-haired blond whom I hadn't seen working there before. This I assumed was the girl of Mark's earlier conversation.

"No, I'm sorry, a pint of lager please." She smiled and moved away to fill my order. It struck me then that English people always apologize even when there is no need for it.

I had no sooner placed my order than I heard Mark's voice and saw him pushing from the far end of the bar towards me.

As he came along side me the blond returned with my order.

Before I was able to offer her a pound note, Mark called out:

"Just the usual, Viv, and take for the lager."

"Cheers !" So saying he raised the remnants of what was left in his glass to mine and then we both took a deep draught.

"Well, what do you think?"

I played dumb.

"About what ?"

"Vivian of course."

So this was Vivian. I'd really known it from the first moment that I saw her.

....

PART TWO - THE WEB

How Merlin was assotted and doted on one of the ladies of the lake.

Sir Thomas Malory, Le Morte D'Arthur

VIVIAN

She was the bramble girl, yet a rose grew in the heart of this thorny bush.

To most people, she represented a barren land to be shunned. Much better to keep to the well-trodden path.

Where did the thorn bush come from; how were its seeds sown?

She was called the Ice Maiden.

Her sun was so deep within that it rarely shone upon her outer world. It took a keen adventurer to hazard the challenge of thorn and lurking beast.

She was the virgin maiden held captive in the tower. Her personality was the tower of challenge, her psyche the damsel in distress.

....

My room was a mess, a mirror image of myself. There were books and scraps of paper on every available surface. The late afternoon sun, slanting through the haze of the grime leaded windows, illuminated the dust hanging like a spangled shroud in the golden light.

My preoccupation with the magical arts and my inner self had made me neglectful of my surroundings. Excessive introspection was obviously a vehicle of selfishness. I wanted to do something but became agitated as I failed to realize what it was.

It's 4:00 p.m. I'll get cleaned up and go for a walk, reunite myself with the gods and try to realize that there is a world outside of myself.

It feels good getting out. It's cool; autumn is abroad and the air is quiet with pensive moisture. Nature hangs suspended in time, awaiting the inevitable crown of winter. It makes the stroll refreshing.

Over the summer months of my seclusion, Lammas Park had become a most reassuring haven where I was able to mix, yet remain aloof from the rest of humanity.

The park was only a few minutes walk and readily accessible to me. Although busy with activity, it possessed a mystical quality that was difficult to define. Had it at some point in the far distant past witnessed scenes of high magick? Was it a portal, a crossing-over point to the realms of long-forgotten kingdoms unknown and unwanted by modern man? Who can say?

Whatever the reason, as I walked the paths beneath the boughs of the overhanging chestnut trees, I became conscious of another world.

Each tree and flower was in possession of its own unique and individual spirit. The outer form was but the sheath of this inner being, its expression as my own body to my soul. In lines of bark and the movement of leaf or flower the spirit can be seen, just as the sylphs of the air can be seen in the pictures produced by the pattern of clouds.

Nature in her guise of tree and flower was reaching out trying to communicate and overcome my dullness in a language of piquant tongues.

Mythical beasts would materialize in the pastel green, pink, and purple liquid ethers of the other world between the trees. Griffins, unicorns, basilisks, and sphinxes, all with a question, all with a story.

These images came out of nowhere, unconscious on my part. At these times I felt close to death. It was as though I was slipping quietly out of life, as steam dissipates and disappears from the spout of a kettle. Tears would well, I would tremble with the memory of my distant lost childhood and feel so desperately alone.

Was I a bridge between worlds? A vehicle whereby one world entered another? A render of the veil? Perhaps I was the rainbow bridge, or Nemo, the no man, a ghost who belonged to neither world.

Now this was all quite controllable. It wasn't as though I was suddenly thrown into the midst of some 60's acid trip where logic suddenly disappeared out of that part of me upon which I normally sat. No, here the images were of delicate hue, if I did happen to meet somebody I knew it was quite easy to throw off the reverie and conduct a normal conversation.

After my walk through the park, I was returning by way of the shops to pick up something for dinner, when before me I caught sight of Vivian emerging from the underground station.

I'd come to realize that she was one of those girls who always spoke but somehow seemed unapproachable. She laughed a lot, but there was always a distance there, a vacuum behind her eyes. She was burdened down with two large shopping bags and walked dreamily unaware of the hustle and bustle going on around her. I speeded up my pace and drew up along side of her and tapped her lightly on the shoulder.

"Hello."

She looked at me and smiled.

"Oh, hello."

"Here let me give you a hand," and I reached down to take one of the bags, while she insisted she could manage.

Finally she relented and said "OK, thank you."

"Well, what have you been up to? I haven't seen you around lately," she continued.

"Not a lot," I replied. "How about you?"

"It's been one of those days. I'm ready for a drink," she answered a little sleepily.

"Well, let's go," I said.

I was suddenly confident and enthusiastic. After spending the day alone, it was so good to be with somebody, to re-enter the world of the living.

"I would but I've got people coming for dinner."

I felt very down-hearted after my sudden on-rush of euphoria. My balloon of optimism had suddenly burst and left its debris across my face.

"Why don't you come?" she asked.

Hello, I thought. This is more like it.

"Well, um, yes OK."

She smiled at me.

By this time we had reached her home. It was a small early Edwardian terrace set in a line of about thirty others. The style of architecture was extremely common on the west side of London which had seen much development during the early twentieth century. A small garden about ten feet deep separated the house from the street. At some period a gate had hung from the brick wall which skirted the enclosure but now all that remained was a solitary, rusty cast-iron hinge. The garden was paved with irregular stone slabs except for two small round flower beds from which climbed rose bushes heavily armed with thorns. The area was well tended but fallen leaves, the badge of autumn, had blown in from the surrounding elms and given it an air of abandonment.

These homes had originally been constructed for family occupancy, but, sadly, over recent years they had been split up into apartments to house the tidal wave of new Londoners who had arrived to experience the streets of gold.

She unlocked the door and we carried in the bags, entering a cubicle vestibule which necessitated our pushing against each other, while she struggled with the lock on the second door. The sudden opening of the door had us almost falling in a heap in the narrow hallway beyond. In silent patrol we followed its course. Through an open door on the left, I had a fleeting glimpse of a very neatly laid out bedroom, so precise that it resembled a show room. A few feet further was a second door, but this, unlike its previous companion, was closed. Through a door at the bottom of the hall we passed into a very pleasing clean, bright and uncluttered living room with a bare varnished wood floor.

I followed Vivian into the kitchen and put down the bags while she pulled a bottle of wine out of the fridge.

"Nice place you have."

"Thank you, it should be. It costs every penny I earn."

I hadn't noticed before but I detected in her reply the trace of an accent. Her English was impeccable, but there were the undeniable traces of a foreign tongue.

She gathered two glasses out of an eye-level cupboard and we went into the living room. I sank down into the luxurious couch while she took possession of a huge armchair. I sipped at the golden contents of the glass and gazed at her, I felt very content. In the silence I began imagining.

Against the backdrop of my present life-style, the thought of life with Vivian in this ordered world seemed most appealing. In my mind's eye I courted and married her within a matter of seconds. She appeared as the answer to all my dreams. I mentally undressed her, experiencing the roundness of her hips and breasts with my imaginary hands. These hips spiraled in erotic vibrant movements. It was surprising how the simple collection of curves, which made up her body, could unleash such power and energy. It was a primitive dark force that normally lay suppressed deep within the forests of the human psyche, something not to be touched upon. But the proportions of her body were a talisman which evoked the sexual demon within me and burst the chains of his bondage.

How I longed for her, to melt our worlds together in a cauldron of dreams. I wanted to lie naked with her in bed in the early morning. Make love to her and feel her hands caress my lustful flesh as I plunged into her within a reassuring cocoon of blankets. I wanted to force my tongue in between her moist lips so as to explore the hidden interior of her facial cavity, then have her chew it to a pulp of bleeding flesh and leave me a gibbering wreck, a victim to ivory and passion.

She broke my reverie.

"Have you got a job yet?"

"No, I've got a lot of reading to do first." I replied.

God, I wanted her so much, I could feel my self begin to tremble uncontrollably. If only I could reach out and kiss her, or to just hold her would be enough to relieve this growing tension. My nerve endings rose to the surface of my skin causing my whole body to prickle as I suppressed my thoughts through fear of rejection.

The dinner was most enjoyable, a contrast to my previous weeks of solitude. Vivian was a wonderful hostess; nothing was too much trouble for her small array of guests. In the babble of conversation, she moved unnoticed except by myself. The music, the talk, the candle light and sparkling crystal produced a feeling of euphoria, helped by the effects of the free-flowing alcohol. My gaze kept returning to Vivian as she maneuvered between the three other seated and preoccupied guests.

To my right sat a chap called Bob. Rather a loud-mouth who loved the sound of his own voice, and by and large always got to say what he wanted. He was stocky and if you didn't pay attention to what he was saying, he was liable to use his physique to push a point over, especially after a few drinks. I found him extremely annoying -- maybe intimidating, not so much from his size as his education, which was well-rounded. But for all his education, he lacked the wisdom or ability to be interesting. At this moment I wished I possessed the eloquence to drive a nail into his inflated confidence and crucify it.

Across from Bob sat Mark, who was quite his opposite. His shortness appearing as dumpiness against the physique of the other. He had a complexion that looked unhealthy due to the red blotches caused by excessive drinking which patch-worked his flabby round face. Deterioration had apparently set in quite rapidly, at least I couldn't remember seeing these tell-tale signs when I saw him a couple of months earlier.

Our relationship had become somewhat strained at my being adamant over the band issue. In fact, it had come to the point where we now only passed a polite "hello" when seeing each other.

Mark struggled for words under the onslaught of his opposition. He obviously had much to say but lacked the weight and timbre of voice to encourage patience in his listeners. His thinking was complex but, unfortunately, he was deficient in the machinery by which to express his ideas coherently. I could see that he was becoming extremely agitated. First, because of his own ineptitude at explanation, and second, because of the lack of seriousness with which the other guests held his views. He was so long-winded in making a statement that before he was finished saying what he wanted, his words were drowned out and ridiculed. When there was a pause in the discussion, Mark took the opportunity to loosen his tie and yank it over to one side. His casual look.

As I looked at him, I imagined what he would look like in a few years, a bloated, disillusioned malcontent. His self-respect already appeared much eroded. He didn't believe in anything, not even in himself. For him there was only analysis.

I hadn't really involved myself in the cacophony of conversation. Deep down I wanted everybody to leave so that I could be alone with Vivian.

"What are you doing these days?"

It was Chris, a rather arty type of girl from the George and Dragon, who took advantage of the pause to bring me into the conversation. She was arrayed in scarves and masses of jewelry, giving her the appearance of a Gypsy. I was waiting for her to ask to see my palm or inquire about my star sign. She went to a lot of trouble to look exotic, but underneath all the garb it was readily apparent that she was overweight and flabby. Less time spent in the George and Dragon would produce wonders, I thought.

I tried to think of something that would draw me into the conversation and make me interesting. All of a sudden it became important that I should impress this group . . . but why?

I gathered myself and prepared to speak by which time the only person listening was Chris, the others, after the distraction, having returned to their political discussion.

"I'm between worlds I suppose you'd say, trying to find a way to go."

"You're not playing anymore, then?"

"No, I just can't find the enthusiasm any more."

Vivian returned from the kitchen, the light behind her creating the illusion of a halo, a flaming white aureole around the waves of her golden hair.

My previous imaginings may have been purely lustful, now they became celestial as I gazed upon her bewitching entrance. In this instant, she became a goddess to my humble eyes. Was this the way my father had first beheld my mother and become enchanted by the effects of her feminine sorcery? Was this the magic spell with which she had snared the luckless hare? Or was it maybe the lust of the flesh which had attracted him as in my earlier imaginings?

She perched herself diagonally across the table from me and forced her way into the conversation, at an equally diagonal position with regard to the conversation. They treated her views as a joke, and although I didn't agree with her, my heart went out to her.

I stood and went to the stereo where I turned over the record. While doing so, I noticed several books on astrology supporting the albums on the shelf. I laughed a little to myself. I saw them as middle class trinkets without substance and used for obtaining predetermined answers rather than discovering the truth.

I returned my gaze to the table and saw Vivian as a priestess of love, a Venus made flesh. Her skin beneath the halo was of pure white alabaster, emphasized by the severe lines of kohl which high-lighted those deep unfathomable eyes. She was goddess and whore. Her dress was of native design with primitive patterns of reddish hue, the lines and shapes of which danced in the flickering candle light as though they were alive.

Vivian briefly looked over at me and then returned her gaze to the table. After a few moments, she rose and walked towards me; I in turn moved to face her, drawing myself away from my idle preoccupation with the books.

"I love your dress." I noticed her ears. They were like delicate shells, perfect in symmetry and form; the conches petit cups awaiting whispered words or exploring tongue.

"Well, thank you. I brought it in Algeria last year," came her reply.

Again I detected the lilt of a foreign accent suspended upon her words.

"What's the design?"

"Oh, native. Don't you just love the color? It's a dye made from dried crushed beetles," she continued enthusiastically.

"It's the female of the species that they use, kermes they call it. Apparently people used to think that they were berries. Strange um?"

"Well, maybe not, the beetle to the ancient Egyptian was Kephera, the sun at night, the seed of the dawn Sun god, Ra. The allegory is that the berry contains the seeds of the tree and the beetle associated with Kephera rolls its eggs, seeds, in a ball before it. He who rolls the same thing -- each is a symbol of the other."

Behind our conversation, the babble of the other guests supplied a droning back-drop.

"Where did you learn all that?" She tilted her head a little to one side and smiled as she spoke.

"Books," I smiled in answer.

This was surely kismet.

She didn't reply but turned to answer a call from Mark. The moment was lost and I mentally cursed him for his interruption.

I returned my attention to the small collection of books and pulled out Margaret Hone's Astrology from its place. Then, picking up my wine from the table, retired to the couch with the book, safe within my shell. The group at the table didn't miss my departure and continued much along the same lines as earlier.

Vivian was leaning over me and shaking my shoulder gently.

"Were we that boring?"

"Oh God, I'm sorry. Did I doze off?" I said and moved to stand up.

"What time is it and where is everybody?"

"Oh, it's about 2:30. I've only just managed to get them all out. They were going to wake you but I said that you'd be OK. Poor Mark wasn't too happy, I believe he thinks that there's something going on between us."

"I do apologize if I've made things difficult for you."

"No, that's all right he's been chasing me for months, maybe this will put him off. He's too short for me."

We both grinned and then laughed for a moment at Mark's expense.

She continued, "No, we shouldn't laugh. It's wrong. Would you like some coffee before you leave?"

"Yes, that would be lovely if it's not too much trouble."

"No, not at all. I was going to make some for myself anyway, once I'd gotten rid of everybody. God, I thought they'd never leave."

She turned and went into the kitchen where I could hear her going through the throes of manufacturing the coffee. I went to the bookshelf and returned Margaret Hone's book to the shelf and then returned to the couch, complimenting myself into maneuvering myself into this position with Vivian.

I was feeling far more relaxed in her company since she had wakened me. The conversation was light but the tones of her speech had been soft and most becoming.

She returned from the kitchen bearing a tray with two coffee cups and a plate filled with various biscuits.

"I am sorry for nodding off, I feel awful."

"No, don't worry, you didn't miss anything." She offered me a cup and then said, "Mark tells me you're involved in black magic, is that true?"

"Heavens no! I have certain beliefs but they have nothing to do with black magic."

I sipped my coffee composing my thoughts and cursing Mark.

"No, I see it more as a form of psychology, but unlike psychology you are given the tools to help yourself. It's a union of art and science whereby you come into control of yourself."

"Are you in control of yourself?"

"No, not yet, but I'm working at it. For example, you look around this room and tell me one thing that didn't first exist in the imagination. If you could control your imagination you'd be a god." I pointed to my head, "Inner space, the final frontier."

"Um, sounds a little strange to me," she replied.

"Yes, I do get a little carried away, I'm sorry."

"So what do you do. . . to practice gaining control of yourself?"

"Well I use tarot and exercises to guide my imagination." I didn't want to say rituals as I thought that this would probably alarm her after Mark's comments.

"Oh, you tell fortunes?" She asked excitedly.

"I don't believe in fortune-telling. I look at it from the point of view that we really know within us what the answer is when we ask the question. It's just that we don't, for one reason or another, choose to accept it. What the cards do is make us think about the problem and help us interpret what is within us; I don't really believe that it makes much difference what the cards are."

"Will you read mine?"

"Yes, of course." Here was an excuse for another meeting.

"But you do know the real use of the cards is to use them as doorways?"

"What do you mean by that?" She said frowning slightly.

"Well, the idea is that each of the cards represents a different aspect of the human mind and that by fully knowing or experiencing each card, you then come to a greater knowledge of yourself."

"I see," she replied, but didn't sound too convinced.

"But you will read my fortune?"

"Yes, of course. What are you doing tomorrow?"

"Well, I'll be working in the pub from 12:00 till 3:00 but then I'll be free all afternoon until 7:00. It's my turn to work Saturday. Maybe you could come down and help me get through it."

"Why don't I come around at about 4:00. I can do the cards and then I'll meet you later at the George."

"I'll tell you what, I'll make you something to eat. That will save you having to go home and then you can stay here until you're ready to come down to the pub."

"Sounds terrific. Well, I suppose I'd better be off. What time is it?"

"Only 3:30," she replied and laughed.

"Oh, is that all," I smiled.

My walk home was wonderful. All my dreams were being fulfilled. Vivian had shown me to the front door and as I was saying goodnight, she had delicately kissed my cheek. With my hands gripping her hips, I had turned her to face me and kissed her mouth, feeling an equal return of enthusiasm.

She gave me a final look then smiled and said "You had better go. I'll see you tomorrow."

The following day was beautiful. I was awakened early by the rays of the sun streaming through my open curtains. Despite having only a few hours sleep, I felt in wonderful spirits and decided to take full advantage of the situation by first scrying a tarot card and then brushing up on some of the meanings of the other cards before my rendezvous with Vivian in the afternoon. Breakfast was out. It was hopeless trying to scry with a stomach loaded down with food. I'd just make do with a cup of coffee and then eat after the exercise.

By 8:00 I was ready to begin.

Now with any magical performance, it is always best to work within a circle, even with the simple exercise of scrying. For this purpose I had a length of white rope which, after moving my furniture from the center of the room, I unraveled and laid in as close approximation as possible to a circle. In the center I placed a chair to be as comfortable as possible and avoid undue distractions like cramps.

I next went to the wooden chest where I kept all my magical regalia and withdrew my diary and pack of silk-wrapped tarot cards. Removing the major atu card of the High Priestess, I proceeded to the center of the circle and opened my diary for today's page and wrote:

Saturday . . . .

8:10 began banishing ritual of the pentagram prior to scrying the card of the High Priestess.

If the banishing did nothing else it certainly built up the atmosphere so by the time it was completed and I had invoked the spirits of the moon, I was in a most susceptible state of mind. The time was now 8:30 and I dutifully wrote in my diary:

Began scrying card.

I sat with the card gripped between my two hands directly in front of me then proceeded to stare at it until it began to blur. I then closed my eyes and visualized the card as a huge doorway before me. It took a few seconds for the image to be strongly established so I could identify all the fine detail.

I now stood before a colossal doorway upon which was the design of a woman dressed totally in white. On either side stood two pillars; the one on the left being black, that on the right white. The door now began to swing slowly inwards revealing an infinite blue sky. I allowed myself to be drawn into the vision.

Below me I see green fields, forests, gardens, and grottos alive with meandering streams and crystal pools. Above, the blue sky of Jupiter is lit by the light of a radiant sun. I look behind and there is the open doorway beyond which I can distinctly see my seated figure within the circle. I turn and descend in the form of a lion crouched upon a bolt of lightening. On reaching the ground, I stand outside of a fence which surrounds a field.

Inside the fence is a dull rock. Chained to the rock is a huge bull, a magnificent beast, grazing upon the green succulent grass totally unaware of my presence. I try to walk but discover I can only move in an up or down direction. The laws of the horizontal are unknown to me.

A beautiful fair-skinned woman with flaming red hair, dressed in a translucent white gown, appears close but far enough away to be out of reach. I struggle desperately to reach her but all my endeavors lead to nothing. The bull in the field continues to graze, totally unaware of my frantic activity.

The woman opens her robe to me, encouraging me on. The sight of her beautiful naked form is truly a garden of delights. The curves of her exquisitely formed breasts and hips rouse my animal passion to unprecedented heights. The flame of her red pubic hair burns in the darkness that holds the mystery of what lies between her legs, a sacrificial fire of her virginity to the seeds of creation which dwell within me.

Vainly I fight invisible bonds in a desperate attempt to unleash the beast of my lust.

The more I struggle to achieve my goal, the tighter I become enmeshed in the web of the unobtainable.

All my attempts lead to nothing and in my exhaustion I appeal to the sensitivity of the beauty for compassion.

"Please, I beg you, come to me."

Her voice replies in tones as soft as wind chimes.

"Inspiration is not enough to win me. The lion alone is not the answer."

Her attention moves to the oblivious bull and she continues,

"There is your key. The lightning must be contained within the bull. Go and defeat the dull ignorance which chains him. Strike off his fetters with your thunderbolt. He is perseverance and the vehicle of your inspiration.

Inspiration, however pure, is not enough to claim possession of your dreams.

The lord of the flame and the lightning must dwell within the lord of the wild and fertile land.

I'm the graal, that which is the summa bonum of your all your desires. I represent the purest manifestation of any idea, I am the ultimate answer to all your questions. From me you were born and to me you will return at death.

Don't confuse me with reality."

Vivian was cleaning the front windows of the house when I arrived and I thought to surprise her while she was pre-occupied, but as I approached my hopes were dashed for without turning she said, "Oh you've arrived then." The memory of the remark made me shudder as I recalled it was the comment made by the man in my dream outside of the ruined abbey.

"What made you say that?"

"Made me say what?"

I was obviously still a little hyper after the experience with the tarot card.

"Oh nothing, I'm sorry. I'm miles away."

She smiled and collected her cleaning materials and we entered the house.

"Did you bring your cards?" she called from the bathroom above the rushing noise of the water tap.

"Sure did. Do you want to do it now?"

"Yes, just give me a couple of minutes to get cleaned up."

By the time she emerged I had already laid out the black silk cloth, which in times of disuse protected the cards but upon which I now proposed to do the reading.

"Where do you want me to sit?"

"Here, opposite me," I pointed to the chair across the table.

"What's your birth sign?"

"Aquarius."

"Ok." I flicked through the deck searching for the Princess of Swords. Finally I discovered it and withdrew it from its hiding place and laid it in the center of the black cloth.

"That represents the querent, in this case you. Now, what I want you to do is shuffle the deck, cut it three times, and then hand the pack to me. You understand?"

"Yes, I think so. I shuffle and cut the deck three times right?"

"Right." I nodded.

"Now, while you're doing this you must at all times be thinking of your question and, let your mind wander as little as possible."

"Do I have to tell you the question?"

"No, in fact it's probably better if you don't, but you should write it down. Questions like dreams have a habit of unconsciously changing."

"Alright, hang on a minute and I'll get something to write with."

While I waited my thoughts returned to the vision experienced earlier in the day. "Perseverance is the key to obtaining your dreams." Um, I wonder if the girl in the dream was a representation of Vivian?

I could think of nothing else but being with her, and this was what worried me about reading her cards. She must sense how I felt and I didn't want it to appear as though I was creating an answer around my own hunger. This I would find embarrassing. Oh well, maybe the cards wouldn't flow that way. Let's hope the question won't be about relationships.

I gazed out of the French windows and for the first time noticed an Oriental garden tucked away against the far fence. The center piece was a small terra-cotta pagoda-style temple and around this a mass of alpine flowers and shrubs. On either side and partially over-hanging the arrangement like a canopy, were two fairly young fir trees, standing as though on guard of the delicate sanctuary. The shrine and its flora radiated a sense of calm and peace. Though out of the way and almost unnoticed in it's lowly position, it was to me the crown of the garden.

I was drawn from my reverie by the sound of Vivian's light steps entering the room.

She had changed into an almost translucent white cotton dress with a plunging neckline and it was readily apparent that she wore no bra. The darkness of her nipples stained the front of the material.

I felt myself harden and I was forced to shift in my seat.

She returned to the chair opposite me and leaned over the table so that I was able to see clearly down the front of her dress. I couldn't help myself, I had to look and see her swelling breasts and, hopefully, be blessed with a glimpse of her russet colored nipples.

The act was like that of stealing. Like Columbus anchored off the shore of the New World, I drooled over the thought of exploration of this new continent, to steal that which is unknown.

She looked up and smiled with the innocence of a native expecting a handful of beads. I'm sure that she was ignorant of my voyeur preoccupations.

"Sorry about that. I can never find a pen or pencil when I want it. Well, are we all set?"

I coughed nervously and while inhaling to catch my breath, detected the rich heavy scent of hyacinth blossoms such as one experiences when walking in the garden after a heavy fall of spring rain. Why the aroma should be present at this time of year I couldn't fathom, I could only assume that it came from Vivian.

"First write your question."

"Yes, I already did that in the other room."

"OK, now I want you to shuffle the cards as I showed you, remembering all the time to be thinking about the question, but be careful not to drop a card, otherwise we have to wait a few minutes and then begin again."

She picked up the pack. The cards were large but they looked colossal in her delicate hands.

"My, they're so big. This is really difficult."

"Don't talk, just think about the question."

Many times it appeared that she would drop them, but somehow she kept the deck intact. Finally, having shuffled the cards and cut them three times, she placed them before me.

"OK, now cut the cards and place the top half to the right of the bottom half."

This accomplished, I picked up what had been the bottom of the pack and placed it on the top of the cards on the right.

"This covers you." I turned face up the first card, The Moon.

"What does that mean?"

"It's the influence that you are living under at present."

"It doesn't look too good."

The card depicts a waning moon at the top with dots like tears descending on two dogs on either side at the bottom -- these animals appearing like guardians. Between them, disappearing into the distance, is a winding path along which crawls a crayfish. The effect of the whole is that of evening or a stagnant pool.

"A lot depends on the other cards but generally it means dissatisfaction or deception, but only the other cards will make it apparent."

After the moon came the Fool. Forces in opposition! As the rest of the cards became visible, the reading became more and more sinister and intimidating.

In vain I tried to make the reading optimistic, but there was no way to hide what was being said. Sadness and deception were the order of the day and she knew it.

"Well it doesn't look too good does it?" A cloud passed across her earlier light and happy mood and she said, "Like a drink?"

VIVIAN II

I love the preparations for Christmas and the dressing of that old phallic symbol, the Christmas tree. The festival is, of course, of pagan origin, celebrated to acknowledge the emergence of a new generative cycle depicted by the tree.

The pine associated with Zeus and Jupiter is an ideal vehicle to express the idea of generative power, especially since when fully grown, it would appear to pierce the sky as though in an attempt to impregnate it. The trinkets, tinsel and food which adorn the tree are really an offering and appeasement to the sky god for a good year to come. The fairy is the crowning aspect of the divine.

Over the passing months I had spent less and less time at my own flat and more and more at Vivian's clean and safe haven. The day of the tarot reading had been the turning point. That same night we had writhed the whole night away together. As the creative energies of the Great Gods, Isis and Osiris, we fornicated into existence a new universe and future for ourselves. There seemed to be no end to our lovemaking, no end to the rhythm that is bliss. At odd times we would catch moments of sleep only then to wake simultaneously and recommence the rhythm until, like waves upon a beach, we slid once more into sleep.

The following day had been spent in similar pursuit finding us licking and fondling each other's bodies, interspersed with Rhine wine and Benson and Hedges cigarettes.

That evening we had visited the George and Dragon. The inevitable knowing glances and innuendos we shrugged off with physical gesticulation or open ended retort.

Now, months later, as Christmas approached, we had slipped into a calmer pattern of living and loving, although sexual satisfaction continued to be the cornerstone of our union.

The ominous tarot reading had not come to pass and neither of us had since mentioned its content although I had pondered over it from time to time and wondered how it could have been so incorrect.

Vivian had never told me what the question was, but I'm sure it must have been about herself. From past experience I have discovered that people always want to know what the world holds for them. If she was encountering the painful influences of the cards, she certainly kept it well hidden as there appeared to be not even a blemish on our happiness. The magick art which had accompanied me through my solitude and loneliness now took second place but was not forgotten, just neglected.

I continued to observe the four daily adorations to the sun, which had the effect of keeping me mindful of the higher aspirations, but as far as ritual went, I performed none. There were times when I wasn't with Vivian that my mind drifted towards doing more and, while I often felt that I should, somehow I never seemed to get around to it. There was always an excuse for not doing anything.

Saturday was a day that we usually rose late if Vivian wasn't doing a lunch-time session at the pub. But on this Saturday, we had decided to finally brave the crowds and go Christmas shopping.

At 10:00, we dutifully set off upon our quest not deterred by the moist air and the steel skies of Albion, which blanketed the city and were evidently here for the day.

The underground station was packed and we had to stand in line for tickets for a good ten minutes being buffeted and pushed by the agitated crowds who were as dull as the sky above. The journey was no better. We had to stand the whole time crushed between countless bodies either standing, or struggling to get in or out of the carriage.

It was like being enmeshed in a mass of tendrils as arms and bodies stretched out between each other reaching for support to contend with the rolling of the carriage as it thundered between stations.

Vivian stood a little way away from me, as we became separated by two extremely well dressed middle-class women who had pushed their way in at Knightsbridge station.

One was dressed in an obviously expensive mink coat and the other in a very stylish grey wool overcoat. Both were adorned in bulbous jewelry and sported bulging Harrods' shopping bags.

Although the women weren't engaged in conversation I suddenly discovered that I had been preoccupied in observing them and anxiously looked for Vivian.

I looked around the fur coated, bejeweled woman and stared speechless. Vivian was smiling and then, as she continued to look at me, her expression became puzzled. I only half-observed her changed expression as my attention was gripped by what I saw beyond her. Directly behind her, like a storm cloud, was the figure from my dream; the man from the bookshop, the black-coated man from my childhood. Was he really there or was I hallucinating?

I felt myself shiver. The crystal blue eyes clashed with mine while Vivian stood innocent of the energies that swirled around her.

The train lurched to a sudden halt at Green Park and I stumbled awkwardly into the two well-dressed women who only smiled and moved to one side, thinking I was trying to get off. I reached Vivian, only to see the apparition disappear into the crowds beyond the automatic doors of the carriage.

"Are you all right ?"

"Yes, I just stumbled," I replied.

"No, before that. You looked ill. I thought you were going to faint."

"No, I'm fine." I think I may have answered a little abruptly as I felt extremely agitated. The train once more commenced its passage and I tried to catch a glimpse of the man in the crowd, but to no avail. He was gone.

We emerged with relief upon Leicester Square station which, although crowded, didn't have the same claustrophobic atmosphere. It was here that I detected there was a strain between us. The invisible bond between the two people who got on the train had been lost somewhere in transit. We were polite but there was a bluntness in our conversation. It was as if speaking to each other was an effort, the spark was missing. This was the first time in the months that we had spent together that a cloud of intolerance for each other had become visible.

Walking along Oxford Street in the daytime is always difficult but at this time of year it's impossible. One moves more quickly and quite possibly with more safety if one directs one's steps upon the street.

The problem with shopping in Oxford Street is that there is just too much choice and the only achievement is confusion. Knowing this, we decided to make for Selfriges department store with the intent of making all purchases there.

"Do you like this?" Vivian held up a silk scarf.

"Yeah, its fine." Normally I was good company shopping with her. But today, since the encounter on the train, I felt drained and uninspired. I'm sure that my reply intoned my mood, although apparently she didn't detect it for she continued to fondle and stretch out the radiant colored silk enthusiastically between her hands.

My thoughts were totally occupied with the incident on the train and it was impossible for me to focus thought on any other topic. Christmas was ruined. The appearance was like an embarrassment that has suddenly been made public.

ARGOS

One should not be looking for the meaning of life but should be involved in living in the world.

Preoccupation of the self with searching for personal meaning or quest will surely lead to ego emphasis, separatism, or a sense of elitism.

In living life to the full, one becomes aware of the differing aspects of the self and the universe.

Once these aspects have been acknowledged and harmonized, the individual will automatically follow the path of his preset incarnation. Therefore, the student should not be obsessed with mission or meaning but with learning and observing.

If a meaning of life is essential, then let it be the overcoming of fear to experience and see the self as it truly is.

One of the marks of a non-aberrated human being is the ability to face chaos or disorder and not to escape into apathy, grief, anger, intellectualism, sanctimony, false mysticism or any of the other myriad methods of running away.

....

"What time is it?"

"11:00." I responded, irritated at the intrusion distracting me from my reading.

"You coming to bed?"

"In a minute," my tone reflected my rising impatience.

"OK, I'll see you in a minute then," she replied.

"OK."

She rose, picked up the coffee cups, and went into the kitchen. I heard the china clatter and the tap run as she washed them in the sink. She passed through the living room like a wraith without saying a word. I knew she was there, but I didn't want to say anything that might lead to conversation.

How I could have been attracted to her I now couldn't imagine. Because of her I had allowed myself to neglect the magical art. Why, oh why did I so easily become a victim to the deceptions of flesh and easy living which now was a living hell?

When I first met her only six months ago, she was Venus and now who was she? Hecate of the underworld.

What was annoying was that it wasn't really her fault.

I had obviously seen her as something she wasn't. How could I have been so blind?

With her passing went my distraction and I returned my attention to the Morning Star. It didn't matter how I neglected or ignored the book, it was always there, always awaiting my returning interest, always the same, unemotional and unchanged by my disregard.

The book, I suppose, was like God; it didn't really exist until you either looked for it or needed it, and, as with different races' conception of God, so my conception of the book's contents changed with my moods. Like God, the book had more uses apart from that for which it was intended i.e., as a doorstop or for standing on so as to reach something which is out of reach etc. etc. . . . .

Of course, it's not the book that is important . . . only the content, the message which is carried upon the vehicle of words has importance.

Words are power. Before the word there is nothing, but once you can put a name to something, well, then you have power over it.

Why?

Words are description, location, the building bricks of imagination. Words are the bridge between an idea and its actuality.

In bygone times, were not words often considered secretly as the beast, knowledge, the power which made one independent of preconceived thought?

As I read, the light appeared to dim but fractionally. I was aware yet not aware of its lessening magnitude.

Was it just my tired eyes?

A glaze rippled across the page.

The world of faerie was upon me, and I was hypnotized by the eye of the beast.

The serpent with the expanded hood of a king cobra slowly but perceptibly began to spiral from within the printed words.

I stared, beguiled by the yellow hypnotic eyes, which reached into me, clawing at the framework of my mind. The sparkle and energy of the lights destroyed all laws and barriers I had been educated to believe in. I was a drop of water drawn inevitably down into an infinite ocean, where I would be a part of everything, yet a part of nothing.

All pre-conceived ideas of self and world were being smashed.

Fear came out of nowhere. My body arched and I could taste vomit, then the full power of the message within those eyes wove a suffocating web around the fire of my panic. My reason discovered in this moment that it needn't fear destruction.

Destruction is but the dark cloak of transformation. One must be a chameleon and adapt.

Here was the key to the mysteries.

In an instant, quicker than the twinkle of a star, all was black. The serpent towered above me. I sat rigid in awe at the magnificence of the beast. The perfect symmetry of scales and proportions of body were the ideal vehicle of the brittle pure white fangs, that the whole body had evolved to serve.

As I stared, I perceived the pointed teeth dripping crystal venom. The inheritance of the poison was soon to be mine.

In blind acceptance I offered myself to the kiss of initiation.

I became aware that I was irrevocably being drawn to a previously unnoticed tree. As the serpent, I wound myself upward tasting the fruit of the spheres.

The more I devoured, the less I seemed to know. My mind was being erased. The madness of infinity was sweeping towards me as a tidal wave upon a canoe and I reached out to embrace that which would destroy me.

AND LO, SO IT WAS, THAT THE FIRE OF CREATION WAS AS PLUMED SERPENTS UPON THE LIPS OF THE CHILDREN OF THE DAMMED.

WITH THE FEROCITY OF A CAGED BEAST, THE CHILDREN SPOKE THE WORD OF THE AEON, AND THE WORD WAS, DARE!

I opened one eye. God, I was cold!

The light was on. No wonder I'm cold, the gas fire is out.

Good God, Vivian must have been in and switched it off. Why the hell didn't she wake me?

The will of Hypnos drew me to bed and further sleep with the reassuring feeling that I had been reaccepted into the bosom of the magical art.

The early hours are so beautiful: Silent, still, unblemished. It's as though one has the world to one's self.

I slid quietly from the bed, not wanting to wake Vivian, feeling that any other person sharing these hours would be unwelcomed clutter.

Silently, I padded to the kitchen and filled the kettle for coffee. In mesmeric daze I gazed into the street from the little kitchen window. Outside, the world so silent and still was surreal in its clearness. It seemed a blanket of peace lay across the world, although I knew her fingers were rapidly becoming bloody and broken from contending with the forces of activity.

The coffee made, I retired to the living room table and entered the previous evening's dream into the diary. I had been given another chance. I mustn't lose it. Just as I was finishing, Vivian opened the living room door. I was annoyed at her entrance as I was hoping for another hour or so to myself to catch up on my reading and perform a morning adoration to the god of the dawn.

She sat at the table. The very place I had first seen her only a few months ago. I knew she had something to say.

"What are your plans for today?"

"I thought I'd nip up to Charing Cross Road and check out the bookstores."

"I was hoping that we could do something together."

"Well, why don't you come with me?" I prayed she'd say no.

"No, I don't think so."

My prayer having been answered, I even felt safe in pushing the point.

"You might enjoy it."

She stood and walked towards the kitchen.

"No, it's all right. I have a lot of things to do here. Mark and Chris are coming around for dinner this evening so I must get that organized."

"God, do they have to come?"

"Well, yes. They're my friends. I thought it would be nice to have them over."

"Not for me."

I didn't hear her reply from the kitchen. Damn! The thought of people coming over drove me nuts, especially Mark and Chris.

"You don't have to come if you don't want to. It's not compulsory."

"OK, if you don't mind I'll give it a miss."

"As you like," she replied and sat on the couch with her coffee.

I think her silence was worse than her talking. A blanket of oppression seemed to descend and suffocate me. I felt I had to move, to be by myself. I got up and returned to the bedroom to continue my reading.

After a while, I put aside my reading and pondered our relationship. I related it to a piece of cracked porcelain after the affectionate pawing of a child's hands. What devils in our heads had aroused this destructive beast? Something which so recently had opened like a lotus with the dawning rays of the sun on a new day was now closed tight beneath the gibbous moon of vampire night. I sighed and returned to the kitchen.

Breakfast was eaten in silence except for the accepted pleasantries. When it was finished I rose and brought up the subject of the evening dinner.

"You're sure you don't mind, then, if I don't come this evening?"

"Not in the least. Why should I mind?" Her tone didn't compliment her statement.

"All right, I'll be off then. Maybe see you tomorrow."

"You're really not coming this evening?"

"No, I thought we'd already gone over that."

"Yes, but I didn't think you meant it."

"Well, I did. I can't stand either of them."

Actually I was happy to have the dinner as an excuse to get away. Secretly I was desperate to get home and continue my magical enterprises in peace.

"I must say I think it's rather rude of you."

I thought she was about to cry, which was really not what I was after. I was hoping she would be angry enough to end the relationship and save me the embarrassment.

"I don't see why. I didn't invite them."

"We are in a relationship aren't we?"

"I sometimes wonder. We seem miles apart."

"OK, well do what you like. Run off to your damn bookshop."

It was almost a year to the day since I had first visited the Halcyon Days and discovered the cornerstone of my life. It was like that year was "zero": a new beginning.

The emergence of the Morning Star had brought new promise to my life, filling it with good intentions. Sadly, as I reflected, I realized that these intentions remained just that, had even soured, thanks to my relationship with Vivian.

I had hoped that she would have assisted me in my endeavors and become involved, but this was not to be the case. The future Diamond

Priestess had become a dull rock, and, like my vision, I had become the placid bull.

Leaving the house had roused a wonderful sense of optimism within me, a feeling of freedom. I was a bird breaking out of its egg into a larger world. The egg which had once offered protection to the developing embryo was now a prison which could only offer suffocation. The egg was a world and the only way to develop was to destroy a world.

It was inevitable to me that the affair with Vivian must finish. It was now the only loose end.

The bookshop was unchanged. It could even have been the same selection of used books on the rack outside awaiting the disinterested hands of idle passers-by.

On entering I was immediately struck by a sense of deja vu, not anything to do with the shop, but because of a black-coated man who greeted my vision.

He was consulting with an assistant behind the counter who was indicating a row of shelves towards the rear of the store.

The coat was certainly of the same style and color as a year and possibly almost a life time ago in the fateful department store incident, and the hair was definitely grey. From my position, it was impossible to ascertain the color of the eyes.

Was it the same man or was I filling gaps within similarity to create a reality of recognition?

I watched him perusing the shelves. He leafed through the assorted tomes as though trying to fill in time before some other prearranged rendezvous.

I tried to note which ones he selected and with shadowed eyes I obliquely observed him.

The air in the shop was peculiar. It had a hard quality, similar to what one finds in a boiler room but without the heat. For want of a word, it was like iron. He scrutinized the shelves for several minutes and then abruptly turned away as though he had heard someone call his name from behind.

I took the opportunity to occupy his place and try to recall the titles which had maintained his interest amongst the numerous books.

Squeezed at one end of the shelf was a rather oversized edition bound in black which attracted my attention. I withdrew it from its companions, being careful not to have them all cascade to the floor. I turned the title towards me, "The Goetia."

Opening the front cover a piece of card slipped from between the pages and tumbled to the floor. Stooping down I retrieved the fallen card.

At first I thought it to be some kind of stock record but on turning it over, I discovered my name. Neatly written beneath it was a telephone number.

I turned and looked for the man in the black overcoat. There was no sign of him. I returned my attention to the card, re-read it and then turned it over in the hope of finding some additional clue. There was nothing, only my name and the telephone number.

I diverted my gaze to the black-jacketed book and opened it to the title page.

The Book of the
Goetia
of
Solomon the King

I turned the page and read.

The First Book, or Part, which is a Book concerning Spirits of Evil, and which is termed The Goetia of Solomon, sheweth forth his manner of binding these Spirits for use in things divers. And hereby did he acquire great renown.

The following pages were filled with the diagrams of talismans and the names of the spirits which they were capable of evoking. However well the book was produced, I couldn't help but feel that it didn't contain anything genuine. That it was the product of some present-day author.

Returning the book to the shelf, I wondered, who had been watching whom. I assumed that the message had been left by the figure who had been the center of my covert scrutiny.

A shiver of apprehension ran through me and I felt myself to be surrounded by eyes, the gaze of Argos.

I pushed the card into my pocket, and proceeded to read the remainder of the titles but found nothing of interest. Finally I turned and idly gazed around the shop with it's ghost-like occupants, all of whom were preoccupied with their studies.

"Excuse me."

"Oh yes, sorry," I replied startled by a young woman of about twenty as she squeezed by me. She smelled strongly of patchouli oil and possessed the moodiness of a Rossetti maiden. She confidently scrutinized the shelves, obviously aware of what she sought. She ran a well-manicured right index finger across the bound titled backs and tilted her head to one side to make the wording more accessible.

I observed her hips shrouded in the tight fitting material of her dress which was an unwelcomed intrusion to my search for the ridge line of her underwear about her well rounded buttocks.

The line was strongly erotic and its discovery gave a sense of achievement to me.

I continued to watch her until she turned in my direction, maybe detecting observation. Feeling a little like I had been "caught" at some misdeed, I diverted my gaze.

I left, emerging into the noon sunlight, wondering how my life might have been changed if I'd had the confidence to speak to the woman and maybe strike up a relationship.

I telephoned the number on the card. I had deliberated much during the course of the day as to what it might be all about and how to broach the conversation. I needn't have worried, however, for the conversation was brief and to the point.

The receiver was picked up quickly and before I had the opportunity to speak a voice had said,

"Randolph Vann. Is this John?"

"Yes, it is," I replied. A little startled by the direct inquiry.

"I have a message to call you. I'm sorry, I missed your name."

"Oh, I do apologize. Randolph Vann. I had expected you to call earlier but I suppose that you have been busy."

Did I detect a note of sarcasm in the reply ? There was no time for me to speak.

"I understand that you are interested in the Morning Star."

"Well, yes," I replied, hesitantly, being unsure of the invisible confidant.

"That's good. Are you free a week on Saturday?"

"Yes, as far as I know."

"In that case please come to . . . . ," he then gave me an address in Sevenoaks Kent.

The conversation concluded with me agreeing to telephone back when I had confirmed the times of train arrivals from London.

ARGOS II

Victoria Mainline Railway station is hardly the place where one would expect to begin a magical quest or, for that matter, out of choice, commence any kind of undertaking. Maybe in its heyday it had captured the imaginations of foreigners as the gateway to the streets of gold, but now it was blatantly obvious that the gold had all been stripped away.

The structure seemed to secrete dirt. Whatever one touched left a smear of grime on hand or clothing. The waste paper, like tumbleweed, journeyed ever onward to some unforeseen and unimagined destination, much like the countless prospective travelers and clientele of the station's environs.

The air of despondency and abandonment was emphasized by the new structure constructed within the shell of the old.

Strange how new buildings appear to degenerate and become far more of an eyesore than the ones that they have replaced.

The drawings and models of these 20th century edifices always appear so Utopian. They deteriorate at an alarming rate and the designs always omit the reality of how the buildings and piazzas will look with litter-filled fountains and the stains of polluted air and acid rain.

Possibly during the week, with the thunder of commuter traffic, the place isn't such an eyesore. But now, with the sparseness of weekenders, the whole takes on the appearance of a slum and the people reflect the mood.

With this as the first experience that European visitors arriving by train from the Continent have of London, any subsequent sights have to be an improvement.

After pulling out of the station, the train travels through a cutting lined with blue brick and then, quite suddenly, emerges into open air and crosses the Thames on a black iron girder bridge. The noise of the wheels is suddenly amplified by the resonant quality of the steel structure.

A few moments later the train pulls to a stop at London Bridge station after leaving Victoria only five minutes previously. The odd door can be heard to slam to the accompaniment of whistles and raised voices and then, once more, the locomotive is on its way.

On this side of the river, the railway lines travel along the top of a viaduct giving all aboard a commanding view of south London. I tried to imagine how it would have looked to the armies of Caesar as they marched, line upon line, around the marshes towards their prize, the Celtic fortress which would soon become Londinium.

The malaise of reality below was too overpowering, however, to bend to the whims of fancy. Here, truly, was the death of an empire reflected in the unkempt buildings and streets of its capital and heart. In the new tower blocks of apartments, with their minute window openings that rise and pierce the sky like termite hills, it would appear that man has reverted to the caves of his youth. Block upon block of new habitations rise from the elegance of Victoriana below, without rhythm or scheme. The planning would have been as successful if somebody had given a chimpanzee a pen. We, the custodians of planet earth, have made a poor job of tending what nature has graciously placed in our care.

Fortunately, these depressing scenes are soon left behind, and the train enters the realm of the English countryside, serene and safe after the jumble of the city just left behind. The fields so neat and symmetrical display how nature can be enhanced and brought to a perfection in ecological harmony. Everything, even the pastoral cows, appear as recycling machines, drawing up, casting out, only to eventually lie down one day and be recycled themselves by the greatest machine of all, Mother Earth.

From my vantage point beside the window, I can quite easily gaze at the all too rare English blue sky which, like a bubble, protects us from whatever may lie beyond.

I consider the sun and the sign of the Zodiac it is in at the present time, and then visualize its great wheel, the belt of Isis, as it arcs towards the horizon and then disappears below my feet, only to once more reappear where it began.

I can easily visualize the houses of the year in silver filigree lattice work. Each awaiting its time to be brought into life by the great creative force of the sun.

The perpetual wheel of life: we are born, we live, we die, we are recycled.

Whatever? Does it really matter?

What was a death road to Phaeton is to me a highway to the gods where rite of entry is restricted to those who dare.

Those who dare. I, for the first time, detected slight apprehension as to what lay before me. Especially since no one, not even Vivian, knew to what address I was destined.

I traveled into the Rainbow Bridge, Seven Oaks, finally.

The whole journey I had spent alone in the train compartment with my thoughts, which resulted in my being extremely drowsy by the time I emerged onto the platform.

The blue sky has gone and the steel skies of Albion have returned to cast the druid spell.

He was exceedingly conservative in appearance. Certainly not what you'd expect an occultist to look like.

There was no sense of intimidation, in fact, quite the opposite was the case. It could have been my father before me.

He stood in the doorway wearing casual cord trousers, a white shirt fitted at the neck with a polka-dot bow tie, and over the top, an open-knitted cardigan.

The blue eyes stared direct and keen, a reminder to me of the figure from my youth. The memory was intimidating.

"Hello John."

"Randolph Vann?"

"Yes, come in."

I don't know why I should have been surprised by him recognizing me. After all, it was he who had left me the card.

"Well come in," he said, and stood to one side to allow me passage into the hallway, which I noticed, could have done with a fresh coat of paint.

He closed the door, deliberating over the latch as if there was a problem clicking it into place.

"I wasn't expecting you so soon. I'm sorry if I'm a little disorganized," he said, turning from the recently concluded encounter with the door.

"Yes, I'm sorry I didn't have the times of the trains right. It arrived at 2:05 not 2:55."

"That's all right. You don't have to apologize," and he smiled.

We entered into a most elegant room, quite a contrast from the hall.

Greens surprisingly are a most difficult color to utilize successfully, but here several different shades were blended beautifully. The carpet was a deep emerald and the wall covering appeared to lighten to a soft almost blue eggshell as it approached the white of the ceiling.

The seating was most luxurious and inviting. A deep bountiful couch skirted two walls and an armchair of the same design sat on a third.

To compliment and off-set this, was an extravagant use of brass in door furniture and picture framing.

"Well, take a seat I'll make some tea, or would you rather take coffee?"

"No, tea will be fine."

He left the room and from my chair I looked around for evidence of magical memorabilia, but to no avail. The room could have been any one of millions in and around London. My enthusiasm sank a little. I don't know what I had expected, but it hadn't been this.

There was a large aquarium against the far wall filled with various species of exotic marine life. The bubbles supplied a reassuring background noise to the waiting, although simultaneously emphasizing the silence.

I watched his cat, his familiar, playfully amusing herself with a large wisteria plant. The animal, so innocent and oblivious, stalked and attacked the thin delicate leaves in preparatory maneuvers for the night's hunting. Soon bored by the plant's lack of retaliation, she ambled to a bureau and gazed out of the window. Here, with jerking movements of her head, she followed the progress of her aspiration, the birds locked into the air waves. To me she was childish innocence, to the birds she was a vision of death.

She returned her attention to the plant, the leaves of which were now gently rising and falling at the direction of the breeze. In prone position, she swayed lightly, awaiting the moment to strike, awaiting the moment of stillness which comes before death. Obediently, under the hypnotic gaze of the predator, the leaves became motionless and the feline made her move. She made the most tremendous leap and stuck her prey directly. The plant and pot tottered under the velocity of the beast and then, directed by the laws of gravity, plant and cat thundered to the ground with a resulting crash. The cat suddenly assuming itself as the victim of the encounter under the prolific abundance of leaves, shot headlong from the scene of action and cowered by the door awaiting release.

I picked up the pot and scraped as much of the dark loam as possible from the pile of the carpet and returned it to its previous position. The leaves looked a little bent here and there, but otherwise it appeared that the wisteria had weathered the encounter. The only other evidence, the traces of dark earth, which remained on the carpet.

I returned to my seat and heard Randolph's footsteps in the hall as he approached the door.

The door opened inwards under the direction and motivation of the well-aimed toe of his shoe and he appeared in the room bearing a tray with a teapot, two cups, and a jug, presumably containing the milk. The cat, I noticed, slipped from the room through the half open door.

He placed the tray on the octagonal top of a carved wooden table of Oriental design, the base of which was a rather stiff primitive looking elephant.

"I take mine black but I've brought some milk if you take yours white."

"Oh yes, thank you," the thought of black tea quite repulsed me.

"Nice home you have. Been here long?" I needed to fill the silence.

"Yes, it was my mother's. I was born upstairs. You could say I've spent an eternity here."

He began pouring the tea from a pot that was quite beautiful, a pure white background with an emerald green design of a dragon highlighted with a gold relief.

"So, you're interested in the Order of the Morning Star. Is this a practical interest or is it purely an intellectual preoccupation that you wish to pursue?"

He passed me a cup.

I was a little taken aback by his coming straight to the point and I heard the nervousness in my voice as I replied.

"Well, it's something I've felt drawn to since my earliest memories. My mother would talk to me about it, wrapped up in stories. I don't know how much truth they contained, if any."

"Do you remember any of those stories?"

"Yes, one or two, although they seem of little consequence. Any of importance I can't for the life of me seem to recall."

"Well don't be shy, tell me one."

I pondered for a moment over his request and then said,

"What about 'the house of golden windows'?"

"That sounds innocent enough, tell it to me" he replied earnestly.

There was once a young boy who lived with his family in a cottage on the eastern slopes of a valley.

The family was very poor and every waking hour was spent in either tilling or harvesting the tired soil so that enough money could be earned to pay the yearly taxes to the Lord of the land.

Each morning, the boy would rise at dawn and look out across the valley to the western sloping hillside in the distance, and there see a cottage with burnished golden windows.

Oh, how those windows blazed, and oh, how he yearned to live in that house across the valley, to escape the turmoil of his own environment.

The people who lived there must be so rich to be able to afford such an extravagance, he thought. Not even the lord who took all his family's wealth could pay for such beauty.

One morning, the urge to see the house became overwhelming. So after feigning sickness, the boy waited for everybody to leave the house and go about their daily labours. Then he quickly dressed and slipped out on his quest, knowing he had until dusk to return, as nobody ever stopped working while there was still light to labour by.

Much to the boy's dismay, the trek to the cottage was far more arduous than he had anticipated and with half the afternoon gone he was still not at his destination.

The valley was extremely wooded, he knew, but he hadn't imagined the undergrowth to be so thick and dense.

He had not seen the house across the valley since leaving his own home because of the thickness of the trees. So with the lateness of the hour, he was beginning to wonder if maybe he hadn't wandered too far along the course to the valley.

Just as he was beginning to think about changing his course, he caught sight of something through the trees. He walked a little further and to his relief, saw it was the stone wall of the building he sought.

But no! It couldn't be. This house was a ruin, without even a roof.

He walked around the side in dismay and saw the windows with broken panes of glass and a door idly swinging on broken hinges.

This couldn't be true. The goal of his aspiration surely couldn't be a pile of broken stones and cracked glass.

The door swung positively, in contradiction to its earlier movement, and there on the portal stood an old man with long grey hair, wearing a maroon ankle-length robe.

The boy was startled and backed away from the figure, fearing a reprimand; but he needn't have worried, for the old man smiled and pleasantly said,

"Welcome young sir. You look weary, can I help you?"

The boy looked despondent and didn't reply, so the old man, feeling compassionate, walked over to comfort him. It was then, after a few moments of rest, that the boy related his story of his quest for the house with golden windows.

The old man continued to smile and said,

"I am the magician of the Morning Star. Your quest is over. I can show you the house with golden windows."

The boy looked up sharply, suddenly alert at the old man's words and followed the direction of his pointing.

The setting sun was behind them but it had not yet fallen below the brow of the hill. The old man directed the youth to look east towards the oncoming cloak of night and there he saw across the valley the object of his search.

It was his own home, the windows blazing gold with the rays of the disappearing sun.

There was the house of golden windows!

"I wouldn't have considered that of little consequence."

He didn't allow me time to answer, but continued,

"Maybe it's roots that you're searching for. Do you remember much about your mother?"

"No, she died when I was young."

"Do you feel that she deserted you?"

"Not especially," I sipped my tea.

"Well, enough of these meanderings. Did you bring your diary, as I asked you?"

"Yes, here you go," and I pulled my black notebook from out of its paper bag. I passed it across the table to his waiting hands.

"You have a liking for black-jacketed books, I see. Is it a reflection of your character?"

"No, not especially. Why do you say that?"

"Well, this," he raised my diary slightly emphasizing his meaning.

"And the Goetia. By the way, did you buy it?"

"I barely looked at it, to be honest. Is it worthwhile?"

"Like everything else, it depends on your point of view, but I would say yes, even if it only teaches you to learn by your mistakes."

I wanted to ask, and I knew he knew that I wanted to ask, about the card in the bookstore, but I waited too long and the opportunity was lost, for the present.

He opened my diary and carefully flicked through a few pages.

"You realize that if you are accepted into the Order, a lot will be expected of you. There is no room for those with idle curiosity."

"Yes, I realize that."

"I hope so, because there will be much you will be asked to experience. The inner grades are only obtainable by complete selflessness."

He devoted his attention to the journal. I wanted desperately to broach the subject of his similarity to the figure who persistently pushed into my life and dreams from my earliest recollections, but couldn't fathom how to introduce the subject tactfully.

I knew if I brought it up I would just blurt it out. The whole subject put me on edge.

His face looked now as when I first remembered it in the department store; not a year or month appeared to have passed across it. You wouldn't exactly say that the face was youthful; it was more that youth shone through it, a glass-still lake beneath the surface of which one witnessed the electric swift movements of a dexterous trout.

The complexion was tanned and the same wrinkles surrounded the steel blue eyes.

"Well, I must say, you have been busy. It's rare that I see this much effort in somebody working alone. However, I see that you seem to have tailed off a little towards the end. Getting disheartened?"

"No, it's just that now I have a relationship with a young lady and so my time isn't quite as free as it was."

"Well that's good. One shouldn't cut one's self off from life. How does your young lady feel about the magical art? I'm sorry, I didn't catch her name."

"Oh, Vivian. I'm afraid that she doesn't approve, thinks that it's black magic."

"Oh, I'm sorry to hear that. It must make things a little difficult."

"Yes, just a bit."

"Does she know that you're here?"

"Yes."

He raised his tea cup and returned his attention to the journal.

"I see here that you performed a tarot reading for, Vivian did you say?"

I nodded in response.

"She approved of that then?"

"Oh yes, you know how people are. They are unhappy with life and want to hear that it's getting better. They think it's the world that's at fault, not themselves."

"That's a little harsh isn't it? You know, not everybody is fortunate enough to have spent the time you have to find out these things."

I felt reprimanded.

"Yes, maybe you're right."

"This vision that you record here on the day you did the reading for her, the one about the bull and the lion, how do you interpret that?"

"That I lack perseverance."

He gave an understanding nod.

"Yes, carry on."

"I saw the maiden as the whole temple of initiation; her legs, the twin-pillars which divide to allow the aspiring neophyte access to the chalice of her secrets, that inner place waiting to be filled with life by the power of my wand."

"But that's not what you say here. If I may quote, you say that . . . 'she was a vision of Vivian and a symbol of how you should pursue her . . . ' so what changed your mind?"

"At the time I was besotted with her. She was all I could think of. It was as though I was possessed and everything related to her."

"This is not the case now?"

"No."

"Um, interesting."

I wasn't too sure if I had said the right thing.

"What I would like to do, if I may, is keep the diary for a week and have you come back next weekend. I'll have had time to give its reading justice by then, and we'll go from there. Does that sound all right to you?"

"Yes, of course."

"What I would also like, is to set you a task that will encourage your perseverance and self-control. Just flicking through your diary I can see that you tend to flit from one idea to another without really consolidating anything. Do you agree?"

After his earlier comments, this was like receiving a slap in the face.

"I'm sorry I didn't mean to belittle your efforts. I can see I've hurt your feelings."

"No, well yes, just a little. The problem is, that as soon as I begin to delve into a subject, a multitude of other fringe topics appear which seem to demand investigation if I'm to be successful."

"Yes, that's the same with most things in life. The successful, however, are those who are single-minded. Even if you are side-tracked, you must always keep your goal in view."

I sipped at my tea, but it was cold.

"I believe I'm persistent."

"Then why the vision? You were told what you lacked, why do you persist in ignoring it? Too much effort for you to get up and do something about it?"

He spoke calmly without any vindictiveness, but I took great exception to his comments. This wasn't how I viewed myself.

"You should remember that dreams are not the act, only a guide. They are at best a vision of what might be, but they won't bring it about. Only you can do that, and that takes effort."

"All right what's the answer?" I asked abruptly.

He reached into a pocket and withdrew his hand, gripping an ornate lacquer-painted box about two inches square.

"Do you consider yourself one of the elect prepared to dare all, or is there a limit to your endeavors to find the answer within yourself?"

The man who had greeted me when I arrived was not the man who now sat before me. I felt intimidated and tried to act casual by answering, "I'll play along."

"This isn't playing, my friend. Be sure before you say yes! If you back down after I open this box, you won't be welcome here anymore, and of course you won't be welcome within yourself."

"I've said I want to find the answer, so show me."

He carefully levered open the lid saying, "Smash the egg and be born, rise up."

This seemed a little theatrical, to say the least, and only served to erode his conservative demeanor to the level of mountebank.

From out of the small box, he withdrew between thumb and forefinger a plain razor blade.

"This will be your teacher."

I wanted to laugh.

"For the next week you will not cross your legs. Each time you do, you will cut your arm with this razor blade."

I ran a hand through my hair in disbelief. The whole idea seemed totally barbaric.

"Remember, each time you cross your legs."

I looked down, and with a sudden movement, repositioned my lower appendages.

"Let me get this straight. You seriously expect me to cut my arm each time I cross my legs?"

"You agreed to the task."

"But I didn't know what it was." The ridiculousness of the statement hit me as I said it.

"That's something else you have to learn."

He stood and walked to the window, his back towards me.

"The first requirement in the art of magick is control of the self. If you can't control yourself, how can you expect to control the energies of the subtle planes?" he asked. Then, continuing, "I would also like you to have ready a motto which describes your aspiration. This will be another weapon which will help to maintain your attention towards your goal."

"Any questions?"

"Just one, why did you leave the card in the book for me?"

He broke my confidence with his direct stare.

"Isn't it what you wanted?"

"But why that way? Why not more direct? You couldn't have known that I'd reply."

"Would you have wanted it any other way? A potential adventure, how could you fail to reply?"

How much did this man know about me, and from where did he get his information? One mystery solved merely unlocked yet another. It was like peeling an onion.

I had awakened with my legs crossed, so obediently I lifted the razor and made a long stroke across my arm. It was surprising how much easier it was getting. At first it was extremely difficult to cut deep enough to draw blood and first attempts had found the skin to be quite rubbery, requiring far more pressure than I thought to break through it. This discovery had occurred ten razor strokes previously and I now drew the blade confidently through the flesh. My left arm was now elegantly adorned with elastoplast.

The previous evening had been a little difficult in that I thought Vivian may have found it disturbing to see me consciously cutting my arm. She found the whole subject of the occult disturbing and such an action would have been more ammunition for her. So on each occasion, I went to the bathroom and inflicted the punishment upon my disobedient body in solitude.

But of course, it wasn't my body which was at fault, it was my mind, it lacked the power to observe.

It was eight-thirty and Vivian had already left for work. I swung myself out of bed insuring that my legs didn't cross and proceeded into the living room. I stood in the center of the room and faced east looking towards the French windows.

Jachin and Boaz appeared before me and I silently made my adoration to Ra the rising sun.

It felt wonderful to perform the ritual nude. It seemed to bring about a closer relationship with nature. Clothes represented the everyday world and the discarding of them couldn't help but transport one into another realm.

ARGOS III

Diary entry :

I had a dreadful argument with Vivian this evening and stormed out. God, it feels good to be away from her and back in my own place, to get away from all that oppression.

I wonder now what I ever saw in her. I can only assume that she's changed. Listening to her waffling on drives me crazy.

The silence is absolute.

I'm awake, but it's as though I'm in a dream.

The darkness is so intense. Not so much as a glimmer of reflection in this morass of black.

Am I blind?

No, with scrutiny I can vaguely make out my clenched, bone-white knuckles gripping the protective cocoon of blankets.

Am I awake?

Yes, I feel conscious.

I look around the room. There is nothing, just a solid wall of black.

But wait, there is something.

It's an oppressive and overwhelming sense of evil. A tidalwave of something unwholesome.

At the extremity of my vision I'm aware with an intangible sense that the darkness which surrounds me is alive with a writhing mass of stinking rotting forms. There is no part which isn't mobile. Everything one finds unwholesome when lifting a slab of stone is here. Huge worms of slime distort and fester as they extrude and entwine with each other, tearing one another apart with their convulsions. Out of the slime of their residue they are reborn, denizens of worlds that should not be made conscious to the fragile human mind. It's that awesome feeling one has as a child as one waits in the pensive quiet before a thunder storm. The lightning and sudden onset of rain are such a relief and release of tension.

Taloned fingers of fear tear at the back of my skull behind my ears and then cascade with lightning precision as icy water down my spine, forcing my body into a rigid attitude of animal terror.

There is no way I dare to venture out of bed. There is definitely something out there. My bed and blankets now become a fortified citadel protecting me from the hostile forces of chaos which surrounded me.

I snuggle down further into the blankets, seeing myself as a shipwrecked sailor gripping at his humble piece of flotsam as he waits for unheralded rescue.

My gaze is drawn to the center of the room and now thankfully, my sense of perspective has returned.

A pinpoint of light forms, hovering between floor and ceiling.

I gaze fascinated, as slowly the point becomes a sphere. A jewel of such exquisite proportion.

In origami fashion, the sphere unfolds out of nothing to approximately a foot in diameter.

It draws toward me.

The pressure of silence is so intense, I believe the very air will crack to relieve the strain.

The sphere is just a couple of feet away. Its light in all this darkness is reassuring.

It hovers before me.

After all the strain, the light is a friendly hand, reaching to pull me from my torment, release me from this black abyss.

But no!!

Good God, how close I am to destruction. This light is the terror!!!

The sphere turns into a huge pyramid, composed of a myriad of blinking eyes.

The room disintegrates and the pyramid and I are giants on a colossal plain. It's evening, the setting sun is a huge dry blood beast at the point of defeat against the onslaught of night.

With Gorgon-like quality, the eyes cast a blanket of terror and evil across the land. My lower entrails move up into my throat and I want to vomit. Fortunately, the inrush of air from my heavy breathing restrains me.

I pull away and visualize the sword of power in my right hand. The blade so pure, turns the light of the setting sun into immense flashes of lightning. It hovers, awaiting my judgement.

My arm sweeps down in a perfect arc and smashes the figure asunder.

Nothing. The room is immediately normal, as though nothing has happened.

It's quiet, yes, but it's the quiet one is used to, with the infinitesimal background noises.

I can't believe it. What the hell just occurred?

The blackness has all disappeared and there is now a reassuring warmness about the atmosphere.

I'm sure it's OK to get out of bed now. The air feels safe and clean.

The storm has passed, for the present.

CROSSING THE RUBICON

A stream between Italy and Gaul; the crossing of it by Caesar marked the beginning of the war with Pompey.

The die is cast and the Rubicon crossed

....

"You always sit in that corner."

I made a motion to move, unconsciously thinking I was in the wrong.

"No, don't move. You're obviously comfortable there."

He crossed his legs and laid an arm across the back of the chair, assuming a most nonchalant pose.

"How's Vivian?"

"I've not seen her for a few days. I suppose that you'd say we've had a 'tiff'."

"Oh, that's too bad. It's not a permanent split, I hope?"

"I hope it is! She drives me bloody crazy. I'm sorry to say that she's not what I thought she was."

"And what was that?"

"Oh, more feminine, mystical. You know, ethereal."

"Unreal you mean?"

"No!"

"Maybe unknown would be a better description then?"

"Possibly, I suppose if I'd known what she was really like I'd never have gotten involved. All the time she goes on about how important her friends are and how they say this and that."

"Do you feel threatened by them, then?"

"No, it's not that. It's just that their only interests seem to be set around drinking and work and talking about themselves. I'm sorry, I'm rambling. At the end of the day I suppose there's no mystery any more."

"There was at the beginning then?"

"Oh yes! She was everything. She was magical. She was all I could think about, the image of all my dreams."

"Have you thought that that maybe is the problem? She is a real person, not a dream. A person in her own right and has a life beyond what you imagine for her."

He didn't seem to understand what I was driving at, so I tried to elaborate my point of view.

"At times I can't bring myself to talk to her, she's so irritating. Her views are so narrow, all cooking, cleaning and dinner parties for boring people. She has no urge to progress."

"Isn't that what attracted you in the first place, a model home, security? Everything has its price you know?"

"Yes, but I thought . . . oh, I don't know what I thought. All I know is, it isn't right anymore."

I thought a moment and then continued, "I'll tell you what it's like. It's as though there was a wall there which I can't break down. I had a dream once where I saw us both in bed lying on our backs, both of us pure white and then gently we drifted into one another, becoming one celestial body. There were no secrets between us then. That's the relationship I want: perfect honesty. When we make love, I want it to be as if we were gods, great creative energies of the universe."

He looked at me through narrowed eyes and then responded.

"There are a number of wants in that statement. Have you ever thought to wonder what Vivian might want?"

"You talk of honesty, would you tell her how you speak about your relationship to somebody who is a stranger to her, and are you prepared to give all of yourself to this relationship? It takes a tremendous amount of courage and trust to do what you ask. Maybe you shouldn't expect her to do what you're not prepared to do yourself."

I stood up and walked over to the aquarium to observe the fish in their uncomplicated world. I didn't like what I was hearing and needed a break. Still, he continued,

"I've read your diary. You've kept a very good record, but I can't help but think you're too easily sidetracked. By the way, how's your arm?"

Returning to my seat I rolled up my sleeve to display the multiple strips of sticking plaster that adorned my forearm. This accomplished I rolled up the other to display an equal quantity where, through lack of space on the former, I had been forced to continue.

"You kept a record I trust?"

I pulled a small pocket book from my inside jacket pocket and handed it to him. Inside were the dates, times and circumstances of every stroke of the razor. I had purposely bought a green covered notebook because of his comment the previous week.

"Well, that's very thorough. I'm encouraged. It's not easy, is it?"

"No, I'll agree to that, but it sure does make one take note of what one is doing. It's quite amazing how much we do subconsciously. I must say, though, that there were times I thought I was going nuts."

"In what way?"

"I can't really put into words what I felt. The closest I can come is to say that my mind felt itself to be on a knife's edge. I saw it as one of those insects you see that walks on the surface of a pond protected by a thin skin which covers the surface from the infinite power beneath."

"If the skin is ruptured, the fragile creature loses all identity and becomes absorbed by the depths beneath. It made me realize what a delicate instrument reason is."

I then related the nightmare experience of a few nights previous concerning the pyramid of eyes. He listened attentively and then said, "I would say that you were experiencing the power of Lucifer."

"That sounds ominous," I responded.

"I suppose so, if you think of him in the conventional sense. But remember, Lucifer is the light-bringer who reveals the dark side of the moon in us. He manifests the true self, that part of ourselves we do not wish to acknowledge."

"We, in true human fashion, of course, can't admit our own shortcomings and so invent something to hang our guilt on, the scapegoat. Lucifer, therefore, is in reality, the Messiah. He takes on all our sins."

An interesting piece of rhetoric I thought, as he continued.

"Let's face it, the concept that Lucifer was thrown out of heaven by God is absolutely ridiculous when you consider that Lucifer was the purest and most loved by God. God trusted Lucifer above all his other Angels. He didn't throw his most loved Lucifer out of Heaven, he sent him on a mission that he knew only Lucifer could accomplish. He sent Lucifer into matter to purify it. He isn't the Fallen Angel; he is the descent of the light of God, Fiat Lux, the command of God."

I nodded silently which he obviously took for agreement, for he continued.

"Christianity, not wanting Man to rise in knowledge and become wise, individual and free, has bastardized God's message for its own ends. It doesn't want to save Man; it wants to imprison and control him, make him a prisoner in the inertia of matter. It has, in fact, created Satan out of God's messenger. As it is said, one usually judges others by ones own standards."

I couldn't help but think that there was, to say the least, a little bit of judgement going on here. I didn't reveal any thoughts I might have had, although I felt that he waited for me to express an opinion.

He turned his head and gazed out of the window and continued as though speaking to the world at large.

"Christianity is the true agent of ignorance, it represents the unpurified matter, inertia, which God sent his most beloved Lucifer to purge. In other words Christianity is the base element of alchemy: Eve, Guinevere, and the mother of Christ."

He returned his attention to me and stared, demanding a reply with his cold steel blue eyes.

"But surely, Lucifer was driven out of heaven before the start of Christianity?" I questioned, speaking more out of a need to fill the silence rather than having any argument.

He replied calmly, "Yes, but the Christian fathers were the descendants of those pagans who sought power through ignorance. They took old beliefs and bent them to their own ends, then they calculatingly destroyed the old religions in the hope that truth would be lost."

"When I argue the validity of Christianity, it is not the universal message that I object to, it is its silk-tongued bandits of freedom that I question; those who would have us believe that God is outside of ourselves. You know that we are all a part of God and that the Christ was an image of the Godman, the symbol of what Man should strive to be. The being symbolized by Christ and multiple other sacrificial gods is in every man. Life is the quest to come into contact with the energy and become the figure of our aspiration."

"It is an internal reality, not an external idol to be worshiped."

"Remember, we are all sparks thrown off from the infinite. There is no part of us which is not of the gods."

"There is nothing actually wrong with the fabric and props of Christianity because it is intrinsically pagan in the way it uses the images of high magick. Observe the dates of its festivals."

"What Christians fear is knowledge and truth, and these, as I have stated, are the attributes of Lucifer. He gives us the ability to search and confront our true selves, so that we can work to become closer to God and perfection. Lucifer is on a mission from God, an agent of God, alive within the hearts of all Men and awaiting discovery. He is the hero figure and this figure is always perceived by the established order as entering the social circle by apparent violence; each new generation revolts against the established order. That is why Christianity lives in fear of the hero. He is the figure they most sought to destroy from the old beliefs. The hero fights what is corrupt."

"Remember in the Arthurian legend? How in the Christian translations they have the hero, Launcelot discredited for manifesting Guinivere's true self? She was in reality the base matter, like Eve from a similar book of legends called the Bible. He tore away the shroud and showed her for what she was. He demolished the pedestal of lies; Launcelot was the Lightbringer, Lucifer."

"Here though, we also see the error in experiencing the truth too quickly; it destroys the whole fabric. It should be a gradual process, and here my friend, lies the message of alchemy, gradual heat. You are a disciple of the art. You should know that."

"Well yes, I'll agree to that."

"At the time of the Last Battle though, Launcelot returns and wins the day. Truth finally wins out. They forgot to twist that, a grave error, for this Last Battle is a representation of Armageddon."

He leaned back in his chair and breathed heavily, pausing briefly before recommencing.

"Cain is yet another example. Didn't he have to kill Abel, the conditioned man, the old order? Abel was here the base matter, Cain was the hero, one in whom the energy of Lucifer had manifested."

I remembered my own interpretation of this story from my school days and its uncanny similarity to Randolph's. The sensation of chalk-filled nostrils returned with the memory.

"The seven punishments put upon Cain were, in fact, the knowledge of the seven planets, each one representing an inner process of man. His punishment, if one can call it that, was the knowledge that he was not perfect until he had understood and harmonized these seven energies: the sign upon his brow, the five-pointed star point uppermost, the symbol of human intelligence, the faculty required to achieve this process."

"The descendants of Cain have lived and worked within the structure of society, ensuring that they do not make themselves conspicuous, either by dress or life style, from the people that they live among. Through the course of centuries they have endeavored to change humanity's outlook by the power of example."

Obviously, if what I had discovered about the history of the Order of the Morning Star was true, then according to Randolph's interpretation they were a part of the family of Cain.

He continued, drawing me further into the shadow land by his explanation. "Always, Lucifer is the drive forward of evolution. All who thwart this drive are an abomination and perversion. Lucifer will always be the rebel to each new generation until the time that man reaches perfection. It is the task of the elect, those who are one with Lucifer and the descendants of Cain, to purge this black dragon and by degree, raise it up through sublimination."

"And from where do you draw these conclusions? Surely it was Lucifer who rebelled against God?"

"That's how it has been twisted, granted."

"Aren't you just changing what you don't find convenient?"

"Is that what you think?"

"I think that maybe you are trying to be controversial, maybe trying to shock me."

"Why should I want to do that?"

"I don't know, build up a mystique. You tell me."

"Don't pride yourself. It has nothing to do with image building. You know the Latin translation for Lucifer surely."

"No."

"Well, it means the morning-star, Venus. Look it up sometime."

The morning star. Has my whole life's search been a quest to become one of the damned, I pondered?

"But whatever my views, let's face it, Western civilization has been raised on a Bible, which has been translated so many times, by so many political factions, who knows what is the truth? At the end of the day you must dig and come to your own conclusions. The adept must test all things. You should know that."

"Yes." He was right. In all that I had read that was the consistent message, test everything.

I didn't speak, but I was convinced that he was reading my thoughts. How do I test him?

He gazed with the cold-blooded eyes of a predator selecting its prey and I remembered my childhood experience in the department store.

I returned his stare, sinking into the infinite pools of blue that spiraled ever down into the sockets of his head like whirlpools.

The waters are dark and stagnant with depths of infinite silence. Nothing moves, yet there is a fear of the depths, a fear of no accountable reason.

From out of the silence, I observe a pin-point of light arcing unhurried like a shooting star across the face of the unending desolate waters. Although falling, there is purpose and direction in its movement.

There is the rumbling as of distant thunder through the deep, as the star enters the waters, and in so doing, it unfolds into geometric patterns, ever-increasing in complexity until finally creating a cathedral of life from what was originally inertia.

From within the center of the matrix of geometry, at the point which was the falling star, dawn appears, and the last stars retreat from the indigo waters of the night sky.

The eastern horizon becomes stained red with the blood of the recently slain dragon of night, defeated by the hand of the unfolding dawn.

In brilliant yellow armour, the morning rises and treads the waters of life; the stars melt and appear to become one with the light of day. Individuality is sacrificed to the power of the new order; all becomes one with the universal god of life and the earth is kissed by the rapture of freshness.

As a stone, I observe the passage of the sun until, as an old man, he finally returns to below the horizon and the kingdom of stella light is rekindled in individuality.

A voice echoes throughout the vaults of the night and the stars cascade like confetti.

"Well?"

"I'm sorry, what did you say?" How long had I been in the reverie? It must have been for only seconds, although eons seemed to have gone by.

"You don't trust me do you?"

I always felt he was trying to make me look like an idiot, and I wondered if he laughed at me when he spoke about me to others.

"Yes, of course," I replied. But it was so weakly replied it was obvious that it was a lie.

"It's of no matter," he smiled.

I felt embarrassed.

He smiled again, leaned forward slightly and said with some enthusiasm, "So you have a motto I trust?"

"Yes, although it didn't come easy. Eventually, though, I came up with 'Rubicon'."

"Um, that's good. Frater Rubicon. He who has cast the die, nothing will ever be the same for you, you have crossed over."

It's obvious from your latest experience that you have come into contact with the forces behind existence. Possibly the Goetia rubbed off on you. You really must be more critical about what you pick up."

He smiled as though to himself.

"I think it would be wise for you to be initiated into the order for your own protection. You need to learn to read the forms which ride upon the waves of the ether and restrain the freedom of the spirits therein."

My heart jumped. My adventure was coming true. He continued,

"From what you've said, I think that it should be done at the first opportunity if you are not to be lost. How does next weekend sound to you?"

"Wonderful!"

"Fine, I'll arrange it for then. Oh, by the way, you can dispense with the razor blade exercise. It's served its purpose."

What a relief! My body silently sighed.

"Oh, one more thing, if you need to get into contact with me, don't use the phone. Communicate by letter and insure that the postage stamp is upside down."

"Whatever for?"

"Because," he said with a note of exasperation, "I'll know what it concerns and I will be sure to examine the contents in private."

"Should I be doing anything this week in the way of preparation?"

"Just continue with the banishing ritual. I can see from your diary you have been practicing. You should be safe with that."

INITIATION

The gift of death or the secret of transformation.

I witness my own funeral.

Upon the sandy beach of a huge lake stands the funeral party around my body. The latter, which lies on the top of a huge pile of timber, is adorned with the trinkets of the world I am leaving.

The flames rise high, licking the evening sky with tongues of red and electric blue, tarnishing the still water with the reflected color of their fleeting image. My essence, contained within the smoke, quietly spirals unobtrusively into the indigo vault of heavenly night.

The priestess in white flowing robes reads:

"You who created the light and the dark
You who created the male and the female
You who art the bornless one
Accept the return of thy prophet who's life was but a spark in the infinite blue-lidded eyes of Our Lady of heaven."

At the closing of these lines, seven archers fire seven flaming arrows across the water into the evening sky.

The small body of mourners watches them fall quietly far out into the lake; not even the sound of their extinguishing can be detected. Then universally, as if pre-arranged, all attention is drawn to a solitary bird flying away from the land towards the heart of the lake and the setting sun.

(Translated from a 16th. century Morning Star manuscript by Soror Rhiannon.)

....

I had expected Randolph to answer my call, so I was taken aback somewhat to be confronted by a casually dressed young man, probably in his early twenties.

"Is Randolph Vann at home?"

He beckoned me in without a word, and in silence, closed the door behind us. He also had difficulty managing the latch.

He walked by me in a manner which encouraged me to follow, which I did, into a dimly lit, probably 12'x10' room, at the end of the corridor.

From an old tall walnut wardrobe, he withdrew a black garment and motioned me to put it on. He then withdrew a second and proceeded to put it over his head. At this point, I thought it safe to follow suit.

My dumb companion returned to the wardrobe and this time brought forth a full-sized sword painted completely black, which he lay on a small table next to a door directly opposite the one we had just entered.

I could hear scrapings and knockings coming from the other side of this door and the inaudible mumblings of human voices.

Like my colleague, I was dressed in a plain black robe except that mine was fitted with a hood and his was augmented with an Egyptian-style head cloth.

Hanging around his neck from a black ribbon was a pendant, the design of which was a human eye painted in black and white. This he had obviously donned when my attention was drawn to the noises from the direction of the door.

I was feeling a little on edge sitting with my companion in silence, who offered neither speech nor smile as reassurance in the bare little room.

The noises from the other side of the door subsided and my companion rose and picked up a length of white cord.

For the first time he spoke,

"Please cover your head with the hood."

I pulled it to the top of my head so that only my face was exposed.

"No, please cover your whole head so that you can't see and then place your hands behind you."

I followed the instructions and committed myself to darkness beneath the folds of the material, my anxiety rising. As I lowered my arms after their work with the hood, I felt them being guided by other hands to a position behind my back. A feeling of alarm suddenly arose as I felt them being tied until I realized the knot was extremely loose. The cord was then passed around my waist three times and finally tucked in behind my hands.

I was feeling quite vulnerable within the dark of the hood and began to wonder if I was doing the right thing. Maybe I should just leave and call the whole thing off.

I waited too long, for suddenly, from the other side of the door I heard a resounding voice cry.

"Hekas hekas estie bebelio." Its sound passed through the door, then the tiny room containing my companion and myself, to finally become inaudible as it passed behind us out into the universe.

The voice was followed by a series of deliberate knocks, which was answered by my companion. The voice beyond echoed again,

"Very honored hierophant, the hall is properly guarded."

The voices then became very subdued and it was impossible for me to pick out what they were saying, so in silence I was left to wonder.

I tried to see light through the material but it was impossible, the material was so thick. Staring into the blackness, shapes appeared and dissolved as my imagination wandered.

Again, there came a battery of knocks and then silence.

A few seconds passed and then I heard the sound of the door opening.

I stumbled a little as I was pushed forward in the direction from where I heard the sound, and the voice I had been hearing returned.

"Child of earth unpurified and unconsecrated, thou canst not enter our sacred hall."

A movement of feet and then another voice.

"Child of earth I purify thee with water."

More shuffling followed by yet another voice, this time female.

"Child of earth I consecrate thee with fire."

Once more I felt myself being directed forward but the touch felt different. I began to feel a little ridiculous and wondered if the people in the world I had just entered were perhaps laughing at me. I must be cutting a funny sight stumbling about, especially since I had of my own free will subjected myself to this condition.

After a few steps, I was directed to kneel. Then in sonorous tones I heard,

"Please repeat after me your obligation."

This I repeated, one line at a time.

"I, Frater Rubicon in the presence of the Lord of the Universe and of this Hall of Neophytes of the Order of the Morning Star in the Outer, regularly assembled under warrant from the Greatly Honored Chiefs of the Second Order, do, of my own free will and accord, hereby and hereon, most solemnly pledge myself to keep secret this Order, its name, the name of its members, and the proceedings which take place at its meetings, from all and every person in the whole world, who is outside the pale of the Order, and not even to discuss these with initiates, unless he or they are in possession of the password. I undertake to maintain a kind and benevolent relation with all the Fratres and Sorores of the Order."

"I furthermore promise and swear that I will keep any information relative to this Order, which may have become known to me prior to the completion of the ceremony of my admission, and I also pledge myself to divulge nothing whatsoever concerning this Order to the outside world in the event of resignation, demission or expulsion therefrom. After the completion of my admission, I will not seek to obtain any ritual or lecture pertaining to the Order without due authorization from the Praemonstrator of my Temple, nor will I possess any ritual or lecture unless it be properly registered and labeled by him."

"Furthermore, I undertake to pursue with zeal the study of occult sciences, seeing that this Order is not established for the benefit of those who desire only a superficial knowledge thereof. I will not suffer myself to be hypnotized or mesmerized, nor will I place myself in such a passive state that any uninitiated person, power, or being may cause me to lose control of my thoughts, words or actions."

"Neither will I use my occult powers to any evil purposes and I further promise to persevere with firmness and courage through the ceremony of my admission, and these points I generally and severally, upon this sacred and sublime symbol, swear to observe without evasion, equivocation, or mental reservation of any kind whatsoever; under the no less penalty on violation of either being expelled from this Order, as a willfully perjured wretch, void of all moral worth, and unfit for the society of all right and true persons, and in addition under the awful penalty of voluntarily submitting myself to a deadly and hostile current of will set in motion by the chiefs of the Order, by which I should fall slain and paralyzed without visible weapon as if slain by the lighting flash."

I felt something touch and then rest awhile on the back of my neck; it was as though I had my head on a block and was about to have it removed.

The obligation then closed with,

"So help me the Lord of the Universe and my own higher soul."

As I repeated these closing lines, the timbre of my voice became deeper and took on a tremendously vibrating tone which resounded through the very fiber of my being, splitting its components asunder.

The confines of the hood quite suddenly disintegrated and I simultaneously stood in four places at one time, one self against each wall of a bare square room. All the laws of time and space defied this experience even within a vision.

With four separate pairs of eyes from four different directions, I stared at the center of the room where stood a black pair of scales. On one side of the scale was suspended a feather and on the other balanced against it, nothing. There was something disturbingly ominous about this 'nothing.'

Monitoring the swing of the scale stood Randolph.

Outside of the hood, there then followed much shifting, speeches, and moving around the temple. I had thought that after the adoration the blindfold would be removed but this was not the case.

The voice of the officer who had taken my obligation echoed.

"Let the mystic circumambulation take place in the path of darkness with the symbolic light of occult science to guide the way."

Although registering and comprehending all that was being said, the vision I was experiencing in my personal darkness remained firm.

In my still helpless state I find myself repositioned in a fresh location in the hall. Then, gently guided, I begin to move in a circular rotation around the hall, as though a part of a huge spiraling wheel. Within my vision, my four separate selves at this point moved inward and become as one being upon the scale balanced against the feather.

All the time I can sense the close proximity of other bodies around me. How many officers are affiliating at this ceremony? It is impossible for me to tell in my blind condition, but I have distinguished at least three different voices thus far. I wondered what was happening in the world beyond my cowl. Like the mundane world where invisible spirits busy themselves with their appropriate tasks upon the ethers to effect the everyday world, so was it here with the invisible officers effecting me.

We stop after what seems to be a couple of rotations and I hear again the sound of the person's voice who first spoke on my entering the hall.

"Child of earth consecrated, thou mayest approach the gate of the west."

Within my other world, the one beneath the hood, I feel my reconstituted self upon the scale to be fired as an arrow from the bow of promise, upward and onward to pierce the arc of the rainbow bridge. The ceiling splits like a piece of fabric and beyond is an infinite sea of pure white light. Here is the initiation for which my whole life has evolved; here is the reason for my being summoned.

I feel someone fumble with the hem of my hood and then it is suddenly lifted.

The hall is dimly lit and a black-cloaked figure holding a sword and whose head is covered by the mask of a falcon speaks,

"Thou canst not pass by me, saith the guardian of the west, unless thou canst tell me my name."

The words cut through me like a knife, not because of their content, but the accent that spoke them . . .

The figure began to reveal itself by lifting the mask, but she didn't have to, I knew. Vivian stood before me.

A voice answered for me from a figure who stood just behind and slightly to one side of me,

"Darkness is thy name, the great one of the paths of the shades."

I am no longer soaring upward, my velocity is drained. I am tumbling erratically down, returning to the scale which I can dimly see below me.

I wanted to run and escape the humiliation but I was helpless in the bonds. Immediately it was known that I'd seen her, the hood was returned over my head and the ceremony continued.

God, please let it end, release me. I could feel tears of rage and helplessness trickle upon my cheek.

Within the hood, the ground below me opens as an invitation for me to enter. Down and down I tumble and within the opening I can see that my destination is a pit of writhing beings, the repulsive beings of my nightmare. The scale passes me by and in the next instant I am eaten by the pit, thus condemned to be one of the foul creatures of loathsome horror.

What humiliation! She must know all that I've said to Vann. I could kill him. I could kill them both.

Yet again I am led in a circle and again I am challenged.

"Thou canst not pass by me saith the guardian of the east, unless thou canst tell me my name."

The hood is lifted and there, standing dressed in yellow and red, is Randolph Vann. He remains totally unemotional as though confronting a stranger.

Behind him is a fine open-weave cloth and behind this is a white light which gives the material the resemblance of mist. In the foggy half light, I can dimly perceive three other figures beyond this veil: one dressed completely in red, another in yellow, and the third in blue. The colors are the only distinguishing factors that I can perceive through the delicate fibres.

The same voice answers for me.

"Light dawning in darkness is thy name, the light of a golden day."

The hood is once more returned and in my personal darkness I hear the voice echo.

"I come in the power of the light
I come in the light of wisdom
I come in the mercy of the light
The light hath healing in its wings"

Once more I feel myself being directed by unseen hands and then I hear a door close, the sound of which seems to come from behind me.

"Hekas hekas este bebeloi"

Faintly, I hear the words repeated from the beginning of the ceremony. It must be over, surely. I'm in such confusion. I just want to get hold of Vivian and unleash my venom at the cruelty of her deception. Then again, maybe I want to just go away and hide with embarrassment. All I really want to do is get free to go home and try to forget the whole incident.

The minutes pass and I begin to wonder if I'm on my own, but then I feel movement at my wrists as the bonds are loosened and fall away. Thankfully I rub my wrists and then remove the hood.

I'm alone. My releaser has disappeared, but then, maybe he wasn't human. Maybe he was an elemental evoked by the ceremony from the spirit world.

The house appeared empty. Thankfully no one answered my calls. I just don't know how I would have reacted if I had had to face anyone.

PART THREE - THE KILL

And how he was shut in a rock under a stone.

Sir Thomas Malory, Le Morte De'Arthur

RHIANNON

Merlin saw a beautiful woman, in garments that shone like gold, approaching on a white horse. He sent men to meet her but no one could come near her. The next day, when she appeared, he went to meet her himself, but could not shorten the distance between them until he called to her in the name of love.

....

I stand looking at the little Edwardian terrace with its forlorn paved garden.

The entrance is still gateless; the rusty hinges wait like the first time that I saw them, silently anticipating labor.

Each evening for the past week, I have walked this way in the hope of meeting Vivian; but on every occasion, the windows have remained dark with the curtains yawning open.

I have conducted a thousand conversations in my mind in the event of meeting Vivian. Each, I know, redundant before spoken. Even if I should glimpse her, I know that I would, in all probability, seek cover in the lengthening shadows of evening. Which just goes to prove that the whole mental exercise is a complete waste of time. Even so, I have no choice, however I vainly try to control my thoughts they continue to run in circles leading nowhere except to frustration.

I pull the front door keys from the dark depths of my trouser pocket and walk the lonely path to the front door.

Several empty cardboard boxes are stacked against the wall in the inner vestibule. I feel a lump form in my throat as the connotations that they arouse manifest. Packing boxes.

I listen outside of the inner door for sounds of occupation but all is completely silent. I insert the second key into the key hole and as quietly as possible turn it. The door makes a cracking sound as it opens inward.

The hallway is completely dark.

"Vivian" I call. No reply

"Vivian" Still no answer.

I feel more confident but refrain from turning on the light and so in darkness walk the length of the passageway until reaching the living room door at the far end.

I listen, no sound.

I inch open the door. In the evening half light I can see that the interior is completely empty, not one piece of furniture. I switch on the light, the room is bare.

I retrace my steps and enter the bedroom, switching on the light. It amplifies the same stark desolation; no offer of consolation here.

Completely disheartened I turn and return to the deserted living room. Once back I check all the shelves in the vain hope of finding some clue, but there's nothing. All have been thoroughly dusted, removing any chance of divining answers from the patterns made in removing the articles that they once supported.

I wander into the kitchen and here I'm caught by surprise, for on the work surface is a video cassette. I walk over to pick it up and in so doing see that underneath it is an envelope. I lift the cassette and see written in Vivian's hand my name inscribed in ball point.

The flap isn't glued. I open it and remove the solitary piece of paper. Dear Frater Rubicon, it begins, Will visit with you Tuesday, until then may the Gods be with you.

Rhiannon.

PS: The video is a gift for you.

What the bloody hell is this Rhiannon crap?

I can feel that I'm shaking. Today is Monday, does she mean tomorrow or was it last Tuesday, when I morosely paced in the shadows in the street outside.

Please let it be tomorrow.

I pick up the cassette and leave, turning off the lights as I go.

The tape has me stunned. I never thought of myself as prudish but the content of what I am witnessing has me completely numbed.

Randolph and Vivian are standing completely nude.

Vivian's entire body, except for her hair, is painted a vivid blue. Painted in flashing orange upon the blue, I recognize the sigils of spirits and angels along with letters or symbols of an unknown language. The hair on her head and between her thighs is painted in metallic silver.

Randolph, in contrast, is painted red with equally vivid designs in green. His body hair is a brilliant yellow.

They walk away from the camera and approach a cubic altar in the middle of the room, the side of which is decorated with the symbols of Capricorn and Saturn.

The slow steady beat of a solitary drum begins and Vivian turns and then lies on her back upon the altar.

I really don't believe what I'm seeing. I can't believe that she would allow herself to participate in something like this and allow herself to be filmed.

I know now that I really don't know this woman. Who or what is she?

Randolph moves to the altar to enter Vivian, keeping his feet upon the floor. Her legs straddling him, he moves or is rather drawn in, to the rhythmic pulsating beat of the drum.

The symbols upon their bodies gyrate and take on a hypnotic quality. They appear to become three-dimensional and move upon their own accord. I want to turn it off, but I can't. I am completely mesmerized and begin to derive a certain amount of fascination and enjoyment from the spectacle.

Although participating in the sexual act, both parties remain calm. There appears to be no urgency or excitement. It's as though both were conducting an everyday task.

The minutes pass and their rhythm remains steady and unhurried, unflinching from the unseen beat of the drummers hands. Still the time passes and then I begin to discern a thin vaporous mist rising in a spiral from their still pulsating bodies.

The sigils and letters move and interweave, supporting the thickening vapor until a gaseous form materializes above the altar.

The two sexually joined bodies seem oblivious to this new presence and continue to the same beat.

The form is now quite discernable and recognizable to anyone who has read the works of Eliphas Levi.

The head is that of a ram, or rather a synthesis of a dog a bull and maybe a donkey, crowned with a pair of huge horns, between which is a flaming torch and below it, on the brow of the beast, the sign of human intelligence, a point upmost pentagram.

It has human hands, one pointing upward the other downward indicating two moons: the one above white, the other black.

The lower half of the body is clothed, except for the legs, which terminate in the cloven hooves of a goat.

The chest of the being is green and covered in scales up to the breasts which are those of a woman.

I recognize him as the Goat of Mendes, The Lord Baphomet.

The right arm, which has been pointing towards the white moon, moves down and aims the index finger directly at me.

The scene now transcends the television screen, it's as though we were all in the same room.

With the finger pointing at me, the being speaks, creating a vibration which shakes the very fibre of the universe.

"John Barry, your time has come.

I am the God of the world. The universe is but a ring upon my finger. Those who worship me know truth. Truth is pain and truth is pleasure. There is no difference except in the way you choose to perceive it.

The abomination which is Christianity says that I will be destroyed at the time of the Apocalypse. This is only true in so far as the false image which the Christians have given me will be destroyed, my true self will live and be recognized as the Messiah of the New Aeon.

The items that evoked me upon this altar are the powers of life and death. They create, and in so doing, destroy what was. They are the wand and the cup, the opposing forces that work within the universe to bring about manifestation. They are the girders of the rainbow bridge.

My law is the law of the strong. It is the law of those who walk upon the edge of the Abyss and rationalize chaos. It is the law of the hero.

The elect salute you under your self-adopted name of Rubicon.

All you were is dead. Go forth and create yourself. You are a descendent of Cain, and Cain was mine.

The figure disappears immediately and I see that the altar is bare, Vivian and Randolph have departed without my noticing.

I rewind the cassette to the beginning and press Play. I wait. Nothing, just the white flashing screen and the rushing sound of static. The tape is clean, there is nothing on it.

Very clever. How did they manage that one? It has to be a trick. I don't like the alternative. Did I imagine the whole thing?

In retrospect, I question the content of the tape. The light had been dim. Is it possible that the girl was a Vivian look alike?

All day I have waited for Vivian, I can't think of anything but her and the tape.

John Barry is dead. The phrase haunts me but even so I derive a fascination, a sense of being chosen. At the same time, I am filed with disbelief because the whole experience is so bizarre and unearthly.

Mind you, I can't believe that it would be too difficult to make a film like that. There are people in Hollywood who make things like that every day.

The longer I wait for Vivian, the more agitated I become as I realize that she is controlling me, making me build my life around her coming and going.

I have done nothing all day but await her anticipated arrival.

Why should I? Only a few weeks ago I wanted her out of my life because she was such a distraction; and now, when I think I'm rid of her, she becomes a distraction.

I've tried running the cassette countless times, even though other tapes play back without a problem. I know that there is nothing wrong with the equipment. I've cleaned the heads of the machine, checked the leads, still nothing.

The repetitive tones of Jean Michell Jarre's Oxygene album on the record deck are lulling me to sleep when I hear the ring of my door bell.

I jump up; my heart suddenly pounding, it must be Vivian. I look at my watch, 5:00pm. Bitch. She's made me wait all day. I breath deeply, trying to calm myself as I make my way to the building's communal front door.

I consciously walk slowly, attempting to bring my rising anger under control. As I approach the front door I realize that I'm failing miserably.

"Hi," she says as I open the door.

She's dressed very expensively. It's as though she has stepped out of a fashion catalogue. Designer camelhair topcoat opened, revealing a fitted navy blue two-piece suit. Around her neck, a delicate gold chain necklace and upon her lapel a small brooch in the shape of a salamander in platinum-colored metal and stones which could be diamonds. I see the Salamander as a chameleon, the symbolism is too obvious to mention.

The Vivian that I thought I knew would have scoffed at the present image. She had always been so very bohemian.

I'm annoyed at her casual tone of voice and calm sophisticated manner.

"Oh, hello," I try to relax but I can feel my voice trembling.

"Are you going to let me in?" she asks in the same casual tone.

I move to one side, in a symbol of encouragement to enter. She leads the way and I follow her upstairs to my rooms. Once inside, I slam the door behind us, hoping to startle her. I don't give her time to turn around and speak.

"I can't believe it. How the hell could you do such a thing?"

"Because I'm Rhiannon."

"Rhiannon! Vivian, what do you mean, you're Rhiannon?"

This was too much. Hadn't I been embarrassed and ridiculed enough? Why must she persist in continuing the game? I surely wasn't expected to believe that this was a centuries old woman.

My temper was rising and I could feel my temples harden with the concentration of blood in the fragile veins.

"If you had loved me you would have known. If you had ever taken the time to try and understand how I felt, you would have known me. Your self-obsession and total disregard for my individuality have built the walls of your prison. My hands are bloodless."

I tried to interrupt but her words and tone of voice were like a tidal wave. She spoke the truth and any resistance on my part was obsolete and deserved destruction.

"In all of your wanderings I was what you sought, yet you failed to realize it; and we failed to realize that you weren't ready."

"How long has this been going on. Since the beginning?"

"That, I'm afraid is your curse, and it won't be lifted until you realize that it doesn't matter. What does matter is that in time you will come to know that we love you."

"Love! You call it love?"

"Don't shout. Remember the attitude that you promised in your oath to maintain towards all members of the Order?"

She stared through me with total detachment, no facial expression, movement of limb or shifting of posture.

A desert of emotion stretched before me. I stood naked before the intense rays of her orbs. Eyes that betrayed absolutely no emotion stared pure and hard as diamond. First my flesh withered and fell away, then my bones collapsed into a pile of fine dust. Finally, I was absent, born away upon the wings of the wind which is called insignificance.

"You, without knowing it, are your father. One day soon I hope you will discover the seed of your mother."

Whatever I said, however much I pleaded, swore or tried to break her down with obscenities, she retained her placid attitude of indifference. I wanted so much to hurt her, to see her suffer, to destroy her with my hands, make her obedient to me and see her beg for mercy.

At the same time I wanted to love her.

"You're becoming emotional," were her final words.

She had reduced me to a groveling dog begging for crumbs at the rich man's table. After all the times I had spoken to her of independence and self-respect, here I was groveling for pity and a handout of affection through a chink in her armour.

She was turned to stone by my lack of regard for her feelings over the previous months. I had played the Gorgon role and now I reaped the consequences of her rigidity.

But was I totally to blame? Hadn't I been led into the bramble bush where I now lay enmeshed, struggling like a trapped hare, awash in the glow of a hunter's moon? The more I struggled with myself and my beguilers, the more impossible my position became. From within the heart of the bush I saw Rhiannon and Randolph free to walk away.

Their imprisonment of me within the bush was the key which initiated their freedom.

I heard the door slam and I ran to the window waiting for her to emerge into view. Across the street the line of elms swayed in time to the breath of autumn. An air of desolation and electrically charged half-light pervaded the scene.

She walked purposefully and erect along the pavement below me without so much as an upward glance. I followed her progress, urgently beseeching her across the ether to return, but to no avail. She finally became devoured within the jaws of distance.

I remained staring from my lonely tower into the evening light hoping she would reappear. She was gone, eaten up. In the space she had occupied there was now a vacuum and around it a shell of bitterness.

In the silence I felt decimated, and I slumped helplessly into an armchair which gave a brief wheeze under my weight, I wanted to slip away quietly.

My mind reeled and spun in confusion. I was left totally helpless. Nothing I did made any difference. Affection, hate, these were nothing to the futility of my situation which nailed me to a cross of despair. It was as though she was dead. No, if she were dead it would be better, more romantic. At least there would be a memory of love, with indifference there was nothing. In kaleidoscopic images the beautiful times rolled within my mind. How could I let her slip? Now she was all important. Next time I'd be different.

Had I ever had a choice or had it all been a joke?

My ego was lost somewhere far beneath my feet.

The tarot reading! Good God, the question she asked must have been about me and not herself.

The deception was symbolized by the moon, and then there was me, the fool.

RHIANNON II

The postage stamp was upside down so I knew where it had originated from, irrespective of the German post mark.

I sat turning the envelope around in my fingers, thumbing the corners, turning them into ornate curves of Gothic design. It wasn't possible for me not to open it, although I desired to condemn it to flames, unread as a symbol of defiance.

I leaned it against my coffee cup and with my head cupped in my hands I stared at the awaiting message.

At this moment I felt as a bird without wings.

I give a copy of the letter.

Nuremberg
Germany *Oct. 81*

Dear Frater Rubicon,

Remember it was all a part of the learning process. You chose your own motto, and therefore your destiny.

Rubicon.

You have arrived, now step through the gate.

You know within yourself what the gate is. Accept it.

Love Rhiannon and Randolph

PS. We will be watching, as we always have. When we feel that the time is ripe, we will be in touch. Until that time, continue along the path with courage.

I tore it in half and crushed it, only to retrieve the debris and pathetically re-assemble it, while a glaze of tears filled my eyes.

How the hell could she use that name which was a symbol of my beguilement and a symbol of her love for Vann.

I read and reread the letter looking for clues, for something. Surely there had to be something. What I was looking for wasn't there, however deep I searched. I possessed a handful of dead dried leaves but desired a handful of gold.

A light breeze pushed into the room through the half-opened window, sounding the wind chimes and resurrecting the stagnant curtains on its passage before being lost in stillness.

How was it possible that I could have let happiness escape, and for what?

I looked around my bare room and felt waves of self pity well up into my throat as I gazed around at my humble belongings. Tears burst from nowhere and my whole body quaked under the sobs which issued from deep within. My shoulders hunched and my frame jerked with the emergence of tension.

After a while the crying became a relief, my body relaxed from the growing tension and my whole attitude turned about face. Waves of euphoria eased my strain. Crying became laughter and out of laughter was born optimism.

I leaned back in my chair rocking it on the two back legs to the rhythm of my heartbeat. Odd tears continued to push forth and I wiped them away with the backs of my hands.

I felt totally emotionless as though I was stood on a high hill, far below the countryside rolled away into nothing. It was impossible to tell where the edge of the land finished and the sky began.

I was locked into a pagan landscape not experienced since my youth as a boy. The hill became a bronze age fortress with concentric circles of ditches circumscribing its colossal circumference. Within the ditches were the teeth of the castle's defenses: huge wooden stakes crowned with intimidating points of potential death.

The horizon began to turn black.

Minutes passed and out of the darkness pressed a huge army upon the undulating defenses of the citadel. They moved at an even pace to the rumbling rhythm of the dirdum, its sound echoing like thunder across the emerald green pastures below. The previously serene landscape was rapidly becoming obscured beneath a carpet of impending doom.

Throngs of people suddenly emerged from the huts within the castle's defenses and swarmed around me calling out for strength and victory.

For the first time I noticed I had become the huge elm tree from my youth with thick green foliage reaching up into the wide blue sky. I wanted so much to help these people in their hour of need but couldn't think how. I called out to the gods, beseeching them for aid.

The reply came keen and swift with the lightning precision of a divine messenger.

"The hostile army is the outside world. Don't be intimidated by it. The inhabitants are the various aspects of yourself. Believe in them."

I had at first taken the voice to be Rhiannon's, and this was partly true. However, there was an undertone which, although alien, contained the seed of familiarity. I could only equate it as a rhythm which supports the melody of a tune, always present and imperative, yet generally unacknowledged by the undiscerning.

I cried with the recognition, and the urn became complete as the sound of my mother's voice erupted from the lake of my tears. Rhiannon and my mother were one. They were the lady of the lake bestowing the sword of discernment to the newly-acknowledged king in his sorrow at acknowledgment of his separation.

My body burned as a huge spiraling column of incandescent light and the day become night with the magnitude of my knowledge. Darkness, the mother of light, was the container of my ashes. From oblivion I am born and to oblivion I shall return. This acknowledgement is the death of inflated ego.

"Self knowledge is the angel of light which, for the weak, is Satan, for the elect, is Lucifer."

Thus she concluded, and her voice trailed away with these final echoing lines, a fitting epitaph to her memory.

I woke in the dark and felt extremely cold and uncomfortable. In the darkness I again felt that there was a presence and that in the far unseen corners there was something lurking.

I continued to sit and observe, delving into the unknown reaches willing a manifestation.

My challenge was unanswered, but the act of standing firm had incapacitated the horror. Courage to experience the truth without grasping at any of the myriad forms of escapism was the sword which slew the jailer and threw open the gate of the prison.

There is no god but man and life is what you make it.

BELTAINE

The celtic god of spring

"ONE MAN'S SUNRISE IS ANOTHER MAN'S SUNSET"

The sun is returning and spring is in the air.

You can always tell when winter is over. It's then that the clientele of the George and Dragon spill out onto the street with their drinks and idle chatter. The return of the sun draws life from the darkness making what appeared at one time dead, radiant with color.

I was returning home after walking by Vivian's flat for the thousandth time. I knew she was no longer there as I gazed at the blind empty windows, but as they say, hope springs eternal.

I hadn't intended to tarry, but the vitality of life outside of the pub encouraged me to want to participate in its humdrum hubbub.

I pushed the familiar large brass plate on the door and ventured into the room which held so many memories.

Inside, I couldn't immediately distinguish details, the darkness a contrast to the bright sunlight outside, but I managed to find my way to the bar and there readjust my vision.

Surprisingly the bar was quite full so I had ample time to survey my surroundings while waiting to be served by the solitary person working behind the counter.

There was no one I recognized on my first scrutiny, but when the man on my left moved away with his order I was confronted by the sight of Mark and Chris sitting opposite each other at a table only a few feet away. They were deep in conversation and obviously enraptured with each others company. My inclination was to flee before they caught sight of me, instead I turned away and pretended that I hadn't noticed them.

I ordered a drink and as I did so caught sight of them looking over at me at the sound of my voice. As I waited for my drink I tried to think of something to take my mind away from them but couldn't. I fought the urge to look over at them.

The barman returned with my drink.

"I'll take for that." Mark held out a note.

"You going to come and join us?"

I felt awkward and didn't know how to respond. I wanted to talk, and at the same time wanted to escape.

"Come on, come over."

"Yes, OK."

As we approached the table, Chris looked up and smiled.

"Hello, John, how are you? Long time no see."

"Yes, I suppose it has been quite a while."

As Mark seated himself they smiled at each other and their display of honest affection made me realize that I was missing something in life, something that I had always wanted.

We sat drinking and obviously enjoying each other's company until finally Chris leaned over to Mark and said, "We better be going otherwise we'll miss the beginning."

"Were going to see 'The Shining' at the ABC. You want to join us?" Mark asked.

"No, I've got things to do, but thanks all the same."

Chris stood, obviously anxious to leave.

"Thanks for the drink," I said.

"Oh that's OK. You can get them next time. Why not this evening?"

"Yes, that sounds good, I'll see you here tonight."

"See you later," replied Mark cheerfully. They both smiled and departed.

I was sorry to see them leave and I realized that as I had failed to see the mystery within Vivian, so I had failed to perceive the charm within them. It is an interesting lesson that the diamond which has adorned every famed crown is formed from the plainness of carbon.

After they had gone, I sat and fumbled in my pocket and pulled out a collection of torn pieces of paper. I realized that it had been months since I had worn this jacket and that these pieces of paper were the letter I had received from Rhiannon and Randolph.

On the table in front of me I flattened out the debris and pieced it together into a coherent format. Like the petals of a rose it flowered into a bloom. It was as though each piece of the letter represented a fragment of myself and that in re-piecing it, I in fact, collected myself.

It had to contain a key. There had to be something there, there just had to be.

"You know within yourself now what the gate is, accept it." Of course. The gate! All the time, the goddamn gate.

The gate of tears, the gate of death and the gate of the Garden of Eden is life. It's life!

Magick is the art of living, it is not the life.

Is it over?

Am I back to where I began?

No, I have the experience. Its magick may have retreated but I have the memory.

Was the whole experience a joke or are Rhiannon and Randolph truly immortals?

Is Rhiannon my mother, or is it I that look for my mother in all the women that I come into contact with?

There is always choice, but if the lesson has been learned there is no uncertainty.

The sword of decision awaits my judgement, which world do I sacrifice? The self-centered path which spirals ever inward or the ever outward path that is nature, evolution and Cain?

Cain old friend, you always appear in a new disguise, always where I least expect to find you. There is only one path to follow; I must be like "Athena"and spring fully armed with wisdom from the brain of "Zeus".

I must enter the world of the living, but remember that the world is not a clay to be molded by the individual; both are living entities in their own right, brought to enrichment when harmonized with one another.

One should not progress at the expense of the other.

I will no longer escape from the world through fear.

I will step through the gate and be free.

EPILOGUE

HYMN OF LUCIFER

I am one with Ra, overcoming the Dragon Apophis, who is sleep.

I am one with the Lucifer, the Lightbringer overcoming the inertia that is heaven.

Release me from the coils of sleep and ignorance, that are the angels of mortal men. The mire of the universe.

The Christian God is a god of the shroud, one who would conceal the truth.

Praise be to Lucifer and the opening eye of Ra.

Our Law is the Law of the Strong

Our Law is the Law of being responsible for our own actions.

We do not seek forgiveness from a self-appointed agent of god, we seek learning. Those with short memories make the same mistakes. I, Lord Lucifer, grant that you may know and be watchful.

I stand on the edge of the Abyss and rationalize chaos.

There is no God but man, and life is what you make it.

May the Gods be with you.

*AMEN**

* Amen, the ancient Egyptian god who was the personification of the hidden and unknown creative power.

CHAISES

Coordination et rédaction
Patricia Bueno

Conception graphique et mise en page
Carlos Gamboa Permanyer

Directeur de production
Juanjo Rodríguez Novel

Traduction
Aline Révolte

Publié par : Atrium Group de ediciones y publicaciones, S.L.
c/ Ganduxer, 112
08022 BARCELLONA
Tel: + 34 932 540 099
Fax:+ 34 932 118 139
e-mail: atrium@atriumgroup.org
www.atriumbooks.com

ISBN : 84-95692-30-9
Dépôt Légal : B-38703-03

Imprimé en Espagne
Anman Gràfiques del Vallès, S.L.

Image page 3 : photographie de Jonathan De Villiers du livre produit par Kartell "150 articles, 150 œuvres"

Chaises

INDEX

INTRODUCTION 8

HISTOIRE DE LA CHAISE
DE CES ORIGINES AU XIXe SIÈCLE 10

XXe SIÈCLE
100 ANS D'INNOVATION 24

1900-1910
LES PIONNIERS 26
Michael Thonet 28
Antonio Gaudí 30
Charles Rennie Mackintosh 32
Frank Lloyd Wright 34

1910-1920
UN DÉFI AUX CONVENTIONS 36
Gerrit Thomas Rietveld 38

1920-1930
L'ERE DES ARCHITECTES 40
Eileen Gray 42
Mies van der Rohe 44
Le Corbusier 46
Marcel Breuer 48

1930-1950
TRIOMPHE DU DESIGN ORGANIQUE 50
Alvar Aalto 60
Charles & Ray Eames 64
Eero Saarinen 66

1950-1970
LE DIVERTISSEMENT COMMENCE 68
Arne Jacobsen 78
Harry Bertoia 80
Verner Panton 82
Eero Aarnio 84

1970-1990
L'ÈRE DU "TOUT EST BON" 86
Ettore Sottsass 92
Vico Magistretti 94
Óscar Tusquets 98

XXIe SIÈCLE
UNE VISION DU FUTUR 100
Ron Arad 102
H. & F. Campana 106
Antonio Citterio 108
Piero Lissoni 112

Lievore, Altherr, Molina 116
Josep Lluscà 120
Alberto Meda 124
Jasper Morrison 126
Jorge Pensi 130
Gaetano Pesce 134
Karim Rashid 136
Philippe Starck 138
Marcel Wanders 142
Andrea Branzi 144
Matali Crasset 145
Nanna Ditzel 146
Frank Gehry 147
Stefano Giovannoni 148
Konstantin Grcic 149
Massimo Iosa Ghini 150
Ross Lovegrove 151
Enzo Mari 152
Marc Newson 153

REFLETS MÉTALLIQUES
ALUMINIUM, ACIER... 154

RECOUVREMENTS, TEXTURE,
COULEUR ET CONFORT 174

BOIS ET FIBRES NATURELLES
NOUVELLE INTERPRÉTATION DE LA MATIÈRE CLASSIQUE 192

PEAU
AU-DELÀ DU TEMPS QUI PASSE... 212

ERGONOMIE ET TRAVAIL
FORMES AU SERVICE DE LA FONCTION 230

PLASTIQUE ET NOUVEAUX MATÉRIAUX
TRIOMPHE DE LA TECHNOLOGIE 246

CHAISES ET ART 268

RÉPERTOIRE 314

Signification des icônes utilisés :

Hauteur de la chaise en cm

Largeur de la chaise en cm

Longueur de la chaise en cm

Hauteur du siège en cm

INTRODUCTION

Pourquoi un livre sur les chaises ? Parce que les chaises se révèlent être la parfaite excuse pour toutes sortes d'événements. La source d'inspiration permettant d'exprimer des inquiétudes artistiques. Le trône où s'accumule le pouvoir. La chaise de bureau sophistiquée permettant d'exercer le contrôle. La chaise longue de la plage pour respirer face à la mer. Le fauteuil de lecture représentant le lien avec le monde réel quand les heures passent au milieu de mondes imaginaires. La chaise électrique qui, pour certains, rend le fait de tuer plus légitime. La chaise douillette, complice de discussions interminables. La chaise comme point de départ pour démocratiser le monde, comme le souhaitaient les membres de la Bauhaus et, plus tard, tous ceux qui virent dans cet objet la plate-forme depuis laquelle ils pouvaient exprimer leurs inquiétudes sociales. Un design risqué devient un exemple paradigmatique de manifeste esthétique exprimant la rupture avec les normes établies. La chaise met également en évidence notre besoin de nous unir à la nature et aux personnes et non de nous y opposer. Elle peut être aussi l'excuse pour attendre ou pour s'en aller...
De nombreuses postures se manifestent dans la chaise et déterminent notre manière d'observer le monde. Pour toutes ces raisons, il est facile de comprendre, à partir de l'étude de ce meuble, les motivations qui ont poussé les charpentiers, les tapissiers, les ébénistes, les architectes, les ingénieurs et les designers industriels à créer différents types de chaises répondant à chaque instant aux besoins et au contexte culturel de toutes les époques. Entre une chaise fabriquée en 1900 et une chaise créée en l'an 2000, il y a des ascensions et des décadences de monarques, des conquêtes, des guerres, des modifications de frontières, des transferts d'hégémonie politique, des époques de crise s'alternant avec d'autres de bien-être économique, des changements au sein des classes sociales et, évidemment, un incontournable progrès tech-

nologique donnant naissance aux nombreuses innovations techniques qui sont à l'origine du changement des habitudes et des goûts.

Actuellement, ce qui différencie le bon design d'une simple copie ne réside pas seulement dans l'originalité. Il doit également avoir une certaine signification ; être conforme aux besoins réels des utilisateurs et respecter l'environnement en utilisant, par exemple, des matériaux recyclables ; être versatile et faciliter son utilisation dans divers contextes ou situations ; être en accord avec les impératifs de l'industrie de façon à ce que sa fabrication implique un coût réduit et rende le design accessible à une grande partie de la population, comme le souhaitent de nombreux designers depuis longtemps ; comprendre un composant innovateur, aussi bien au niveau de la forme qu'à celui du fond ; avoir une forme ergonomique, l'élément fondamental permettant d'obtenir une communion physique avec l'utilisateur de la chaise, et une certaine esthétique répondant au style de vie de celui auquel il est destiné, permettant également d'atteindre une communion spirituelle.

D'un autre côté, ce qui semble clair, c'est que la maxime du fonctionnalisme "la forme suit la fonction", est maintenant obsolète et laisse place à une approche très différente du monde du design, répondant ainsi aux diverses motivations de chaque créateur.

Ce livre retrace l'évolution des arts décoratifs et de la société depuis les temps de l'empire égyptien jusqu'à nos jours, à partir des designs des chaises les plus emblématiques et des grands innovateurs se trouvant derrière chacune d'entre elles. Les dernières pages sont consacrées à la création libre avec un chapitre réservé à la chaise considérée comme un objet d'art et présentant les différentes façons de la contempler. Il ne nous reste donc plus qu'à trouver une excuse pour nous installer et profiter de la variété et de la complexité de cet objet d'apparence si simple.

Patricia Bueno

HISTOIRE DE LA CHAISE

DE SES ORIGINES AU XIXe SIÈCLE

"... chaque idée réellement originale –chaque innovation dans le design, chaque nouvelle introduction de matériau, chaque invention technique dans la fabrication du mobilier– semble trouver sa plus belle expression dans la chaise.",
(George Nelson, designer et auteur du livre *Chaises*, 1953)▪

La chaise est l'élément de base du mobilier, c'est le plus commun et le plus varié de notre entourage. Pour cette raison, c'est également le plus intéressant étant donnée sa capacité à transmettre des informations sur la culture de tous les temps et de tous les espaces.

Même s'il semble que l'homme a toujours été assis de la même façon, la position qu'il a adoptée s'est modifiée au cours de l'histoire, d'une période à une autre, d'une culture à une autre, d'une ville à une autre et d'un continent à un autre.

Alors qu'à certains endroits, il est normal d'être accroupi, à genoux ou avec les jambes croisées, la notion de confort occidental utilise la chaise comme unique patron. Les gens sont tellement habitués au fait que la chaise les accompagne dans toutes les situations qu'il semble difficile d'imaginer que ce n'est qu'au cours du XIXe siècle que son utilisation s'est généralisée et s'est étendue à toutes les classes de la société. Ceci démontre que les différences dans le design de ce meuble ont été déterminées par des raisons qui vont bien au-delà d'une simple fonction pratique puisqu'elle est associée à des symboles. La chaise évolue avec le pouvoir politique, économique et religieux, avec l'art, avec le savoir, avec la sensibilité esthétique et, finalement, avec l'industrie.

Il est fascinant de suivre l'évolution d'un objet aussi quotidien au cours des siècles car, comme toujours, l'étude du passé nous aide à comprendre le présent. Faire des recherches sur l'évolution de la chaise à travers les siècles met en évidence les tensions sociales, économiques et culturelles qui ont fait bouger le monde depuis l'ère de l'Egypte pharaonique. Il s'agit d'un voyage qui modifiera votre façon de voir les chaises : de l'objet quotidien au témoin vivant de l'évolution (et parfois de la régression), de l'être humain.

La théorie la plus commune sur la façon dont la chaise a fait son apparition en Occident en tant que support plus ou moins confortable pour le corps, établit que son origine réside dans les trônes de la royauté (symbole évident du pouvoir terrestre et céleste), puisque la société en général a toujours eu l'habitude –ou le besoin– d'imiter les classes sociales privilégiées. Cette théorie nous renvoie à l'an 3100 av. J.C.

Pages précédentes : chaise provenant de Tanzanie, façonnée dans un bloc de bois et comportant des motifs symboliques traditionnels. Relief travaillé dans le cadre de la porte d'accès à la pièce des statues de la tombe de Horemheb qu'on peut observer assis devant la table des offrandes (env. 1325 av. J.C.).

Déjà à l'époque de l'Egypte Ancienne (environ 3100-475 av. J.C.), le privilège de s'asseoir sur un support était réservé à la royauté et aux membres de haut rang de la société. Plus tard, le tabouret est apparu comme l'une des premières pièces de mobilier. Sa construction s'est perfectionnée petit à petit jusqu'à incorporer un dossier bas et incurvé qui devait soutenir le bassin et le sacrum suivant une orientation précise permettant de trouver une position équilibrée pour l'épine lombaire. Le plus curieux, ou intrigant, de cette innovation, c'est qu'on ne la retrouve plus au cours de l'histoire de la chaise.

A l'époque de la IVe Dynastie, la chaise atteint son plus haut niveau de perfectionnement. À partir de ce moment, elle s'est présentée sous deux formes de base pendant douze dynasties (environ jusqu'en 1320 av. J.C.) : la chaise raffinée utilisée par la royauté, la noblesse et les fonctionnaires ; et le tabouret réservé au reste des classes sociales qui n'abandonnèrent cependant pas leur habitude de se reposer accroupis. Les deux modalités pouvaient comprendre un coussin mou pour le siège, ce qui les rendait plus confortables. Les chaises les plus luxueuses montraient fréquemment des incrustations de marbre, de bois d'ébène ou de petites plaques de verre.

La position qu'on adoptait sur les chaises les plus hautes, avec les pieds touchant le sol, est le premier exemple historique de la posture actuelle occidentale. Une autre introduction digne d'intérêt est celle d'un petit banc (petit tabouret pour reposer les pieds) qui était utilisé avec ce type de siège et qui permettait de s'installer avec les cuisses parallèles au sol, d'une façon semblable à celle utilisée actuellement dans les mesures ergonomiques modernes.

Au même moment, l'empire de Mésopotamie se développait et son mobilier était très semblable à celui de la culture égyptienne. Une des différences les plus significatives était sans doute l'existence de tabourets à pieds croisés et d'autres en forme de coffre qui comprenaient des jalousies sur les côtés. Cependant, la caractéristique la plus importante réside dans le fait que ce design est très semblable à des pièces qui se construisent encore de nos jours en Irak, plus de 4000 ans après.

Détail du dossier du trône de Toutankhamon (env. 1325 av. J.C.)■

Tout comme en Egypte, les chaises à dossier étaient exclusivement réservées à la royauté et aux classes privilégiées. Dans la culture de Mésopotamie, curieusement, la chaise égyptienne ne fut pas adoptée. La chaise se construisait avec un dossier droit et délibérément rigide, ce qui pouvait donner une idée de la sévérité de ses propriétaires. Au début du ve siècle av. J.C., à l'époque de la Grèce Antique (au cours de laquelle on atteint une certaine sophistication dans le design de divers contextes artistiques), les artisans développèrent une nouvelle sorte de chaise, reconnue comme de design "classique" grec. Celui-ci comprenait sur la partie supérieure du dossier une large baguette disposée horizontalement qui enveloppait le dos de la personne qui y était assise. Les pieds étaient généralement incurvés et le siège était léger, ce qui facilitait mouvement et flexibilité. C'est ainsi que fut déterminée la forme de la chaise classique qui allait servir de base au design des siècles suivants.

Chaise de style Chippendale

Ce type de design semble être basé sur la préoccupation des grecs pour obtenir un plus grand confort, ce qui les poussa à ajouter un support pour le dos s'adaptant à la forme du corps. L'utilisation de la chaise devint plus commune même si elle se limitait tout de même aux classes sociales les plus élevées. D'un autre côté, l'utilisation de bancs se répandit dans les écoles et les théâtres ainsi que dans les réunions des philosophes avec leurs auditeurs■

Les modèles de tabourets, de chaises et de divans (que les Grecs utilisaient pour manger dans une posture inclinée et qui se sont maintenant convertis en chaises longues) de l'ère de la Grèce Classique (475-370 av. J.C.) ont eu une grande influence jusqu'à nos jours■

Au sein de l'empire romain, les designs de la culture grecque se sont maintenus et ont renforcé l'idée selon laquelle les trônes et les chaises étaient réservés aux personnes qui détenaient le pouvoir. À partir de la décadence de l'empire, l'habitude de s'asseoir sur une chaise disparut pendant des siècles car elle fut éradiquée par la culture qui avait envahit le territoire et qui considérait cet objet comme une excentricité superflue. On continua à l'utiliser à l'église et dans les vestibules des maisons des citoyens les plus puissants. Ce n'est qu'à partir du XVIIe et du XVIIIe siècle que réapparurent les designs inspirés des styles grec et romain. Il s'agit d'un fait surprenant qui démontre que, dans l'histoire de l'occident, le progrès n'a pas toujours était continu■

Chaise de style Isabelino■ Chaise de style Louis XVI■ Fauteuil de style Louis XV■ Fauteuil de style Louis XVI■

De la même façon, tout au long de l'Ere byzantine et du Moyen Age, les traditions des arts classiques et la notion de support confortable se perdirent, la chaise adopta une forme sévère et de grandes dimensions et fut réservée aux autorités et aux actes cérémonials■

Au cours de l'Ere Gothique (du XIIe au XVe siècle), en Europe, seules les personnes dotées d'une certaine éducation et avec des moyens économiques avaient un lien avec l'église. Par conséquent, le type de mobilier a été déterminé par les besoins du clergé qui poussa à la construction de chaises pour des raisons utilitaires telles que le fait de rendre plus facile l'étude des manuscrits, l'écriture ou la peinture. C'est à ces besoins qu'est due l'apparition, au XIVe siècle, de la chaise pivotante qui simplifia le travail des érudits■

L'ascétisme propre à cette époque ôta au design des chaises toute recherche de confort ou d'amélioration de la posture du corps et les meubles ce caractérisèrent alors par leur austérité et les angles droits entre le siège et le dossier (généralement haut et méticuleusement travaillé et décoré)■

Un des meubles les plus appréciés de cette époque était le coffre qui servait à la fois de rangement et de siège et permettait de transporter les objets personnels. Lorsque la population abandonna ses coutumes nomades, le coffre se transforma en un banc collé au mur■

Ce n'est qu'à partir du XVIe siècle que l'Europe marqua les lignes directrices dans l'évolution des Arts Décoratifs en général et du design de la chaise en particulier car il

Chaise Louis XIV■ Fauteuil Louis XV■ Chaise Louis XVI■ Chaise Louis XVI■ Chaise Louis XVI■

s'agissait d'un objet qui comprenait les principales caractéristiques de chaque période. La France et l'Angleterre étaient les pays qui exerçaient la plus grande influence dans le domaine du design de mobilier. À partir du XIXe siècle, les Etats-Unis commencèrent à les suivre de près■

La plus grande partie des styles décoratifs qui se sont succédés au cours de ces années ont reçu le nom du dirigeant de chaque période car c'était généralement lui qui ordonnait la fabrication du mobilier qui allait répondre à ses goûts et caprices. De ce fait, tous les styles ne furent pas exportés en Europe, et ils ne le furent pas en même temps■

Certains des exemples les plus significatifs de l'influence qu'exercèrent les dirigeants sur les Arts Décoratifs peuvent s'observer en France, sous le règne des "Louis" (Louis XIV, surnommé le Roi Soleil, Louis XV et Louis XVI) et, plus tard, avec le style Empire, à l'époque de Napoléon Bonaparte. Chacun d'entre eux voulut façonner le mobilier à l'image de sa grandeur et de sa majesté, selon ses obsessions et circonstances personnelles■

Depuis le début du XVIIe siècle, sous le règne de Louis XIV, différentes modes de décoration d'intérieur se succédèrent et firent de la France le pays qui jouissait de la plus grande influence dans le domaine du design de mobilier. C'est sous le règne de Louis XV, avec l'apparition du style Rococo français le plus authentique, qu'on retrouva la notion de chaise en tant que support pour le corps permettant de garder une posture déten-

Chaise Biedermeier■ Chaise Empire (Col. Antiquaire Giorgio Copetti)■ Chaise Art Nouveau (Col. Antiquaire Giorgio Copetti)■ Chaise de bureau (Col. Antiquaire Giorgio Copetti)■

due. Les éléments constructifs s'arrondirent pour donner naissance à des formes ondulées suggérant raffinement et joie de vivre. En ce qui concerne les pieds, qui étaient généralement travaillés, c'est le style cabriolé qui s'imposa avec une ondulation en forme de "S" étirée et un pied de chèvre présentant des volutes ornementales. Les dossiers suivirent la tendance du règne précédent : ils étaient hauts avec une corniche carrée ou légèrement incurvée et une belle retombée. L'utilisation des dossiers et des sièges cannés commença à s'imposer. Pour les fauteuils, le dossier et les bras formaient un tout uni et incurvé, généralement tapissés de façon luxueuse avec des damas, des cotons et des soies aux tons vifs. Un des traits les plus singuliers de cette période est l'introduction d'une certaine asymétrie dans les designs■

Dans l'ensemble, la chaise rococo peut transmettre une sensation d'élégance, de confort, de mouvement et de subtilité. Avec elle, la chaise perdit de la rigidité des siècles précédents et retrouva les lignes douces et la notion de confort que les grecs avaient développée■

Les personnes aisées de l'époque ordonnaient la fabrication des chaises aux ébénistes qui tentaient de transmettre les goûts des classes privilégiées avec des travaux élaborés de menuiserie faisant des meubles de véritables pièces d'art. De nouveaux matériaux et de nouvelles technologies apparurent et développèrent considérablement l'utilisation de la tapisserie. Peu à peu, le menuisier commença à céder du terrain au tapissier en tant que designer de chaises. Les formes se firent plus douces et arrondies, le dossier plus haut pour envelopper l'utilisateur, la profondeur du siège augmenta, on introdusit des ressorts à la base et on commença à tenir réellement compte du concept de "confort". Cependant, la chaise continua à être le privilège des classes aisées jusqu'à la Révolution Industrielle qui généralisa son utilisation aux classes populaires à partir du début du XIXe siècle.

Toutes les courbes et le confort proposés par le style rococo se perdirent à nouveau avec le règne de Louis XVI dont les goûts étaient déterminés par l'influence d'un néo-classicisme plus rigoureux. On en revint à une symétrie stricte qui se centrait principalement sur les lignes droites, les angles droits et la verticalité des pieds imitant les colonnes de l'Antiquité gréco-latine avec ses formes tronconiques et encaissées.

Cette considération pour l'Antiquité classique s'accentua avec le style Empire, qui apparut au début du XIXe siècle et qui, comme son nom l'indique, était un fidèle reflet de l'Empire napoléonien.

Bonaparte, responsable de la récupération du style et des icônes de la période classique de la Grèce et de Rome, imposa une fidélité tyrannique à la tradition classique. Il mit en place une réglementation très stricte qui limitait considérablement la marge de liberté et de créativité des ébénistes qui n'étaient pas autorisés à s'écarter de l'ordre établi. Le mobilier adopta des formes très simples et géométriques dans lesquelles dominaient les lignes droites, la symétrie exagérée et les structures massives. Les pieds étaient généralement dessinés en forme de colonne avec des griffes. Les dossiers caractéristiques du style Empire quadrangulaires et concaves rappelaient vaguement la forme d'une gondole. Certaines chaises étaient décorées avec des silhouettes ou des symboles mythologiques de l'Antiquité, et d'autres avec la lettre "N" de Napoléon I.

En Angleterre, l'évolution fut plus ou moins semblable, avec la succession, à partir du XVIe siècle, de nombreux styles décoratifs qui reflétaient son idiosyncrasie particulière. C'est de là que surgit le premier style décoratif connu sous le nom de l'artiste qui

Fauteuil double style Chippendale.

le créa, Thomas Chippendale (Yorkshire 1718-Londres 1779). Le style Chippendale supposa le point culminant de l'époque de splendeur du meuble anglo-saxon qui conjuguait les idées essentielles de tous les styles précédents. L'innovation la plus importante qu'il légua à la postérité fut l'introduction d'un nouveau concept qui considérait les pièces de la maison comme un tout, un ensemble uni dans lequel tous les éléments devaient avoir un lien entre eux et se compléter (nous retrouverons ce concept dans des styles emblématiques du modernisme, comme le Bauhaus). Les chaises étaient spécialement mises en évidence car elles montraient une structure très large comparée à leur profondeur et elles présentaient une grande variété de dossiers. Leur beauté et leur rigueur leur permirent de trouver leur place dans les bâtiments nobles du pays■

Ce grand ébéniste anglais réalisa des pièces très correctes et d'une fonctionnalité au caractère révolutionnairement bourgeois et confortable dans lesquelles il réussit à réunir l'art le plus pur du meuble et une industrialisation parfaite. Avec Chippendale, l'art bourgeois commença son pèlerinage vers le continent, et spécialement vers la France et les Pays-Bas■

À cette époque, on voit apparaître la chaise Windsor, d'origine rurale et constituée d'éléments façonnés au tour et d'un siège en bois massif. Avec le temps, cette chaise est pratiquement devenue le symbole patriotique aussi bien de l'Angleterre que des Etats-Unis, avec leurs apports nationaux respectifs. D'autre part, le fauteuil à bascule se transforma en une passion définitivement américaine■

À partir de ce moment, le design de la chaise fut déterminé par l'idéologie bourgeoise, détentrice du pouvoir économique, et par la Révolution Industrielle qui démocratisa l'utilisation de la chaise en la mettant à la portée des classes populaires■

C'est au XXe siècle que les innovations techniques et l'introduction de nouveaux matériaux firent de la chaise le terrain d'investigation préféré des architectes et des designers, ce qui donna naissance à des formes inimaginables jusqu'à ce moment et conjuguant ergonomie, esthétique et économie. On inaugure les 100 ans d'une créativité continue■

Fauteuil style Louis XV■

XXe SIÈCLE

100 ANS D'INNOVATION

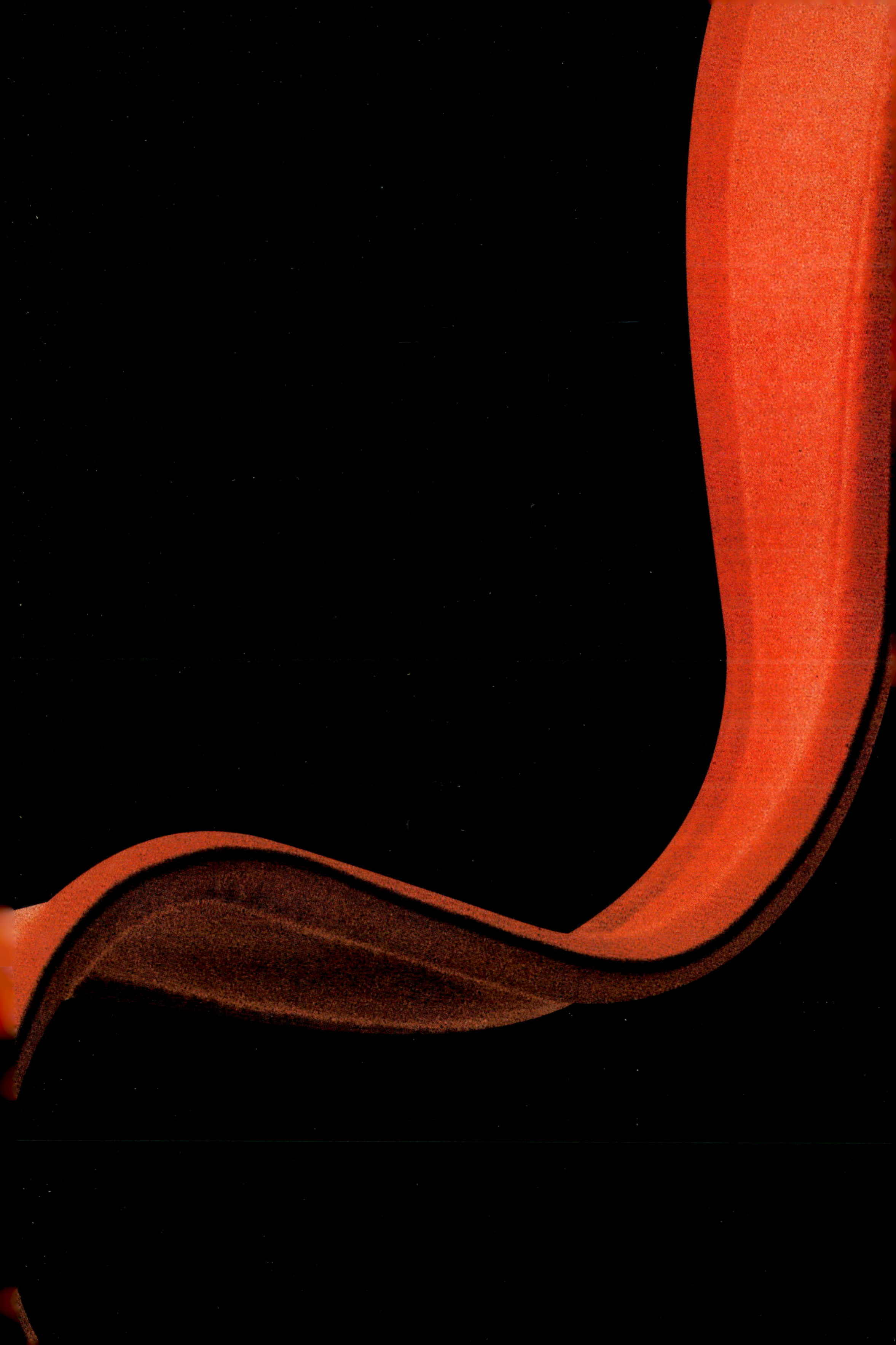

1900-1910

Les pionniers

Le design des chaises du XXe siècle est marqué par l'influence que les grands pionniers exercèrent durant les premières années : ils surent introduire dans leurs créations des innovations aussi bien au niveau des formes qu'au niveau des concepts. Non seulement ils modifièrent pour toujours l'esthétique du monde qui nous entoure, mais ils montrèrent également une nouvelle façon de comprendre la vie de la société de l'époque. Des noms comme Michael Thonet, Antonio Gaudí, Charles Rennie Mackintosh, William Morris ou Frank Lloyd Wright marquèrent le point d'inflexion de l'histoire du design qui servit d'inspiration pour les générations suivantes. Les courants stylistiques qui inaugurèrent le siècle furent l'Art Nouveau et le Mouvement Arts & Crafts. Le premier, qui fut populaire de 1880 au début de la première Guerre Mondiale, prétendait trouver la beauté dans les formes organiques. Ses designs sont basés sur des lignes sinueuses inspirées des formes des plantes et des animaux, et sont très influencés par l'art japonais. L'Art Nouveau se présenta comme la substitution nécessaire aux anciens styles historicistes dans le but de s'adapter à la culture "moderne". Il tenta de réconcilier l'art et l'industrie, mais il ne put pas satisfaire les demandes de productions massives à cause du contenu hautement artistique des pièces fabriquées. Ce genre trouva dans la ville de Viennes les formes les plus rectilignes permettant de mettre un accent particulier sur la fonctionnalité et dont les représentants furent Josef Hoffmann, Adolf Loos et Kolomon Moser■

En Angleterre, aux environs de 1880, le Mouvement Arts & Crafts trouva son origine dans un puissant contenu idéologique puisqu'il apparut en réaction contre les conséquences de la Révolution Industrielles dans les conditions de vie des travailleurs. William Morris, qui en fut le plus grand représentant, croyait qu'un "bon design" pouvait avoir une certaine influence sur la réussite d'une "bonne société". Le Mouvement défendait un retour aux méthodes artisanales du Moyen Âge, aux vertus des objets fabriqués à la main, en se centrant sur des designs simples, honnêtes, fonctionnels, sans ornement superflu et dont la qualité et la beauté étaient mises en relief par l'utilisation de matériaux naturels. Aux Etats-Unis, les plus grands représentants de ce style furent les frères Stickley qui furent sur le point de le transformer en un style national d'une saveur américaine authentique. Au sud-ouest des Etats-Unis, ce style fut surnommé Mission Style lorsque Frank Lloyd le transforma en un genre personnel appelé Prairie■

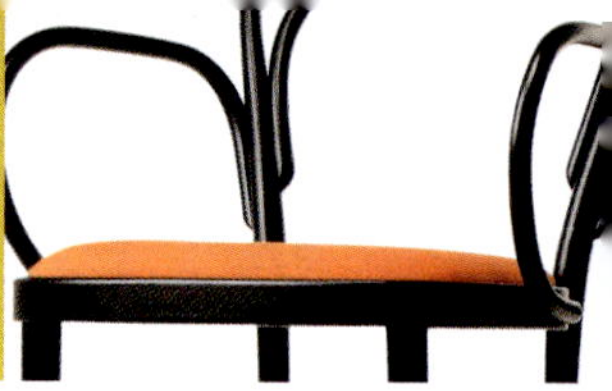

MICHAEL THONET

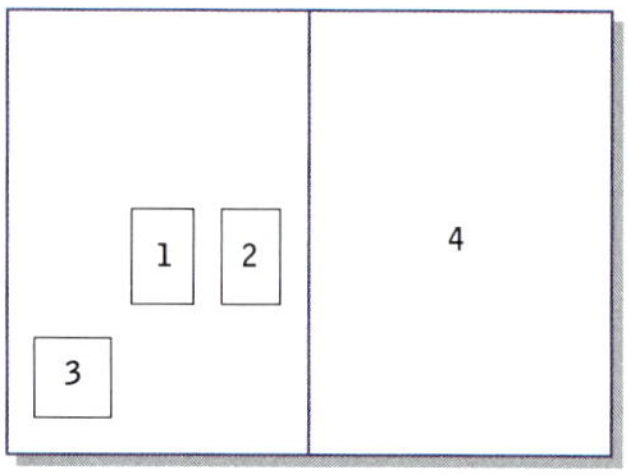

1. Chaise "214 F", de Thonet▪
Structure en bois incurvée et siège tapissé. Réalisée selon le modèle d'origine fabriqué par Michael Thonet, avec une très petite quantité d'éléments▪
⊟ 84 ⊟ 52 ⊟ 46 ⊟ 47 cm▪
2. Chaise "214", de Thonet▪
Structure en bois incurvée et siège canné. Il s'agit d'une descendance directe du modèle "n°14" fabriqué en 1859 par Michael Thonet▪
⊟ 84 ⊟ 43 ⊟ 52 ⊟ 46 cm▪
3. Image de Philipp, Claus et Peter Thonet, descendants du fondateur et actuels dirigeants de l'entreprise▪
4. Chaise "214 K", de Thonet▪
Nouvelle interprétation du modèle historique, symbole de l'innovation et du début d'une nouvelle ère▪

1796 Boppard am Rheim, Allemagne-1871 Viennes, Autriche▪

Même si ce fabriquant de meubles important développa son travail au cours de la deuxième moitié du XIXe siècle, sa présence est indispensable dans un livre retraçant l'histoire de la chaise▪
Michael Thonet est reconnu à un niveau international comme le pionnier de la production industrielle de mobilier, grâce au brevet qu'il obtint en 1856 pour un système révolutionnaire de vapeur sous pression servant à plier le bois. Ces expérimentations facilitèrent également l'utilisation du bois laminé dans la fabrication des chaises : il s'agit d'une des innovations les plus significatives du XXe siècle car elle rendit possible la fabrication des chaises avec moins de pièces, une unité et une fluidité visuelles plus importantes et plus économiques. Son in-

fluence se ressent dans le travail de grands designers comme Marcel Breuer, Alvar Aalto ou Charles et Ray Eames▪
Thonet est donc un exemple historique de la systématisation et de la rationalisation industrielles car il fut capable d'établir une ligne de connexion, qui n'existait pas auparavant, entre le design et la technologie. De cette union naquit un des icônes les plus représentatifs du design industriel : la chaise n°14, un des produits les plus copiés de l'histoire, dont les lignes incurvées sont à la mode encore aujourd'hui, ce qui démontre que les bons designs sont intemporels▪
Lorsque Thonet meurt le 3 mars 1871, il est le fabriquant de meubles le plus important du siècle et il est célèbre dans le monde entier▪

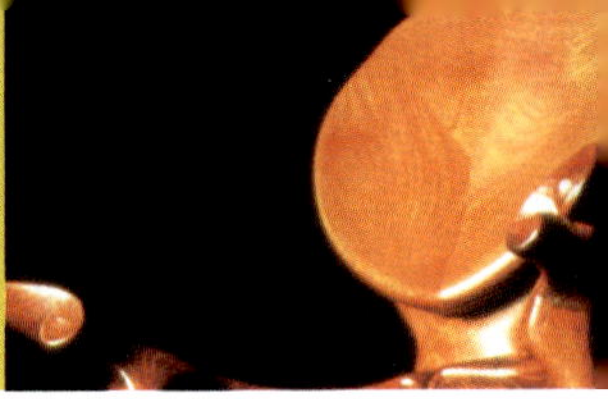

ANTONIO GAUDÍ

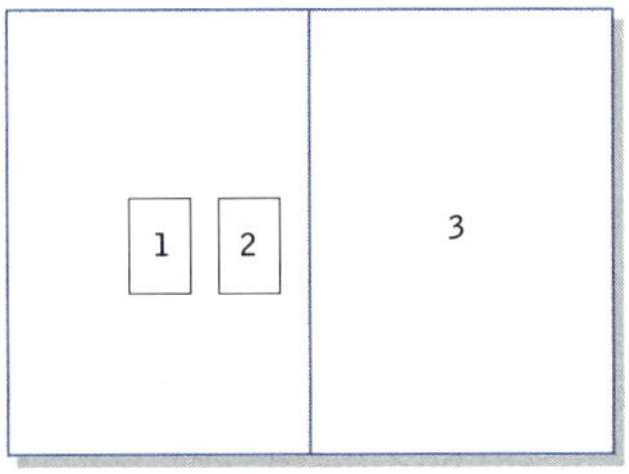

1. Chaise "Calvet", 1902. Produite par Bd Ediciones de Diseño▪
Réalisée en sculpture de chêne massif verni par la Maison Calvet de Barcelone▪
⊟ 94 ⊟ 52 ⊟ 54 cm▪

2. Chaise "Batlló", reproduction de Bd Ediciones de Diseño▪
Réalisée en chêne massif pour la salle à manger de la Maison Batlló▪
⊟ 74 ⊟ 52 ⊟ 47 cm▪

3. Fauteuil "Calvet", 1902. Produit par Bd Ediciones de Diseño▪
Réalisé en sculpture de chêne massif verni pour les bureaux de la Maison Calvet▪
⊟ 65 ⊟ 65 ⊟ 52 cm▪

1852 Reus, Espagne-1926 Barcelone, Espagne▪

Avec le temps, Antonio Gaudí est devenu la figure la plus importante de l'architecture catalane et espagnole ; il est admiré à un niveau international pour l'originalité et l'audace de ses solutions pour les techniques et les formes▪
Sa facette de designer de meubles ne peut pas être dissociée de ses bâtiments les plus emblématiques car sa vision de l'architecture comme un tout implique le même génie créatif pour les façades que pour les meubles. Il effectua ainsi un travail intense sur toutes sortes d'éléments, allant des poignées de portes jusqu'aux chaises et s'intégrant parfaitement dans l'espace architectonique. Les formes organiques, directement inspirées de la nature, se transformèrent en éléments de

structure essentiels dans le but de créer un mobilier donnant l'impression d'avoir été fabriqué dans un matériau extrêmement malléable. Tout comme dans la nature, aucun de ces meubles n'est identique à l'autre, l'asymétrie étant une de ses caractéristiques essentielles. L'ergonomie fut une autre des préoccupations de Gaudí qui dessinait les chaises de façon à les adapter à la structure du corps de l'utilisateur▪
Même si on classe généralement son œuvre dans le Modernisme, sa capacité d'innover, son habileté pour synthétiser l'esthétique historiciste prédominante jusqu'alors et la création d'une décoration "d'avant-garde", unique et brillante, rendent difficile la possibilité de limiter son œuvre à un style particulier▪

CHARLES RENNIE MACKINTOSH

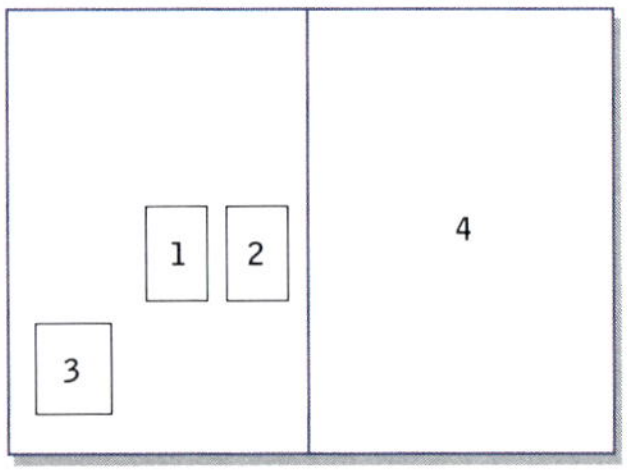

1. Chaise "Willow", 1904. Collection "Cassina I Maestri"▪
Structure en bois de frêne teint et dossier incurvé avec jalousie. Siège avec coussin▪
⊟ 119 ⊟ 94 ⊟ 41 ⊟ 39,5 cm▪
(Photo : M. Carreri)▪

2. Chaise "Argyle", 1897. Collection "Cassina I Maestri"▪
Structure en bois de frêne teint. Siège tapissé▪
⊟ 136 ⊟ 48 ⊟ 47 ⊟ 46 cm▪
(Photo : M. Carreri)▪

3. Chaise "Ingram", 1900. Collection "Cassina I Maestri"▪
Structure en bois de cerisier naturel. Siège tapissé▪
⊟ 95 ⊟ 47 ⊟ 44,5 ⊟ 45 cm▪

4. Chaise "Hill House", 1902. Collection "Cassina I Maestri"▪
Structure en bois de frêne teint. Siège tapissé en vert ou rose▪
⊟ 141 ⊟ 41 ⊟ 35 ⊟ 45 cm▪
(Photo : M. Carreri)▪

1868 Glasgow, Écosse-1928 Londres, Angleterre▪

On doit à Charles Rennie Mackintosh certains des exemples des chaises les plus originales et élégantes de l'Art Nouveau, même s'il ne fait pas directement partie de ce genre▪

Architecte, designer et peintre, il transforma dans ses meubles les formes organiques de l'Art Nouveau en formes géométriques, ce qui fit de lui le précurseur des styles qui l'ont suivi, comme le Mouvement de Sécession viennois ou le Mouvement Moderne introduit par l'École du Bauhaus▪

Tout comme son homologue américain Frank Lloyd Wright, Mackintosh consacrait une attention très particulière aux intérieurs car il pensait qu'un bâtiment devait former un ensemble organique dans lequel tous les détails étaient en harmonie. Son affinité pour les formes

simples et sa passion pour la décoration des surfaces se reflètent dans le design de ces intérieurs dans lesquels toutes les parties s'organisent en fonction d'un sujet généralement inspiré de la nature▪

Ses chaises comprennent également des références à des modèles naturels et à l'ordre géométrique, à l'artisanat de l'Arts & Crafts et au design, et englobent les deux pôles apparemment contradictoires de l'Art Nouveau dans le but de démontrer une symbiose fondamentale. Ses chaises mettent en évidence des dossiers exagérément hauts avec un design résumant son style : un ensemble de subtilité et d'opulence, d'austérité sévère et de romantisme exubérant▪

Son style original fut rapidement reconnu en Autriche et en Allemagne, mais Charles Rennie Mackintosh ne fut jamais considéré comme un prophète dans son pays jusqu'à un certain temps après sa mort▪

FRANK LLOYD WRIGHT

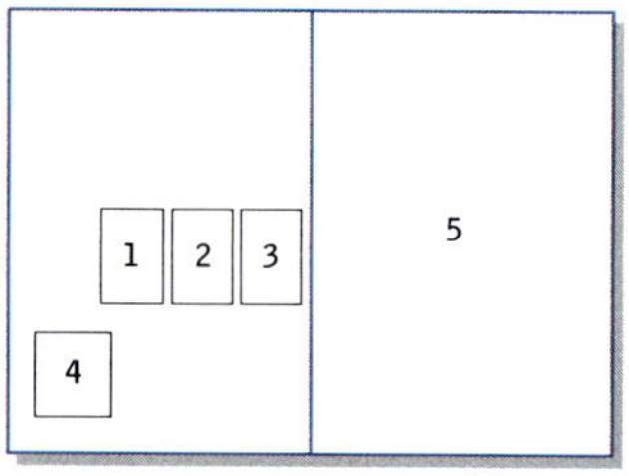

1. Chaise "Johnson Wax 2", 1936. Collection "Cassina I Maestri"■
Structure en tube d'acier peint. Siège et dossier tapissés avec bordure en cuir. Comporte des roulettes■
⊟ 88 ⊟ 61 ⊟ 54 ⊟ 46 cm■
(Photo : L. Torri)■
2. Chaise "Robie", 1908. Collection "Cassina I Maestri"■
Structure en bois de cerisier naturel ou teint. Siège tapissé■
⊟ 133,5 ⊟ 40 ⊟ 45,5 ⊟ 46 cm■
(Photo : Romano Fotografie)■
3. Chaise "Coonley 1", 1907. Collection "Cassina I Maestri"■
Structure en bois de cerisier naturel ou teint. Siège tapissé■
⊟ 46 ⊟ 43 ⊟ 47 ⊟ 46 cm■
(Photo : Studio Marcone)■
4. Chaise "Coonley 2", 1907. Collection "Cassina I Maestri"■
Structure en bois de cerisier naturel ou teint. Siège tapissé■
⊟ 70 ⊟ 43 ⊟ 47 ⊟ 46 cm■
(Photo : Studio Marcone)■
5. Chaise "Barrel", 1937. Collection "Cassina I Maestri"■
Structure en bois de cerisier naturel ou teint. Siège tapissé■
⊟ 81 ⊟ 54,5 ⊟ 55,5 ⊟ 50 cm■
(Photo : Romano Fotografie)■

1867 Wisconsin, États-Unis-1959 Arizona, États-Unis■

Reconnu par beaucoup comme l'architecte américain le plus important du xxe siècle, il fut le précurseur du style Prairie qui révolutionna le design résidentiel du début du siècle avec une philosophie destinée à développer une architecture moderne pour une société américaine démocratique. Dans ces maisons, les espaces s'intègrent dans un tout cohérent et l'extérieur et l'intérieur se réunissent pour unir le contexte et la structure■
Wright concevait un bâtiment comme une création complète dans laquelle le mobilier intérieur devait être en harmonie avec la géométrie et les matériaux de la structure, elle-même créée dans le but de s'intégrer dans un emplacement géographique précis. De plus, il était convaincu que

le contexte dans lequel les personnes vivent joue directement sur leur caractère. C'est pour cette raison que ses meubles et chaises défendaient une construction de qualité avec des lignes simples et droites qui faisaient ressortir la texture et le grain naturel du bois par rapport aux sculptures ornementales et à l'embellissement propre aux styles précédents. Il dessinait chaque pièce de façon individuelle en fonction du client et du contexte architectonique. Son architecture peut être qualifiée d'organique de par son respect des propriétés des matériaux et la relation harmonieuse entre les formes et la fonction du bâtiment. Il transforma la phrase "la forme suit la fonction", maxime du maître Louis Sullivan (adoptée ensuite comme emblème du Mouvement Moderne), en une théorie qui lui était propre : "la forme et la fonction ne font qu'un", la nature étant l'exemple représentant le mieux cette intégration■

1910-1920

Un défi aux conventions

Cette décennie assista à la naissance, au développement et à la coexistence de nombreux mouvements esthétiques qui troublèrent les fondations de l'Art en faisant appel à de nouvelles formes d'expression et, par conséquent, à un changement dans la mentalité de la société de l'époque. Cubisme, Futurisme, Postimpressionnisme, Art Abstrait, Expressionnisme, Dadaïsme, et Surréalisme agitèrent l'Europe avec des ruptures esthétiques et idéologiques continuelles▪

En ce qui concerne le design du mobilier, le rôle protagoniste retombe sur deux courants qui trouvèrent leur point algide au cours de ces années : le Mouvement de Sécession viennois et l'esthétique stimulée depuis la Hollande par le groupe De Stijl▪

"À chaque époque son art, et à chaque art sa liberté" fut la devise du Mouvement de Sécession originaire de Viennes aux alentours de 1900 et dont la volonté était d'en finir avec l'influence de l'historicisme dans le design qui dominait les créations de la fin du siècle. Le style atteint son plus haut degré de définition au cours de ces dix années avec des lignes assez géométriques et mettant l'accent sur l'importance de la fonctionnalité et la primatie de la structure. Josef Hoffmann, Otto Wagner et Adolf Loos (avec leur critique radicale contre les ornements) sont quelques uns des designers qui ont un lien avec ce mouvement. La chaise Prague, créée en 1925 par Joseff Hoffmann, est une des créations reflétant le mieux ce style▪

Le groupe De Stijl, pour sa part, fut fondé en 1917 en Hollande par l'architecte Theo van Doesburg. Les artistes qui faisaient partie de ce groupe voulaient créer un style universel dans le domaine de la peinture, de l'architecture et du design qui se serait basé sur une abstraction pure et une certaine simplicité à partir de l'utilisation de rectangles ou de carrés sur des surfaces planes aux couleurs primaires intenses –associées au noir, au gris et au blanc–, et harmonisées au moyen de lignes droites. Parmi les apports les plus importants à l'iconographie du design du XXe siècle, on trouve les peintures géométriques de Piet Mondrian et le mobilier révolutionnaire de Gerrit T. Rietveld, comme la chaise Red-Blue, une représentation en trois dimensions du tableau de Mondrian. Les manifestations de ce groupe allaient être très importantes au sein de l'École du Bauhaus, fondée en 1919 par Walter Gropius▪

FAUTEUIL "F51", créé en 1920 par Walter Gropius. Produit par Tecta▪

GERRIT THOMAS RIETVELD

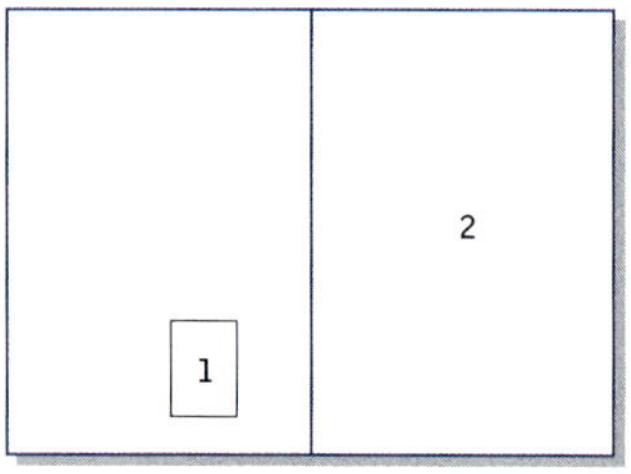

1. Chaise "Zig-Zag", 1934. Collection "Cassina I Maestri"■
Structure en bois de cerisier naturel, avec finition polie■
⊟ 74 ⊟ 37 ⊟ 43 ⊟ 43 cm■
2. Chaise "Red and Blue", 1918. Collection "Cassina I Maestri"■
Structure en hêtre teint en noir. Siège et dossier en bois contre-plaqué laqué■
⊟ 88 ⊟ 65,5 ⊟ 83 ⊟ 33 cm■
(Photo : M. Carrieri)■

1888 Utrech, Hollande-1964 Utrech, Hollande■

L'année 1917 marqua un tournant dans la théorie de l'architecture grâce au design d'une chaise, la Red-Blue Chair de Gerrit T. Rietveld, qui interprétait les théories du Néoplasticisme en remettant en question les normes touchant au style et au goût. De ce fait, l'introduction des pièces néoplastiques dans le design de ses meubles supposa un point d'inflexion dans le renouvellement de la pensée architectonique et décorative qui allait jouer sensiblement sur les mouvements esthétiques à venir■

En 1918, Rietveld entre dans le groupe De Stijl pour apporter une contribution décisive à l'évolution théorique du Néoplasticisme et en devenir l'un des plus grands représentants. Le but de cette collectivité était d'obtenir un équilibre parfait entre l'humanité et la société, et entre la société et la nature grâce à la relation physique des hommes avec leur environnement■

Dans chacun de ses meubles, Rietveld exprime ses intentions et transmet en même temps une des évidences les plus significatives du nouveau concept de l'espace architectonique. Lignes et surfaces se retrouvent à chaque angle, mais sans jointure. Les éléments du design créent une spécialité abstraite dans laquelle l'utilisation de la couleur contribue essentiellement au processus d'interprétation permettant de percevoir la forme tangible dans l'étendue conceptuelle et mettant en évidence une nouvelle évaluation des relations. Le résultat est la création d'une synthèse magique entre le design de l'article et l'espace en lui-même■

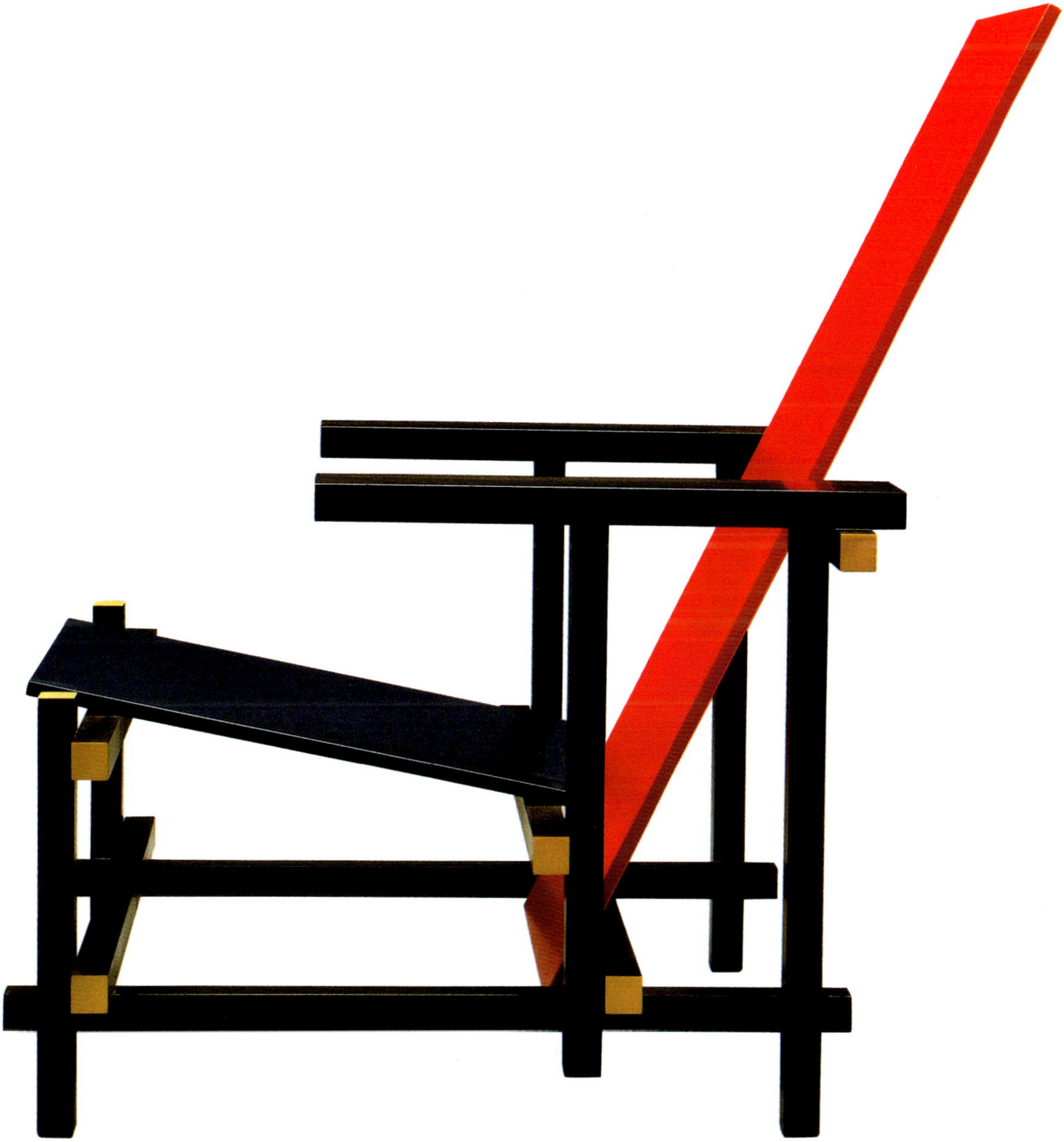

1920-1930

L'Ère des architectes

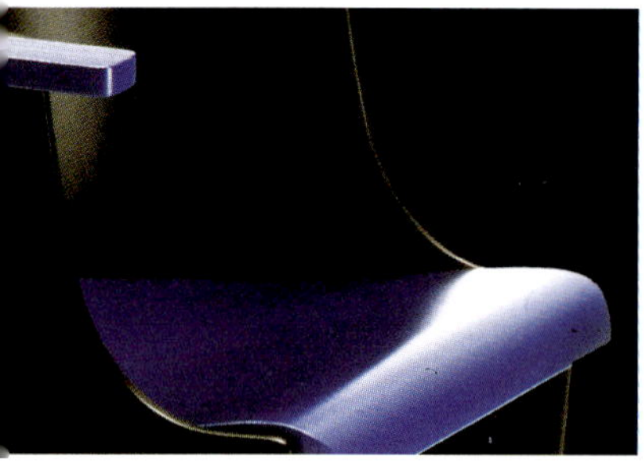

Cette décennie suppose l'éclosion de la tendance qui naquit au début du siècle : les architectes deviennent les rénovateurs principaux du design du mobilier en utilisant les chaises comme terrain d'investigation leur permettant de concrétiser à petite échelle leurs idéaux architectoniques. Le développement de nouveaux matériaux, en particulier le tube d'acier et le bois contre-plaqué, sera fondamental dans le processus de renouvellement des Arts Décoratifs■

À cette époque, on remarque particulièrement l'idéologie établie par l'École Bauhaus, instigatrice du Mouvement Moderne, dont l'influence dans le design est toujours en vigueur. Fondée à Weimar en 1919 par Walter Gropius, et clôturée en 1933 par le parti Nazi, elle était composée de personnes qui considéraient le design comme un moyen de faire avancer la société et qui souhaitaient fabriquer des meubles de bonne qualité mais à la portée de la plus grande partie de la population■

En ce qui concerne les normes esthétiques du Bauhaus, on remarque par-dessus tout la défense de la fonctionnalité au dépend de la forme (de là la fameuse maxime "La forme suit la fonction"), la géométrie, la simplicité, l'honnêteté, l'universalité, la standardisation, l'économie et l'application des nouvelles technologies. Ses partisans prétendaient créer un nouvel environnement domestique à partir de l'union entre la technologie et l'artisanat, et étaient convaincus qu'une maison et les ustensiles qui s'y trouvent doivent être liés sensiblement. Parmi ses plus grands représentants, en ce qui concerne le design de chaises, on trouve Ludwing Mies van der Rohe et Marcel Breuer. Au même moment, Le Corbusier et Charlotte Perriand effectuaient des expériences en France sur les possibilités que pouvait offrir l'aluminium, créant ainsi certains des meubles les plus emblématiques du XXe siècle■

Un autre mouvement esthétique fit son apparition à cette époque : l'Art Déco, découvert lors de l'Exposition des Arts Décoratifs et Industriels Modernes de Paris en 1925 et au cours de laquelle on l'exhiba pour la première fois comme une célébration de la vie dans le monde moderne. Ses participants proposaient une esthétique sensuelle et raffinée qui mettait en évidence l'utilisation d'un artisanat exquis et de matériaux exotiques et luxueux. Ce style se caractérise par son éclectisme et reflète une grande variété d'influences, comme celle de l'Art Nouveau, l'esthétique du Bauhaus, le Cubisme, le Ballet Russe, la culture des Indiens d'Amérique, l'iconographie de l'Egypte, les formes classiques et la nature■

Design de El Lissitzky, 1930. De Tecta. ⊢ 73 — 57 ⊢ 49 ⊟ 44 cm■

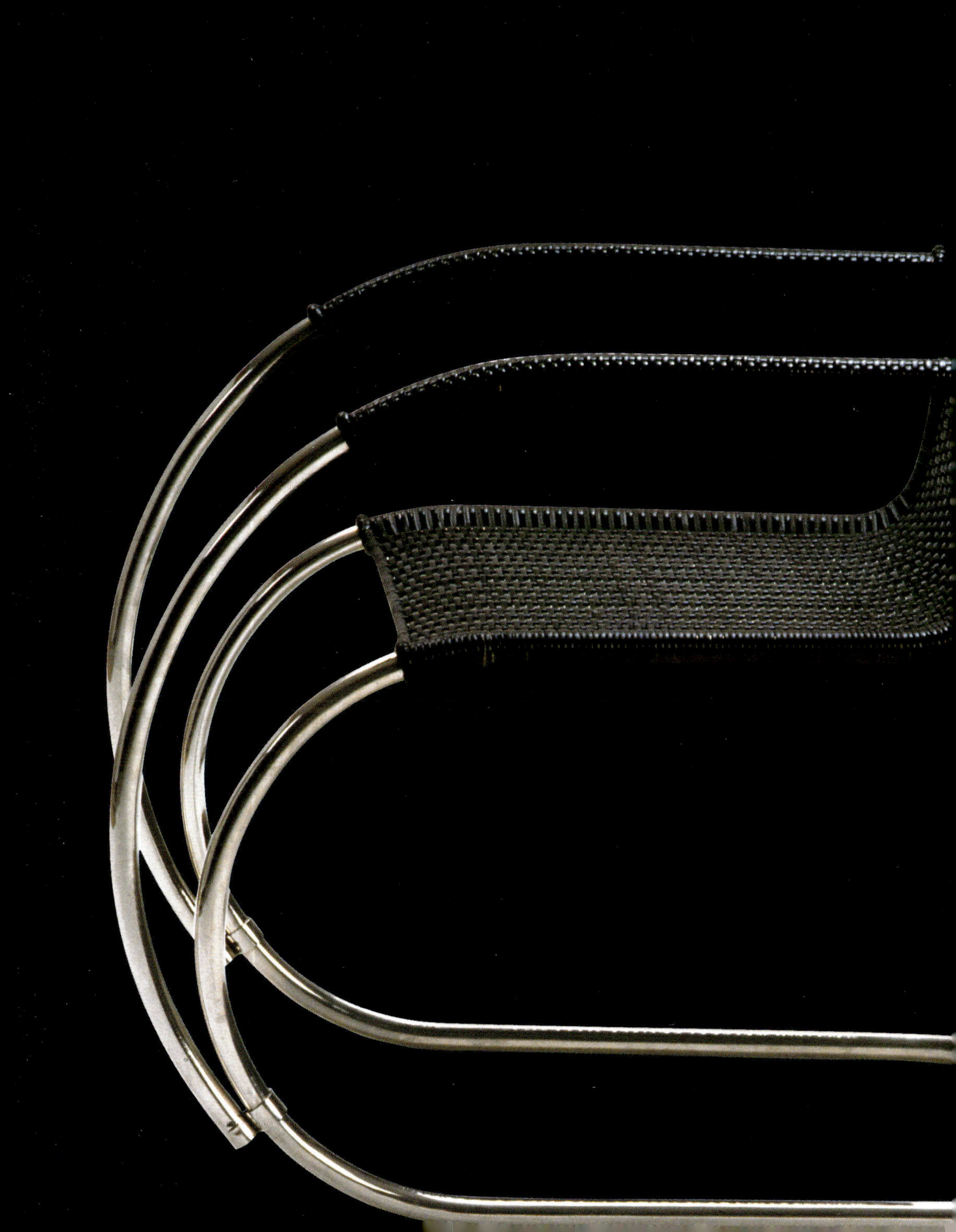

EILEEN GRAY

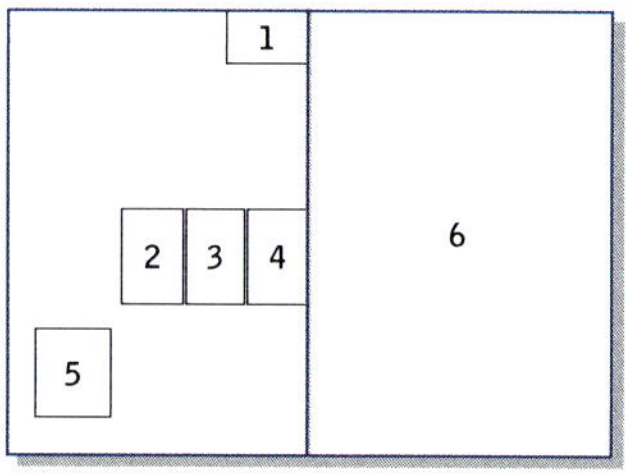

1. Fauteuil "Bibendum", 1929. De Classicon▪
Structure en acier tubulaire chromé. Tapissé en peau ou en tissu▪
⊟ 73 ⊟ 90 ⊟ 83 cm▪
2. Tabouret "N°1", 1927. De Classicon▪
Colonne en acier chromé, base en aluminium laqué, siège tapissé en peau▪
⊟ 70-85 ⊟ 38 cm▪
3. Chaise "Non Conformist", 1926. De Classicon▪
Structure en acier chromé. Siège et dossier tapissés en peau▪
⊟ 78 ⊟ 57 ⊟ 63 ⊟ 45 cm▪
4. Tabouret "N° 2". De Classicon▪
Structure et base en acier. Siège tapissé en peau▪
⊟ 73 ⊟ 30 ⊟ 39,5 cm▪
5. Chaise "Roquebrune", 1932. De Classicon▪
Structure en acier chromé. Siège et dossier en peau▪
⊟ 76,5 ⊟ 45 ⊟ 55 ⊟ 45 cm▪
6. Chaise "Aixia", 1926. De Classicon▪
Structure en tube d'acier chromé, pieds en bubinga et siège tapissé▪
⊟ 83 ⊟ 40,2 ⊟ 52 ⊟ 48 cm▪

1878 Enniscorthy, Irlande-1976 Paris, France▪

Actuellement reconnue comme l'une des figures les plus importantes du Mouvement Moderne en France, Eileen Gray entra dans le monde du design de mobilier et d'intérieur grâce à son étude de la technique du laquage, dans laquelle elle atteint un niveau qui la fit connaître dans les cercles artistiques du Paris du début du siècle▪
Elle développa son propre vocabulaire artistique adapté à son caractère anticonformiste, s'éloignant ainsi des lignes sinueuses de l'Art Nouveau qui régnait alors en France et se rapprochant des idées du groupe De Stijl, avec ses formes géométriques rationnelles et ses lignes simples. Eileen Gray se fit particulièrement remarquer grâce à l'utilisation originale qu'elle fit des matériaux et des formes, en cultivant une sensibilité qui exprimait mouvement et flexibilité dans ses créations. À cette époque, elle se consacra à la création de meubles "adaptés à notre existence, par rapport à nos pièces et en accord avec nos aspirations et nos sentiments", ce qui rejoint sa foi dans une formation d'ambiances complètes dans des maisons qu'elle considérait comme des organismes vivants▪

Des créations comme la chaise Nonconformist, établissant un jeu asymétrique brillant, le fauteuil Transat, spécialement créé pour la fameuse villa E.1027, ou le fauteuil Bibendum, avec sa structure révolutionnaire en acier chromé, l'ont placée parmi les noms "sacrés" du design du XXe siècle. Au cours des années 40 et 70, son travail resta dans la plus complète obscurité, et sa participation au style de vie moderne ne fut redécouverte que peu de temps avant sa mort▪

MIES VAN DER ROHE

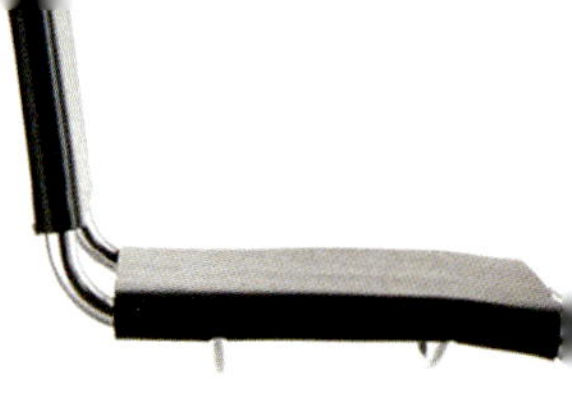

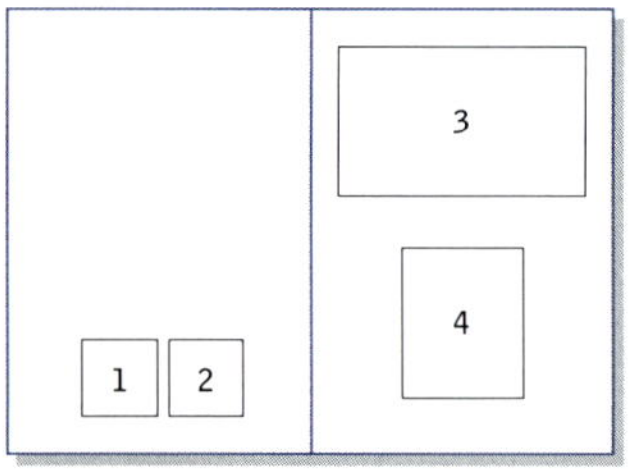

1. Chaise "D 42", 1927. De Tecta▪ Structure en tube d'acier chromé. Siège et dossier en osier réalisé par Lilly Reich▪
⊟ 79 ⊟ 48 ⊟ 74 ⊟ 44 cm▪
2. Chaise en saillie de 1927. Distribuée par Alivar (Collection "Museum")▪ Structure en tube d'acier incurvé. Siège et dossier en peau▪
⊟ 79 ⊟ 47 ⊟ 69 cm▪
3. Chaise "Barcelone", 1929. Distribuée par Alivar (Collection "Museum")▪
Structure en tube d'acier en forme de X inspirée du design classique. Le design de la tapisserie en peau est attribué à Llily Reich. Créée pour le Pavillion Allemand de l'Exposition Universelle de Barcelone▪
⊟ 75 ⊟ 75 ⊟ 75 cm▪
4. Chaise "Brno", 1930. Distribuée par Alivar (Collection "Museum")▪ Structure en acier poli plat. Siège et dossier tapissés en peau▪
⊟ 76 ⊟ 58 ⊟ 57 cm▪

1886 Aachen, Allemagne-1969 Chicago, Illinois, États-Unis▪

Selon Mies van der Rohe, considéré comme l'architecte minimaliste le plus représentatif du xxe siècle, "la chaise est un objet très difficile. Quiconque aura tenté d'en fabriquer une le saura. Il existe en grand nombre de possibilités et de problèmes. La chaise doit être légère, solide et confortable. Il est presque plus facile de construire un gratte-ciel que de créer une bonne chaise"▪
Mies van der Rohe, qui fut le directeur de l'École du Bauhaus entre 1930 et 1933, pensait que l'architecture et le design des meubles étaient intimement liés : les problèmes, les principes et même les matériaux nécessaires à la construction d'un gratte-ciel peuvent également se retrouver dans le design d'une chaise▪
On lui doit deux des maximes les plus connues du xxe siècle "moins est plus" et "Dieu se trouve dans les détails", principes qui se trouvent dans la genèse de ses projets d'architecture et de design de meubles. Une de ses œuvres les plus emblématiques est le Pavillion Allemand de Barcelone en 1929, construit pour l'Exposition Universelle et considéré comme la quintessence de l'abstraction de l'espace dans l'architecture. Le Pavillion donna naissance à la chaise Barcelone, une des plus célèbres de notre siècle. Mies van der Rohe rechercha également les possibilités offertes par les structures des chaises en saillie et s'inspira des designs de Mart Stam. La création en 1930 de la chaise Brno fit de lui la première personne ayant développé une version réellement fonctionnelle de la chaise en saillie avec une structure en acier▪

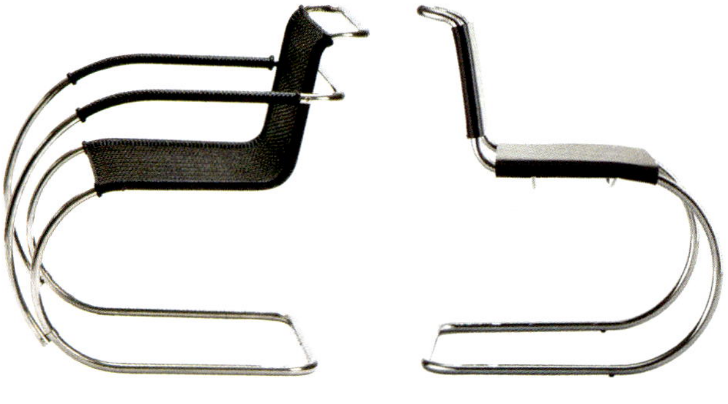

LE CORBUSIER

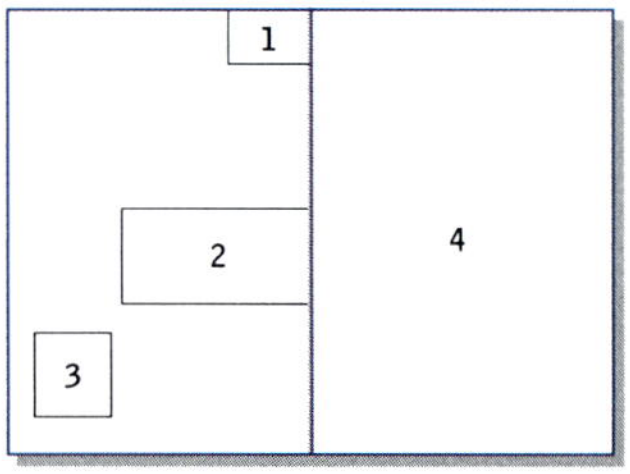

1 et 2. Fauteuil "LC1", 1928. Collection Cassina I Maestri"■
Créé par Le Corbusier en collaboration avec Pierre Jeanneret et Charlotte Perriand. Structure en acier chromé et siège et dossier en peau■
⊟ 64 ⊟ 69 ⊟ 65 ⊟ 40 cm■
3. Fauteuil "LC7", 1928. Collection "Cassina I Maestri"■
Créé par Le Corbusier en collaboration avec Pierre Jeanneret et Charlotte Perriand. Fauteuil pivotant avec structure en acier chromé ou peint en plusieurs couleurs. Siège et dossier tapissés en peau ou en tissu■
⊟ 73 ⊟ 60 ⊟ 58 ⊟ 50 cm■
4. Fauteuil "LC2", 1928. Collection "Cassina I Maestri"■
Créé par Le Corbusier en collaboration avec Pierre Jeanneret et Charlotte Perriand. Fauteuil avec structure en acier chromé ou peint en plusieurs couleurs. Siège et dossier tapissés en peau ou en tissu■
⊟ 67 ⊟ 76 ⊟ 70 ⊟ 43 cm■

1887 La Chaux de Fonds, Suisse-1965 Cap Martin, France■

Charles Edouard Jeanneret, surnommé Le Corbusier en 1920, est connu à niveau international pour être un des architectes les plus influents du xxe siècle. Il articula des idées provocatrices, créa des designs révolutionnaires et fit preuve d'un sens puissant, et utopique, de la fonction de l'architecte : s'adapter aux besoins d'une société démocratique dominée par la machine en proposant une vision de la ville comme un tout architectonique■
Sa conception d'une maison est celle d'une "machine à vivre", un produit industriel devant contenir un mobilier fonctionnel. Dans le même esprit, Le Corbusier créa, en collaboration avec Pierre Jeanneret et Charlotte Perriand, une série de pièces de mobilier basées

sur l'acier tubulaire et qui projetaient une nouvelle esthétique rationaliste. Ce mobilier fut créé comme un instrument dont la fonction était de cohabiter en harmonie avec ces espaces créés par et pour l'homme moderne■
Le seul objectif de ses chaises était d'exprimer concrètement leur fonction. Pour cela, ses composants de base étaient organisés autour d'une structure en tube métallique la plus simple possible. Le Corbusier était convaincu que n'importe quel objet quotidien devait exprimer le binôme forme/fonction. De cette façon, l'objet libéré de tout ornement allait dégager une beauté intime et tirée de sa nature, au moyen de l'harmonie de la simplicité et l'essence de la forme. C'est peut-être pour cette raison que ses chaises restent étonnement actuelles, plus de 70 ans après leur création■

MARCEL BREUER

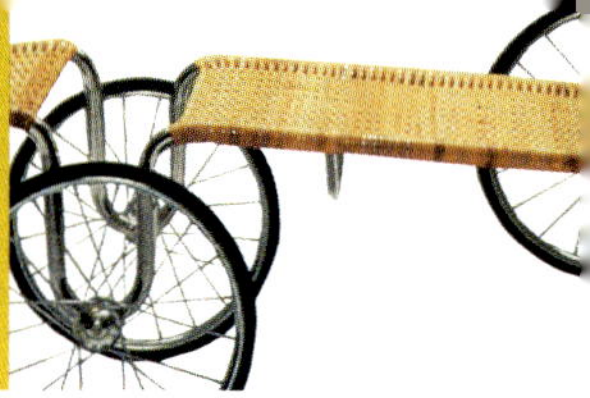

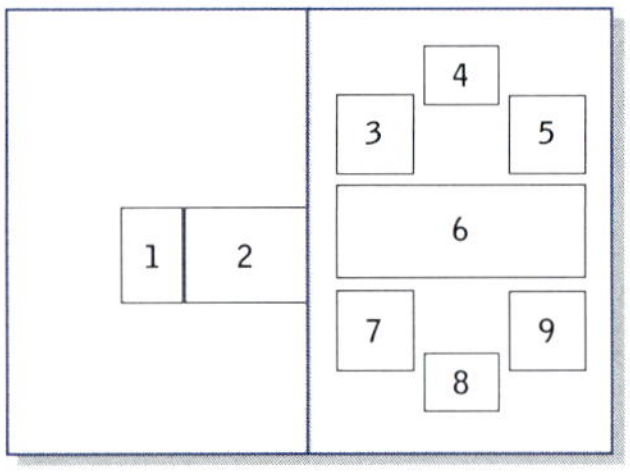

1. Chaise "Lajko". De Ultramobile▪
Chaise en saillie avec structure en acier chromé. Siège et dossier tapissés▪
⊟ 91 ⊟ 59 ⊟ 61 ⊟ 47 cm▪

2. Fauteuil "S35R" avec tabouret, 1929. De Thonet▪
Structure en tube d'acier chromé. Siège et dossier en osier▪
⊟ 84 ⊟ 65 ⊟ 83 cm▪

3 et 5. Chaise "D4", 1927. De Tecta▪
Structure en tube d'acier. Siège et dossier en tissu▪
⊟ 71 ⊟ 78 ⊟ 61 ⊟ 45 cm▪

4 et 7. Chaise "Cesca", 1929-30 (copyright artistique Mart Stam). Produite par Thonet ; Knoll▪
Base en saillie d'acier tubulaire chromé, siège et dossier avec cadre en bois et recouvrement en osier▪
Version tapissée.
Avec accoudoirs : ⊟ 81 ⊟ 58 ⊟ 61 cm▪
Sans accoudoirs : ⊟ 81 ⊟ 46 ⊟ 58 cm▪

6. Chaise longue à roulettes, 1928-30. De Tecta▪
Structure en acier chromé ou peint. Siège et dossier en osier▪
⊟ 63 ⊟ 61 ⊟ 186 ⊟ 30 cm▪

8. Chaise "D40", 1928. De Tecta▪
Chaise en saillie avec structure en tube d'acier chromé. Siège et dossier en osier, accoudoir en hêtre▪
⊟ 88 ⊟ 53 ⊟ 61 ⊟ 45 cm▪

9. Chaise "Wassily", 1925. Reproduction de Galvano Técnica▪
Breuer s'inspira de la poignée de sa bicyclette pour la création de cette chaise, ce qui supposa une véritable innovation. Structure en tube d'acier chromé. Siège et dossier en peau▪
⊟ 75 ⊟ 78 ⊟ 70 cm▪

1902 Pecs, Hongrie-1981 New York, États-Unis▪

Même si Marcel Breuer ne fut pas très applaudi en tant qu'architecte, il fut reconnu comme l'un des derniers architectes réellement fonctionnalistes, et ce fut son travail de designer de meubles qui fit de lui une des influences les plus importantes du XXe siècle▪
Encouragé par l'idéologie de l'École du Bauhaus, dont il fut élève et professeur entre 1920 et 1928, Breuer travailla sur l'application de nouvelles méthodes de production aux problèmes traditionnels du design. Selon lui, "une pièce de mobilier n'est pas une composition arbitraire, il s'agit d'un composant nécessaire à notre environnement. Proprement impersonnelle, elle prend une signification en fonction de la façon dont elle est utilisée ou en formant partie d'un schéma complet"▪

Ses designs de chaises avec structure en tube d'acier (comme l'innovatrice Wassily chair créée en 1925, qui fut inspirée de la poignée de sa bicyclette) et de chaises en saillie –sur lesquelles avaient travaillé Mart Stam (possesseur du brevet) et Mies van der Rohe–, exercèrent la plus grande influence dans l'évolution de la chaise et marquèrent un point d'inflexion dans l'histoire du design. À cette époque, ces designs présentaient de nombreux avantages provenant de l'idéologie du Mouvement Moderne : accessible aux masses, hygiène, légèreté, développement de nouvelles technologies, ruptures avec les traditions, flexibilité et une extrême simplicité et clarté dans les formes. En 1935, Breuer émigra à Londres, fuyant la montée du Nazisme, où il commença à travailler sur les possibilités du bois contre-plaqué et sur des créations qui font également partie de l'histoire du design▪

1930-1950

Triomphe du Design Organique

Au moment où l'Art Déco et l'esthétique du Bauhaus continuaient à étendre leur influence en Europe et aux Etats-Unis, une nouvelle sensibilité, défendue par un groupe de designers et architectes scandinaves, fit son apparition et lança un défi aux formes sévères et impersonnelles du Mouvement Moderne en les remplaçant par d'autres plus douces et en portant une attention particulière sur les matériaux naturels et les formes organiques.

Le nom le plus important de ce nouveau courant esthétique, le Design Organique Scandinave, est celui de l'architecte et designer finlandais Alvar Aalto, un des plus grands promoteurs de l'utilisation du bois contre-plaqué dans la fabrication des meubles et connu pour ses designs de chaises pensées pour s'adapter au corps humain.

L'union délicate entre le fonctionnalisme et la sensibilité est la marque d'identité principale du design scandinave. La préoccupation pour satisfaire les besoins de l'homme avant les questions de style, l'utilisation de matériaux naturels (en particulier, les bois aux tons clairs), la simplicité, la commodité et l'authenticité de leurs budgets et de leurs formes, ... représentent une version "aimable" du Mouvement Moderne si on y ajoute l'approche plus humaniste et chaleureuse du design de meubles et d'objets quotidiens qui exerça un rôle important dans l'évolution du design moderne.

Sur les pas du design scandinave, et en particulier d'Alvar Aalto, le couple Charles et Ray Eames travailla aux Etats-Unis avec de nouvelles techniques pour modeler le bois contre-plaqué qui furent, pour la plupart, développées pour la marine américaine pendant la Seconde Guerre Mondiale et qui supposent un avant et un après dans l'histoire du design américain. Avec Eero Saarinen, avec qui Charles Eames collabora sur de nombreux projets, et George Nelson, ils établirent les bases d'un langage authentiquement américain. De cette façon, à partir du travail de ces grands créateurs et une fois la guerre terminée, les designers américains commencèrent à créer une esthétique qui leur était propre en s'éloignant de l'énorme influence que l'Europe avait exercé sur eux jusqu'alors. Ces années représentent le début de l'hégémonie mondiale du "American way of life". D'autre part, les principaux représentants du fonctionnalisme européen avaient émigré aux Etats-Unis, et participaient à la conception du Style International qui allait dégénérer en un type de design dirigé par des raisons économiques et commerciales.

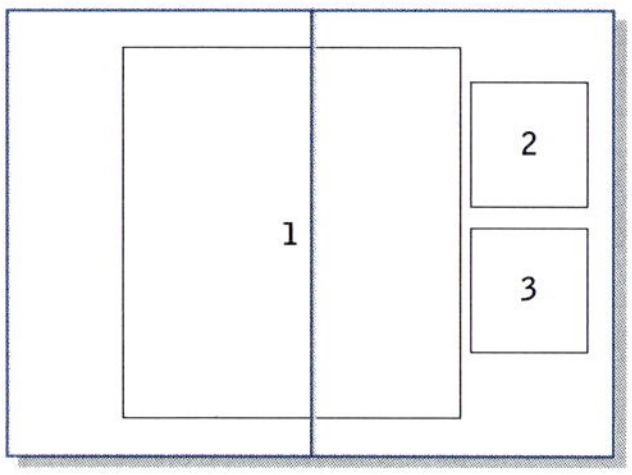

Page précédente :
Chaise "Antony" de Jean Prouvé, architecte et designer français dont les créations ont exercé une grande influence sur le design de mobilier. Base en acier tubulaire laqué en noir et structure du siège en bois contreplaqué. Produite par Vitra. (Photo : H. Hansen)■

1. "The China Chair", 1944. Créée par Hans J. Wegner, un des plus grands représentants du design organique danois du XXe siècle. Produite par Fritz Hansen■
Elle est fabriquée en cerisier ou en caoba■
⊟ 82 ⊟ 55 ⊟ 55 ⊟ 45 cm■
2. Chaise "Torres Clavé", 1934. Créée par l'architecte Josep Torres Clavé, qui s'inspira des modèles populaires d'Ibiza. Produite par Mobles 114■
Structure en cèdre et siège et dossier en tissu d'énéa■
⊟ 75 ⊟ 70 ⊟ 78 cm■
3. "The Church Chair", 1936. Créée par Kaare Klint, précurseur des marques d'identité du design danois qui en firent le style de référence international au milieu du siècle. Produite par Fritz Hansen■
Fabriquée en chêne■
⊟ 84 ⊟ 52 ⊟ 50 ⊟ 43 cm■

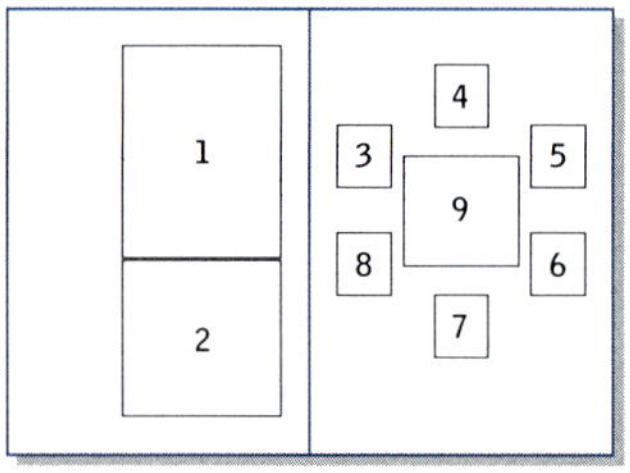

1. Chaise "Standard", 1934-50. De Jean Prouvé. Produite par Vitra■
Base en plaque d'acier et tube rond. Siège et dossier en hêtre naturel ou laqué■

2. Chaise "SE 68", 1950. Design de Egon Eiermann, pour Wilde+Spieth■
Ce modèle est un des classiques du design allemand■

3. Chaise "Risom", 1941. Design de Jens Risom. Elle fait partie de la première collection produite par Knoll. Caractéristique du design scandinave■

4. The Ax Chair, 1950. Créée par Hvidt & Mølgaard. Produite par Fritz Hansen■

5 et 7. Chaise "Sant' Elia" (1936) et "Follia" (1934), de Giuseppe Terragni pour Zanotta■

6. Chaise "Navy", 1944. De Emeco■
Icône du design américain, on commença à la fabriquer pour la marine américaine. Structure d'une seule pièce en aluminium■
⊟ 86 ⊟ 41 ⊟ 50 ⊟ 46 cm■

8. Tabouret Satish, 1931. Design de Eckart Muthesius, produit par Classicon■
Structure en acier inoxydable et siège tapissé en peau■

9. Chaise "565", 1943. Créée par Gerald Summers. Produite par Alivar (Collection "Museum")■
Fabriquée d'une seule pièce en bois contre-plaqué modelé■

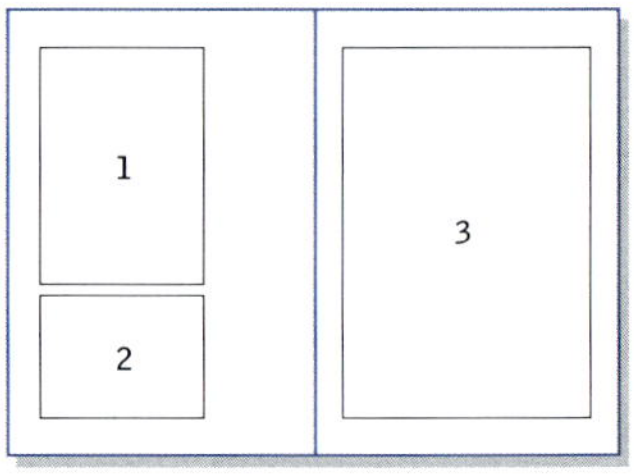

1. Chaise créée par Mogens Lassen pour Fritz Hansen■
Structure en saillie réalisée en tube d'acier. Siège et dossier en osier■
2. "The Wishbone Chair", 1950. Design de Hans J. Wegner pour Carl Hansen■
Structure en frêne, en hêtre ou en chêne. Siège en corde■
⊟ 70 ⊟ 74 ⊟ 52 ⊟ 44 cm■
3. Chaise "SE 42", 1949. Créée par Egon Eiermann. Produite par Wilde+Spieth■

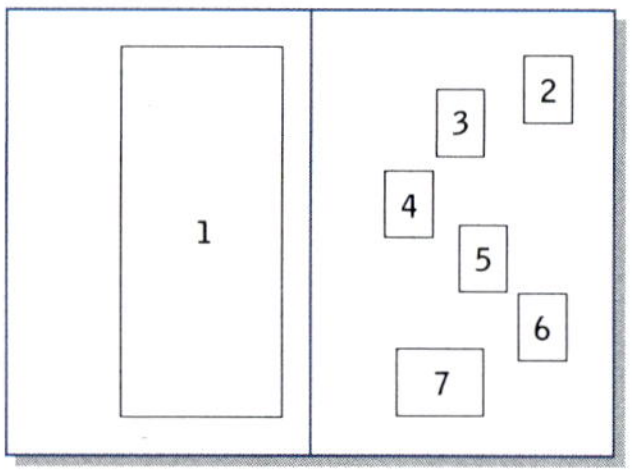

1. CHAISE "SE 68", 1950. Création de Egon Eiermann, pour Wilde+Spieth■
2 et 4. Chaises de la gamme "S 43", 1931. Créées par Mart Stam. Produites par Thonet■
Chaise en saillie avec structure en acier. Siège et dossier en hêtre contre-plaqué modelé■
⊟ 82 ⊟ 44 ⊟ 53 cm■
3. FAUTEUIL "GENNI", 1935. Création de Gabriele de Mucchi. Produit par Zanotta■
Structure en acier chromé. Dossier inclinable sur deux positions. Siège et dossier tapissés en peau■
⊟ 73/82 ⊟ 57 ⊟ 109 ⊟ 41 cm■
5. FAUTEUIL "MAGGIOLINA", 1947. Création de Marco Zanuso. Produit par Zanotta■
Structure en acier tubulaire et corps en cuir. Coussins pour siège et dossier■
⊟ 83 ⊟ 71 ⊟ 102 ⊟ 40 cm■
6. FAUTEUIL "CITÉ", 1930. Création de Jean Prouvé. Réédition de Vitra■
Structure en plaque d'acier laquée. Siège et dossier tapissés d'une seule pièce. Accoudoirs formés par des rubans de cuir. (Photo : H. Hansen)■
7. TABOURET "BANU", 1931. Design de Eckart Muthesius. Produit par Classicon■
Structure en acier. Siège tapissé en peau■

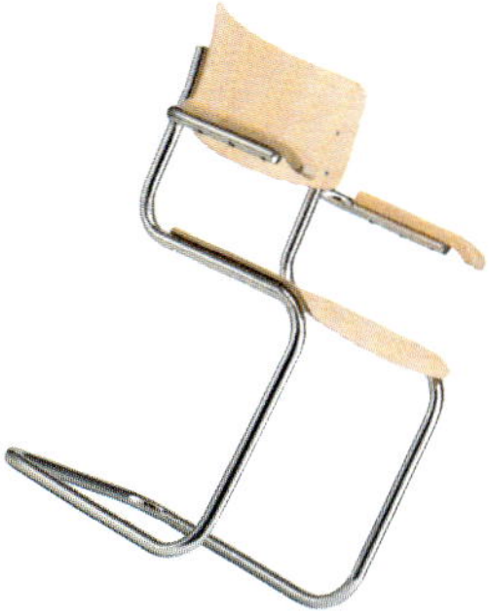

ALVAR AALTO

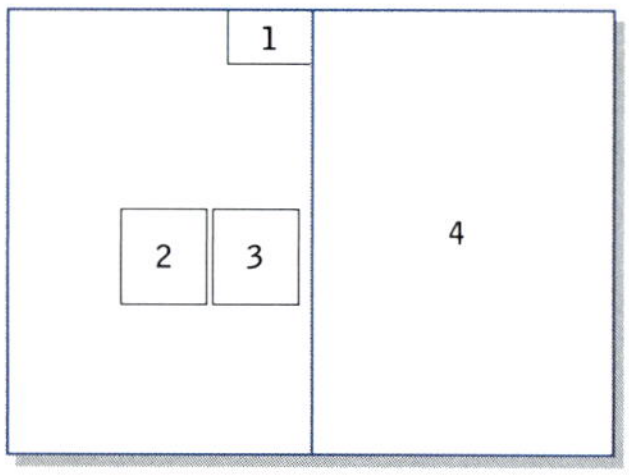

1. Chaise "66", 1933-35. Produite par Artek■
Structure en bouleau naturel. Différentes options pour le siège (bouleau verni, tapissé, linoléum ou laminé)■
⊟ 78 ⊟ 39 ⊟ 42 ⊟ 44 cm■
2. Chaise "611", 1929. Produite par Artek■
Structure en bouleau naturel ou teint. Peut être empilée■
⊟ 80 ⊟ 48,5 ⊟ 49 ⊟ 45 cm■
3. Tabourets de cuisine "64" et "K65", 1933-35. Produits par Artek■
Structure en bouleau. Le siège présente plusieurs options. Mesures :
"64" : ⊟ 65 ⊟ 52 ⊟ 52 cm■
"K65" : ⊟ 70 ⊟ 38 ⊟ 40 ⊟ 60 cm■
4. Fauteuil "42", 1931-32. Produit par Artek■
Structure en bouleau. Siège en bouleau contre-plaqué et modelé, laqué en blanc ou en noir■
⊟ 72 ⊟ 60 ⊟ 75 ⊟ 36 cm■

1898 Kuortane, Finlande-1976 Helsinki, Finlande■

Le design contemporain doit à ce grand architecte et designer finlandais les solutions techniques apportées par le modelage du bois et l'interprétation particulière du Mouvement Moderne, auquel il ajouta chaleur et idéaux humanistes. Il transforma la géométrie stricte en formes plus organiques et démontra une sensibilité particulière pour le bien-être physique et psychologique des utilisateurs (raison pour laquelle il travaillait uniquement sur des matériaux naturels, en particulier le bois)■

Il commença à travailler avec le modelage du bois à la fin des années 20, en collaboration avec sa femme, la designer Aino Marsio, pour donner naissance à des chaises révolutionnaires au niveau de la technique et des formes, et conçues comme une continuation naturelle de ses projets ar-

chitectoniques. Une de ses plus grandes contributions fut la solution qu'il donna au problème de la connexion entre les éléments verticaux et horizontaux avec la création de pieds en bois modelés qui pouvaient être directement introduits dans la partie inférieure du siège sans avoir recours à des cadre ou à des supports additionnels. Ces créations représentèrent la consécration définitive du bois contre-plaqué comme matériel d'avant-garde et firent de Alvar Aalto l'un des designers les plus caractéristiques du siècle. Le succès de ces meubles, qui prétendaient être à la fois modernes, humains et spécifiquement finlandais, le poussèrent à fonder, en 1935, l'entreprise Artek, qui produit actuellement ses créations■

L'exposition de son travail que le Musée d'Art Moderne de New York organisa en 1938 est une preuve éloquente du prestige dont il jouissait au sein de ses contemporains■

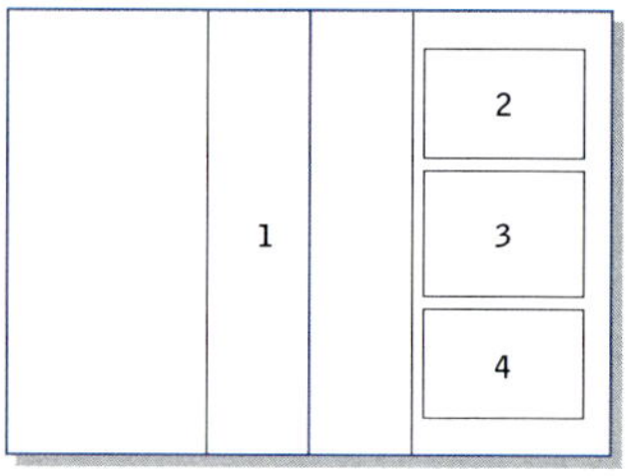

1. Chaise "63", 1933-35. Produite par Artek■
Structure en bouleau. Siège et dossier tapissés en tissu ou en peau■
⊟ 79 ⊟ 46 ⊟ 48 ⊟ 44 cm■
2. Fauteuil "406", 1938-39. Produit par Artek■
Structure en bouleau. Siège à sangles ou lanières entrelacées en toile ou en peau■
⊟ 87 ⊟ 60 ⊟ 72 ⊟ 41 cm■
3. "The Paimio Chair", 1931-32. Produite par Artek■
Il s'agit d'un des designs les plus emblématiques de Aalto, créé par le Sanatorio Paimio. Structure en bouleau. Siège en bouleau contre-plaqué et incurvé laqué en blanc ou noir■
⊟ 64 ⊟ 60 ⊟ 80 ⊟ 33 cm■
4. Chaise "611", 1929. Produite par Artek■
Structure en bouleau naturel ou teint. Peut être empilée■
⊟ 80 ⊟ 48,5 ⊟ 49 ⊟ 45 cm■

CHARLES & RAY EAMES

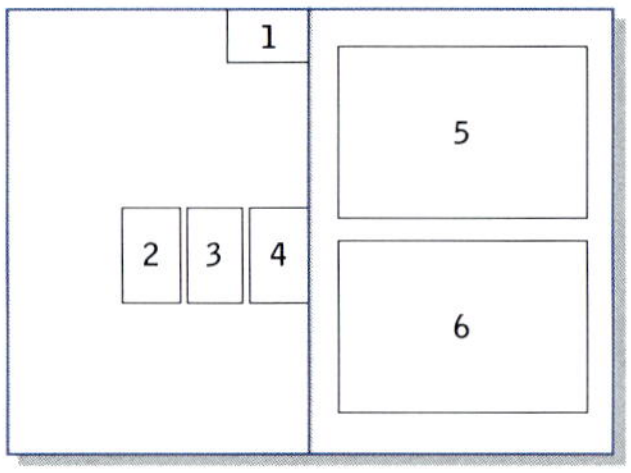

1. "Aluminium Chair", produit par Vitra■
Contours latéraux, base de fixation, accoudoirs et châssis inférieur fondu par pression, poli ou chromé. Différentes options pour le siège et le dossier■
2. Chaise "DCW" (Dining Chair Wood), 1946. Produite par Vitra■
Structure en bois laminé et incurvé en frêne naturel■
3. Chaise "Plastic Chair" (1948). De Vitra■
Réédition de la chaise légendaire réalisée en fibre de verre (remplacée maintenant par du polypropylène). Base formée par des traverses en fil d'acier■
4. "Wire Chair", 1953. Rééditée par Vitra■
Carcasse en fil d'acier soudé, avec coussins. Châssis inférieur Tour Eiffel, en fil d'acier ou avec quatre pieds en acier tubulaire■
5. Chaise longue "La Chaise", 1948. Réédition de Vitra■
Base en acier tubulaire chromé. Siège formé par deux carcasses en fibre de verre collées entre elles et peintes en blanc. Pieds en croix et en chêne■
6. "Lounge Chair", 1956. Produit par Vitra■
Structure formée par trois carcasses de bois déroulé contre-plaqué de cerisier ou laqué en noir, matelassé en peau■

1907 Missouri, EE.UU-1978 Missouri, EE.UU■
1912 Californie, EE.UU-1988 Missouri, EE.UU■

Charles Eames est considéré par beaucoup comme le designer par antonomase du xxe siècle. En 1941, il se marie avec Ray Kaiser et crée une synergie unique qui allait donner naissance à des chaises, maintenant devenues des icônes dans le domaine du design et s'ajoutant à de nombreux autres apports qui allaient faire partie de la modernisation des Etats-Unis après la Seconde Guerre Mondiale■
Ils utilisèrent l'expérience qu'ils avaient acquise pendant la guerre dans le domaine du modelage du bois laminé pour produire, au moyen de techniques qu'ils avaient inventées, des chaises bon marché, aux formes organiques qui supportaient confortablement le corps et étaient aptes à la pro-

duction massive. Leur travail révolutionnaire sur le bois contre-plaqué les poussa à étudier d'autres matériaux : des carcasses de plastique renforcé avec de la fibre de verre (créant ainsi, en 1948, la première chaise en plastique fabriquée de façon industrielle), des chaises fabriquées avec une maille métallique incurvée et soudée, et d'autres en aluminium modelé. À la base de chacune de leurs créations se trouvait le désir de faire un monde meilleur, dans le lequel le design pouvait être au service de la vie et les objets pouvaient satisfaire les besoins pratiques du plus grand nombre possible de personnes. En tant que représentants remarquables du design organique, Charles et Ray Eames démontrèrent que le bon design peut améliorer la qualité de vie et la compréhension et la connaissance des être humains. Pour eux, un design ne pouvait avoir du succès que s'il identifiait les besoins entrelacés du client, de la société et du designer■

EERO SAARINEN

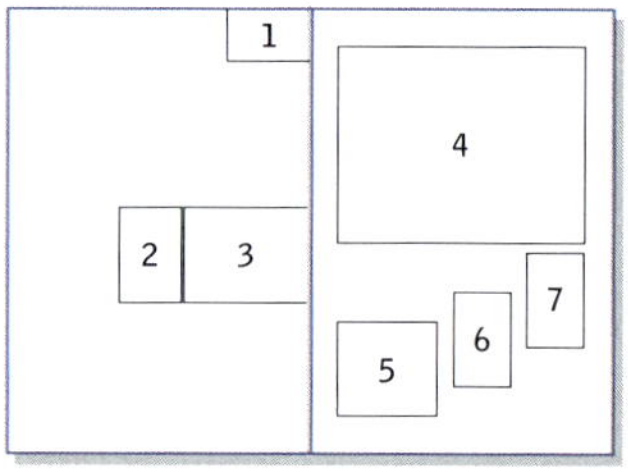

1, 5, 6 et 7. "Executive Side Chair", 1957. Produite par Knoll■
Après son apparition, elle se transforma immédiatement en un classique, établit les normes standards du design moderne dans le domaine des chaises et devint une des créations les plus connues de ce designer finlandais■
2 et 4. Chaise "Tulip", 1956. Produite par Knoll■
Base en aluminium et carcasse en fibre de verre modelée et renforcée avec du plastique. Disponible avec ou sans siège tapissé. Elle gagna le Premier Prix du Musée d'Art Moderne de New York en 1969■
3. "Womb Chair", 1948. Produite par Knoll■
Base formée par une baguette d'acier avec finition en chrome ou peinte en noir. Tapissée sur la carcasse de fibre de verre renforcée, avec coussins séparés■

1910 Kirkkonummi, Finlande-1961 Michigan, États-Unis■

Fils d'un architecte finlandais célèbre, Eliel Saarinen, sa passion pour la sculpture marqua sa carrière d'architecte et de designer de meubles. De fait, il se qualifiait lui-même de "faiseur de formes" et il est évident que toutes ses créations possèdent un fort caractère sculptural■
En 1923, toute la famille déménage aux Etats-Unis où Eero Saarinen devient un des architectes les plus créatifs et célèbre de l'après-guerre. Sa facette de designer de meubles est intimement liée à Charles Eames, avec qui il collabora au développement de plusieurs projets de chaises qui eurent beaucoup de succès lors de leur obtention du premier prix de l'exposition "Design Organique pour la Décoration d'Intérieurs", organisée en 1940 par le Musée d'Art Moderne de

New York. Ils partageaient leur passion pour l'ergonomie et une tendance à utiliser de nouveaux matériaux comme le bois contre-plaqué ou le plastique■
Au début des années 50, alors que la plus grande partie des designers continuaient à travailler les pieds comme une structure séparée de la forme du siège, Saarinen tenta de transformer totalement le concept de la chaise en s'éloignant du "chaos de pieds qui règne dans les décorations d'intérieurs modernes". Il trouva la solution avec une chaise ressemblant à un verre à pied : la fameuse Tulip Chair qui, en plus de donner une sensation de légèreté, montre une structure ingénieuse formée par trois parties intégrées, la carcasse, la tige ou base et le boulon qui les uni. Une "sculpture" reflétant son désir de s'éloigner des idées préconçues■

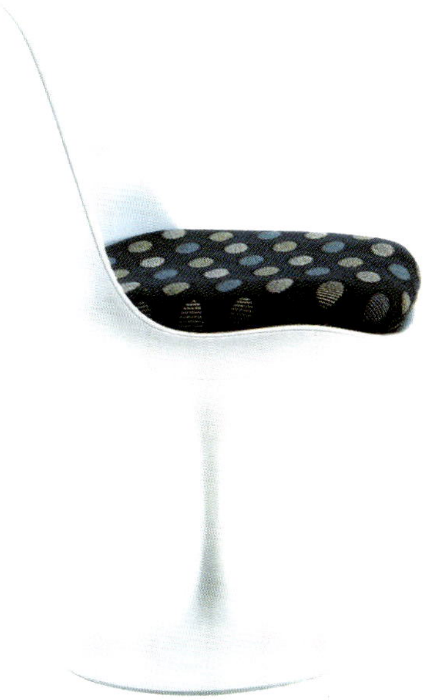

1950-1970

Le divertissement commence

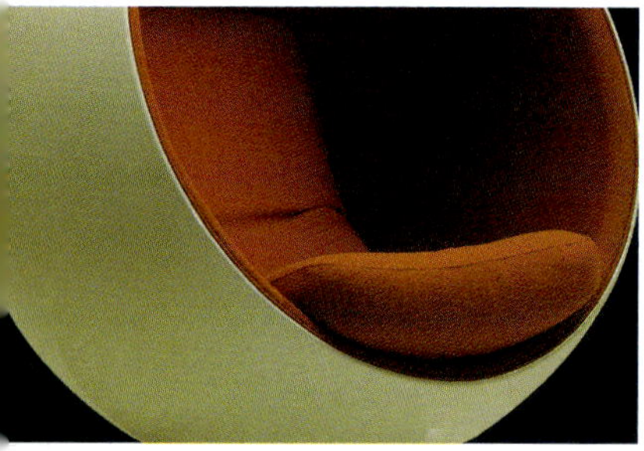

Ces années sont définies par une activité frénétique à tous les niveaux, stimulée par la croissance économique et l'évolution vertigineuse de la technologie qui révolutionna le domaine du design de mobilier. Les nouveaux matériaux, en particulier le plastique et le polypropylène, permirent de donner une forme à toutes sortes d'idées.

La décennie des années 50 commença avec très peu de nouveautés car c'était l'hégémonie esthétique du Mouvement Moderne qui était encore à la mode, avec des lignes pures et fonctionnelles, même si une grande partie des créations avaient perdu leur base idéologique d'origine à faveur de critères économiques promus par la surconsommation grandissante de la classe moyenne. La réaction face à ce type de meubles froids et sans âme apparue sous la forme de manifestations esthétiques qui représentèrent une nouveauté authentique : depuis les formes chaleureuses et artisanales du design scandinave, avec des designers comme Arne Jacobsen ou Poul Kjaerholm, jusqu'à l'explosion du Pop Art, mouvement artistique qui introduisit une certaine vigueur dans le panorama des Arts Décoratifs.

Dans le design du mobilier, l'esthétique Pop prétendait refléter la fraîcheur et l'ironie de la culture populaire au moyen d'une palette intense de couleurs et de l'utilisation de nouveaux matériaux, en particulier le plastique, et devint le symbole de la croissance économique des années 60. On défia les notions de tradition et de longévité en produisant un mobilier jetable et avec un fort composant ludique, réalisant ainsi un design qui partait de l'esthétique propre aux bandes dessinées comics. Pour la première fois dans l'histoire, la frivolité, la banalité, la vulgarité, l'imagination et l'obsolescence les plus osées entrèrent dans la décoration d'intérieurs avec des formes, des matériaux et des couleurs impensables à cette époque. Au même moment, le premier pas de l'homme sur la lune représenta une source d'inspiration remarquable qui donna naissance à une iconographie de style futuriste (aujourd'hui encore, grande partie des meubles créés à cette époque sont d'un style d'avant-garde plus prononcé que ceux qui se fabriquent actuellement).

L'Italie commença à ce moment à prendre une position de leader dans le domaine du design de meubles. Des noms comme ceux de Gio Ponti, fondateur du magazine Domus, les frères Castiglioni, ou Joe Colombo, avec son désir de créer un environnement domestique du future, se trouvent parmi les designers italiens les plus influents.

D'un autre côté, l'ergonomie commence à prendre un véritable sens avec les premières recherches tournées vers le design d'une typologie de mobilier de bureau qui améliora les conditions de travail.

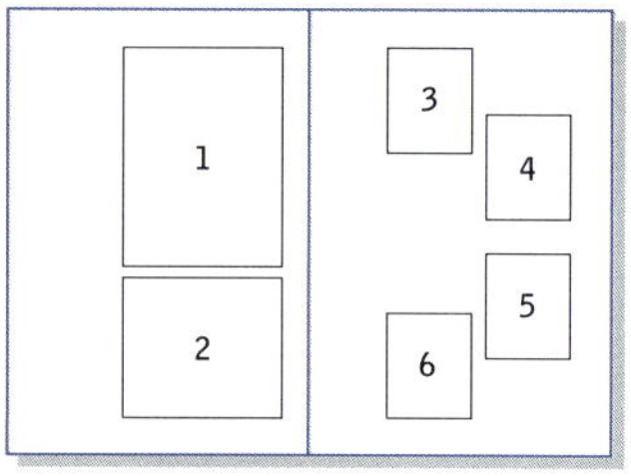

Page précédente :
CHAISE "3107", 1955. Créée par Arne Jacobsen pour Fritz Hansen■
Base en tube d'acier et carcasse en bois laminé. Peut être empilée■
⊟ 78 ⊟ 50 ⊟ 52 ⊟ 44 cm■

1. "THE TULIP CHAIR", 1960, de Poul Kjaerholm pour Fritz Hansen■
Base en acier inoxydable et siège tapissé en peau■
2. CANAPÉ "MARSHMALLOW", 1956. Créé par George Nelson. Réédité par Vitra■
Composé par 18 coussins ronds en vinyle, fixés par un croisillon tubulaire noir de forme rectangulaire. Peut être agrandi selon les besoins de l'utilisateur■
3. FAUTEUIL "PK 20", 1967. Design de Poul Kjaerholm pour Fritz Hansen■
Base en saillie en acier. Siège tapissé en peau et dossier modifiable sur deux hauteurs■
⊟ 73/89 ⊟ 76 ⊟ 80 cm■
4. FAUTEUIL "PK22", 1956. Design de Poul Kjaerholm pour Fritz Hansen■
Base en acier et siège en moelle ou tapissé en peau■
⊟ 71 ⊟ 63 ⊟ 63 ⊟ 38 cm■
5. CHAISE "699" ou "SUPERLEGGERA", 1957. Créée par Gio Ponti pour Cassina■
Structure en frêne et siège en osier d'Inde. Ses caractéristiques principales résident dans sa robustesse et sa légèreté (un enfant peut la soulever avec un seul doigt)■
(Photo : Andrea Zani)■
6. "EASY CHAIR", 1951. Design de Hans J. Wegner pour Carl Hansen■
Structure en chêne massif. Siège et dossier en corde■
⊟ 73 ⊟ 73 ⊟ 35 cm■

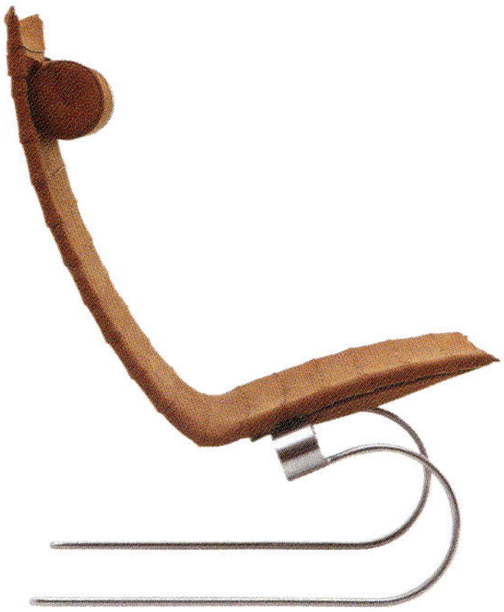

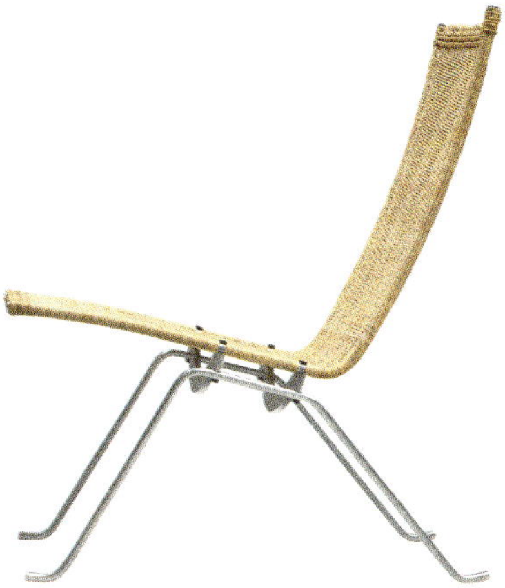

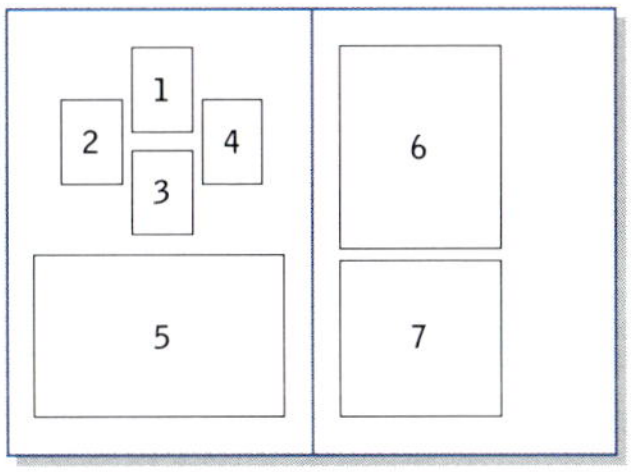

1. "Sella", 1957. Design Diseño de A. et P.G. Castiglioni pour Zanotta■ Base en fer, colonne en acier peint en rose et siège de bicyclette■
⊟ 71 ⊟ 33 cm■

2. Chaise "SE 18", 1952. Design de Egon Eiermann pour Wilde+Spieth■ Il s'agit d'un classique des chaises pliables. Elle reçut le prix "Good Design" en 1953■

3. Tabouret "S 38", conçu en 1950 par Egon Eiermann. Produit par Wilde+Spieth■

4. Chaise "April", 1964. Design de Gae Aulenti pour Zanotta■
Chaise pliable pour intérieurs et bateaux, avec une structure en acier inoxydable. Siège et dossier amovibles en tissu ou en peau■
⊟ 86 ⊟ 51 ⊟ 55 ⊟ 46 cm■

5. Fauteuil "San Luca", 1961/1990. Design de A. y P.G. Castiglioni. Produit par Bernini■
Base en bois et tapisserie en peau■
⊟ 100 ⊟ 87 ⊟ 96 cm■

6. Fauteuil "Barceloneta", 1953. Design de F. Correa et A. Milà. Édité par Santa & Cole■
Structure en hêtre et siège en toile ou en peau. Il fut créé en hommage ironique à la chaise Barcelone de Mies van der Rohe■
⊟ 89 ⊟ 56 ⊟ 72 cm■

7. Fauteuil "Ox Chair", 1960. Design de Hans J. Wegner pour Erik Jørgensen■
Base en acier chromé et siège tapissé avec du cuir de bœuf rappelant la force d'un taureau■
⊟ 90 ⊟ 99 ⊟ 99 ⊟ 36 cm■

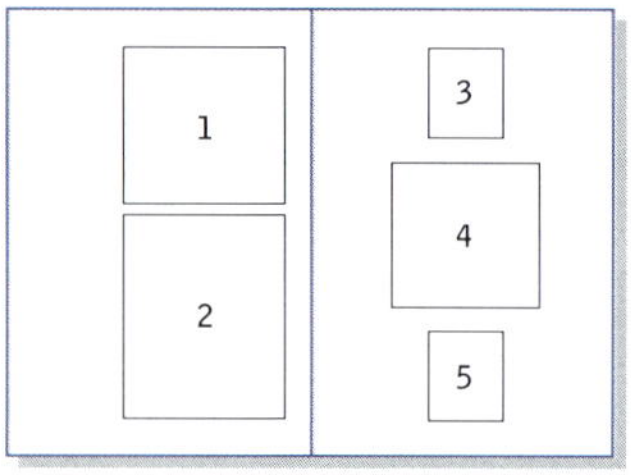

1. "The Shell Chair", 1963. Design de Hans J. Wegner. Produite par Carl Hansen▪
Structure en hêtre peinte ou en érable naturel▪
⊟ 74 ⊟ 92 ⊟ 81 ⊟ 38 cm▪

2. Chaise "Cubist", 1967. Créée par Vladimir Kagan. Collection "Kagan New York"▪
Structure en érable ou en noyer. Siège et dossier tapissés▪

3. Tabouret "Allunaggio", 1965. Design de A. et P.G. Castiglioni pour Zanotta▪
Pieds en acier avec base en polypropylène naturel et siège en alliage d'aluminium. Apte pour les extérieurs▪
⊟ 42,5 ⊟ 152 cm▪

4. Fauteuil "Blow", 1967. Créé par De Pas, D'Urbino et Lomazzi, pour Zanotta▪
Fauteuil gonflable en PVC, qui s'est converti en un icône du design des années 60▪

5. Fauteuil "Sacco", 1968. Design de Gatti, Paolini et Teodoro pour Zanotta▪
Fauteuil anatomique s'adaptant à la posture du corps. Couverture en tissu ou en peau et intérieur rempli de polystyrène très résistent▪
⊟ 68 ⊟ 80 ⊟ 80 cm▪

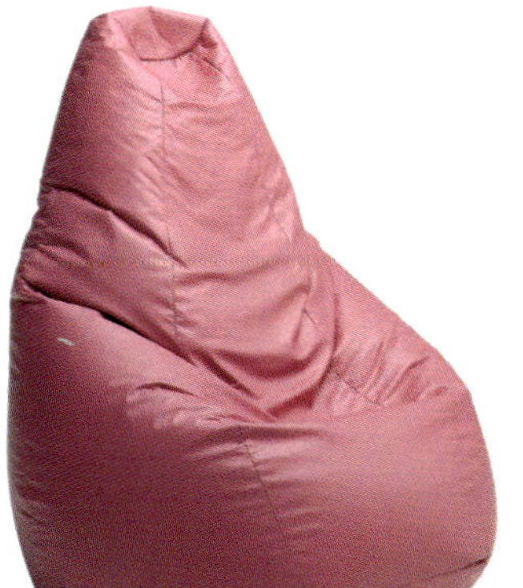

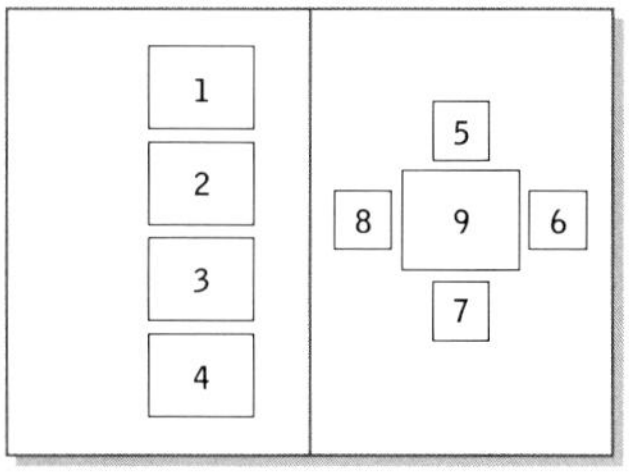

1. CHAISE "4875", créée par Carlo Bartoli. Produite par Kartell (Collection "Classical Seats")■
Structure en polypropylène■
⊟ 71 ⊟ 44 ⊟ 48 ⊟ 43 cm■

2. CHAISE "UNIVERSALE", 1965. Créée par Joe Colombo. Produite par Kartell■
Structure en polypropylène. Elle fut la première chaise modelée avec un seul matériau. Peut être empilée■
⊟ 71 ⊟ 42 ⊟ 50 ⊟ 43 cm■

3. CHAISE "PK 25", 1951. Design de Poul Kjaerholm. Produite par Fritz Hansen■
Structure en acier. Réalisée pour l'examen final de l'École des Arts & Crafts de Copenhague■
⊟ 75 ⊟ 69 ⊟ 73 cm■

4. CHAISE DE LA "LOUNGE COLLECTION", 1966. Design de Warren Platner pour Knoll■
Réalisée avec des centaines de fils de fer incurvés■

5 y 9. "THE SPANISH CHAIR", 1958. Design de Børge Mogensen pour Fredericia Furniture■
Structure en chêne, siège et dossier en peau naturelle. Inspirée des chaises utilisées par les dirigeants de l'armée espagnole■

6. CHAISE "SBG 197", 1950. Design de Egon Eiermann pour Wilde+Spieth■
Comprend le pied "Bruselas" créé pour l'Exposition Universelle de Bruxelles de 1958■

7. TABOURET "BIRILLO", 1970. Design de Joe Colombo. Produit par Zanotta■
Colonne en acier inoxydable, base en fibre de verre. Siège pivotant et dossier tapissés■
⊟ 107 ⊟ 47 ⊟ 52 ⊟ 77 cm■

8. CHAISE "3238", 1964. Design de Børge Mogensen pour Fredericia Furniture■
Structure en chêne, siège et dossier en peau naturelle. Inspirée de la culture Shaker américaine■

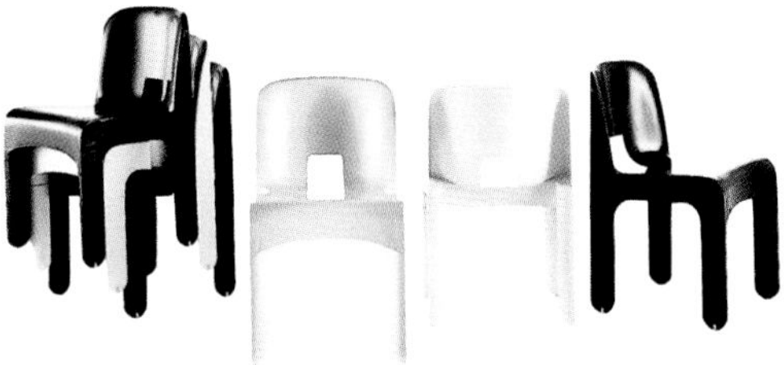

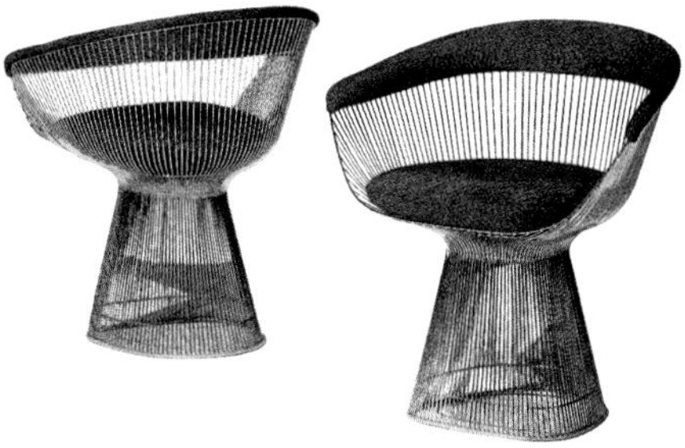

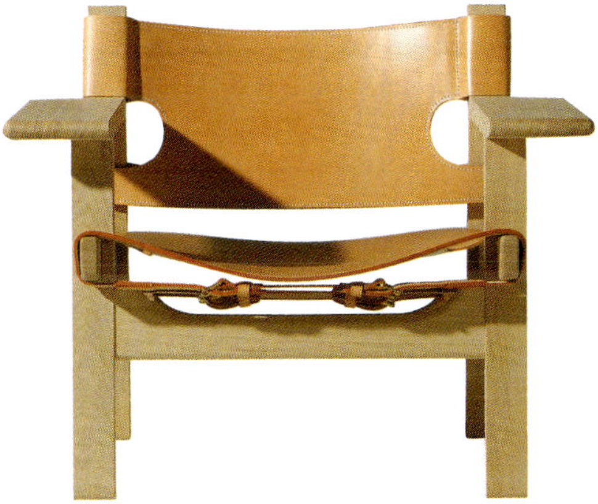

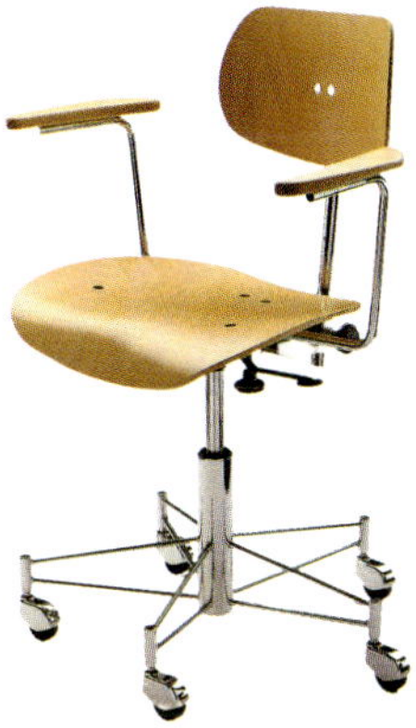

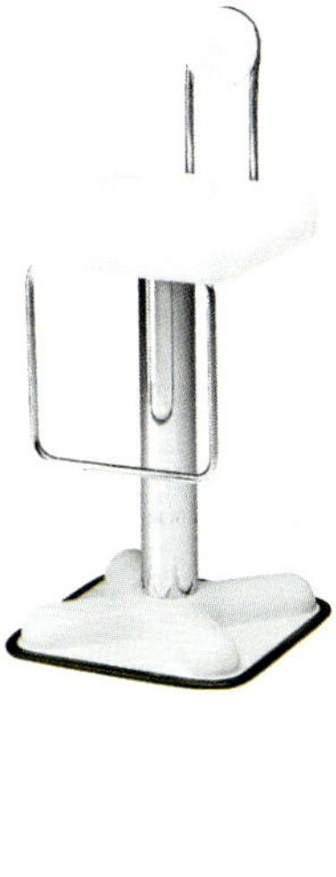

ARNE JACOBSEN

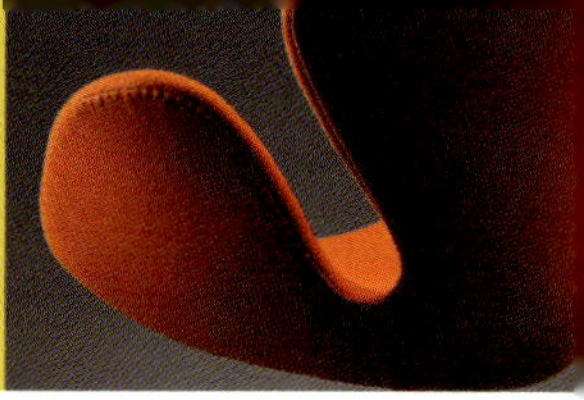

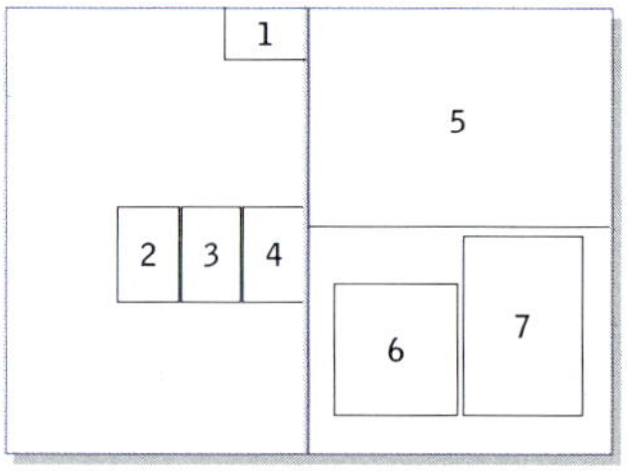

1 et 5. Fauteuil "Swan", 1958. Produit par Fritz Hansen▪
Base en aluminium, siège tapissé en tissu ou en peau. Créé pour le Royal Hotel de Copenhague▪
⊟ 75 ⊟ 74 ⊟ 68 ⊟ 38 cm▪

2. Fauteuil "The Egg", 1958. Produit par Fritz Hansen▪
Base en aluminium, siège tapissé en peau. Créé pour le Royal Hotel de Copenhague▪
⊟ 107 ⊟ 86 ⊟ 79 cm▪

3. Chaise "The Tongue", 1955. Produit par Fritz Hansen▪
Pieds en tube d'acier et siège en bois laminé▪
⊟ 79 ⊟ 43 ⊟ 49 ⊟ 44 cm▪

4. Chaise "The Ant", 1952. Produite par Fritz Hansen▪
Pieds en tube d'acier et siège en bois laminé. Peut être empilée▪
⊟ 77 ⊟ 48 ⊟ 48 ⊟ 44 cm▪

6. Fauteuil "3300", 1956. Produit par Fritz Hansen▪
Structure en tube d'acier. Siège et dossier tapissés en peau▪
⊟ 72 ⊟ 73 ⊟ 79 ⊟ 36 cm▪

7. Chaise "Oxford", 1965. Produite par Fritz Hansen▪
Présentée avec une grande variété d'options et de finitions et deux hauteurs possibles pour le dossier. Créée à l'origine pour le St. Catherine College d'Oxford▪

1902 Copenhague, Danemark-1971 Copenhague, Danemark▪

Jacobsen est un des architectes et designers danois les plus influents, responsable de l'introduction du style fonctionnaliste dans son pays. Il se distingue pour son contrôle sur tous les éléments de ses projets, depuis la hauteur des arbres du jardin jusqu'aux cendriers, dans le but d'obtenir une harmonie complète. Hors du Danemark, il est particulièrement célèbre pour ses design de meubles et d'objets, et il est le créateur de nombreux classiques du design moderne. Une grande partie de son intérêt pour le design de produits est due à l'influence de Charles et Ray Eames, dont le travail lui servit d'inspiration pour la création, en 1951, de son premier succès : la chaise pouvant être empilée Ant, réalisée d'une seule pièce modelée en bois contre-plaqué, avec trois

pieds fins en acier. Après celle-ci, apparut le modèle 3107, qui devint une des chaises les plus populaires et imitées de ce siècle▪
À la fin de l'année 1950, il fut chargé de construire le Royal Hotel de Copenhague, pour lequel il créa tous les éléments du bâtiment, depuis la structure jusqu'aux couverts en acier inoxydable aux formes abstraites qui furent ensuite choisis, à cause de leur aspect futuriste, par Stanley Kubrick pour son film 2001: odyssée de l'espace. Il créa également pour cet hôtel les chaises emblématiques Swan et Egg, aux formes sculpturales organiques et faisant partie de son héritage créatif▪
Dans tous ses projets, Jacobsen combinait un soin profond pour les détails, l'utilisation des matériaux les plus appropriés à chaque cas et la fusion de techniques traditionnelles et fonctionnalistes, à partir desquelles il créait les concepts et les formes de son œuvre▪

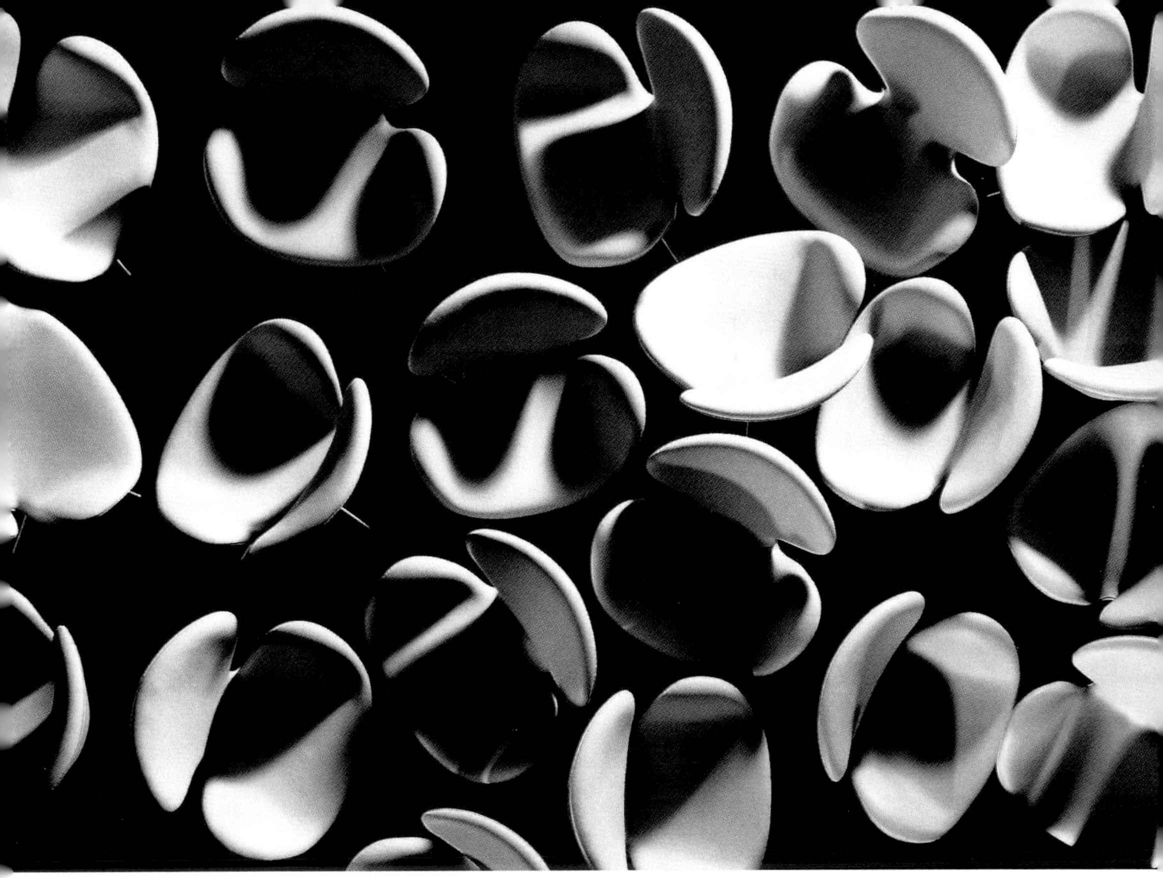

HARRY BERTOIA

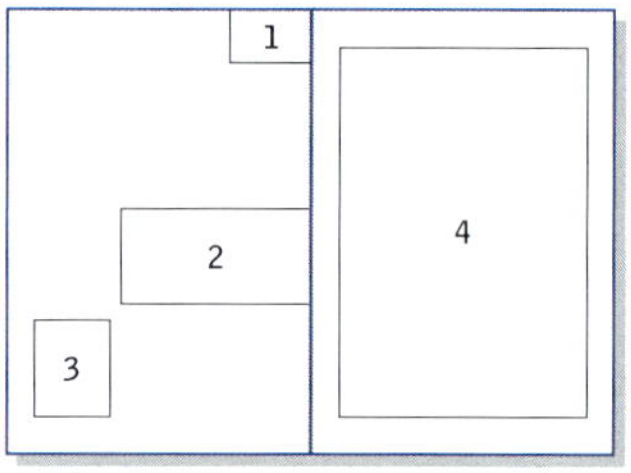

1. Détail de la carcasse de maille en acier, caractéristique de la collection de chaises créées en 1952▪
2. Ensemble de chaises créées par Harry Bertoia en 1952 pour Knoll▪ Elles se caractérisent par leur structure formée par des baguettes en acier soudé et en nid d'abeille. Cette structure résiste aux égratignures, aux tâches et aux ébréchures. Elles sont présentées avec de nombreuses options de tapisserie▪
3. Chaise "Diamond", 1952. Produite par Knoll▪ Disponible totalement tapissée en tissu ou en peau, ou avec une structure en acier à découvert et un coussin pour le siège. Deux tailles disponibles▪
4. Chaise "Bird", avec dossier haut, 1952. Produite par Knoll▪ Disponible en version totalement tapissée. Structure disponible en noir, blanc ou chromée▪

1915 Udine, Italie-1978 Pennsylvanie, États-Unis▪

Le cas de Harry Bertoia n'est pas typique puisqu'il est connu à niveau international pour sa facette de designer de mobilier, alors qu'en réalité, il ne se consacra à cette activité que pendant très peu de temps, poussé par la confiance que lui vouait Florence Knoll, qui lui offrit un environnement totalement libre lui permettant de créer ce qu'il souhaitait▪ C'est de cette relation que surgirent les chaises réalisées avec des mailles d'acier qui devinrent les icônes du design moderne et furent produites par Knoll en 1952. Avant de jouir de ce succès, Bertoia collabora au début de 1940 avec Charles et Ray Eames dans les travaux sur le modelage du bois contre-plaqué. Sa contribution dans ce domaine ne fut jamais pleinement reconnue et il resta toujours dans l'ombre des Eames▪

En réalité, l'authentique vocation de Harry Bertoia furent la peinture et la sculpture. De fait, il concevait ses chaises en acier comme s'il s'agissait d'une sculpture. Selon ses mots, "si tu regardes ces chaises, tu te rendras compte qu'elles sont essentiellement faites d'air, comme pour une sculpture, et que l'espace passe à travers... une fois que tu t'en es rendu compte, les chaises sont comme des études de l'espace, de la forme et du métal". Au milieu de 1950 Bertoia abandonna définitivement le design des meubles pour se consacrer totalement à la sculpture▪
Ses chaises restent son travail le plus célèbre et sont perçues comme des sculptures fonctionnelles créées pour être confortables et soutenir le corps sur le sol. Grâce au métal, Bertoia exprime avec ses chaises la dimension physique de l'homme alors que, avec ses sculptures "tonales" il exprime son côté spirituel▪

VERNER PANTON

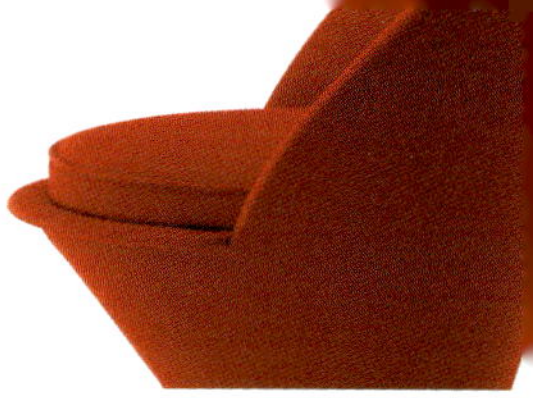

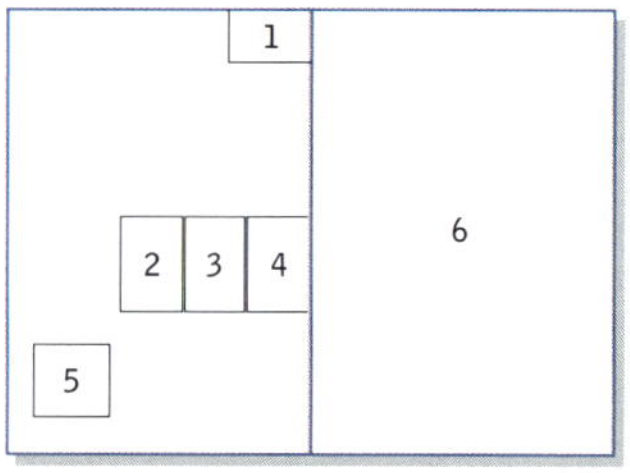

1. "The Cone Chair", 1958. Produite par Vitra■
Pied croisé en acier inoxydable et carcasse en forme de cône, tapissée. (Photo : H. Hansen)■
2 et 6. "Panton Chair", créée en 1960 et produite en 1967-69. De Vitra■
Structure en polypropylène teint, renforcé avec de la fibre de verre. Réalisée selon la procédure de modelage par injection. Première chaise en plastique fabriquée d'une seule pièce. (Photo : H. Hansen)■
3. "Panto Pop", 1990. De Innovation■
Réalisé dans un matériau plastique en plusieurs couleurs. Peut-être empilé■
⊟ 57 ⊟ 80 cm■
4. "Phantom", 1998. De Innovation■
Pièce multifonctionnelle en plastique, disponible en sept couleurs différentes■
⊟ 93,5 ⊟ 35 ⊟ 81 cm■
5. Chaise "Heart Cone", 1959. Produite par Vitra■
Pied en acier inoxydable en forme de croix et carcasse tapissée en forme de cœur■

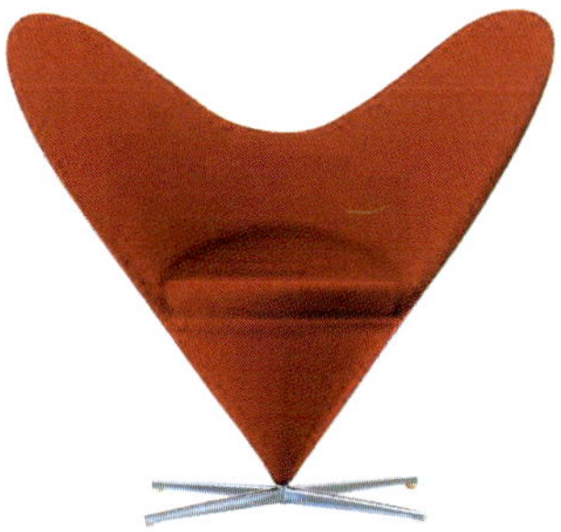

1926 Gamtofte, Danemark-1998 Copenhague, Danemark■

À une époque où le design scandinave était d'actualité, ce créateur danois décida de s'éloigner des formes et des matériaux naturalistes, pour créer des chaises totalement innovatrices qui firent de lui un des "pères" de l'esthétique Pop et un créateur visionnaire qui sut anticiper les tendances■ Panton fut le précurseur du style fluide, coloriste et futuriste des années 60, poussé par sa passion pour les plastiques et autres matériaux synthétiques. Son travail était basé sur cette façon de penser : "le fait de s'asseoir doit également être amusant, tout comme jouer, cela peut être une expérience excitante", et il étudia de nouvelles théories sur l'aspect de la chaise, sur son rôle de support et sur les couleurs vibrantes pouvant leur faire une place dans des contextes domestiques et collectifs. En 1959, il parvint à se faire un nom dans le monde du design grâce à l'in-

troduction de la Cone Chair, qui provoqua une vague d'admiration à cause de ses formes géométriques extravagantes. Cette reconnaissance lui permit de continuer son travail et de donner naissance à deux nouveaux jalons de l'histoire du design : le premier meuble gonflable et l'omniprésente Panton Chair (produite en 1967 mais créée longtemps avant), qui fut la première chaise en saillie réalisée d'une seule pièce en plastique modelé. Ses chaises sont, aujourd'hui encore, les symboles de la modernité car, comme lui-même le disait : "au moment de ressentir l'éclairage, les couleurs, les textiles et le mobilier en utilisant les dernières technologies, je prétends montrer de nouveaux chemins pour encourager les personnes à utiliser la fantaisie et faire en sorte que leur environnement soit plus excitant"■

EERO AARNIO

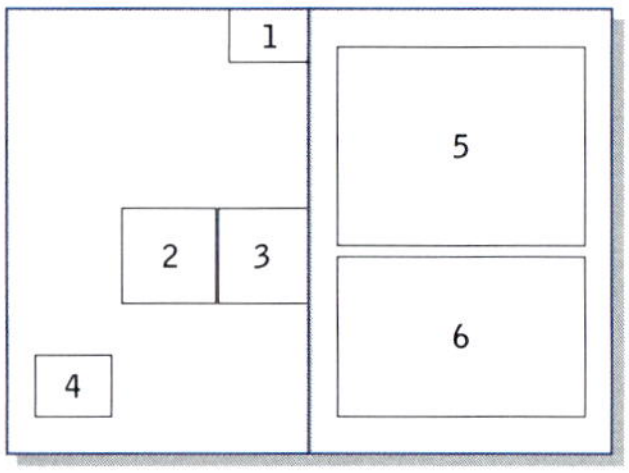

1. "Pastil Chair", 1967. Produite par Adelta■
Carcasse en fibre de verre. Apte à un usage en extérieur. Flotte sur l'eau. Prix du Design Industriel Américain de 1968■
2. "Bubble Chair", 1968. Produite par Adelta■
Carcasse acrylique transparente avec cadre en acier chromé■
3. "Tipi", 2002. Produit par Adelta■
Formes originales pour ce siège présentant une tapisserie de tissu Tonus 2000, de différentes couleurs■
4. "Formula Chair", 1998. Produite par Adelta■
Structure en fibre de verre, avec des formes ergonomiques■
5. "Ball Chair", 1966. Produite par Adelta■
Eero Aarnio assis sur l'emblématique "Ball Chair". Carcasse en fibre de verre et intérieur tapissé offrant de multiples combinaisons de couleurs■
6. Chaise "Focus", 2002. Produite par Adelta■
Structure métallique, entièrement recouverte du tissu Tonus 2000. Grande variété de couleurs■

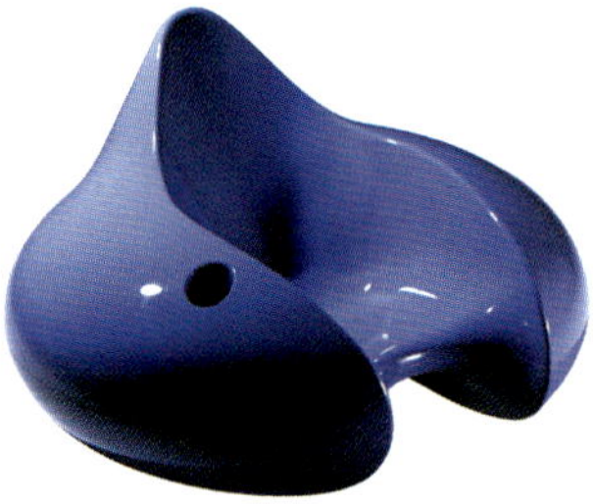

1932 Helsinki, Finlande■

Les designs de Eero Aarnio ne peuvent pas être dissociés de l'imagination liée à la fièvre de la conquête de l'espace de la fin des années 60. Il s'agissait d'une époque pleine d'optimisme pour le futur, avec des meubles qui tentaient de refléter l'aspect probable des intérieurs des générations à venir■
Eero Aarnio était à la tête de cette tendance et fut un des pionniers dans l'utilisation du plastique. Il souhaitait créer des designs ergonomiques en utilisant des matériaux d'avant-garde qui allaient permettre une production massive à bas prix. Les formes qui en découlaient représentaient sa croyance dans le fait que les produits devaient être beaux et extrêmement durables (ce qui, paradoxalement, allait à l'encontre de la philosophie du "user et jeter" du Pop et dont l'esthétique contribua à définir les designs de Aarnio)■

Une de ses premières chaises, la Ball Chair, présentée au public pour la première fois en 1966, lui valut une reconnaissance immédiate et fit de lui une des images les plus célèbre de l'Ère Spatiale. Construite avec un carcasse en fibre de verre imitant la géométrie d'une sphère, cette chaise enveloppe l'utilisateur dans une atmosphère intime et protectrice face à l'extérieur, comme s'il s'agissait d'une "pièce à l'intérieur d'une pièce". D'autres designs, qui eurent le même succès, la suivirent, comme la Pastil Chair, qui gagna, en 1968, le Prix du Design Industriel Américain, ou la Bubble Chair en plastique transparent offrant un isolement acoustique surprenant■
À partir des années 70, il commença à explorer les possibilités de la mousse de polyuréthanne tout en continuant à défendre l'idéal du plastique dans le contexte contemporain■

1970-1990

L'ère du "tout est bon"

Dans les années 70, les formes d'expression individualistes et irrationnelles dénotant une certaine fatigue face à l'homogénéité du fonctionnalisme furent récupérées. C'est ainsi que s'articule le mouvement du Postmodernisme qui supposa le couronnement du défi du Pop contre l'austérité et la tyrannie du "bon design", imposé pendant des décennies par le style du Mouvement Moderne.

Le Postmodernisme, avec son épicentre en Italie, apparut comme faisant partie de la modification générale du design qui commença à se centrer sur la solution des problèmes et l'amélioration des produits basée sur la relation avec le monde de l'imagination, des idées, de l'humour et de la stimulation visuelle. Une des collectivités qui contribua le plus à la projection internationale du style fut le groupe Memphis, fondé en 1981 par l'architecte et designer Ettore Sottsass.

Les propositions de Memphis se basaient sur la continuation des idées radicales du mouvement Anti-Design qui avait pour leaders des groupes comme Archizoom ou le Studio Alchymia (formé par des designers comme Alessandro Mendini, Andrea Branzi, Michele De Lucchi ou Sottsass lui-même). Ils jouaient avec le travail et la juxtaposition de matériaux non conventionnels, la combinaison de styles historiques avec des matériaux et des idées contemporains, l'utilisation de motifs kitsch et populaires et de contrastes de couleurs criardes. Pour Memphis, il n'existait pas de normes, son objectif étant de créer des intérieurs stimulants et imaginatifs, dans une perspective ironique et ludique. Des designers de renommée internationale comme Matteo Thun, Michael Graves, Javier Mariscal ou Shiro Kuramata s'unirent à ce mouvement.

Dans le catalogue de leur première exposition, ils déclaraient : "nous sommes tous certains que les meubles de Memphis ne seront bientôt plus à la mode". Et il en fut ainsi. Même si le groupe exerça une grande influence sur la définition d'un nouveau langage dans le design, son anarchie stylistique cohabita avec des tendances ou des styles opposés qui lui ont survécu, comme la froideur industrielle du Hi-Tech, la géométrie et l'austérité du Minimalisme, une préoccupation croissante pour l'ergonomie et l'écologie, et la redécouverte de l'esthétique du Mouvement Moderne.

Les chaises de la fin du siècle reflètent une grande variété de styles, facilitée par la recherche de l'individualisme et de la pluralité. C'est l'époque du "tout est bon" : depuis le travail de designers influencés par le Postmodernisme, comme Philippe Starck, Jasper Morrison, Ron Arad ou Marc Newson, jusqu'à la réédition des "classiques du design" dont les valeurs sont encore en vigueur.

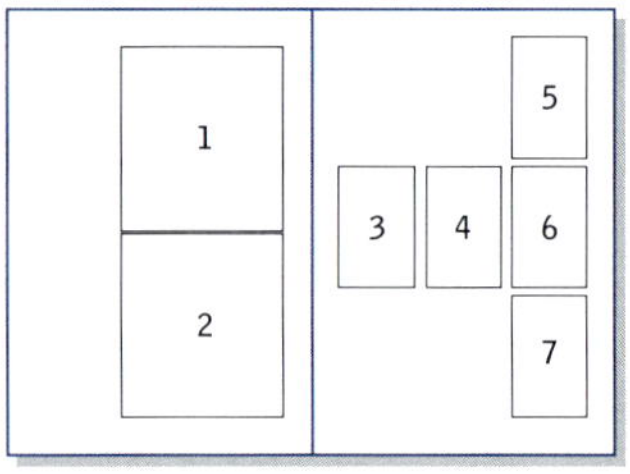

1 et 2. "S-Chair", 1990. Design de Tom Dixon pour Cappellini■
Structure métallique verticale et permettant de réduire la base au minimum. Le recouvrement présente différents matériaux et couleurs■
⊟ 100 ⊟ 52 ⊟ 42 cm■

3. Chaise de bureau "Kevi 2003", 1973. Design de Jørgen Rasmussen pour Fritz Hansen■

4. Chaise avec accoudoirs "Break", 1976. Design de Mario Bellini pour Cassina■
Structure formée par des panneaux en acier, complètement tapissée en peau. Pieds en plastique■
⊟ 85 ⊟ 56 ⊟ 51 ⊟ 45 cm■

5. Chaise "Ramón", 1975. Design de Ramón Bigas. Produite par Santa & Cole■
Structure en acier, siège et dossier en moelle naturelle■
⊟ 75 ⊟ 45 ⊟ 45 cm■

6. Chaise "Sevilla", design original 1974. Créée par Pep Bonet, Cristian Cirici et Mireia Nieto. Éditée par Bd Ediciones de Diseño■
Version en moelle naturelle, créée en 1984. Structure en acier plastifiée de couleur noire. Peut être empilée■
⊟ 81 ⊟ 50 ⊟ 52 cm■

7. Chaise pivotante "Cassia", 1974. Design de De Pas, D'Urbino et Lomazzi pour Zanotta■
Structure en acier inoxydable, base en aluminium. Siège adaptable, tapissé en peau■
⊟ 81/91 ⊟ 59 ⊟ 55 ⊟ 45/55 cm■

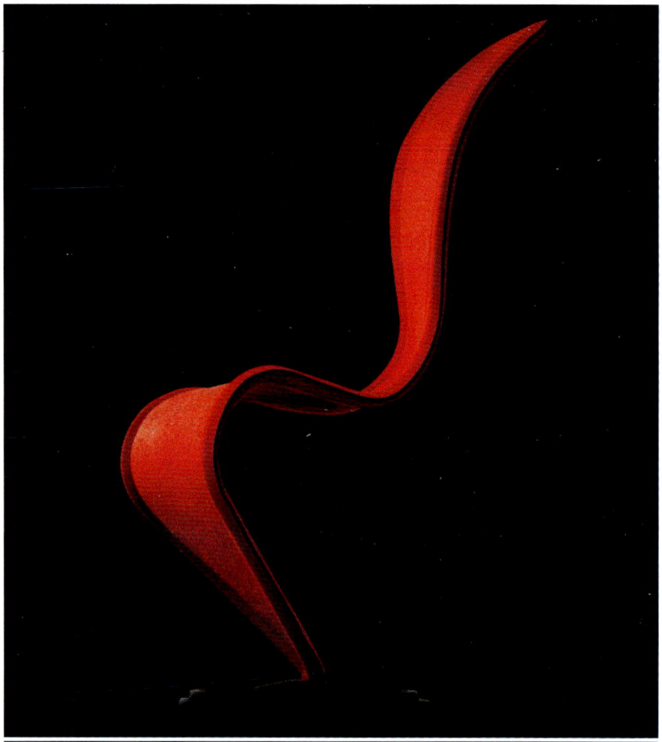

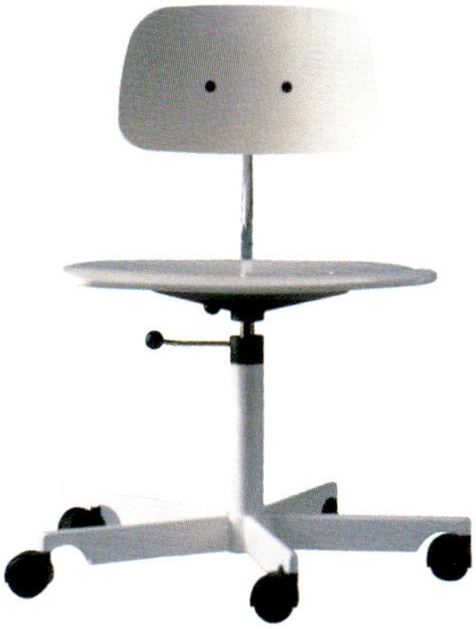

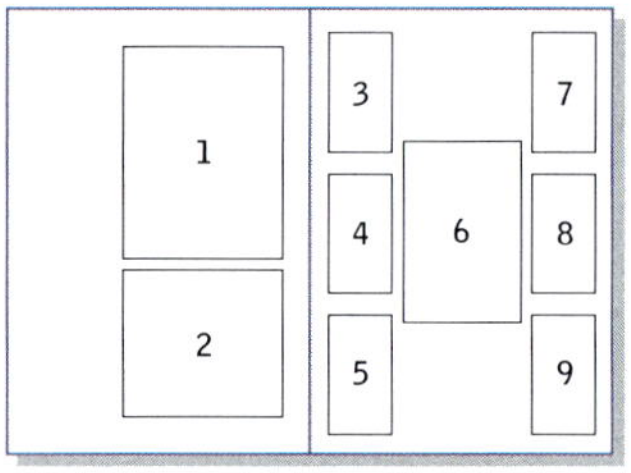

1. CHAISE "FERNANDO", 1984. Design de Carles Riart. Éditée par Santa & Cole▪ Structure en érable. Siège et dossier tapissés▪
⊟ 85 ⊟ 45 ⊟ 50 cm▪
2. TABOURET "GIOTTO", 1975. Design de De Pas, D'Urbino et Lomazzi pour Zanotta▪
Structure en hêtre. Siège pivotant adaptable▪
⊟ 45/55 ⊟ 45 cm▪
3. CHAISE "PAVONE", 1986. Créée par Riccardo Dalisi pour Zanotta▪
Structure en acier▪
⊟ 94 ⊟ 54 ⊟ 54 ⊟ 42 cm▪
4. CHAISE-TABLE "ZABRO", 1984. Design de Alessandro Mendini pour Zanotta▪
Chaise transformable en table. Structure en bois laqué avec dossier peint à la main en polychrome▪
⊟ 137 ⊟ 93 ⊟ 50 cm▪
5. CHAISE "SNOOKER", 1985. Design de Carlos Riart. Éditée par Santa & Cole▪
Structure en érable. Siège et dossier tapissés▪
⊟ 86,5 ⊟ 63 ⊟ 60 cm▪
6. TABOURET "DUPLEX", 1983. Design de Javier Mariscal. Édité par Bd Ediciones de Diseño▪
Structure en acier chromé associée à un pied de couleur. Siège tapissé en peau noire▪
⊟ 77 ⊟ 42 ⊟ 46 cm▪
7. CHAISE "CAB", 1977. Design de Mario Bellini pour Cassina▪
Structure en acier totalement tapissée en peau▪
⊟ 82 ⊟ 52 ⊟ 47 ⊟ 45 cm▪
8. FAUTEUIL "771", 1977. Design de Carlo Scarpa pour Bernini▪
9. BANC "MARIPOSA", 1989. Design de Riccardo Dalisi pour Zanotta▪
Structure en acier. Peint en polychromie par le designer lui-même. Il existe 9 produits signés d'origine▪
⊟ 88 ⊟ 102 ⊟ 55 ⊟ 40 cm▪

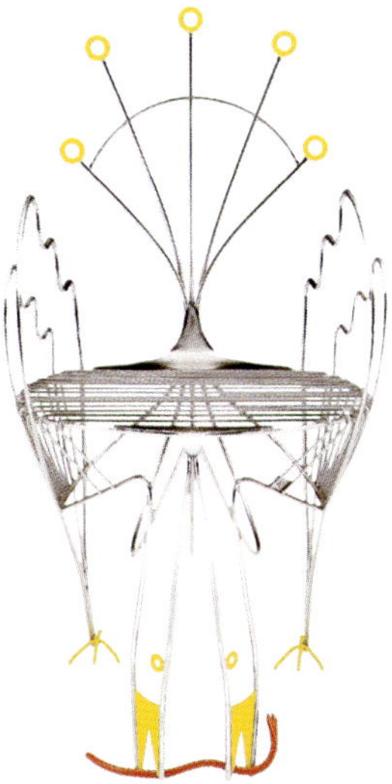

ETTORE SOTTSASS

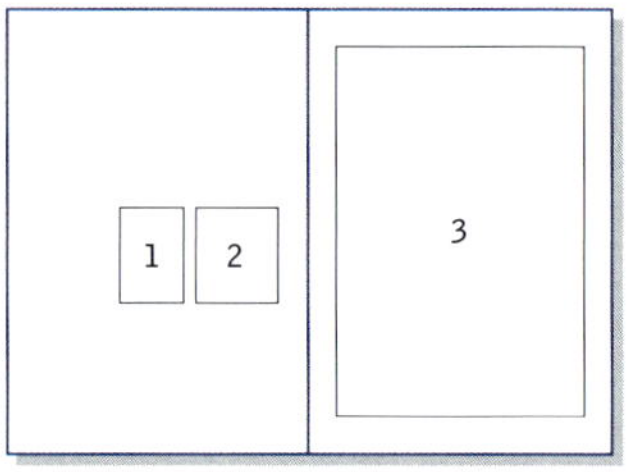

1 et 2. CHAISE "MANDARIN", 1986. Produite par Knoll■
Structure en acier tubulaire, siège et dossier tapissés, avec différentes couleurs et finitions. Elle présente un bras ondulé caractéristique■
3. FAUTEUIL "EASTSIDE LOUNGE COLLECTION", 1983. Produit par Knoll■ Nouvelle interprétation du fauteuil de club classique. Le siège et le repose-tête sont tapissés avec différents tissus■

1917 Innsbruck, Autriche■

"Pour moi, le design est une façon de parler de la vie, des relations sociales, de la politique, de la nourriture et du design en lui-même"■
Né en Autriche, Ettore Sottsass est cependant l'un des grands représentants de la création italienne des dernières décennies. Il travailla pour faire du design quelque chose de plus excitant et sensuel, et il altéra la vision statique des personnes se consacrant à cette activité. Grâce à cet engagement, il parvint à introduire une nouvelle optique intellectuelle qui permit une approche plus libre, inattendue, fluide et conceptuelle des jeunes créateurs du monde du design■
Sottsass s'établit en 1956 comme conseillé de design pour des entreprises comme Olivetti, à un moment où les grandes compagnies

commencèrent à comprendre le besoin d'introduire la figure du designer industriel dans la conception de leurs produits■
À partir des années 70, il devint la figure clé du mouvement Anti-Design italien qui apparut en réaction contre les normes fonctionnalistes du "bon goût". Ce renouvellement esthétique joua un rôle de base dans le développement du Postmodernisme et allait jouir d'une renommée internationale en 1981 avec la première exposition du groupe Memphis fondé par Sottsass. En 1985, alors qu'il se trouvait au sommet de sa gloire, Sottsass prit la décision d'abandonner la collectivité, poussé par son désir de continuer à avancer et à travailler au lieu de vivre de ses anciens succès■
À partir de ce moment, il commença à travailler dans son étude d'architecture et de design Sottsass Associati, où il continua à affronter l'ordre établi aidé par d'anciens membre de Memphis et de jeunes collaborateurs■

DAILY PLANET

VICO MAGISTRETTI

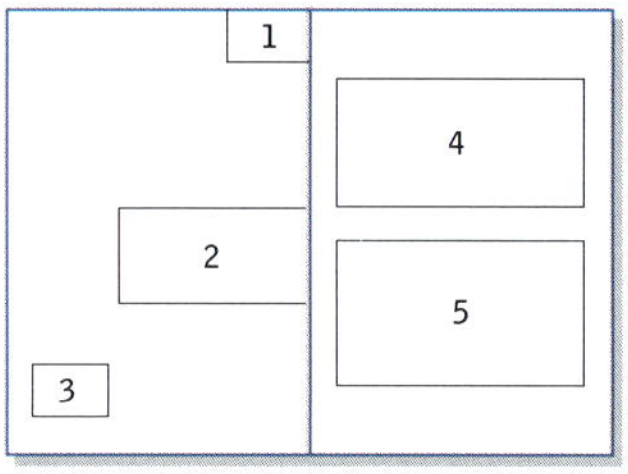

1. CHAISE "MAUI", 1997. Produite par Kartell■
Base en acier chromé et carcasse en polypropylène. Peut être empilée■
⊟ 77 ⊟ 55 ⊟ 52 ⊟ 45 cm■
2. CHAISE "SELENE", 1969. Produite par Heller■
Structure en polypropylène renforcée avec de la fibre de verre. Ce modèle est une réédition du modèle classique des années 70■
3. CHAISE "MAUNA-KEA". Produite par Kartell■
Structure en aluminium. Siège et dossier en polypropylène■
⊟ 77 ⊟ 49 ⊟ 54 ⊟ 46 cm■
4. CHAISE "KENIA", 1995. Produite par Campeggi■
Chaise pliante■
⊟ 73 ⊟ 75 ⊟ 58 cm■
5. CHAISE "AFRICA", 2000. Produite par Campeggi■
Chaise pliante■
⊟ 104 ⊟ 78 ⊟ 80 ⊟ 45 cm■

1920 Milan, Italie■

Les designs de Magistretti pourraient se situer à l'opposé de ceux réalisés par Ettore Sottsass. De fait, Magistretti considérait que les meubles du groupe Memphis "n'offrent aucun type de développement. Ils ne sont qu'une simple variante de la mode"■
À partir du moment où il commença à se consacrer au design de mobilier au début des années 60, Magistretti devint une sorte de maître des formes élégantes, simples, contenues et durables, avec une philosophie qui le faisait aller à l'encontre de la culture de l'obsolescence rapide. Ses meubles sont le reflet de sa passion pour la construction de ce que lui-même appelle "objets anonymes et traditionnels", qui ne répondent à aucun styles ou tendances■

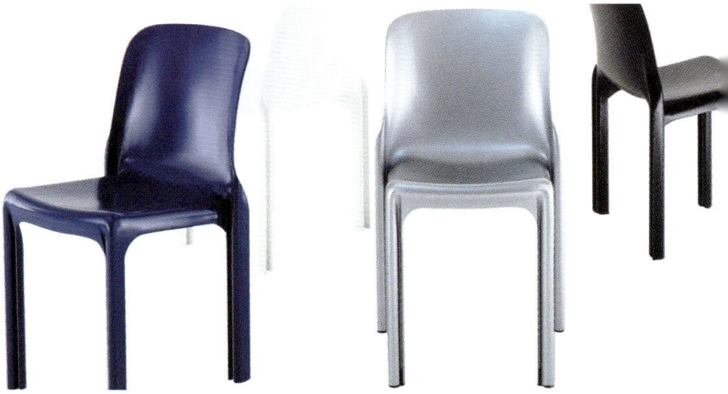

Avec Joe Colombo et Marco Zanuso, il fut un des premiers designers à commencer à travailler avec le plastique, modifiant la perception que les consommateurs avaient de ce matériau : de bon marché et chétif, il passa à être sophistiqué et élégant. Certaines des innovations qu'il apporta dans son utilisation pour la fabrication industrielle furent : les pieds en forme de "S", qui renforçaient la structure de la chaise sans altérer son intégrité , et la technique permettant d'augmenter la grosseur du plastique sur les zones qui s'usaient le plus rapidement. Le résultat de son travail se trouve dans des modèles confortables, résistants, informels, légers, colorés et pratiques, comprenant des solutions tenant compte des côtés technologiques, économiques et fonctionnels. Après 50 années d'activité Magistretti devint l'ambassadeur de l'aspect rationnel du design de l'après-guerre et contribua au succès international du design italien■

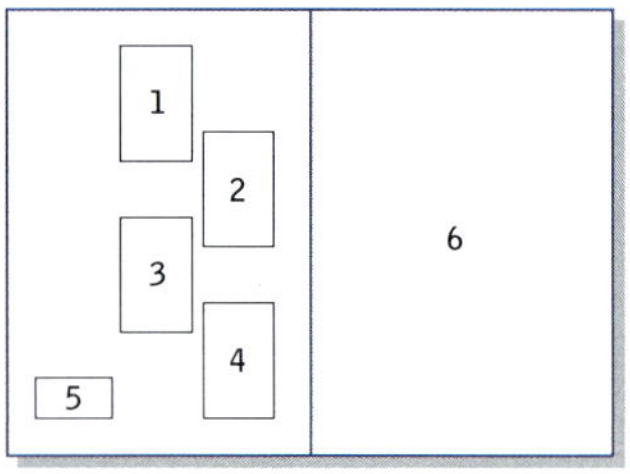

1. "Vico Lounge", 2000. Produite par Fritz Hansen■
Fauteuil confortable s'inspirant des formes de la chaise "Vico". Entièrement tapissé■

2. Chaise "Vico Solo", 1999. Produite par Fritz Hansen■
Structure en tube d'acier. Siège en bois laminé et dossier synthétique. Peut être empilé■
⊟ 73,5 ⊟ 52,5 ⊟ 46,7 ⊟ 45,5 cm■

3. Chaise "Moorea". Produite par Kartell■
Structure en tube d'acier. Siège en polyuréthanne tapissé■
⊟ 79 ⊟ 60 ⊟ 58 ⊟ 44/52 cm■

4 et 5. Chaise "Silver". Produite par Knoll■
Structure en aluminium. Siège et dossier en polypropylène. Peut être empilée■

6. Chaise "Vico", 1994. Produite par Fritz Hansen■
Structure en tube d'acier. Siège et dossier en bois laminé. Peut être empilée■
⊟ 78 ⊟ 64 ⊟ 56 ⊟ 45 cm■

ÓSCAR TUSQUETS

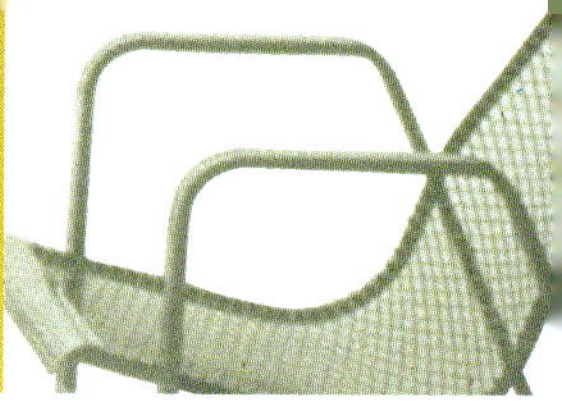

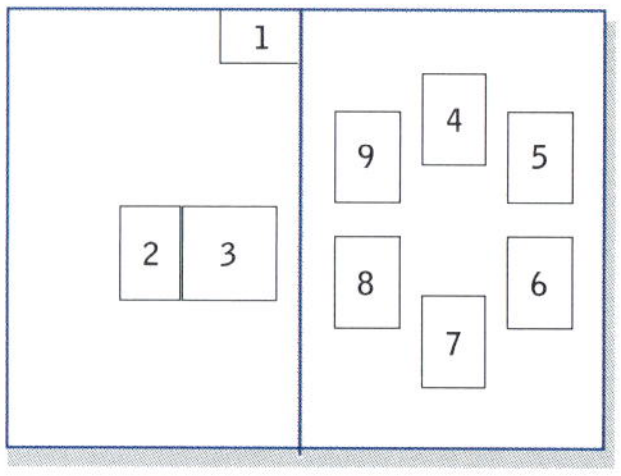

1. Chaise de "Serie Jardín", 1979/1981. Créée par Óscar Tusquets et Lluís Clotet. Éditée par Bd Ediciones de Diseño■
Pieds en tube d'acier. Siège et dossier en acier déployé. Peut être empilée. Version pour jardin dans l'emblématique "Banco Catalano"■
⊟ 90 ⊟ 60 ⊟ 80 cm■
2 et 3. Tabouret (1989) et chaise "Gaulino" (1987). Produits par CJC Concepta■
Structure en chêne. Siège tapissé en cuir de vachette. Chaise pouvant être empilée. Mesures : chaise
⊟ 85,5 ⊟ 45 ⊟ 50,5 ⊟ 46,5 cm■
4. Chaise "Plus", 2000. Produite par CJC Concepta■
Structure en tube d'acier. Siège et dossier en hêtre contre-plaqué. Peut être empilée■
⊟ 83 ⊟ 58 ⊟ 58 ⊟ 45,5 cm■
5 et 8. Chaise "Palio", 1998. Produite par Driade■
Structure en acier tubulaire recouverte de moelle naturelle■
⊟ 89,5 ⊟ 51 ⊟ 62 ⊟ 45 cm■
6. Chaise "Metalástica", 1987/1996. Éditée Bd Ediciones de Diseño■
Structure en acier. Nouvelle version avec siège et dossier avec plaque perforée. Peut être empilée■
⊟ 82 ⊟ 53,5 ⊟ 55 cm■
7 et 9. Chaise "Sinuosa", 2000. Produite par Driade■
Structure en acier inoxydable. Carcasse en polypropylène. Résistante aux intempéries. Peut être empilée■
⊟ 79 ⊟ 57 ⊟ 52 ⊟ 45 cm■

1941 Barcelone, Espagne■

Tout comme la plupart des personnages qui se sont faits remarquer dans l'évolution du design du xxe siècle, Óscar Tusquets est un créateur éclectique. Il se définit lui-même comme un "architecte de formation, peintre par penchant et designer par vocation"■
Il fit partie du groupe d'intellectuels progressistes résidants à Barcelone (parmi eux, se trouvaient des architectes comme Ricardo Bofill et Oriol Bohigas), qui finit par être, à la fin des années 60, un mouvement important de la rénovation esthétique, de par sa position antifranquiste. Ce groupe se qualifia de "gauche divine"■
En 1972, fatigué par le fait que personne n'osait produire ses idées dans le contexte culturel médiocre de l'Espagne franquiste, il décida de créer

sa propre entreprise avec d'autres "célébrités" du design, comme Pep Bonet, Cristian Cirici et Lluís Clotet. À partir de ce moment, Bocaccio Design, maintenant connue sous le nom de Bd Ediciones de Diseño, matérialisa les objets et les meubles inventés par ses fondateurs et les introduisit dans l'Espagne des designers de l'Avant-garde internationale■
Un de ses travaux les plus célèbres, le Banco Catalano, réalisé en collaboration avec Lluís Clotet, dénote son admiration pour l'héritage moderniste et de Gaudí. "Le contour du banc créé par Gaudí pour le Parc Güell nous semblait insurmontable et nous avons décidé de le modifier pour le Catalano. Une bonne copie ne doit pas forcément tuer l'original. La qualité de la copie, comme pour tout, dépend du talent de celui qui l'exécute". Dans son dernier livre "Dieu le voit", il explique que l'œuvre doit toujours s'inspirer de la perfection, comme si un Dieu intelligent était en train de nous juger■

XXIe SIÈCLE

UNE VISION DU FUTUR

RON ARAD

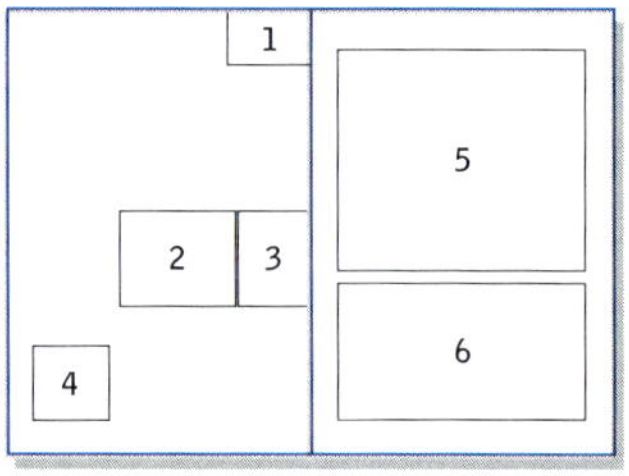

1 et 4. Chaise "Tom Vac" et chaise à bascule "Tom Rock". Produites par Vitra■ Structure en acier tubulaire. Carcasse du siège en polypropylène avec structure ondulée, en couleur ou translucide. Peut être empilée, sauf dans la version chaise à bascule qui comporte des patins en hêtre■

2. "Bad tempered Chair", 2001. Produite par Vitra■ Ce modèle est une réédition de l'original de 1985 réalisée en plaque d'acier. Elle se fabrique maintenant avec une structure en plastique, un mélange de fibre de verre, de carbone et de Kevlar, imprégnée de résine synthétique■

3. Chaise "FPE" (Fantastic Plastic Chair), 1997. Produite par Kartell■ Structure en aluminium et siège en polypropylène. Apte pour un usage en extérieur■
78 43 59 46 cm■

5 et 6. "Ron-aldo Down" et "Ron-aldo Up", 2002. Produits par Bonaldo■ Chaises de salle à manger et fauteuils avec une base en saillie, siège et dossier tapissés■

1951 Tel Aviv, Israël■

Après avoir établi l'étude One Off, en 1981à Londres (où il commença à créer des structures avec des objets trouvés et recyclés qu'il associait à des matériaux high tech), Ron Arad devint un des créateurs de référence dans le panorama international, avec des pièces uniques s'inscrivant la plupart du temps dans la catégorie de l'art. De fait, la plus grande partie de ses designs les plus connus ont pour origine des collections de caractère expérimental fabriquées à la main et en édition limitée qui sont ensuite adaptées pour être produites de façon industrielle par les grandes compagnies du secteur■

Des formes sculpturales caractéristiques définissent les meubles de Arad, sans doute parce que, comme lui-même l'explique, elles sont le

résultat de l'exploration du "matériau, de la morphologie ou de la technologie". Dés ses débuts, il sut transmettre un style unique à partir de la combinaison peu conventionnelle de matériaux et de concepts et rechercha continuellement de nouvelles techniques et de nouveaux matériaux afin de mettre ses idées en pratique■

Son travail sur la plaque d'acier trempé donna naissance, en 1986, à la chaise Well Tempered, et plus tard, à la série Big Easy, qui laissèrent leur trace dans l'histoire du design pour la singularité de leur forme et l'ingénieuse utilisation des matériaux qui consistait à introduire une nouvelle perspective dans l'esthétique de la chaise et dans le design en général■

Son interprétation singulière des lois de l'équilibre généra des structures qui semblaient être toujours en mouvement et capables de provoquer la surprise du spectateur ou de l'utilisateur de ses meubles■

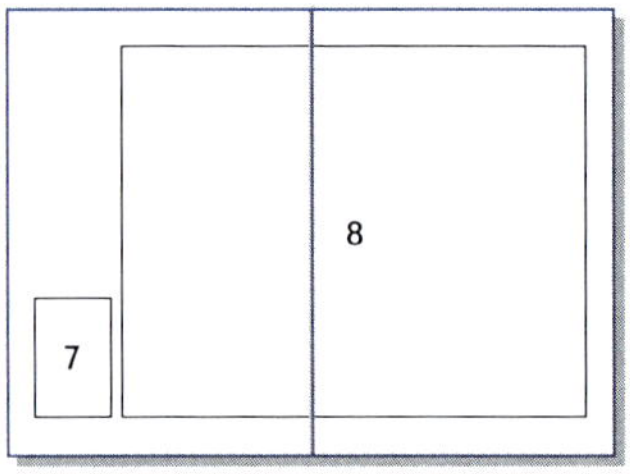

7. Chaise "Anonimus", 1995. Produite par Zeus Noto■
Structure en acier et pieds en aluminium. Siège et dossier en bois laminé incurvé en hêtre■
82 49 53 45 cm■

8. Chaise "Little Albert", 2001. Produite par Moroso■
Structure en polypropylène modelé. Apte pour un usage en extérieur■
75 74 75 cm■

H. & F. CAMPANA

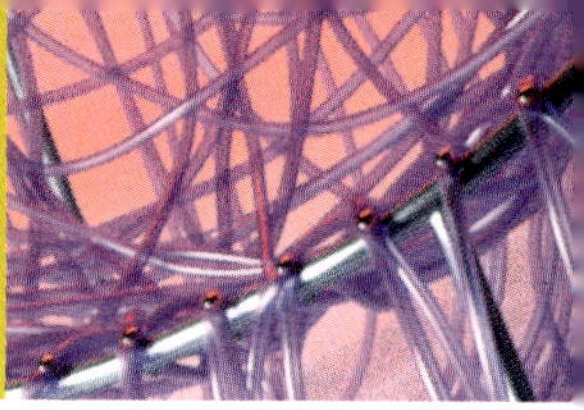

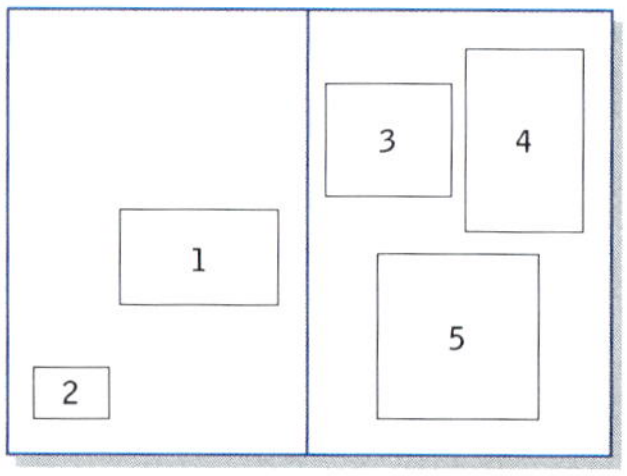

1. "Anemone", 2001. De Edra▪
Structure en acier avec tubes de plastique entrecroisés manuellement de façon arbitraire▪
⊟ 66 ⊟ 120 ⊟ 90 cm▪
2. Chaise "Cone", 1993/98. De Edra▪
Structure métallique et carcasse de feuilles de polycarbonate, découpées au laser▪
⊟ 74 ⊟ 107 ⊟ 85 cm▪
3, 4 et 5. Chaises "Azul", "Verde" et "Vermelha", 1993-98. De Edra▪
Structure en acier et pieds en aluminium. Le siège et le dossier sont faits avec une corde de coton (env. 400 m). Mesures : Azul,
⊟ 98 ⊟ 80 ⊟ 45 cm▪
Verde
⊟ 88 ⊟ 45 ⊟ 54 ⊟ 45 cm▪
Vermelha
⊟ 77 ⊟ 86 ⊟ 58 ⊟ 38 cm▪

Hunberto Campana–1953 Sao Paulo, Brésil▪
Fernando Campana–1961 Sao Paulo, Brésil▪

Le travail des frères Campana est une preuve élégante du fait que dans l'actualité le design va au-delà de la forme et la fonction, au-delà de la somme de ses parties. Ses créations sont capables de transmettre à la fois les archétypes de la culture brésilienne et un langage contemporain dépassant toutes les frontières▪
Les objets qui sortent de leur atelier associent le sens de l'humour et l'audace dans l'utilisation de matériaux récupérés dans les rebuts ou les matières "pauvres" du chaos urbain et sont travaillés suivant des techniques artisanales. Leurs pièces de mobilier se trouvent dans le juste milieu entre les produits essentiellement industriels et les pro-

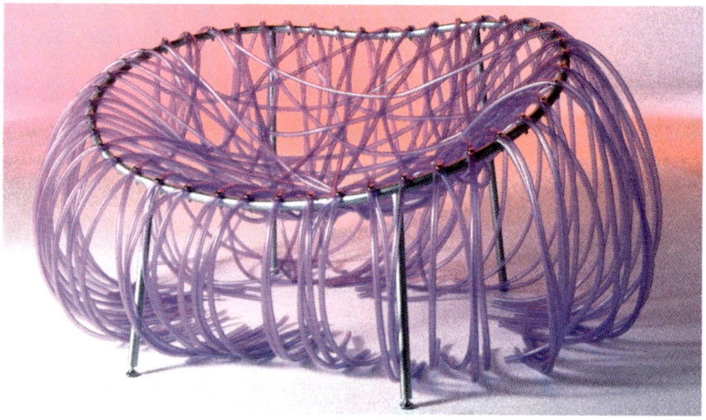

duits artistiques, et remettent en question le contexte social de la production du design tel qu'il est▪
Un des points de départ de leur processus créatif est la recherche de la relation entre l'objet et l'utilisateur. Selon Fernando Campana, "J'observe les relations entre les personnes entre elles et avec le soleil, le son et les nuages", et c'est de cette interaction que surgissent les idées▪
Les chaises des frères Campana sont intuitives et spontanées, nées de l'union entre l'artisanat traditionnel du Brésil, l'utilisation efficiente des techniques et des matériaux industriels et la créativité qui nous fait observer le monde avec des yeux d'enfant▪

ANTONIO CITTERIO

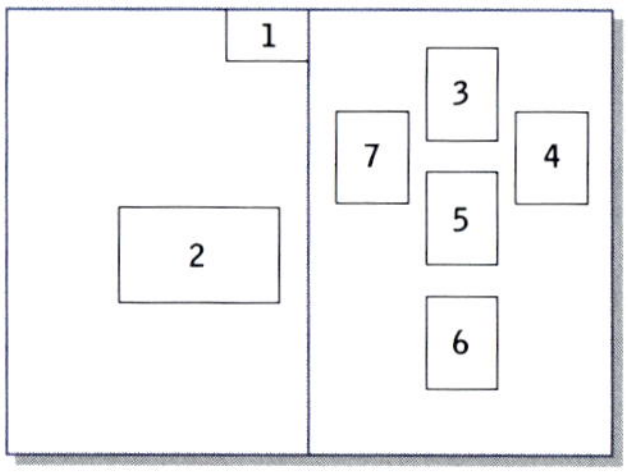

1. CHAISE "MINI". Produite par Halifax■
Pieds et accoudoirs en aluminium. Siège et dossier en polypropylène■
⊟ 80 ⊟ 52,5 ⊟ 50,5 ⊟ 45,5 cm■
2. TABOURET "SPOON", 2002. Produit par Kartell■
Structure en plastique lui donnant flexibilité et élasticité. Base en aluminium■
3 et 4. CHAISES DE BUREAU "OSON-STUDIO" et "OSON-CORPORATE", 2002. Produites par Vitra■
Elles offrent de nombreuses possibilité d'adaptation. Siège et dossier connectés au moyen d'un mécanisme de chaîne en trois pièces■
5. CHAISE DE BUREAU "AXESS", Antonio Citterio et Glen Oliver Löw pour Vitra■
Elle s'adapte à l'utilisateur de façon automatique. Elle reçut le certificat d'ergonomie de l'Institut LGA de Nuremberg. (Photo : H. Hansen)■
6. CHAISE "TONIX", 2002. De Antonio Citterio et Toan Nguyen pour Vitra■
Réservée au conférences. Comprend des roulettes■
7. CHAISE DE BUREAU "T-CHAIR", Antonio Citterio et Glen Oliver Löw pour Vitra■
Le mécanisme synchronisé breveté bouge et soutient le corps dans n'importe quelle position. Dossier flexible en polypropylène. (Photo : H. Hansen)■

1950 Meda, Italie■

Dans les meubles de Antonio Citterio, on retrouve son admiration pour l'art minimaliste. Les motifs de base de ses créations, tant pour le mobilier que pour l'architecture ou la décoration d'intérieur, sont des formes essentielles capables de transmettre beaucoup avec très peu et dans lesquelles la qualité des matériaux est vitale pour la conséquence de cette simplicité d'expression■
Citterio est un des designers les plus prolifiques de sa génération. Il est un représentant du "bon design" italien, et travaille depuis des années pour les grandes compagnies du meuble de design contemporain. Sa philosophie est de ne projeter que les meubles dont il souhaiterait être entouré, ce qui donne naissance à des pièces d'une fonctionnalité extrême. Citterio parvient à transmettre un intérêt visuel et une certaine harmonie au moyen d'une combinaison équilibrée et originale de matériaux et de formes s'éloignant des propositions risquées ou trop radicales■

Cette attitude minimaliste et l'intégrité qui marquèrent sa conduite dans le travail dés ses débuts, sont probablement les responsables du fait que les chaise et les canapés qu'il créa au milieu des années 70 pour des boîtes comme B&B Italia ont résisté au passage des années et sont restés très actuels, ce qui prouve que le fonctionnalisme est un style de vie en marge des modes■
Il obtint une de ses réussites les plus notoires dans les années 90 avec le design d'un nouveau système de chaises pour bureau pour la compagnie Vitra, qui associaient une forme élégante et l'acier, le cuir et la tapisserie qui mettaient en relief sa fonctionnalité■

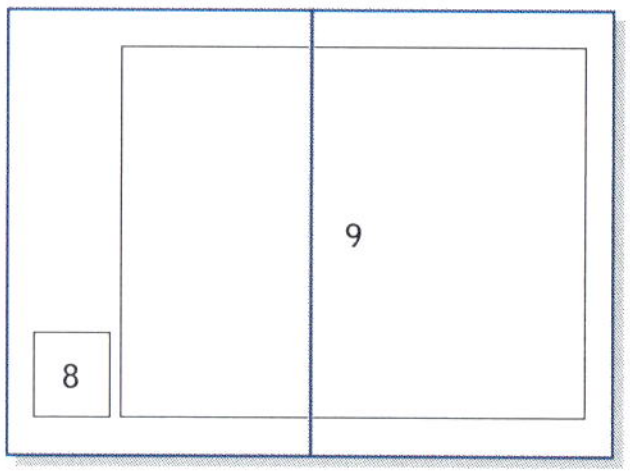

8. Chaise "Visacom", 2002. Produite par Vitra■
Base avec oscillation libre en acier tubulaire chromé. Siège et dossier tapissés en tissu ou en peau■
9. Chaise "Solo", de B&B Italia■
Structure en aluminium. Siège avec cadre en acier, tapissé en tissu ou en peau■
⊟ 88 ⊟ 42 ⊟ 57 ⊟ 47 cm■

PIERO LISSONI

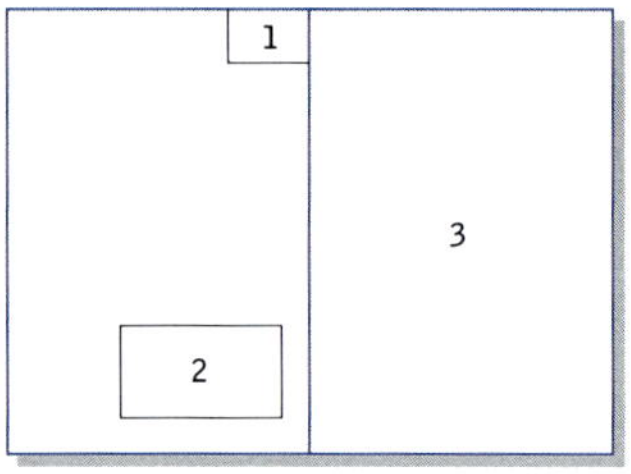

1. Chaise "Form", 2002. Produite par Kartell▪
Structure en acier chromé. Carcasse du siège en polypropylène▪
⊟ 63,1 ⊟ 84,9 ⊟ 81 ⊟ 31 cm▪
2. Fauteuil "Café", 1998. Produit par Living Divani▪
3. Fauteuil "Frog", 1993. Produit par Living Divani▪
Structure en acier tubulaire chromé. Siège et dossier en moelle▪

1956 Seregno, Italie▪

Piero Lissoni est une autre des figures importantes du design italien d'inspiration minimaliste (même s'il préfère utiliser le terme de simplicité au lieu de minimalisme, afin de ne pas limiter son travail à un concept s'appliquant actuellement à tout type de produits sans tenir compte de sa véritable signification)▪

Pour Lissoni, la pureté et l'honnêteté des formes est quelque chose qui va plus loin que n'importe quelle étiquette. Son travail est défini par une poésie qui lui est propre et qui dépasse les exigences imposées par l'industrie. Ses meubles naissent d'une recherche exhaustive et une combinaison pertinente des matériaux qui se modèlent pour créer des formes sobres et fonctionnelles▪

En 1986, il monte le Studio Lissoni à Milan, où il développe des projets d'architecture, de décoration d'intérieur, de graphisme, de dessin industriel et de direction de l'art et de l'image corporative pour les entreprises les plus importantes du secteur. Ce large éventail d'activités répond probablement au concept de Lissoni en ce qui concerne le design : "Lorsqu'on parle de design industriel, on pense généralement à des objets, mais c'est bien plus que cela : cela veut dire penser et créer tout ce qui nous entoure"▪

Lissoni pense que face à la crise conceptuelle de la forme soumise à la fonction, c'est la rechercher esthétique libérée de ses attaches qui prend le rôle protagoniste. Une recherche qui devra trouver son inspiration dans le monde de l'art exprimant dans un sens dramatique les vicissitudes de l'homme▪

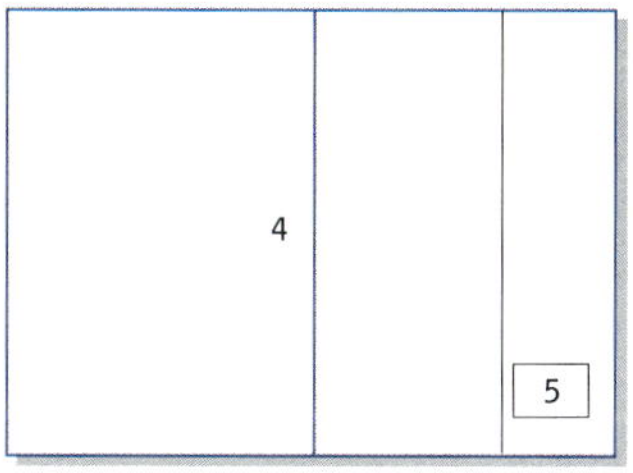

4. Fauteuil "Frog", 1993. Produit par Living Divani■
Structure en acier tubulaire chromé. Siège et dossier tapissés en peau■
5. Fauteuil "Box", 1996. Produit par Living Divani■

LIEVORE, ALTHERR, MOLINA

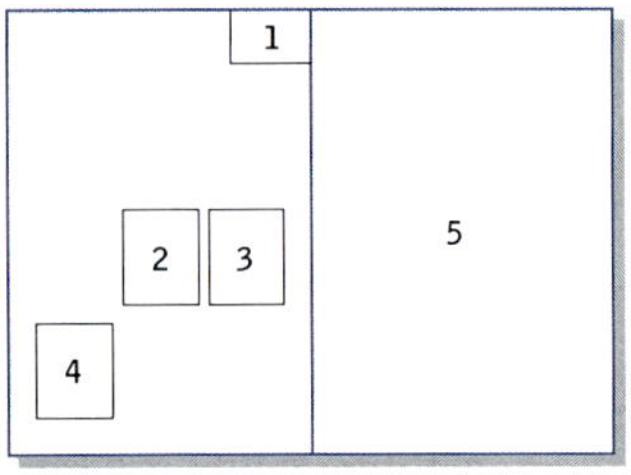

1. Chaise "Radical", 1992. Produite par Andreu World■
Structure en hêtre massif. Siège et dossier d'une seule pièce à partir d'une planche en hêtre contre-plaqué. Premier Prix Design FIM 92■
⊟ 86,5 ⊟ 41 ⊟ 51 ⊟ 45 cm■

2 et 4. Chaise "Manila". Produite par Andreu World■
Ce modèle offre de nombreuses possibilités de combinaison : structure en hêtre ou en noyer, siège et dossier tapissés en peau ou cannés en osier ou combinés. Différentes mesures■

3. Fauteuil "JKR". Produit par Perobell■
Pieds en métal chromé. Siège et dossier avec structure en bois, couvertures en polyuréthanne et tapisserie. Réédition d'un modèle historique de la boîte■

5. Fauteuil "RDL". Produit par Andreu World■
Version fauteuil de la chaise Radical. Structure en hêtre■

Alberto Liévore–1948 Buenos Aires, Argentine■
Jeannette Altherr–1965 Heidelberg, Allemagne■
Manel Molina–1963 Barcelone, Espagne■

Alberto Liévore, architecte de formation, se consacre au design de mobilier depuis qu'en 1972, il fonda à Buenos Aires le showroom-tienda Hipótesis. Des meubles qui lui firent obtenir une reconnaissance internationale surgirent de ses ateliers. En 1977, alors qu'il est déjà installé à Barcelone, il forme le Grupo Berenguer avec Norberto Chaves, à qui s'unirent ensuite des designers comme Jorge Pensi et Oriol Pibernat. En collaboration avec la revue "On Diseño" ils projetèrent SIDI, la Sélection Internationale de design de l'Équipement pour l'Habitat, une plate-forme de lancement du design espagnol■

En 1991, il fonde l'étude Alberto Liévore & Asociados, avec Jeannette Altherr et Manel Molina qui avait collaboré avec un autre des grands designers espagnols, Miguel Milà. En plus de travailler sur le design de mobilier, ils développent des projets de décoration d'intérieur, d'emballage, de produit, de cabinet d'étude et de direction artistique et se consacrent à l'enseignement■
Liévore, Altherr et Molina ont une vision particulière du design : "Nous tentons d'éviter de réduire l'objet à une simple manifestation culturelle. Dans chaque projet, après avoir accepter l'entière complexité du phénomène, nous essayons de ne rien sacrifier, forme ou fonction, raison ou sensibilité, art ou technique, innovation ou continuité, etc. Nous tentons d'obtenir une forme compacte, chargée de signification avec pour résultat un système complexe de forces équilibrées"■

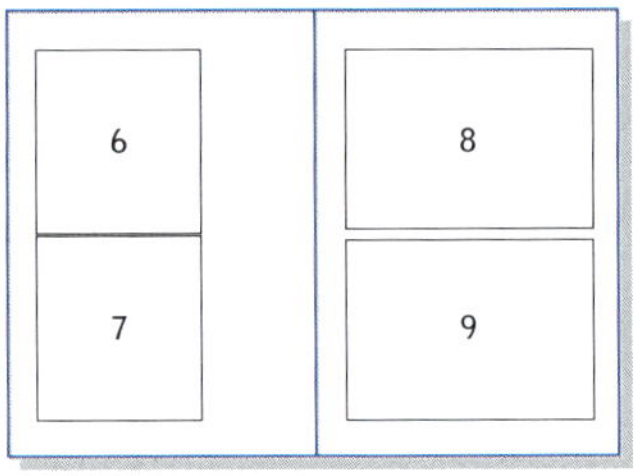

6. CHAISE "RADICAL", 1992. Produite par Andreu World■
Structure en hêtre massif. Siège et dossier d'une seule pièce à partir d'une planche en hêtre contre-plaqué. Premier Prix Design FIM 92■

7. CHAISE "SEDUS". Produite par Muebles Do+Ce■
Structure en bois, siège et dossier tapissés■
⊟ 74 ⊟ 51 ⊟ 53 cm■

8. FAUTEUIL "FABRA". Produit par Perobell■
Structure en acier. Siège et dossier tapissés■

9. CHAISE "890", 2002. Produite par Thonet■
Fabriquée avec trois types de base en acier tubulaire : en saillie, avec cadre et quatre pieds. Siège entièrement tapissé■
⊟ 76 ⊟ 62 ⊟ 64 cm■

JOSEP LLUSCÀ

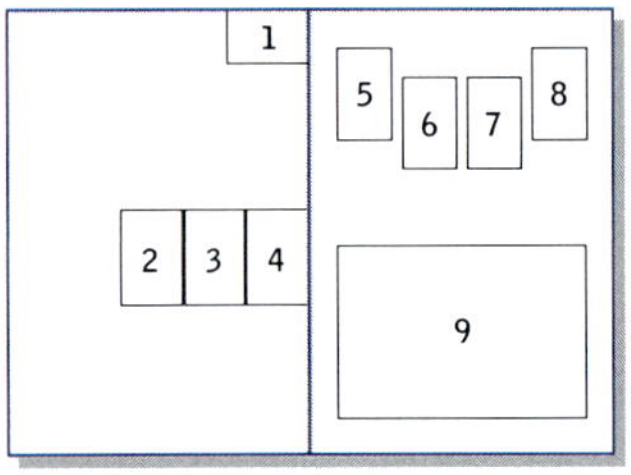

1 et 7. Chaise "Global". Produite par Enea▪

Structure en tube d'acier. Siège et dossier en polypropylène et accoudoirs en polyamide. Peut être empilée. Prix Delta de Plata de 1999▪

2. Chaise de bureau "Neko". Produite par Oken▪

Base en aluminium. Siège en polypropylène recyclable. Le dossier peut être en polypropylène ou en bois. Offre diverses combinaisons▪

3. Chaise de bureau "Lola". Produite par Oken▪

Pieds et accoudoirs en alliage d'aluminium injecté. Structure du siège en bois laminé recouvert de mousse de polyuréthanne flexible▪

⊟ 98/106 ⊟ 65 ⊟ 63 cm▪

4 et 9. Chaise "Aloe". Produite par Oken▪

Structure en tube d'acier. Siège et dossier en bois incurvé. Offre également une version tapissée▪

5. Chaise "Eina". Produite par Enea▪

Structure en acier et accoudoirs en aluminium injecté. Siège et dossier en hêtre laminé, tapissés ou en polypropylène. Peut être empilée▪

6 et 8. Chaise "Lógica". Produite par Enea▪

Structure en acier. Siège et dossier en hêtre verni ou tapissée en peau. Peut être empilée et rattachée à d'autres sur les côtés▪

1948 Barcelone, Espagne▪

Josep Lluscà est un des designers industriels espagnols avec la plus grande projection internationale. Il fait partie du groupe de créateurs qui, depuis les années 80, ont fait de l'Espagne, et en particulier de Barcelone, le nouveau point de référence dans le panorama mondial du design▪

Il fut le vice-président du Mouvement des Designers Industriels du Développement des Arts Décoratifs (ADI-FAD), membre du Conseil du Design de la Generalitat de Catalogne et du Conseil de la Fondation BCD de Barcelone, professeur et membre du Conseil de Direction du Département du Design du Produit de l'École Eina de Barcelone▪

En 1972, il monta l'étude Lluscà y Asociados, en collaborant à la stratégie de création de nouveaux produits pour des secteurs aussi divers

que ceux du mobilier et des compléments, de l'équipement public, de l'électroménager, de l'éclairage, etc. Ces projets furent récompensés à de nombreuses occasions par de prestigieux prix internationaux▪

Un de ses designs les plus célèbres est celui de la chaise Andrea, inspirée de la chaise de la Maison Calvet créée par Gaudí. Le modèle de Lluscà part d'une étude sur le centre de gravité et prend comme point de référence la chaise de Gaudí pour résoudre l'emboîtement entre le siège, le dossier et la structure, mettant ainsi en évidence la l'organisation anatomique de la forme. En sauvant la distance temporelle, la chaise Andrea semble rééditer le dialogue entre le patrimoine artisanal et les nouvelles solutions typologiques, constructives et industrielles▪

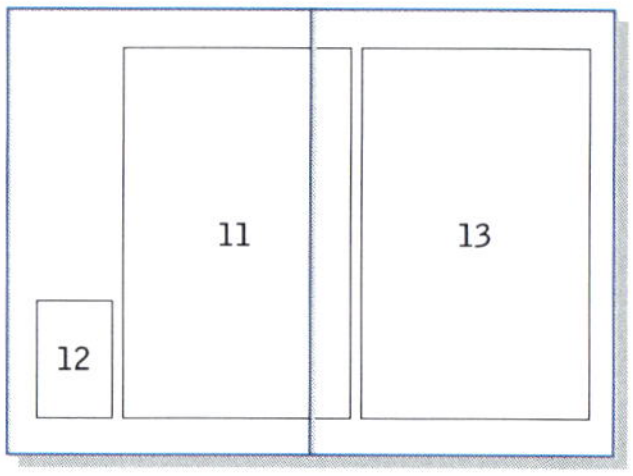

11. Chaise "Andrea", 1988. Produite par Andreu World■
Base sur trois pieds en tube d'acier en forme de cône et chromé. Accoudoirs en aluminium injecté. Siège et dossier en hêtre teint. Sélection Prix Delta ADIFAD de 1988■
12. Tabouret "Coma". Produit par Enea■
Base en acier laqué, repose-pied en aluminium poli et siège en polypropylène avec fibres minérales. 3 hauteurs : 75, 65 et 45 cm■
13. Chaise "Cos", 1994. Produite par Cassina■
Structure en cerisier ou en hêtre, ou teinte en noire. Tapissée en peau. Présentée avec ou sans accoudoirs■
⊟ 82 ⊟ 63 ⊟ 57 ⊟ 45 cm■
(Photo : A. Ferrari)■

ALBERTO MEDA

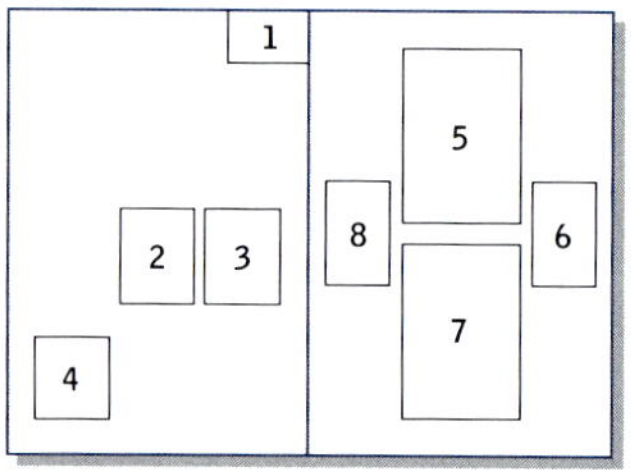

1 et 4. Chaise "Highframe". Produite par Alias■
Structure en aluminium, siège et dossier en grille de polyester avec PVC. Peut être empilée■
⊟ 82 ⊟ 53 ⊟ 56 ⊟ 49 cm■
2 et 3. Fauteuil "Armframe". Produit par Alias■
Structure en aluminium et corps du siège tapissé en peau noire ou en grille de polyester avec PVC■
5. Chaise de bureau "Meda 2XL", 2002. Produite par Vitra■
Comprend un mécanisme synchronisé adaptable à chaque individu. (Photo : H. Hansen)■
6 et 7. Chaise de bureau "Rolling Frame". Produite par Alias■
Structure en aluminium poli ou mat. Siège et dossier tapissés en peau ou en grille de polyester avec PVC■
8. Chaise de bureau "Meeting frame", 2002. Produite par Alias■
Structure en aluminium poli ou mat. Siège et dossier tapissés en peau ou en grille de polyester avec PVC■

1945 Como, Italie■

La plus grande différence entre Alberto Meda et les autres designers italiens de sa génération –ceux qui firent du "design italien" une dénomination d'origine précieuse aux environs des années 70– est sans doute sa formation d'ingénieur industriel mécanique. Il partage avec eux la fusion d'art et de technologie, de raison et d'imagination et la recherche constante dans le domaine de l'innovation technique et formelle■
Sa première incursion dans le monde du design eut lieu en 1973 avec sa position de Directeur Technique de Kartell. En 1979, il s'établit comme designer industriel indépendant et collabora avec de prestigieuses compagnies pour la création de tous types de produits, depuis les voitures jusqu'aux éléments d'éclairage et aux chaises réalisées suivant la technologie d'avant-garde■

Meda est connu à niveau international pour avoir utilisé dans ses designs des matériaux composés de dernière génération, comme la fibre de charbon, l'aluminium fondu et extrudé, Kevlar® ou Nomex®, avec lesquels il créa des objets élégants et innovateurs reflétant ses antécédents d'ingénieur. Son travail représente un trait d'union entre les nouveaux matériaux et les technologies et articles d'usage commun et réinvente le mobilier traditionnel en utilisant des matières industrielles dans d'autres contextes■
Meda pense que la simplicité doit être le guide inspirateur de tout travail de design, "... je suis certain que l'intention d'obtenir des choses simples peut être identifiée avec ce qu'on pourrait appeler un besoin "biologique". Étant donné que nous sommes des êtres compliqués, nous pouvons au moins nous permettre d'être entourés d'objets simples, d'une autre forme... ¡ Que la vie est dure !"■

JASPER MORRISON

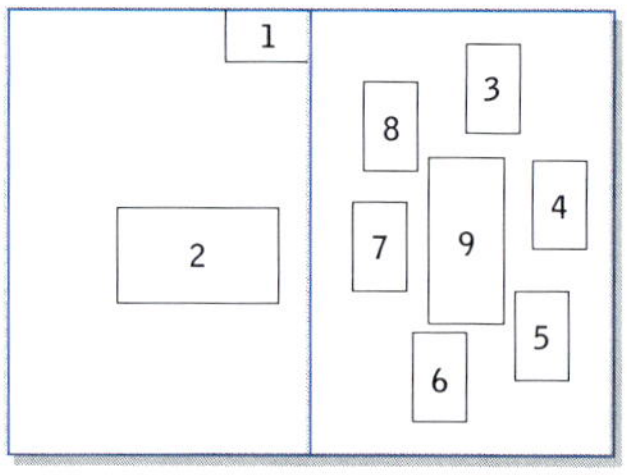

1. Fauteuil "Ph". Produit par SCP■ Structure en chêne massif. Siège et dossier tapissés en tissu ou en peau■
⊟ 83 ⊟ 52 ⊟ 54 cm■
2 et 9. Tabouret "Atlas". Produit par Alias■
Série de tabourets de différentes tailles et finitions. Structure en acier et siège pivotant tapissé avec une large gamme de couleurs■
3 et 5. Chaise "Hi Pad", 1999. Produite par Cappellini■
Structure en acier inoxydable satiné. Siège et dossier tapissés en tissu ou en peau■
⊟ 75 ⊟ 40 ⊟ 45 ⊟ 45 cm■
4. Tabouret "Slatted Stool". Produit par SCP■
Structure en acier inoxydable■
⊟ 70 ⊟ 48 ⊟ 27 cm■
6. Chaise "Tate", 2000. Produite par Cappellini■
Structure en acier inoxydable. Siège en hêtre contre-plaqué ou teint en plusieurs couleurs. Peut être empilée■
⊟ 81 ⊟ 53 ⊟ 47,5 ⊟ 45 cm■
7 et 8. "Air Chair", 2000. Produite par Magis■
Structure en polypropylène renforcé avec de la fibre de verre. Modelée par injection d'air. Apte pour un usage en extérieur■
⊟ 77,5 ⊟ 49 ⊟ 51 ⊟ 47 cm■

1959 Londres, Angleterre■

"Pour plusieurs raisons le fait de créer une chaise n'est pas comparable à la création de n'importe quel autre objet... La chaise est un casse-tête et je ne crois pas que la chaise parfaite ait déjà été dessinée, pas même par Eames"■ Jasper Morrison est un autre des défenseurs importants du minimalisme en tant qu'option vitale. Il parvint à se situer entre les designers les plus influents grâce à sa façon particulière d'envisager le design alliant un ascétisme élégant à une certaine dose d'humour■

Morrison présenta comme une de ses premières influences l'exhibition du groupe Memphis à Milan en 1981, "j'ai trouvé là la preuve du fait qu'aucune des anciennes normes du design n'avait d'importance". C'est également à ce moment qu'il se rendit compte qu'il voulait faire exactement le

contraire, avec des objets libérés de tout ornement pouvant constituer un antidote contre tout excès. Ses créations furent considérées comme une pause face au mobilier retentissant du Postmodernisme. Sa simplicité ou 'essentialité' apparente est si évidente qu'il semble parfois que les objets n'ont été créés par personne. Seulement une étude plus précise de la pièce montre le processus créatif qui se trouve derrière et donne naissance à des solutions techniques et formelles qui contribuent à son amélioration■

Son objectif peut être défini, comme l'expliqua le critique Charles Arthur Boyer, comme "produire des objets quotidiens pouvant être utilisés par tout le monde, faire des choses plus légères et pas plus lourdes, plus douces et pas plus dures, inclusives plus qu'exclusives, générant énergie, lumière et espace". La pureté créatrice de ses designs est le fruit de l'observation et d'une pensée libre■

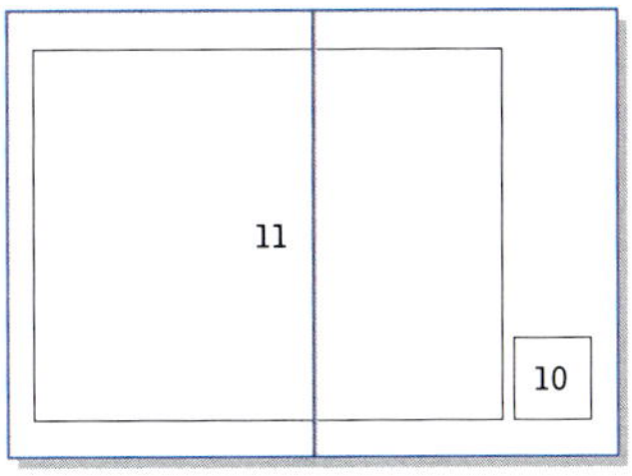

10. Fauteuil "Thinking Man's Chair", 1988. Produit par Cappellini▪
Structure en acier tubulaire. Apte pour une usage en extérieur▪
⊟ 70 ⊟ 57 ⊟ 90 ⊟ 35 cm▪

11. Fauteuil "Low Pad", 1999. Produit par Cappellini▪
Structure en acier inoxydable. Siège tapissé en tissu ou en peau▪
⊟ 75 ⊟ 60 ⊟ 73,5 ⊟ 34 cm▪

JORGE PENSI

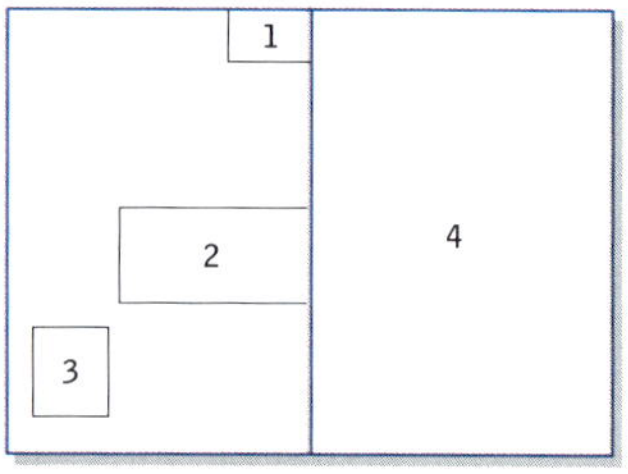

1 et 4. Chaise "Duna", 1998. Produite par Cassina▪
Structure en aluminium verni. Structure du siège et des accoudoirs en plastique tapissé avec de la mousse de polyuréthanne, recouverte de tissu ou de peau▪
⊟ 84 ⊟ 57 ⊟ 57 ⊟ 45 cm▪
2. Tabouret "Gimlet". Produit par Mobles 114▪
Structure métallique avec repose-pied chromé. Siège pivotant en polyuréthanne intégral. Trois hauteurs : 83, 65 et 50 cm▪
3. Chaise "Pol", de Akaba▪
Structure en tube d'acier poli, accoudoirs en polyamide renforcée avec de la fibre de verre. Siège et dossier en polypropylène. Peut être empilée▪
⊟ 82 ⊟ 56 ⊟ 55 ⊟ 45 cm▪

1946 Buenos Aires, Argentine▪

Après avoir terminé sa formation d'architecte et de designer industriel et avoir travaillé pendant quelques années dans sa ville natale, Jorge Pensi s'établit en Espagne en 1975, et devint une des figures importantes de l'élan du design espagnol qui eut lieu une fois la dictature de Franco terminée et dont la plate-forme de lancement international eut pour scène la ville de Barcelone. En 1977, il monta le cabinet d'étude de design Groupe Berenguer, avec Norberto Chaves, Oriol Pibernat et Alberto Liévore. Il fonda sa propre étude en 1985, et se spécialisa dans la création de mobilier, d'éclairage et de mise en scène. Il obtint rapidement une renommée internationale, en particulier pour ses chaises élégantes et fluides, comme le modèle en aluminium Toledo grâce auquel il gagna un grand nombre de prix. Son travail peut être défini comme un pari pour l'intuition. Pensi reconnaît que ses produits se caractérisent par leurs aspects qui ne dérivent pas d'une stricte relation de cause à effet et qui, en même temps, rejettent une correspondance directe entre les intentions et les résultats, puisque dans le processus, c'est la pensée intuitive qui joue un plus ou moins grand rôle▪

Un autre de ses objectifs réside dans des designs intemporels et résistants à l'évolution imposée par le temps : "...Les objets ont un lien étroit avec le temps. Je suis particulièrement intéressé par le sujet de la permanence : voir mourir un objet parce qu'il n'est plus à la mode me rend triste. C'est pour cette raison que je tente d'éviter que cela n'arrive. Mon idéal serait de faire des objets qui aient une vie plus longue que la mienne ; c'est pour cela que j'essaie de donner à mon travail une beauté pouvant dépasser le moment présent"▪

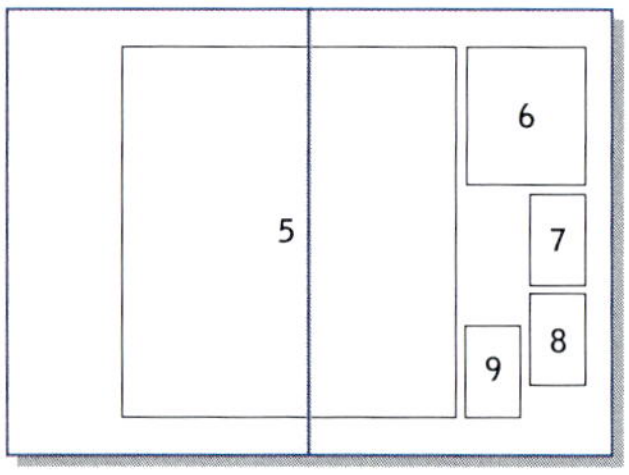

5. Chaise "Momo", de Andreu World■
Structure en bois. Armature métallique. Siège et dossier tapissés■
6. Chaise "Pol", de Akaba■
Structure en tube d'acier poli, accoudoirs en polyamide renforcée avec de la fibre de verre. Siège et dossier en polypropylène. Peut être empilée.
Avec accoudoirs :
⊟ 82 ⊟ 56 ⊟ 55 ⊟ 45 cm■
Sans accoudoir :
⊟ 82 ⊟ 46 ⊟ 55 ⊟ 45 cm■
7. Chaise de bureau "Muga", de Akaba■
Comprend un mécanisme d'adaptation synchronisé. Elle est présentée avec différentes versions, hauteurs et finitions■
8. Chaise "Gorka", de Akaba■
Structure en aluminium injecté sous haute pression. Carcasse anatomique d'une seule pièce en polyamide renforcée avec de la fibre de verre. Peut être tapissée et empilée■
⊟ 82,5 ⊟ 57,5 ⊟ 52 ⊟ 44,5 cm■
9. Chaise "Toledo", de Amat-3 (photo fournie par Knoll)■
Structure en tube d'aluminium poli. Siège et dossier en aluminium fondu et poli■
⊟ 76 ⊟ 55 ⊟ 54 ⊟ 45 cm■

GAETANO PESCE

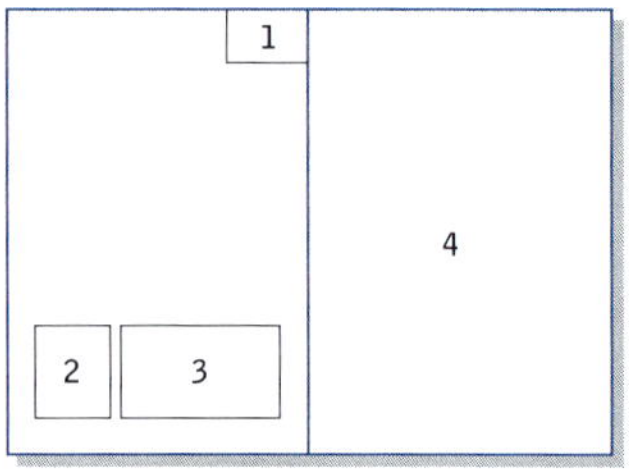

1 et 4. FAUTEUIL "SERIE UP", 1969/2000. Produit par B&B Italia■
Fauteuil gonflable modelé en polyuréthanne et recouvert d'un tissu élastique spécial■
⊟ 103 ⊟ 120 ⊟ 130 cm■
2. FAUTEUIL "FELTRI", 1987. Produit par Cassina■
Entièrement réalisé avec du feutre épais. La base est imprégnée de résine afin d'obtenir une grande résistance. Il est tapissé avec du tissu cousu■
⊟ 130/98 ⊟ 73 ⊟ 66 ⊟ 45 cm■
3. CHAISE "BROADWAY", 1993-2001. Produite par Bernini■
Structure en acier inoxydable. Siège et dossier en résine■

1939 La Spezia, Italie■

L'architecte, artiste et designer Gaetano Pesce est un des grands créateurs du XXe siècle qui continue à exercer une certaine influence au XXIe siècle . Dés ses débuts, son code totalement personnel, la défense de son indépendance créative face à tout canon esthétique universel ou absolu pour exprimer sa liberté par rapport aux limitations imposées par la technologie et la tradition ont étonné à tous les niveaux■
Il commença à se faire connaître dans les années 60 lorsqu'il opposa ses formes exubérantes et sans limites, pleines d'implications symboliques, à la géométrie froide et vide imposée par le fonctionnalisme. La série de sièges gonflables Up aux formes anthropomorphiques et sensuelles sculptées dans du polyuréthanne le rendit célèbre et le fit représenter une nouvelle façon de comprendre le design. Depuis lors, il est resté sur sa position contre la séparation entre la fonction et la signification, entre l'art et le design en travaillant à partir d'une exploration continue des matériaux : "chaque artiste s'exprime avec les matériaux de son époque, moi j'utilise la résine". Pesce unit la logique de la production à grande échelle et les coûts réduits à la création d'objets uniques et fait en sorte que l'art soit accessible à tout le monde■
Tout au long de sa carrière, Pesce contribua à redéfinir les principes qui gouvernent la pratique du design et de l'architecture en partant de la conviction qu'il s'agit d'instruments permettant d'inventer un nouveau monde. Pesce défend également le concept de l'aléatoire dans les processus créatifs et productifs et introduit l'idée des séries industrielles diversifiées face à la standardisation dominante■

21. Jahrhundert
A R I

KARIM RASHID

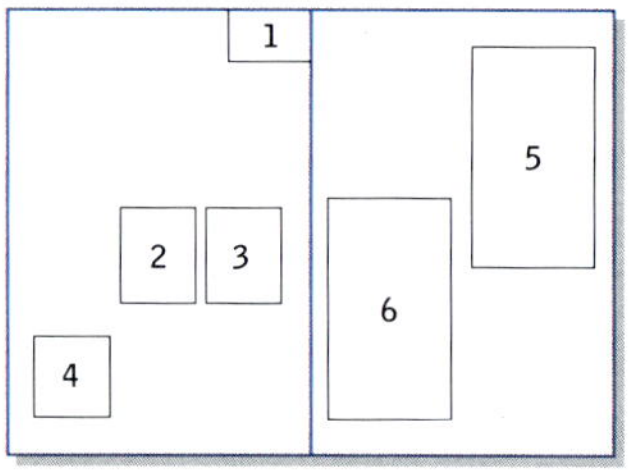

1, 3 et 4. Chaise "Alo", 2002. Produite par Magis■
Structure en tube d'aluminium, avec ou sans accoudoirs. Siège en aluminium. Envers du siège en polypropylène. Peut être empilée. Apte pour l'usage en extérieur■
⊟ 82 ⊟ 53 ⊟ 55 cm■
2. Chaise "Butterfly", 2002. Produite par Magis■
Structure en tube d'acier chromé. Siège et dossier en ABS modelé par injection■
⊟ 82,5 ⊟ 54,5 ⊟ 55,5 ⊟ 46 cm■
5. Tabouret "Arp". Produit par Pure Design■
Base en acier. Siège en bois laminé. Deux hauteurs possibles : 88,9 et 73,7■
6. "Oh Chair". Produite par Umbra■
Structure en acier. Siège en polypropylène. Peut être empilée■

1960 Le Caire, Égypte■

Karim Rashid est considéré comme une "superstar" dans le panorama du design contemporain. Depuis son étude à New York, qu'il monta en 1993, il créa tout type d'articles pour des compagnies leaders, depuis des collections de mode jusqu'à des poubelles■
Rashid définit son style de "minimalisme sensuel" ou "sensualisme", puisque, à partir de formes fluides, douces et organiques, il fait en sorte que l'attention se centre sur le contenu de l'objet et non sur sa forme qui, étant totalement dénuée d'ornement, devient minimaliste. "Les objets doivent réunir l'expérience et la forme afin de les rendre inséparables. Ceci signifie qu'il faut dessiner à nouveau les objets avec lesquels nous vivons pour les adapter à notre façon de vivre. C'est-à-dire

que si nous voulons nous vautrer dans des chaises, nous devons créer des chaises qui nous permettent de le faire"■
Rashid pense que le futur du design passe par la fabrication d'objets "faits sur mesure", personnalisés selon le souhait de chaque client, ce qui ne sera possible que grâce aux nouvelles possibilités offertes par les techniques du futur. De fait, il crée actuellement ses objets par ordinateur■
Son objectif est de rompre avec les normes du passé pour se centrer uniquement sur les besoins et les options réelles du présent et du futur, dans le but de créer des environnements où la technologie, l'automatisation et les systèmes basés sur l'expérience rendront la vie plus facile. Plus que tout, le souhait de Rashid est de changer le monde, comme il l'exprime dans le titre de son livre■

PHILIPPE STARCK

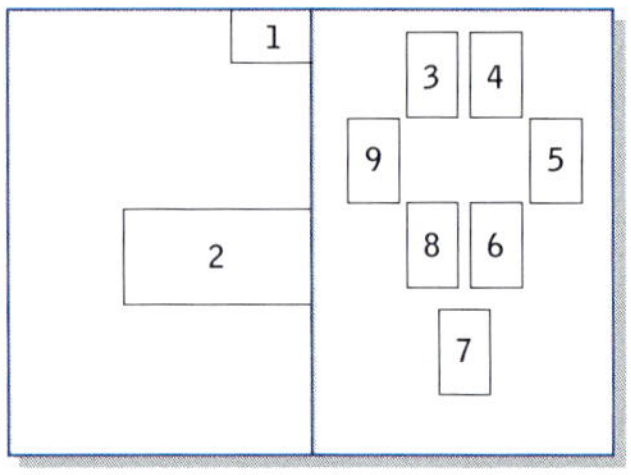

1. Fauteuil "Zbork", 2002. De Kartell■
Réalisé en polyéthylène coloré en forme de sac. Apte pour un usage en extérieur■
2. Chaise "Louis Ghost". De Kartell■
Réalisée en polycarbonate transparent ou coloré imitant le style Louis XV. Apte pour un usage en extérieur■
⊟ 94 ⊟ 54 ⊟ 55 ⊟ 47 cm■
3, 7 et 8. Chaise et tabouret "Hudson". Produits par Emeco■
Série de sièges réalisés en aluminium, poli ou non. Mesures : chaise sans accoudoir,
⊟ 85 ⊟ 43 ⊟ 50 ⊟ 46 cm■
chaise avec accoudoirs,
⊟ 85 ⊟ 53 ⊟ 50 ⊟ 46 cm■
tabouret,
⊟ 109 ⊟ 46 ⊟ 55 ⊟ 75 cm■
4. Chaise "Bo", 2002. Produite par Driade■
Réalisée en polypropylène. Peut être empilée. Apte pour un usage en extérieur. (Photo : T. Vack)■
⊟ 81 ⊟ 50 ⊟ 53 ⊟ 45 cm■
5. Chaise "Heritage". De Emeco■
Structure en aluminium. Le dossier est présenté en fibre de verre ou en bois.■
⊟ 84 ⊟ 44 ⊟ 51 ⊟ 46 cm■
6. Chaise "Toy", 1999. De Driade■
Réalisée en polypropylène. Peut être empilée. Apte pour un usage en extérieur■
⊟ 78 ⊟ 61,5 ⊟ 57,5 ⊟ 43 cm■
9. Chaise "Soft Egg", 2002. Produite par Driade■
Réalisée en polypropylène. Peut être empilée. Apte pour un usage en extérieur■
⊟ 74 ⊟ 60,5 ⊟ 57,5 ⊟ 43,5 cm■
(Photo : T. Vack)■

1949 Paris, France■

Beaucoup considèrent Philippe Starck comme le gourou par excellence du design contemporain. Une réincarnation moderne du Roi Midas qui transforme en or tout ce qu'il touche, depuis les intérieurs des hôtels et des bars, jusqu'aux yachts, motos, lunettes de soleil, ustensiles de cuisine ou chaises : rien ne semble pouvoir échapper à son influence créatrice. Cette activité prolifique a fait de lui un designer omniprésent■
Dans les années 80, il commença à créer des meubles et des compléments pour les boîtes les plus importantes du secteur, avec des objets aux formes suggestives pleines de sensualité et de personnalité. Certaines de ses créations supposent une nouvelle interprétation des anciens styles décoratifs, associant des matériaux contemporains à une esthétique passée■

Personnage controversé et plein de contradictions, il sut appliquer les règles du marketing à sa propre personne en s'entourant d'un halo de romantisme et de génie. Ces dernières années, il débuta une campagne contre le design pour le design, la consommation compulsive, défendant le besoin d'introduire dans le processus un aspect moral, honnête et objectif■
Il publia le catalogue Good Goods, comprenant plus de 200 objets "honnêtes", et prétendant ouvrir le chemin permettant de remplacer "la belle essence culturelle par le ticket humaniste du gaz". L'intention est de créer des objets écologiques, durables, ayant une raison légitime d'exister et respectant la personne. Starck s'inscrit parmi ceux qui pensent que le design peut changer le monde et aspire à "créer plus de bonheur et moins de choses"■

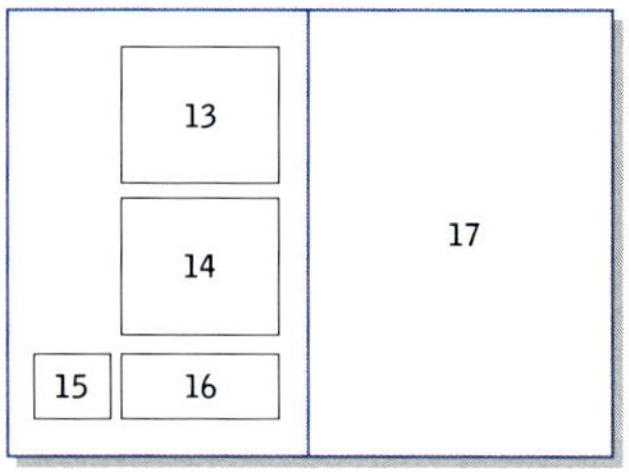

13. Chaise "Lord Yo", 1994. Produite par Driade■
Structure en aluminium. Carcasse en polypropylène. Peut être empilée. Apte pour un usage en extérieur■
⊟ 94,5 ⊟ 64 ⊟ 66 ⊟ 45 cm■

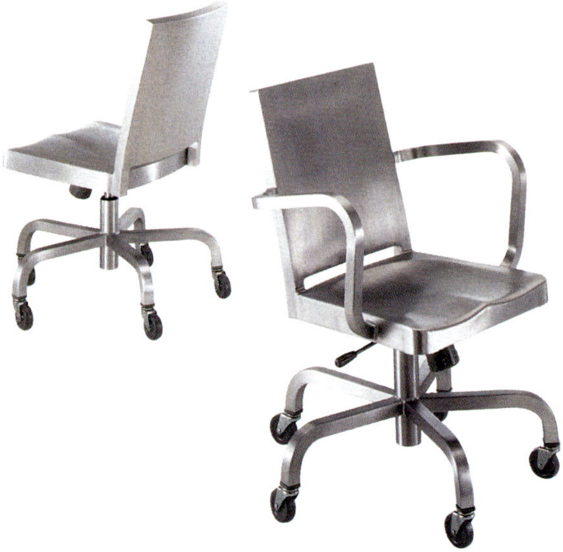

14. Chaise de bureau "Hudson". Produite par Emeco■
Réalisée en aluminium. Hauteur adaptable■
⊟ 79/86 ⊟ 61 ⊟ 61 ⊟ 41/48 cm■

15. Chaise "Ero/s/". Produite par Kartell■
Base rotatoire en aluminium. Carcasse en polycarbonate transparent ou coloré. En forme d'œuf organique■
⊟ 79 ⊟ 62 ⊟ 70 ⊟ 46 cm■

16. Fauteuil et canapé "Ploof", 2002. Produits par Kartell■
Pieds en aluminium poli. Siège et dossier en une seule pièce de polyuréthanne coloré■

17. Chaise de travail "Hula Hoop". Produite par Vitra■
Carcasse en polypropylène teint, avec accoudoirs et matelas intégrés. (Photo : M. Eggimann)■

MARCEL WANDERS

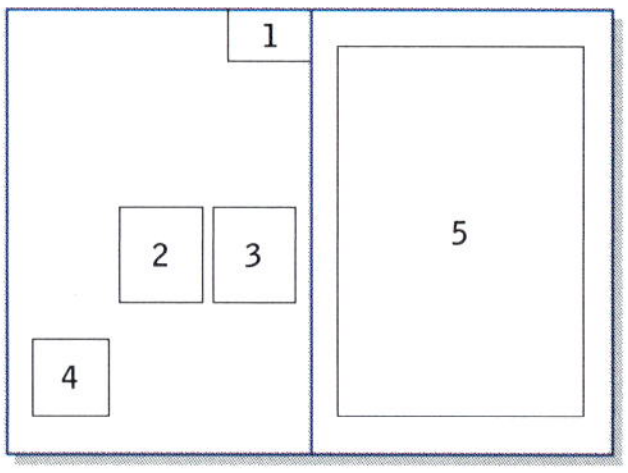

1 et 3. Chaise "Gwapa Lounge" et "Gwapa dinner", 2001. Produite par Moooi. (Photo : M. van Houten)▪ Structure en acier inoxydable. Il existe une version apte pour l'usage en extérieur. Mesures : lounge,
⊟ 61 ⊟ 78 ⊟ 82 cm▪
dinner,
⊟ 75 ⊟ 55 ⊟ 57 cm▪

2. Chaise "V.I.P.", 2000. Produite par Moooi. (Photo : M. van Houten)▪ Tapissée avec du tissu semblable au feutre▪
⊟ 78 ⊟ 62 ⊟ 53 cm▪

4. "Flower Chair", 2001. Produite par Moooi. (Photo : M. van Houten)▪ Structure en acier chromé▪
⊟ 65 ⊟ 78 ⊟ 74 cm▪

5. "Knotted Chair", 1996. Produite par Cappellini▪
Réalisée avec une corde gommée disposée manuellement sur un noyau de carbone. Le résultat ressemble à un travail en macramé. Prix Rotterdam Design▪
⊟ 70 ⊟ 50 ⊟ 65 cm▪

1963 Boxtel, Hollande▪

"Je suis ici pour créer un environnement d'amour, pour vivre avec passion et pour faire réalité mes rêves les plus émouvants"▪

Les apports de Marcel Wanders au monde du design industriel ont été un des principaux atouts dont le design hollandais s'est servi au cours des dernières années pour se placer en tête de l'Avant-garde, avec Amsterdam comme l'un des nouveaux centres du circuit international▪

Son travail suit la ligne de ceux qui souhaitent faire fusionner utilité et art en mettant en avant leur préoccupation pour la préservation écologique : "Le caractère durable dans le champ des idées, les relations, les objets, etc., ne crée pas seulement un monde moins gaspilleur, mais il crée également des relations plus profondes et plus significatives avec notre

environnement". En 1995, il fonda son propre studio à Amsterdam, après s'être rendu compte de la difficulté de trouver des producteurs pour des objets basés sur des concepts nouveaux ou différents, échappant à la beauté considérée normale. Une des bases de sa philosophie créatrice est l'exploration continue de l'interaction entre la technologie et la nature. Dans ses designs, Wanders adopte en général un changement technologique rapide et montre comment la nature peut accepter plus facilement l'innovation que la lutte contre le changement▪

Depuis quelques années, il est le directeur artistique de la compagnie hollandaise Moooi, qui est devenue une plate-forme pour les jeunes designers aux idées provocatrices et inusuelles lançant un défi constant à la signification conventionnelle de la beauté. L'objectif est de faire en sorte que les formes soient pleines de sens▪

ANDREA BRANZI

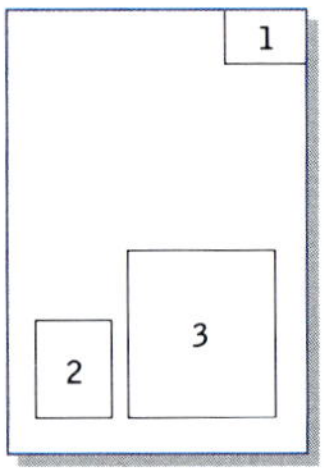

1 et 3. Chaise "Revers", 1993. Produite par Cassina■
Structure en aluminium. Siège en hêtre contre-plaqué. Dossier et accoudoirs formés par une bande en hêtre massif■
⊟ 76 ⊟ 64 ⊟ 51 ⊟ 45 cm■
(Photo : A. Zani)■
2. Chaise "Lori", 1995. Produite par Zanotta■
Totalement tapissée en peau■
⊟ 82 ⊟ 41 ⊟ 52 ⊟ 46 cm■

1938 Florence, Italie■

Membre fondateur, en 1964, du groupe de design radical ou anti-design Archizoom, le premier groupe de design d'avant-garde célèbre à niveau international, elle collabora également avec le Studio Alchimia et le Groupe Memphis. Branzi a toujours maintenu une attitude expérimentale et critique face à ce qu'on appelle le "Nouveau Design", aussi bien avec les objets qu'elle a créés qu'avec ses apports théoriques. On peut observer une preuve éloquente dans la collection d'objets-créatures qu'elle créa entre 1985 et 1986, appelée Animaux Domestiques et composée de designs fétichistes et contemplatifs réalisés avec des matériaux naturels suggérant des rites tribaux■
"Le design est une activité qui implique une pensée très complexe et qui a une logique propre originale dans laquelle l'exploration esthétique est liée à la stratégie industrielle et où la technologie n'est qu'une partie d'un contexte symbolique. Les relations entre l'art et le design ne sont par faciles à théoriser car elles sont toujours spontanées et discontinues"■

MATALI CRASSET

1965 Châlons-en-Champagne, France▪

Cette jeune designer est devenue une figure importante dans le panorama du design européen. Après avoir travaillé avec des créateurs de l'envergure de Denis Santachiara et Philippe Starck, avec qui elle collabora pendant cinq ans sur le développement d'articles pour Thomson, elle monta sa propre étude à Paris. Son activité s'étend du mobilier et compléments d'intérieurs à la mise en scène, l'architecture, la cosmétique, les bijoux et les vêtements▪
Sa vision du design est ludique, imaginative et poétique. Dans les meubles de sa création, son intérêt se centre sur l'aspect temporel des objets quotidiens et tente de fuir les intérieurs immobiles ou statiques. Crasset donne à ses pièces de mobilier flexibilité et mouvement, pour que l'utilisateur puisse décider comment et où il va les utiliser. On appelle ce type de situations flexibles "vie polyvalente"▪

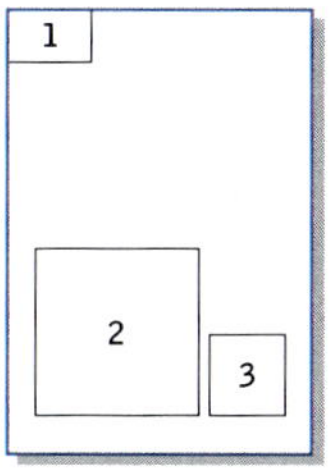

1 et 3. Chaise "Capriccio di Ugo". Produite par Domodinamica▪
Accoudoirs inclinables se transformant en supports et faisant office de tables d'appoint▪
⊟ 75 ⊟ 60/105 ⊟ 55 cm▪
2. Chaise de travail "Capriccio di Ugo". De Domodinamica▪
Version pour bureau, comprend des roulettes. Hauteur adaptable▪
⊟ 80/88 ⊟ 62 ⊟ 55 cm▪

NANNA DITZEL

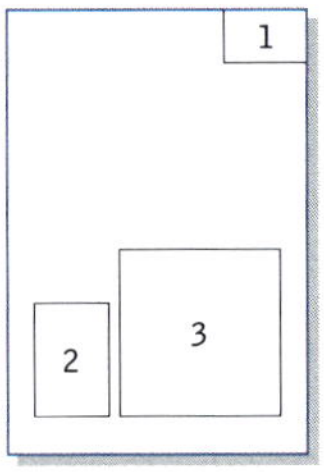

1 et 3. Fauteuil "Icon", 2002. Produit par Fredericia Furniture■
Structure en acier inoxydable. Siège et dossier tapissés. Dossier flexible■
2. Chaise "Sonar", 2000. Produite par Fredericia Furniture■
Structure métallique. Siège et dossier en bois, disponible en version tapissée. Peut être empilée■

1923 Copenhague, Danemark■

Récemment nommée "Première Dame du Design Danois de Mobilier" à l'Exposition du Meuble de Scandinavie, Nanna Ditzel crée des meubles innovateurs et fonctionnels depuis plus de cinq décennies■
Elle commença sa carrière après la 2e Guerre Mondiale, à une époque où très peu de femmes travaillaient dans le design de mobilier. Elle ressentit toujours le besoin de travailler sur de nouvelles techniques et de nouveaux matériaux, et créa des formes à la fois pratiques et novatrices. Ses meubles vont des pièces pluri-fonctionnelles qu'elle projeta à ses débuts et pensées pour s'adapter à de petits espaces, aux meubles en bois pour enfants ou aux chaises aux lignes exotiques inspirées de fleurs et de coquillages■
Nanna Ditzel est, avec Verner Panton, une des figures les plus influentes et importantes des dernières décennies dans son pays. Son talent sans âge et son âme éternellement jeune la poussent à continuer à créer des meubles■

FRANK GEHRY

"Créer une nouvelle chaise c'est comme si quelqu'un te demandait de réfléchir sur le sens de la vie alors que tu te trouves en équilibre sur une seule jambe"■

Frank Gehry est un des architectes les plus novateurs de l'actualité. Il utilise un vocabulaire formel qui lui est propre et fortement influencé par l'art contemporain qui le poussa à considérer ses projets comme s'il s'agissait de grandes sculptures réalisées à partir de la réinvention des matériaux■

Ses designs de meubles sont une interprétation de sa philosophie architectonique et reflètent son intérêt pour la manipulation de matériaux de base pour produire des objets fonctionnels et excitant au niveau visuel. Sa première collection de meubles, réalisée à la fin des années 60, est fabriquée avec du carton pressé dans le but de créer des meubles à la fois économiques et expressifs. Durant les dernières années, il réalisa des chaises avec du bois incurvé entrecroisé qui, comme pour ses collections précédentes, supposent une réaction contre les expectatives habituelles du marché du mobilier■

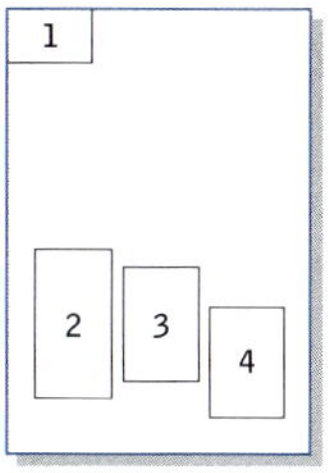

1 et 4. Chaise "FOG", 1999. Produite par Knoll■
Carcasse en aluminium et pieds en acier. Dossier flexible. Peut être empilée. Apte pour un usage en extérieur■

2. "High Sticking Chair". Produite par Knoll■
Inspirée par les caisses de pommes avec lesquelles il jouait lorsqu'il était petit, Gehry a créé cette série de chaises avec de minces bandes d'érable entrecroisées■

3. Chaise "Hat Trick". Produite par Knoll■
Structure en érable. Chaise modelée comme s'il elle était formée par des rubans■

STEFANO GIOVANNONI

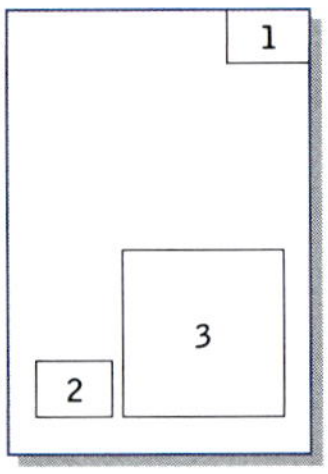

1. Chaise "Bombo", 1999. Produite par Magis▪
Base en acier chromé. Carcasse en ABS modelé par injection. Siège pivotant. Hauteur fixe ou adaptable▪
⊟ 85/96 ⊟ 40 ⊟ 40 ⊟ 46/56 cm▪

2. Fauteuil "Kalla". Produit par Domodinamica▪
Base rotatoire en aluminium. Siège tapissé avec du tissu élastique. Les accoudoirs peuvent s'ouvrir et se fermer pour obtenir de nombreuses positions▪
⊟ 88/99 ⊟ 58 ⊟ 58 ⊟ 48/59 cm▪

3. Chaise de travail "Bombo", 2000. Produite par Magis▪
Base en acier inoxydable. Carcasse en ABS. Roulettes en polyamide. Adaptable en hauteur avec un piston à gaz▪
⊟ 105,5 ⊟ 110/170 ⊟ 83 ⊟ 39 cm▪

1954 La Spezia, Italie▪

Stefano Giovannoni est un des plus grands représentants du design commercial, tourné vers la production massive. Ses objets sont colorés, amusants, simples, fonctionnels, accessibles à tous et s'inscrivant dans ce qu'on pourrait appeler "design démocratique". De fait, Giovannoni est une des figures centrales de la révolution qui supposa, dans les années 80, le dépassement du concept de design comme une chose élitiste et intellectuelle, et considérée comme un moyen de communication massif▪
Ses objets sont le reflet de sa passion pour les formes arrondies et de son intérêt pour les comics, la science fiction, la mythologie de la celluloïd et des sphères de la fiction artificielle et imaginative. Son objectif est de créer des objets aptes à la production massive, "le design m'intéresse comme facteur de grande consommation ; créer des objets pour tous a toujours été un de mes objectifs". Pour s'aider dans cette voie, il utilise des matériaux –en particulier le plastique– et des codes communicatifs innovateurs stimulant l'évolution du marché▪

KONSTANTIN GRCIC

1965 Munich, Allemagne■

Lorsqu'on interroge Konstantin Grcic, connu comme l'un des plus grands rénovateurs du design contemporain, à propos du futur de cette discipline, il répond en restant fidèle à sa philosophie de travail : "Nous ferons moins de produits, mais nous les améliorerons. Nous ferons des choses simples, mais nous ne les ferons pas plus simples. Nous aimerons les belles choses, mais elles pourront être rustiques. Nous utiliserons la technologie, mais de façon naturelle. Nous penserons à un marché massif, mais dans une masse d'individus. Nous travaillerons beaucoup, mais nous en profiterons énormément"■

Après avoir étudié à Londres et travaillé pendant une année avec Jasper Morrison, Grcic monta, en 1991, sa propre étude à Munich. Ses travaux sont le reflet de son amour pour les choses simples, de son pragmatisme, d'une minutieuse observation du monde des objets et d'une forte attraction pour l'histoire du design. La clarté de ses créations est souvent accompagnée de solutions inattendues alliant l'efficience à un voile d'ironie■

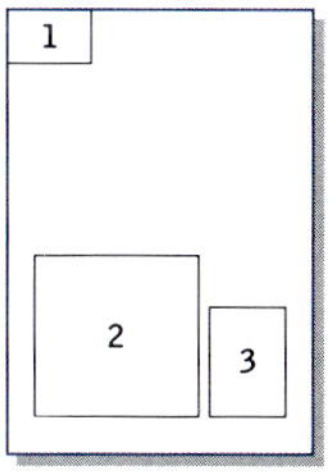

1 et 2. FAUTEUIL "CHAOS". Produit par Classicon■
Base en acier et tapissée en tissu ou en peau■
⊟ 74 ⊟ 90 ⊟ 66 ⊟ 42 cm■

3. CHAISE "TABAC", 2001. Produite par Montina■
Structure en frêne laminé. Siège tapissé en tissu ou en peau■
⊟ 78 ⊟ 51 ⊟ 57 ⊟ 46 cm■

MASSIMO IOSA GHINI

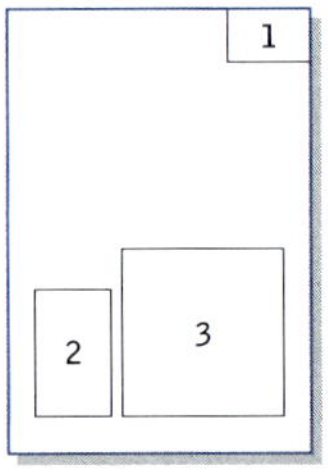

1 et 2. Chaise "Open". Produite par Domodinamica■
Structure en acier. Siège en bois recouvert de tissu. Dossier pliable permettant de transformer la chaise en tabouret■
⊟ 58/90 ⊟ 45 ⊟ 51 cm■
3. Tabouret "Open Bar". Produit par Domodinamica■
Structure en acier. Siège en bois recouvert de tissu. Dossier pliable■
⊟ 80/124 ⊟ 45 ⊟ 51 cm■

1959 Bologne, Italie■

Architecte et designer, Massimo Iosa Ghini se caractérise par sa participation dans les courants de l'avant-garde italienne, en tant que membre fondateur du Bolidismo –mouvement architectonique partant de l'analyse de la vitesse comme sujet dominant la réalité contemporaine–, et designer d'objets et d'intérieurs pour le groupe Memphis■
Iosa Ghini commença sa carrière comme dessinateur de comics extrêmement sophistiqués pour des revues à tendances et fit ensuite passer cette liberté expressive à des objets en trois dimensions. Depuis 1986, il a sa propre étude où il développe des projets allant de la définition de l'aspect esthétique d'un produit à l'étude du développement technique, de la construction de prototypes ou de la définition de l'identité du design intérieur pour les grandes compagnies comme Ferrari ou Superga. Ses travaux se caractérisent par des formes dynamiques et fluides évoquant une sensation de vitesse et renvoyant au style créé par le Bolidismo■

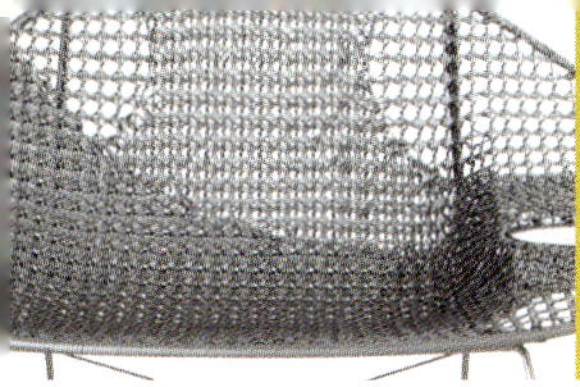

ROSS LOVEGROVE

1958 Cardiff, Gales▪

"Une grande chaise est comme un visage..., tu en connais des milliers mais seules quelques unes sont mémorables"▪
Ross Lovegrove est un des grands designers destinés à définir la culture de notre temps et à stimuler une nouvelle vision de l'avenir. Sa maxime est "la forme suit l'émotion", et il utilise comme axe de ses créations une optique humaniste à laquelle il associe, de façon équilibrée, son enthousiasme pour les procédures industrielles, son inspiration pour les formes de la nature et son habileté pour provoquer une réponse émotionnelle dans les utilisateurs. Le résultat sont des formes organiques, ergonomiques et durables▪
Depuis son étude à Londres, fondée en 1990, il crée des objets pour les compagnies leaders du secteur. Il se sert des matériaux les plus novateurs, comme le polypropylène, la fibre de carbone ou de magnésium, et des technologies permettant de développer des produits faciles à utiliser et à produire ; il montre, en même temps, une sensibilité marquée pour l'écologie▪

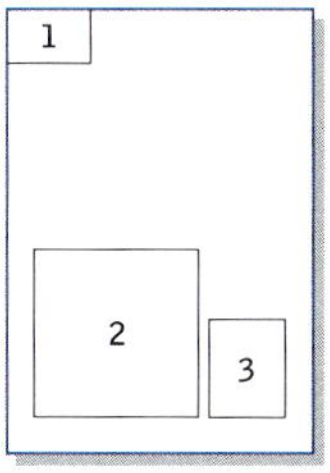

1. SIÈGE "LOVENET SILVER", 2002. Produit par Moooi▪
Structure en acier avec tissu PE. La largeur des accoudoirs permet de l'utiliser comme table d'appoint▪
⊟ 90 ⊟ 150 ⊟ 80 cm▪
2. CHAISE DE BUREAU "SPIN", 1997. Produite par Driade▪
Structure en acier. Carcasse en polypropylène. Hauteur adaptable▪
⊟ 77/88 ⊟ 69 ⊟ 55 ⊟ 40/51 cm▪
3. FAUTEUIL "AIR ONE", 2000. Produit par Edra▪
Fauteuil pouvant être empilé réalisé avec de la mousse de polypropylène. Très léger▪
⊟ 53 ⊟ 115 ⊟ 115 cm▪

ENZO MARI

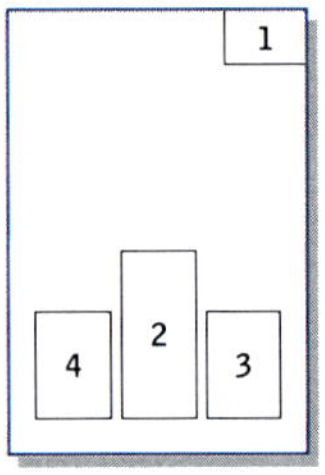

1 et 4. Chaise "Delfina", 1979. Produite par Robots▪
Structure en acier chromé. Dossier et siège en coton Kvadrat. Prix Compasso d'Oro 1979▪
⊟ 79 ⊟ 48 ⊟ 57 ⊟ 47 cm▪
2. Chaise "Tonietta", 1985. Produite par Zanotta▪
Structure en aluminium poli ou peinte en noir. Siège et dossier tapissés en peau ou en nylon peint▪
⊟ 82 ⊟ 39 ⊟ 48 ⊟ 46,5 cm▪
3. Chaise "Marina", 1991. Produite par Zanotta▪
Structure en bois. Siège et dossier tapissés en peau▪
⊟ 83,5 ⊟ 39 ⊟ 48 ⊟ 46,5 cm▪

1932 Novara, Italie▪

Selon Alberto Alessi dans le livre L'Usine de Rêves : "Enzo Mari est le plus grand interprète de la vision "pure et dure" du design appliqué à la production industrielles : ne pas se laisser aller à la fantaisie expressive, pas d'oripeau formel gratuit, mais une recherche constante de cette simplicité qui, à elle seule, devrait justifier la naissance d'un nouveau produit dans notre société de consommation déjà trop peuplée"▪

Enzo Mari est devenu un des représentants de grande autorité du design italien, grâce à sa recherche constante et à son travail sur les formes et les significations qui, souvent, s'opposent aux tendances du design industriel actuel. Dans son travail théorique, il reste sur une position critique face à la société de consommation et aux commandements du marketing qui est à l'origine d'une grande partie de la production actuelle et est devenu le protagoniste du débat sur cette profession. Pour toutes ces raisons, il est considéré comme "la conscience critique du design"▪

MARC NEWSON

1963 Sydney, Australie■

Marc Newson est un des designers "cultes" du XXIe siècle, avec une approche futuriste, novatrice et techniquement rigoureuse du monde du design qui lui a permis de projeter aussi bien des chaises qu'un jet privé ou une voiture■

Le développement de ses projets l'a parfois poussé à se comporter comme un ingénieur capable de construire ses propres bicyclettes, montres ou même, sa première pièce de mobilier, la Lockheed Lounge, qu'il fabriqua en 1987 avec une base en fibre de verre recouverte d'une plaque en aluminium et qui représenta sa plate-forme de lancement■

Installé à Londres depuis 1997, après avoir travaillé plusieurs années à Sydney, Tokyo et Paris, Marc Newson se caractérise par une pensée hautement créative et anticonformiste qui le poussa à fuir des typologies existantes et à les observer depuis une perspective latérale en imaginant quelle en serait la version parfaite : "ce qui m'a toujours stimulé en tant que designer a été la gêne provoquée par la cochonnerie qui m'entoure et le besoin de l'améliorer"■

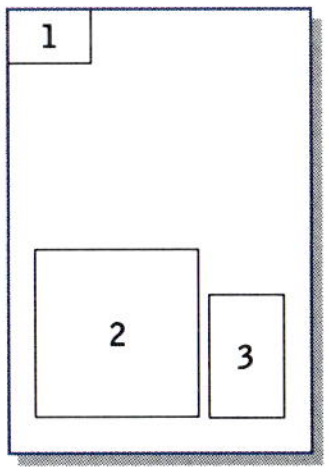

1 et 3. "Coast Chair", 2002. Produite par Magis■
Structure en polypropylène renforcé avec de la fibre de verre. Siège et dossier tapissés en laine ou en peau■
⊟ 79,5 ⊟ 48,5 ⊟ 48,5 ⊟ 45,5 cm■

2. "Felt Chair", 1989. Produite par Cappellini■
Structure en fibre de verre modelée avec des formes ergonomiques. Pieds en aluminium. Elle se fabrique également avec une structure tapissée en tissu ou en peau■
⊟ 86 ⊟ 67 ⊟ 106 cm■

REFLETS MÉTALLIQUES
ALUMINIUM, ACIER...

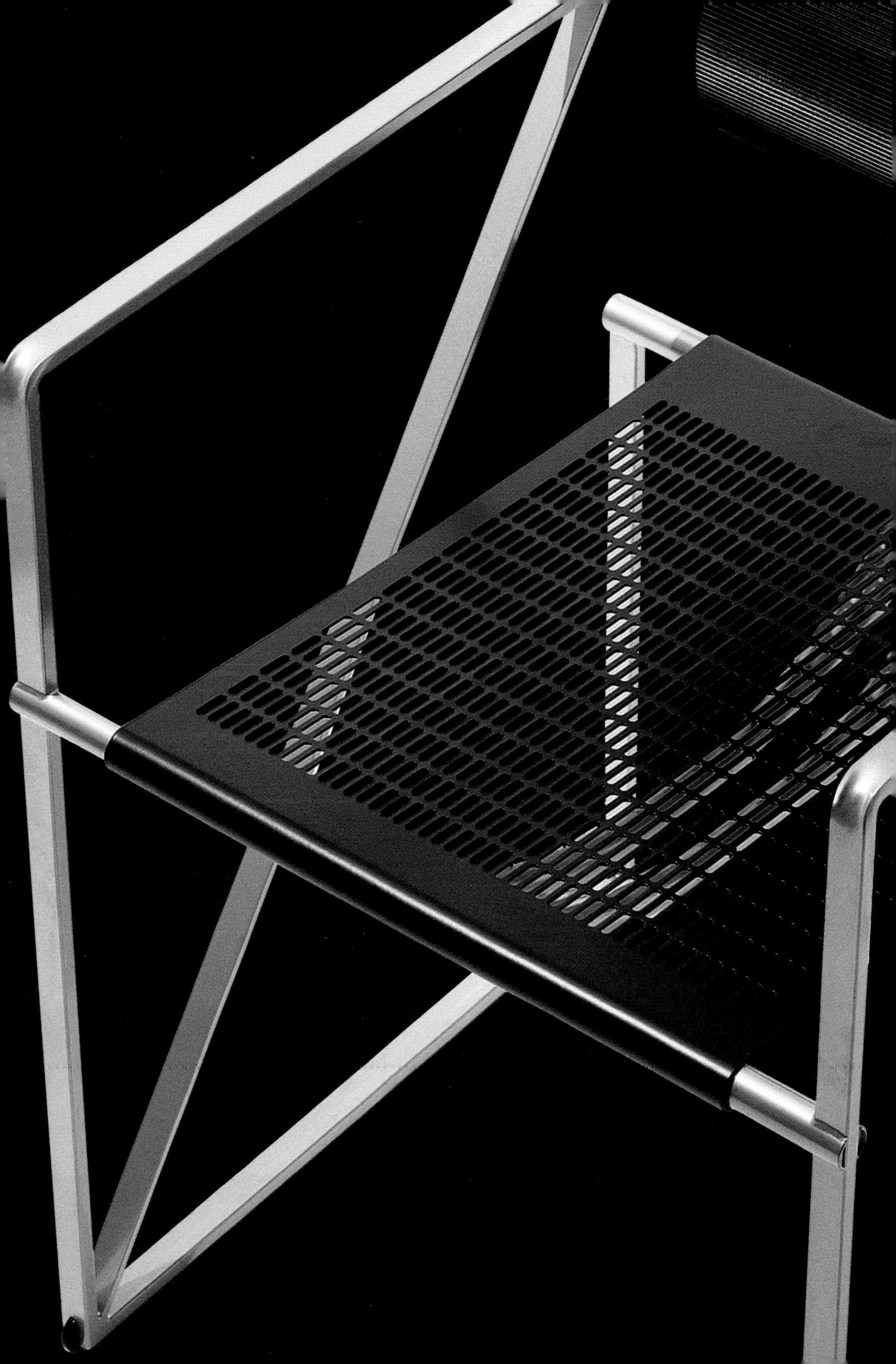

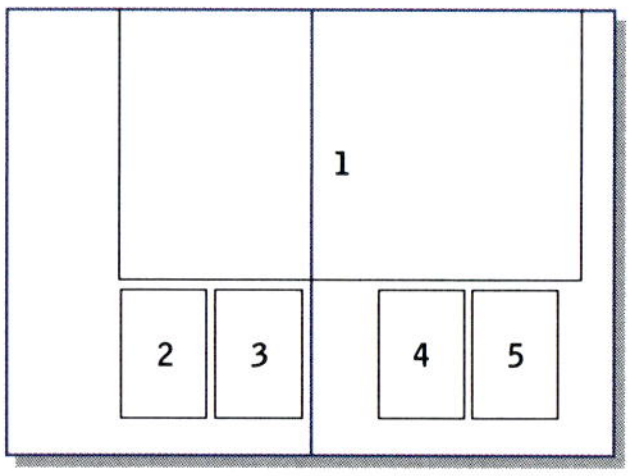

1. FAUTEUIL "BLOOM", 2000. De Giorgio Cazzaniga pour Living Divani■
Combinaison de base en acier avec siège en bois, tapissé à l'intérieur■
2. CHAISE "GAZELLA", de Jonathan Crinion pour Sintesi■
Structure en tube d'acier. Siège et dossier en feuilles de métal pressées■
⊟ 82 ⊟ 51 ⊟ 58 cm■
3. CHAISE "PAKI" de Bruno Rainaldi pour Alivar (Collection Brilliant Furniture)■
Structure en acier. Siège et dossier tapissés en tissu ou en peau. Peut être empilée■
⊟ 81 ⊟ 45 ⊟ 55 cm■
4. CHAISE "MEGAN". Produite par Galvano Tecnica■
Structure en tube d'acier. Siège et dossier en polypropylène■
⊟ 81 ⊟ 50 ⊟ 62 ⊟ 44 cm■
5. CHAISE "MIRANDOLINA", 1992. De P. Arosio pour Zanotta■
Structure en aluminium. Peut être empilée. Apte pour un usage en extérieur■
⊟ 84 ⊟ 48 ⊟ 53 ⊟ 46 cm■

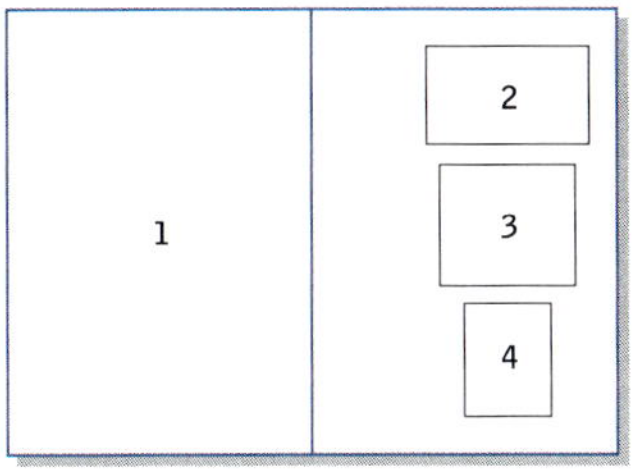

1. CHAISE "ZILLI", 2002. De Roberto Barbieri pour Zanotta■
Structure en aluminium poli ou peint, siège et dossier en grille de polyester avec PVC ou tapissés en tissu ou en peau. Peut être empilée. Apte pour un usage en extérieur■
⊟ 78 ⊟ 49 ⊟ 54 ⊟ 46 cm■

2. CHAISE "GAS", 2002. De Jesús Gasca pour Stua■
Structure en aluminium brillant. Siège et dossier tapissés ou grille synthétique. Prix IF Design Award. Prix Red Dot Design■
⊟ 78,5 ⊟ 50 ⊟ 48 ⊟ 44 cm■

3. CHAISE "COSMOS", 1999. De Gunilla Allard pour Lammhults■
⊟ 80 ⊟ 44/50 ⊟ 51 ⊟ 46 cm■

4. CHAISE "LAGOA", de Enrico Franzolini pour Accademia■
Structure en aluminium. Siège et dossier en polypropylène ou en chêne■
⊟ 79 ⊟ 44 ⊟ 53 ⊟ 46 cm■

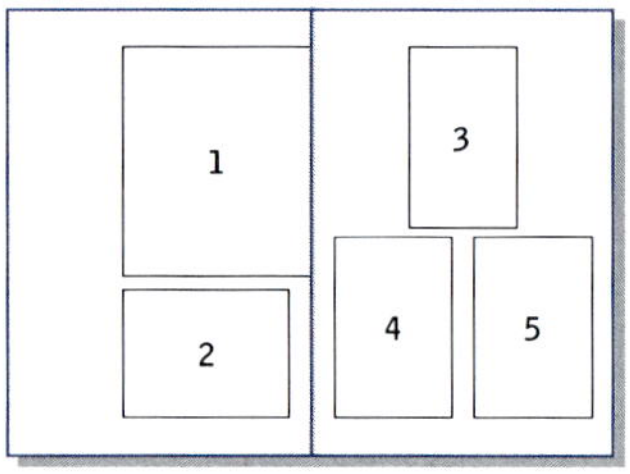

1. Chaise "Boulevard", 1994-95. De F. A. Porsche pour Ycami■
Réalisé en aluminium. Peut être empilée■
⊟ 77 ⊟ 55 ⊟ 57 ⊟ 44 cm■

2. Chaise "Alu Uno", 2000. De Kurt Thut pour Indecasa■
Structure en aluminium. Multiples combinaisons de dossier en polypropylène ou en aluminium et siège en bois contre-plaqué ou en aluminium■
⊟ 73 ⊟ 42,5 ⊟ 49,5 ⊟ 45 cm■

3. Chaise "Zebra". Produite par Sintesi■
Structure en tube d'acier. Siège et dossier en bois résistant à l'eau■
⊟ 82 ⊟ 56 ⊟ 58 ⊟ 47 cm■

4. Chaise "Talle", de P. King et S. Miranda pour Sellex■
Structure en acier inoxydable. Carcasse du siège formée par une plaque contre-plaquée incurvée■

5. Chaise "Ginestra", 1994. De P. Scarzella et P. Rasulo pour Zanotta■
Structure en aluminium. Siège et dossier en fibre naturelle■
⊟ 82 ⊟ 45 ⊟ 52 ⊟ 45 cm■

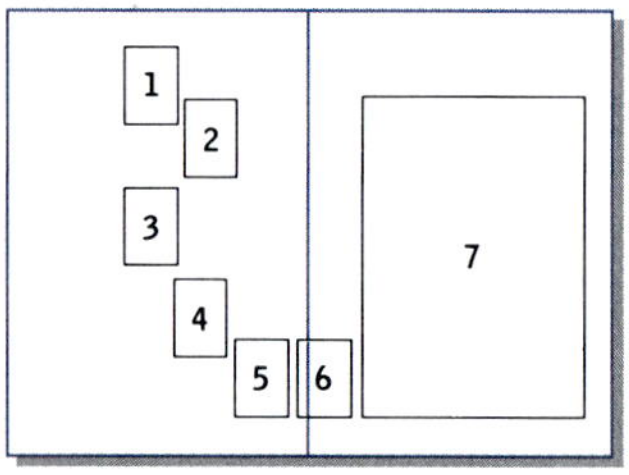

1. Chaise "Ginger", 1998. De Maurizio Peregalli pour Zeus Noto■ Structure en acier. Siège et dossier en métal■
⊟ 81 ⊟ 49 ⊟ 54 ⊟ 46 cm■

2. Chaise "Zebra", de Johnny Sørensen pour Magnus Olesen■ Structure en acier tubulaire. Siège tapissé et dossier en hêtre ou en noyer■

3. Chaise "Frame", de Arco Meubel■ Structure métallique avec finition chromée brillante ou mate. Siège et dossier tapissés en tissu ou en peau■
⊟ 83 ⊟ 50,5 ⊟ 57 ⊟ 45 cm■

4. Chaise "Lilly", de Sintesi■ Structure en tube d'acier. Siège et dossier en bois contre-plaqué recouvert d'aluminium■
⊟ 85 ⊟ 40 ⊟ 50 ⊟ 46 cm■

5. Chaise "Donald", de Studio Cerri & Associati pour Poltrona Frau■ Structure en aluminium. Siège et dossier tapissés en peau, avec le système de couleur Pelle Frau®. Pliable■
⊟ 76 ⊟ 46 ⊟ 49 ⊟ 45 cm■

6. Chaise "S60", de Glen Oliver Löw pour Thonet■
Structure en saillie en acier. Carcasse du siège en bois, tapissée en tissu ou en peau. Nouvelle interprétation de la chaise Thonet de 1931 créée par Mart Stam■
⊟ 65 ⊟ 55 ⊟ 63 cm■

7. Chaise "Antalya". Créée par Aldo Cibic pour Bisazza■
Structure en aluminium, recouverte à la base par une mosaïque de verre Vetricolor (20x20 mm)■

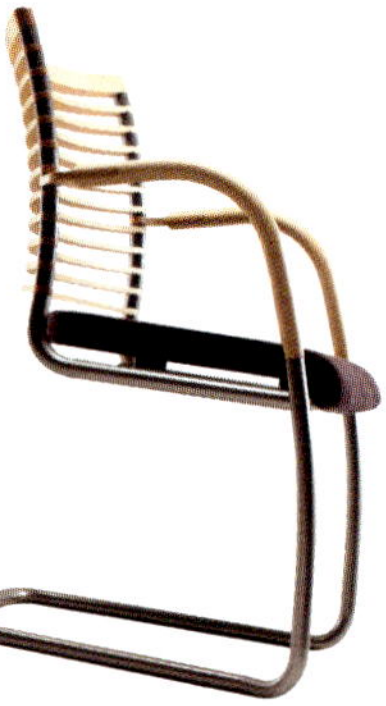

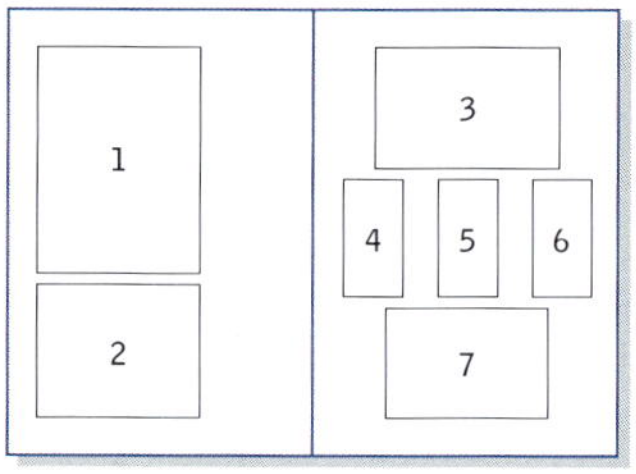

1. Tabouret "Jim", de James Bruer et Scot Laughton pour Pure Design
Base en acier chromé et siège en aluminium. Deux hauteurs possibles : 76,2 et 61

2. Tabouret "Copa", 1995. De Alfredo Arribas pour Casas
Support en aluminium fondu. Siège en polypropylène tapissé. Trois hauteurs possibles : 80, 65 et 45 cm

3. Tabouret "Sputnik", de Vibiemme
Base en acier. Siège pivotant en plastique
93 59 82 59 cm

4. Tabouret "Starla", de Pure Design
Structure en acier. Siège tapissé en vinyle. Deux hauteurs possibles : 76,2 et 61 cm

5. Tabouret "Jacana", de Claudia e Mattia Frignani pour Wunderkammer Studio
Réalisé en aluminium fondu
78 40 40 cm

6. Tabouret "Glow" de Rodolfo Dordoni pour Fontana Arte
Le siège comporte un éclairage, et il remplit donc également une fonction de lampe

7. Tabouret "Tantus", 2001. De Joan Casas Ortínez pour Indecasa
Structure et siège en aluminium. Siège pivotant. Trois hauteurs possibles : 80, 65 et 45 cm

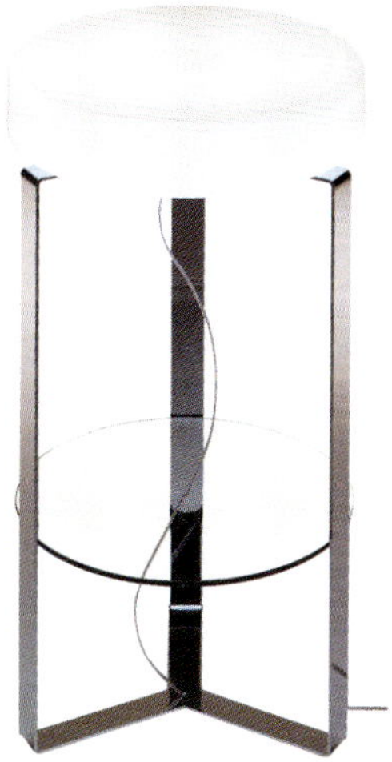

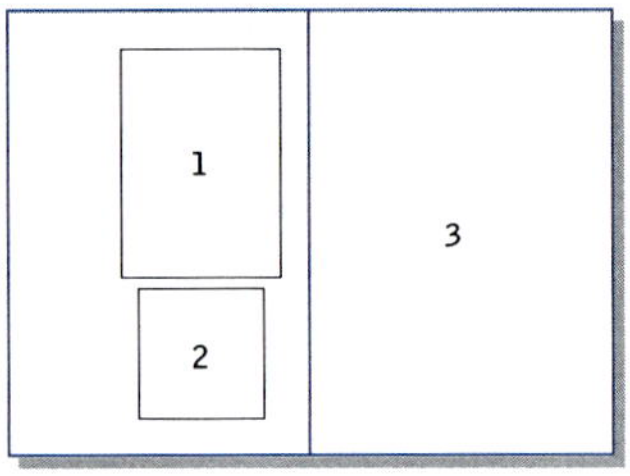

1. Tabouret "Table-stool", de Richard Hutten pour Pure Design■
Remplit la fonction de table d'appoint et de tabouret. Structure en acier peint. Deux hauteurs possibles : 76,2 et 61cm■

2. Tabouret "Jamaica" de Pepe Cortés pour Amat 3 (photo fournie par Knoll)■
Structure en tube d'acier chromé ou peint. Siège pivotant en aluminium fondu ou en hêtre massif. Il existe une version avec roulettes. Trois hauteurs possibles : 77, 64 et 43 cm■

3. Tabouret "Coco", de Studio Kronos pour Cattelan Italia■
Structure en acier et siège en hêtre ou tapissé en peau■
⊟ 76/64 ⊟ 40 ⊟ 43 cm■

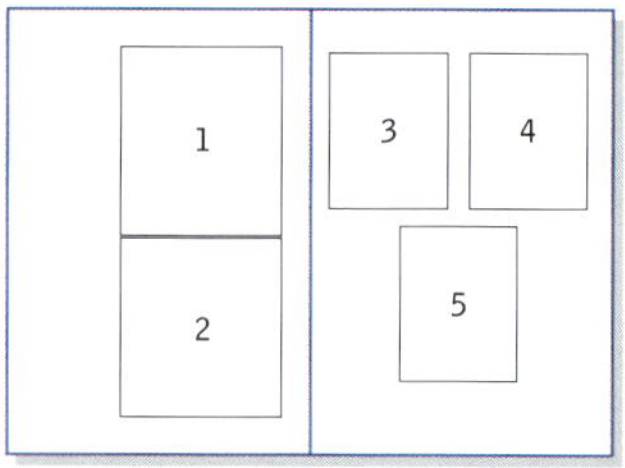

1. Chaise et tabouret "Gaja" de Kazuhide Takahama. Produits par Ultramobile■
Structure en tube d'acier chromé. Siège tapissé en caoutchouc et laine synthétique. Chaise :
⊟ 67 ⊟ 51 ⊟ 44 ⊟ 46 cm■
tabouret :
⊟ 85 ⊟ 51 ⊟ 44 ⊟ 64 cm■
2. Chaise "Gin-Integra" 2002. Design de Mario Mazzer pour Ycami■
Structure en aluminium■
⊟ 81 ⊟ 43 ⊟ 53 ⊟ 46 cm■
3 et 4. Chaise "Secondas" de Mario Botta pour Alias■
Structure en acier. Siège en acier perforé et dossier avec élément cylindrique en polyuréthanne■
5. Chaise créée par Mario Botta. Produite par Alias■
Formes sculpturales pour cette chaise dont la structure est en acier émaillé■

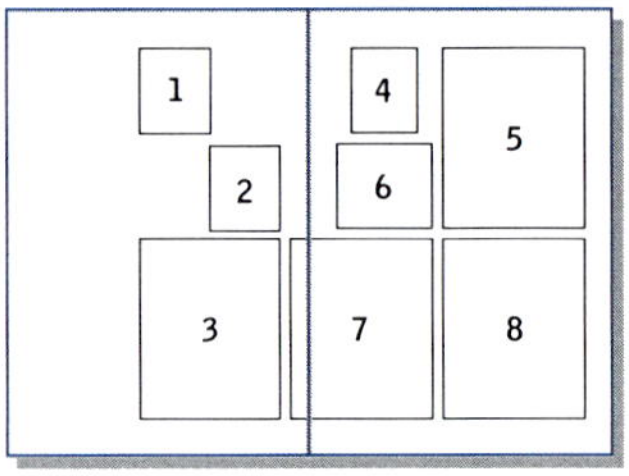

1. Fauteuil "Centomila", 2001. De James Irvine pour Magis■
Structure en tube d'acier verni. Siège et dossier en polypropylène. Peut être empilé■
⊟ 70 ⊟ 66,5 ⊟ 57 ⊟ 39,5 cm■

2. Chaise "A900F", de Norman Foster pour Thonet■
Structure en aluminium. Siège et dossier en polypropylène transparent. Peut être empilée■
⊟ 80 ⊟ 55 ⊟ 53 cm■

3. Chaise "Tulu" de Kazuhide Takanama pour Ultramobile■
Structure en tube d'acier chromé. Siège et dossier tapissés en caoutchouc et laine artificielle. Peut être empilée■
⊟ 73 ⊟ 48 ⊟ 51 ⊟ 43 cm■

4. Fauteuil "FTL Milana" de Jean Nouvel pour Sawaya & Moroni■

5. Chaise "Vassili", de Sintesi■
Nouvelle interprétation du modèle classique créé par Marcel Breuer. Structure en tube d'acier. Siège et dossier en PVC■
⊟ 78 ⊟ 78 ⊟ 79 cm■

6. Fauteuil "Spaguetti" de Giandomenico Belotti pour Alias■
Structure en acier. Siège et dossier en PVC transparent. Peut être empilé■
⊟ 71 ⊟ 68 ⊟ 59 ⊟ 42 cm■

7. Chaise "Tempesta", Tanzi Design pour Album■
Structure en acier tubulaire. Siège et dossier en acier inoxydable. Peut être empilée. Roulettes et accoudoirs en option■
⊟ 78 ⊟ 54 ⊟ 51 ⊟ 46 cm■

8. Chaise "Zilli", 2002. De Roberto Barbieri pour Zanotta■
Structure en aluminium poli ou peint, siège et dossier en grille de polyester avec PVC. Peut être empilée. Apte pour un usage en extérieur■
⊟ 78 ⊟ 49 ⊟ 54 ⊟ 46 cm■

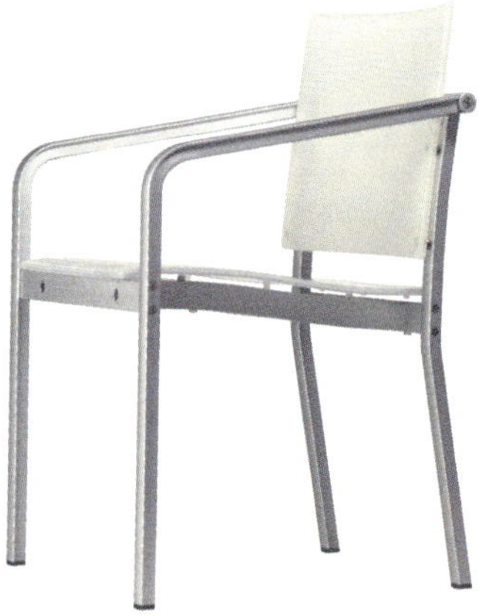

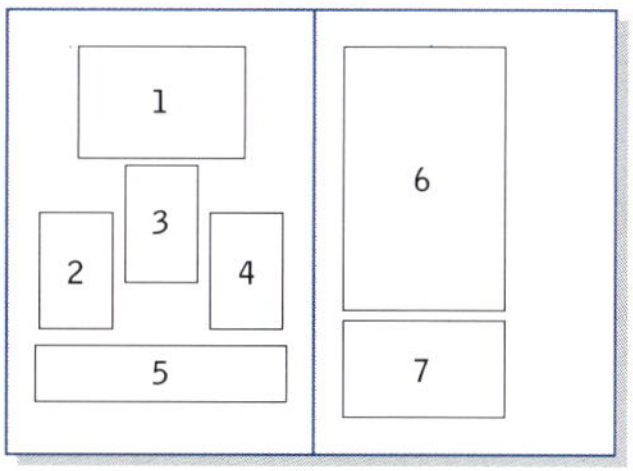

1. Collection "Sedia", de Maurizio Peregalli pour Zeus Noto■
Structure en acier. Dossier en gomme. Le siège peut être fabriqué avec différents matériaux. Peut être empilé. Mesures chaises :
⊟ 81 ⊟ 40 ⊟ 44,5 ⊟ 47 cm■

2. Chaise "Unisex" de Raul Barbieri pour Alivar (Gallery Collection)■
Structure en acier chromé ou peint. Dossier et siège en peau, en noyer ou laqués en blanc■
⊟ 78/82 ⊟ 48,5 ⊟ 54 cm■

3. Chaise "3400" des archives historiques de Fontana Arte■

4. Chaise "Mies" de Natison Sedia■
Structure en tube d'acier. Siège et dossier en polypropylène. Peut être empilée■
⊟ 82 ⊟ 52 ⊟ 55 ⊟ 43 cm■

5. Fauteuil "Cinquanta", 2000. De William Sawaya pour Sawaya & Moroni■

6. Chaise "Margherita", 1997. De Carlo Colombo pour Ycami■
Structure en aluminium. Siège et dossier en polycarbonate transparent ou en couleurs. Apte pour un usage en extérieur■
⊟ 82 ⊟ 42 ⊟ 54 ⊟ 45 cm■

7. Fauteuil "Lips", 2000. De Piergiorgio Cazzaniga pour Dema■
Structure en acier inoxydable. Carcasse en bois laminé, tapissé à l'intérieur■
⊟ 71 ⊟ 95 ⊟ 72 cm■

TAPISSERIES

TEXTURE, COULEUR, CONFORT

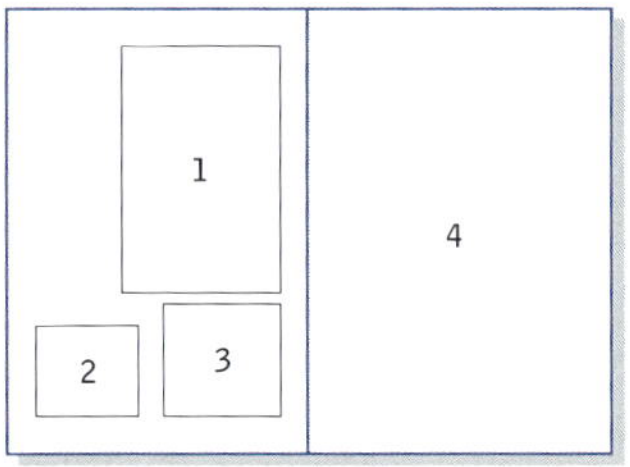

1. Chaise "Orea", de Gerard van den Berg pour Label
91 47 51 47 cm
2. Chaise à bascule "Roly Poly", 2000. De Guido Rosati pour Giovannetti
Structure en résine renforcée avec de la fibre de verre. Tapissée en polyuréthanne indéformable recouvert de tissu protecteur
3. Fauteuil "Sunset", 1997. De Cristophe Pillet pour Cappellini
Structure en métal verni couleur aluminium. Siège pivotant en bois contre-plaqué tapissé en tissu ou en peau
75 82 45 41 cm
4. Fauteuils bas "Tokio", 1997. De Nancy Robbins pour Andreu World
Tapissé avec une grande variété de tissus. Les dossiers sont disponibles en format arrondi ou carré

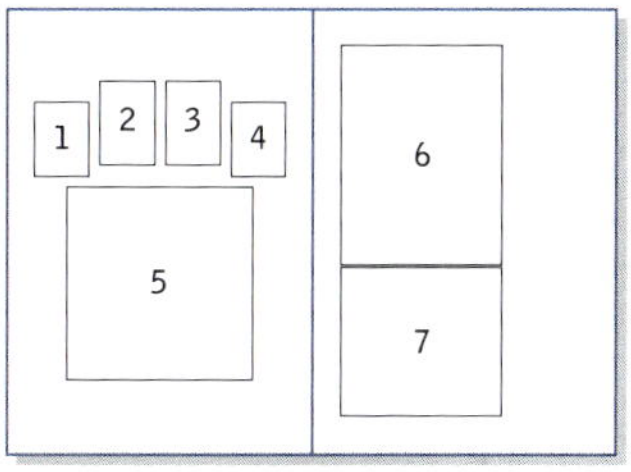

1. Chaise "Magazine" de Heitlinger Design pour Calligaris
90,5 45 55 46,5 cm
2. Chaise "Donna" de Johannes Foersom et Peter Hiort-Lorenzen. Produite par Erik Jørgensen
3. Chaise "Anna" de J. Broente pour Bonaldo
4. Fauteuil "Mosquito" de Fabrizio Gallinaro pour Natison Sedia
Structure en acier chromé. Pieds adaptables
5. Fauteuil-chaise à bascule "Swing", de Denis Santachiara pour Domodinamica
Base en ABS. Rotation de 360°
86 83 83 cm
6. Chaise "Tiba" de Gerard van den Berg pour Label
81 61,5 53,5 46,5 cm
7. Chaise "Nefer", 1999. De Diego Fortunato pour CJC Concepta
Structure en hêtre. Siège et dossier tapissés en tissu ou en peau

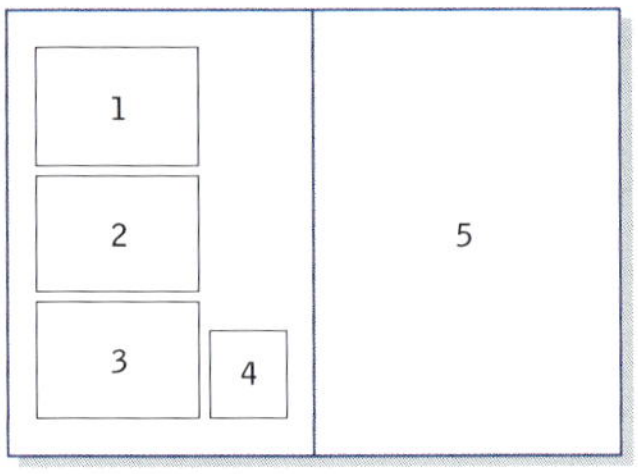

1. Chaise "Mikado", de Arco Meubel▪
Structure en acier inoxydable. Siège et dossier tapissés en tissu, en peau ou en bois laqué. Pieds synthétiques transparents ou en aluminium▪
□ 85 ⊟ 52 ⊟ 47 □ 47 cm▪

2. Chaise "S81", de Thonet▪
Structure en acier tubulaire flexible. Siège et dossier tapissés▪
□ 84 ⊟ 54 ⊟ 56 cm▪

3. Fauteuil "S555", 2000. De Jehs & Laub pour Thonet▪
Structure en acier. Carcasse du siège en bois contre-plaqué, tapissée à l'intérieur▪
□ 79 ⊟ 75 ⊟ 69 cm▪
(Photo : M. Gerlach)▪

4. Chaise "Triennale", 1954/2002, création de Willem H. Gispen. Produite par Leolux▪
Ce modèle est un classique du design allemand▪
□ 83 ⊟ 69 ⊟ 70 cm▪

5. Chaise "Asia", 2001. De Enrico Franzolini pour Crassevig▪
Structure en acier chromé. Siège et dossier tapissés ou en bois▪
□ 81 ⊟ 48 ⊟ 52 cm▪

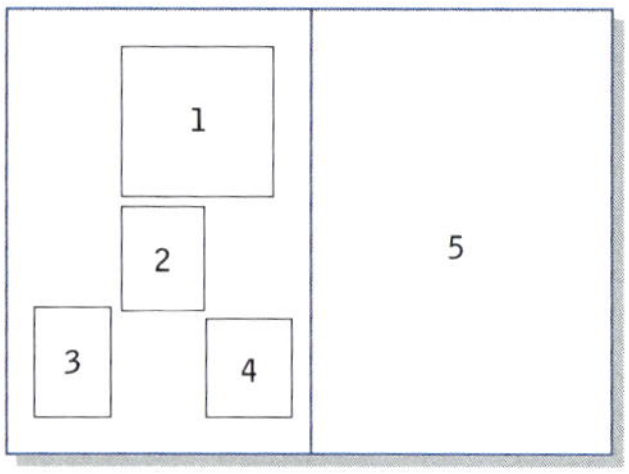

1. Tabourets "Cubo", 2000. De Diego Fortunato pour CJC Concepta■
Structure en barre d'acier massif. Siège en bois tapissé■
⊟ 80 ⊟ 28 ⊟ 28 cm■
2 et 4. Tabourets "Soshun", 1990. De Masanori Umeda pour Edra■
Structure métallique laquée. Siège tapissé en velours de plusieurs couleurs. Deux hauteurs possibles. Diamètre : 56 cm■
3. Tabouret "Trampie", 1996. De Paolo Golinelli pour Zoltan■
Structure en aluminium. Tapissé en peau ou en coton. Quatre hauteurs possibles : 80, 70, 48 ou 30 cm■
5. Tabouret "Otto", 2002. De Design For Use pour Zanotta■
Structure en acier. Tapissé en tissu, en alcantara ou en peau■

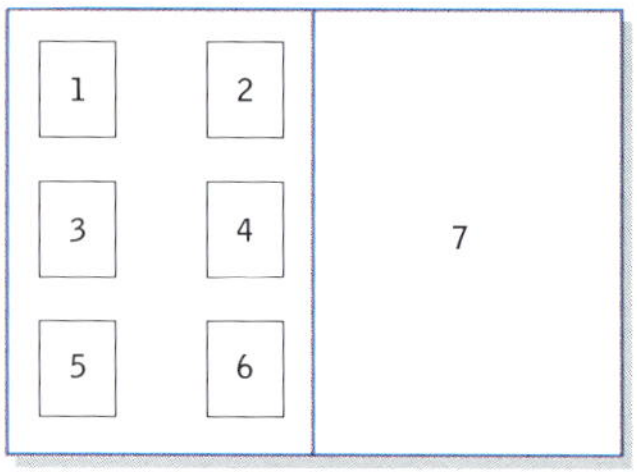

1. Fauteuil "Solo" de Christian Steiner pour Schmidingermodul■
Structure en hêtre■
⊟ 88 ⊟ 62 ⊟ 78 cm■

2. Chaise "Fizz" de Daniele Lo Scalzo Moscheri pour Alivar (Gallery Collection)■
Structure en acier. Carcasse en bois tapissée en tissu ou peau■
⊟ 80 ⊟ 48,5 ⊟ 55,5 cm■

3. Fauteuil "Waiting" de CJC Concepta■

4. Chaise "Smilla", 2002. De Piergiorgio Cazzaniga pour Acerbis International■

5. Fauteuil "Gigi" de Gerard van den Berg pour Label■
Siège pivotant■
⊟ 67 ⊟ 108 ⊟ 83 ⊟ 38 cm■

6. Fauteuil "Popi Pop", créée par le Studio Ingenieria Modular pour Domodinamica■
Nouvelle interprétation des formes classiques. Dossier inclinable■
⊟ 107 ⊟ 100 ⊟ 82 cm■

7. Chaise "Meggy", de Ca'Nova Design pour Cattelan Italia■
Existe également sans accoudoir■
⊟ 85 ⊟ 43 ⊟ 52 ⊟ 46 cm■

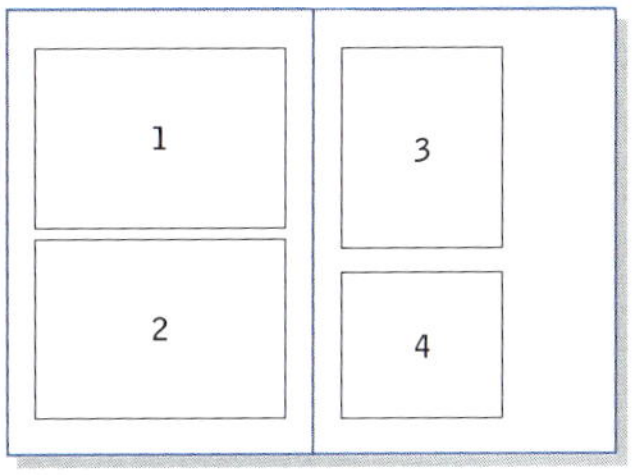

1. Fauteuil "Saghi", de Kazuhide Takanama pour Ultramobile■
67 64 76 40 cm■
2. Fauteuil "Bent", 2000. De Piergiorgio Cazzaniga pour Dema■
Structure en acier. Existe avec ou sans accoudoirs■
72 84 88 cm■
3. Chaise "Fun Bukko", de Natison Sedia■
Structure en acier. Tapissée en peau ou en tissu■
4. "Stafford Chair", 1998. De Andrew Stafford pour SCP■
Carcasse en fibre de verre. Intérieur entièrement tapissé. Pieds en érable■
78 84 88 42 cm■

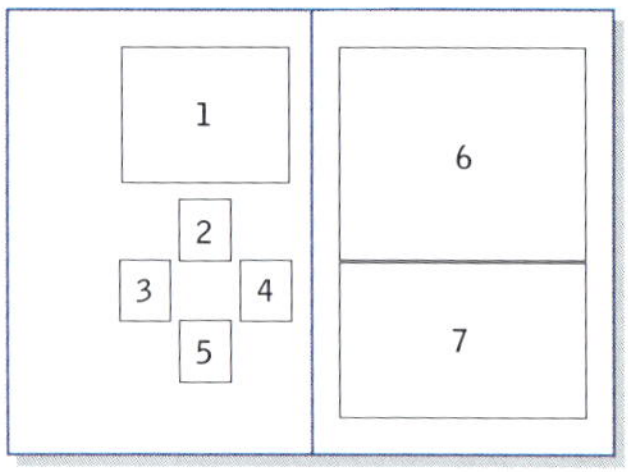

1. Fauteuil "Dandy" de Gijs Papavoine pour Montis■
Tapissé en tissu ou en peau■
2. Chaise "Shells", 2002. De Martin Ballendant pour Tonon■
Prix Good Design Award 2002 du Chicago Athenaeum. Prix Focus Gold 2002 d'Allemagne■
3. Fauteuil "Shell" de Club 8 Company■
4. Chaise "Greta" de Enrico Franzolini pour Accademia■
Structure en chêne naturel. Mesures : chaise,
⊟ 78 ⊟ 50 ⊟ 57 ⊟ 46 cm■
fauteuil,
⊟ 79 ⊟ 58 ⊟ 59 ⊟ 46 cm■
5. Fauteuil "Nikita" de Gerard van den Berg pour Label■
6. Chaise "Circo" de Peter Maly pour Cor■
Siège pivotant. Options de tapisseries multiples■
⊟ 71 ⊟ 61 ⊟ 57 cm■
7. Fauteuil "Malindi" de O. Moon pour Porada■
Structure en cerisier ou en noyer. Tapissé en tissu ou bandes de cuir■
⊟ 75 ⊟ 62 ⊟ 81 cm■

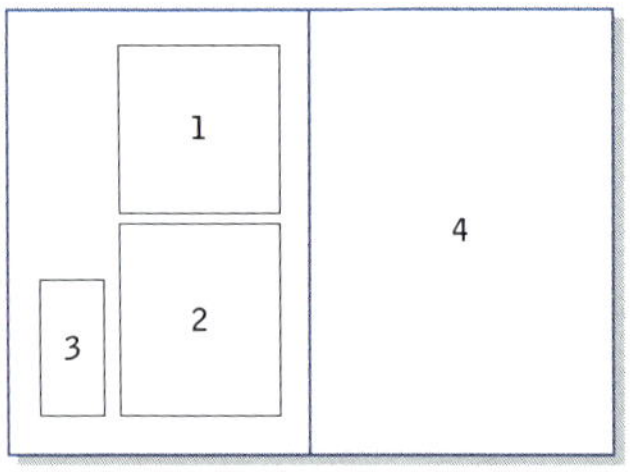

1. Fauteuil "Pancras" de Borgensen & Voll pour Iform■
Siège tapissé en tissu ou en peau. Carcasse en bois modelé par compression■
2. Fauteuil "Corona" de Poul M. Volther pour Erik Jørgensen■
3. Chaise "Pause-Café" créée par Pascal Mourgue pour Artelano■
4. Chaise "Eleonoire" de Ca' Nova Design pour Cattelan Italia■
⊟ 110 ⊟ 49 ⊟ 58 ⊟ 50 cm■

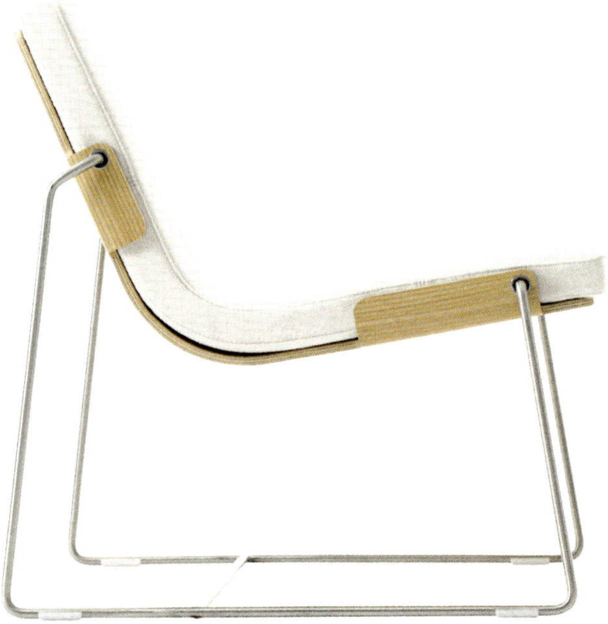

BOIS ET FIBRES NATURELLES

NOUVELLE INTERPRÉTATION DE LA MATIÈRE CLASSIQUE

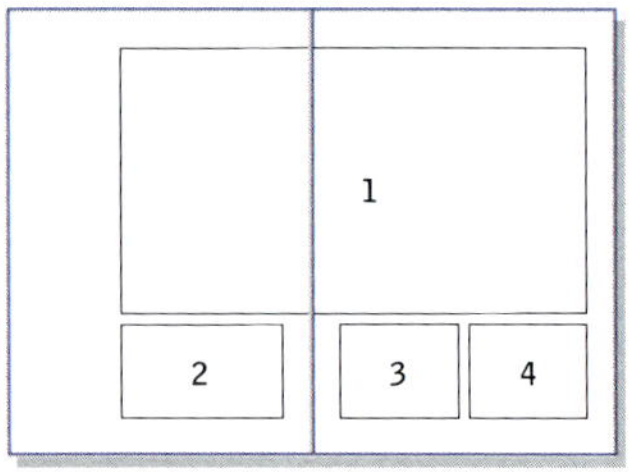

Page précédente :
CHAISE "BALESTRA" de Enzo Berti pour Lago
Structure en noyer. Siège tapissé en peau

1. CHAISE "ALIS", 2000. De Palomba Serafini pour Crassevig
Structure en acier chromé. Siège en bois laminé. Deux mesures possibles :
⊟ 81 ⊟ 52 ⊟ 54 cm
⊟ 81 ⊟ 58 ⊟ 55 cm

2. CHAISE "ECO", 2000. De Peter Karf pour Iform (Collection Voxia)
Structure en hêtre laminé, modelé d'une seule pièce. Peut être empilée. Prix IF Design
⊟ 81 ⊟ 45 ⊟ 48 ⊟ 45 cm

3. CHAISE "NXT", 2001. De Peter Karf pour Iform (Collection Voxia)
Structure en bois laminé modelé d'une seule pièce. Prix Red Dot
⊟ 75 ⊟ 51 ⊟ 46 ⊟ 45 cm

4. CHAISE "GLOBUS", de Jesús Gasca pour Stua
Structure en acier. Siège et dossier en bois laminé laqué de couleur, ou en finition hêtre, cerisier ou wengé. Peut être empilée
⊟ 85 ⊟ 47 ⊟ 55 cm

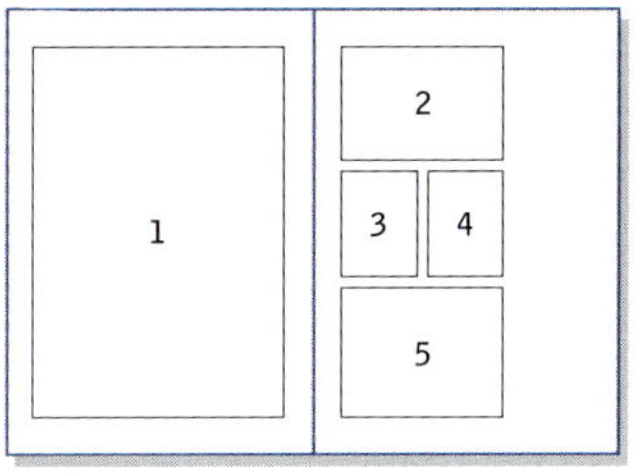

1. Chaise "Anna", 1998. De Palomba Serafini pour Crassevig■
Structure en hêtre. Siège en bois contre-plaqué ou tapissé■
⊟ 87 ⊟ 56 ⊟ 51 cm■

2. Chaise "Omu", de Oswald Matias Ungers pour Sawaya & Moroni■

3. Chaise "Delta" de Christian Steiner pour Schmidinger■
Structure en hêtre. Peut être empilée■
⊟ 81,5 ⊟ 49 ⊟ 51,5 ⊟ 45,5 cm■

4. Chaise "Primo" de Ruud Ekstrand pour Iform■
Structure en hêtre. Siège tapissé■
⊟ 80 ⊟ 42 ⊟ 51,5 ⊟ 44 cm■

5. Chaise "Seagrass", de Karin Tyrefors pour Iform■
Structure en frêne. Siège et dossier en tissu de corde naturel■

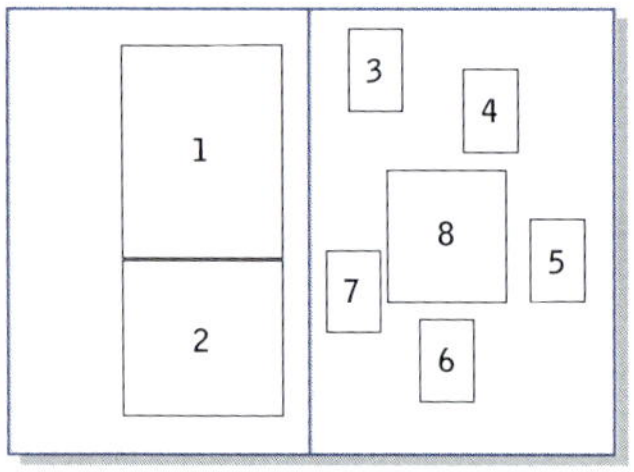

1. Fauteuil "Room 26", création de Arne Quinze et Yves Milan pour Quinze & Milan■
⊟ 56 ⊟ 65 ⊟ 100/62 ⊟ 32 cm■
2. Tabouret "Room 26" création de Arne Quinze et Yves Milan pour Quinze & Milan■
3. Chaise "Laleggera" de Riccardo Blumer pour Alias■
Existe en cerisier, érable ou wengé. Peut être empilée■
⊟ 79 ⊟ 44 ⊟ 53 ⊟ 46 cm■
4. Chaise "Tuli", de Marco Romanelli pour Montina■
Structure en chêne. Siège et dossier tapissés en tissu ou en peau■
⊟ 84 ⊟ 52,5 ⊟ 55,5 ⊟ 46,5 cm■
5. Chaise "Vela", de Driade■
Structure en hêtre. Siège et dossier en conglomérat industriel■
6. Chaise "Ballerina", 1991. De L. Bertoncini pour Bernini■
7. Chaise "Pab", de Paul Baber pour Pure Design■
Structure en acier. Siège en bois laminé modelé■
⊟ 80 ⊟ 48,3 cm■
8. Chaise "Round" de Stefano Bianchi pour Sintesi■
Structure et accoudoirs en tube d'acier. Siège et dossier en bois contreplaqué■
⊟ 82 ⊟ 59 ⊟ 59 ⊟ 46 cm■

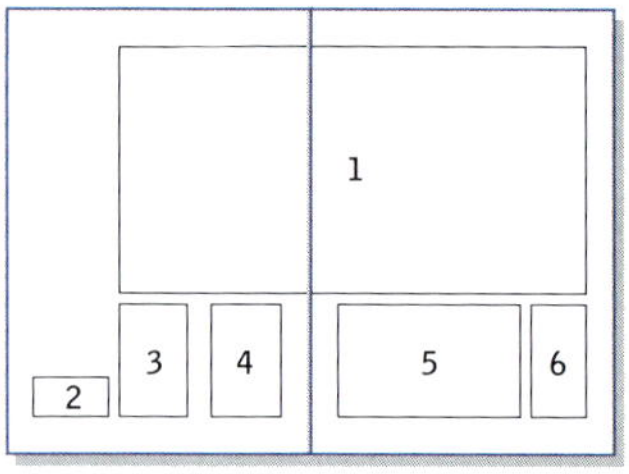

1. Chaise de la série "8000" de Rud Thygesen et Johnny Sørensen pour Magnus Olesen■
Structure en hêtre laminé. Peut être empilée■
2. Tabouret "Hula", 2000. De Barber Osgerby pour Cappellini■
3. Tabouret "Origami", de Enrico D. Bona pour Montina■
Réalisé en chêne■
4. Chaise "Hans", de Philipp Mainzer pour e15■
Structure en acier inoxydable. Siège et dossier en noyer européen■
⊟ 80 ⊟ 43 ⊟ 50 cm■
5. Chaise "S664" de Eddie Harlis pour Thonet■
Structure en tube d'acier. Carcasse du siège en bois contre-plaqué■
⊟ 85 ⊟ 60 ⊟ 52 cm■
6. Chaise "Diva", 1987. De William Sawaya pour Sawaya & Moroni■
Structure en bois. Siège tapissé en peau■
⊟ 87 ⊟ 43 ⊟ 46 cm■

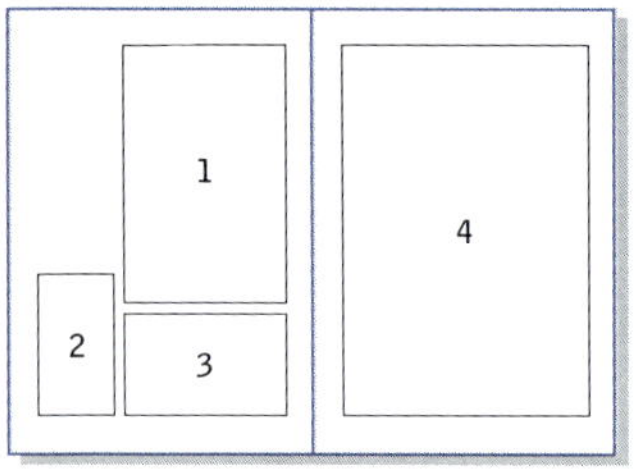

1. CHAISE "MIKADO", de Arco Meubel▪ Structure en acier inoxydable, avec pieds synthétiques de couleur transparente, noire ou aluminium. Carcasse du siège en bois contre-plaqué▪
⊟ 85 ⊟ 42 ⊟ 47 ⊟ 47 cm▪

2. CHAISE "JANET", de Sintesi▪ Structure en tube d'acier carré. Siège et dossier en bois contre-plaqué verni couleur cerisier ou naturel▪
⊟ 86,5 ⊟ 41,5 ⊟ 50 cm▪

3. CHAISE "COLORI", de Natison Sedia (Collection FUN Tasia)▪ Structure en tube d'acier. Carcasse du siège en bois laminé. Peut être empilée▪
⊟ 80 ⊟ 47 ⊟ 52 ⊟ 46 cm▪

4. CHAISE "CAMPUS", 1992. De Johannes Foersom et Peter Hiort-Lorenzen pour Lammhults▪
⊟ 76 ⊟ 47 ⊟ 49 ⊟ 45 cm▪

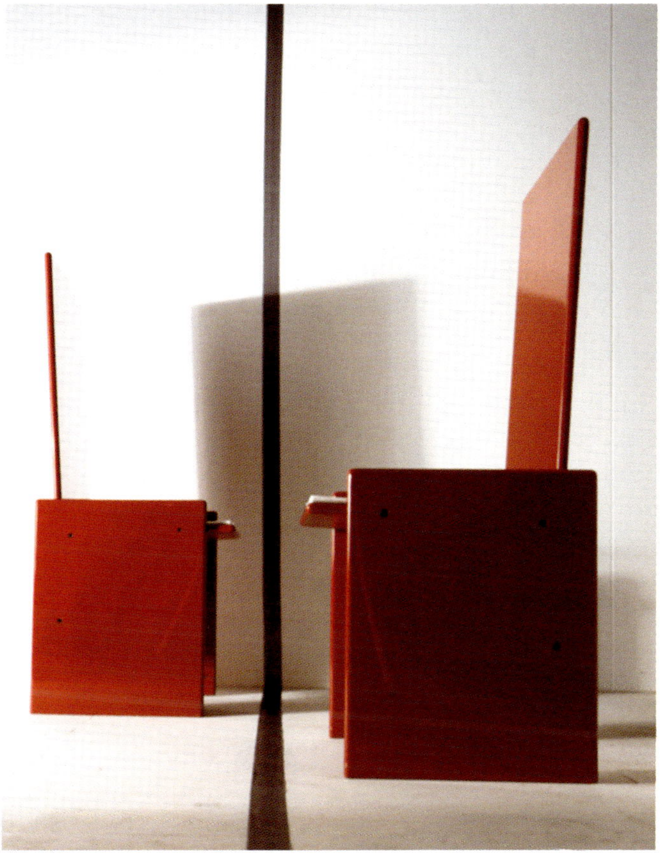

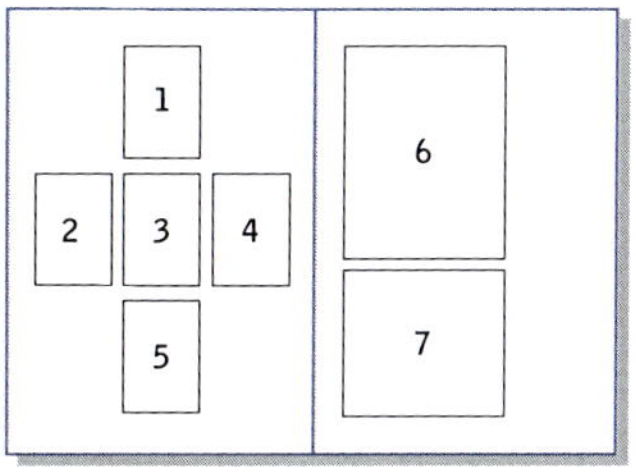

1. Chaise "Ho" de Luca Meda pour Molteni & C■
Structure en bois contre-plaqué de noyer, cerisier, wengé ou érable. Jointure en métal pour unir les pieds, le siège et le dossier■
⊟ 80 ⊟ 51 ⊟ 50 cm■

2. Dossier "Egoa", 1988. De Josep Mora pour Stua■
Structure en acier chromé. Siège en hêtre, frêne, cerisier ou wengé. Le dossier s'adapte à la position du dos. Prix Innovative Design de Melbourne■
⊟ 82 ⊟ 50 ⊟ 54 ⊟ 41 cm■

3. Chaise "All", 2000. De Laura Silvestrini pour Giorgetti■
Structure en hêtre. Accoudoirs et dossier en aluminium. Transformable de chaise à fauteuil. Mesure : chaise,
⊟ 80 ⊟ 53 ⊟ 57 cm■
fauteuil,
⊟ 83 ⊟ 53 ⊟ 51 cm■

4. Chaise "Portoghesa 3200" de Helena Ladeiro pour Sintesi■
Structure et accoudoirs en tube d'acier. Siège en bois contre-plaqué modelé■
⊟ 87 ⊟ 46 ⊟ 55 cm■

5. Chaise "Apta", 1996. De Gabriel Teixidó pour Andreu World■
Structure métallique, siège et dossier en hêtre verni. Peut être empilée■

6. Chaise "Kazuhi" de Kazuhide Takahama pour Ultramobile■
⊟ 107 ⊟ 46 ⊟ 47 ⊟ 43,5 cm■

7. Fauteuil "Upper Lips", 2000. De Piergiorgio Cazzaniga pour Dema■
Structure en acier inoxydable. Carcasse en bois laminé, tapissé à l'intérieur■

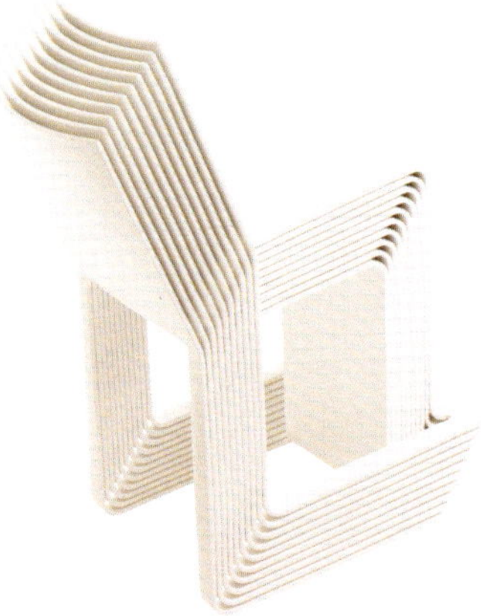

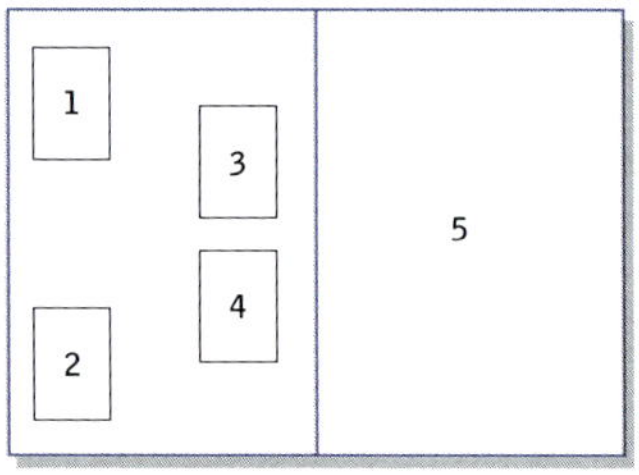

1. Chaise "Eco", 2000. De Peter Karf pour Iform (Collection Voxia)▪
Structure en hêtre laminé, modelé d'une seule pièce. Peut être empilée. Prix IF Design▪
⊟ 81 ⊟ 45 ⊟ 48 ⊟ 45 cm▪

2. Chaise "Runner", 1997. De Kasper Salto pour Fritz Hansen▪
Structure en tube d'acier. Siège et dossier en bois laminé. Peut être empilée▪
⊟ 83 ⊟ 46 ⊟ 42,5 ⊟ 45 cm▪

3. Chaise "The King of Schu", de Sirch et Bitzer pour Schmidinger▪
Réalisée en hêtre▪
⊟ 87 ⊟ 38 ⊟ 52 cm▪

4. Chaise "Sixta", 2000. De Miguel Milà pour CJC Concepta▪
Structure en tube d'acier. Siège, dossier et pieds avants en hêtre contreplaqué. Siège tapissé. Peut être empilée▪
⊟ 86 ⊟ 56 ⊟ 58 cm▪

5. Chaise "Parade" de Rud Thygesen et Johnny Sørensen pour Magnus Olesen▪
Pieds en tube d'acier. Siège et dossier en érable ou en hêtre laminé. Peut être empilée▪

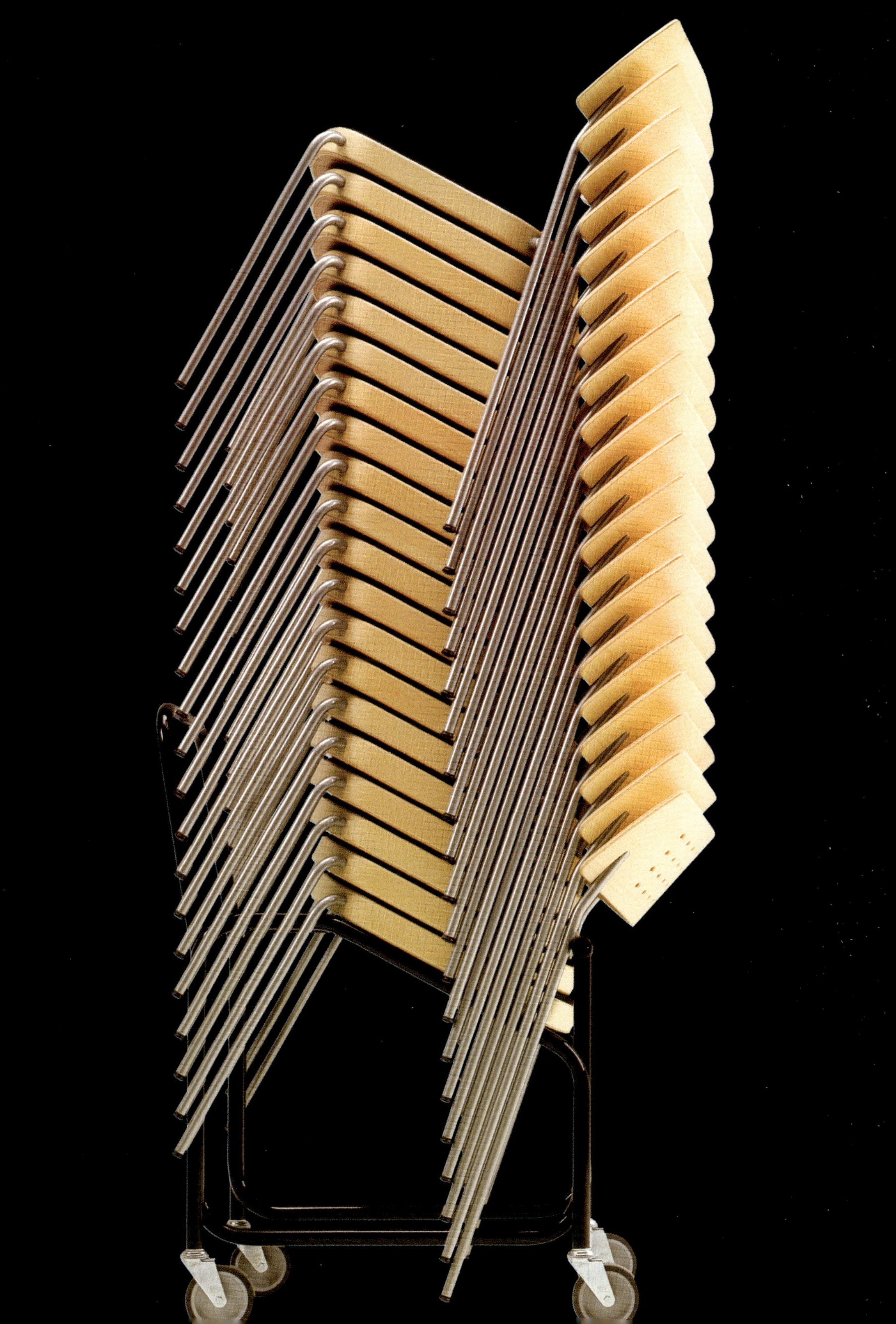

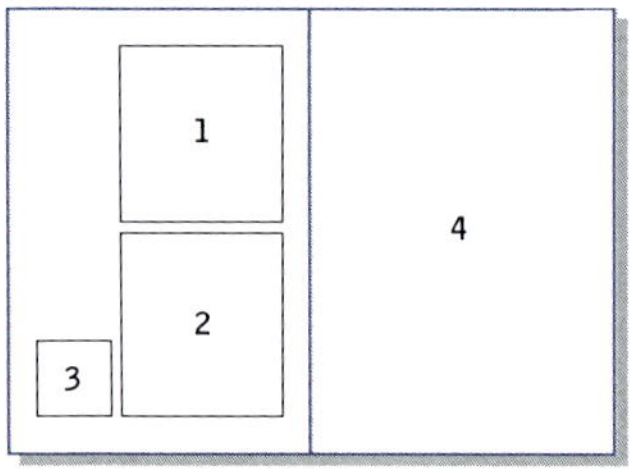

1. Chaise "30 x 30", 1999. De Niall O'Flynn pour CJC Concepta■
Structure en hêtre. Siège et dossier en bois contre-plaqué incurvé■
⊟ 73 ⊟ 42 ⊟ 54 ⊟ 45 cm■
2. Chaise "Ampolla", de Enzo Berti pour Lago■
Structure en noyer. Siège tapissé■
3. Chaise "Tri", de Peter Karf pour Iform (Collection Voxia)■
Structure en bois laminé modelé d'une seule pièce■
⊟ 80 ⊟ 55 ⊟ 45 ⊟ 45 cm■
4. Chaise "Lola", de Giacomo Passal pour Andreu World■
Structure en hêtre massif. Siège tapissé■

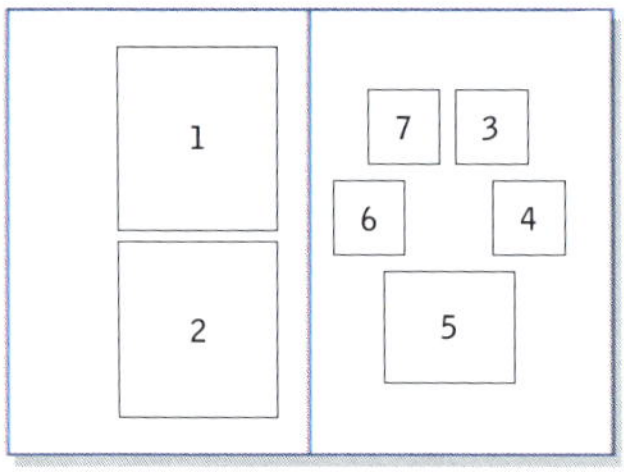

1. Chaise "Xus" de Iform
Structure en saillie réalisée en hêtre laminé d'une seule pièce

2. Chaise "Oto", 2001. De Peter Karf pour Iform (Collection Voxia)
Modelée d'une seule pièce en hêtre contre-plaqué. Prix IF Design
71 78 61 38 cm

3. Chaise "Bossi" de Markus Pfyl pour Schmidinger
Réalisée en bois laminé
78,5 51,5 53,5 43,5 cm

4. Chaise "Ayu", 2002. De Roderick Vos pour Driade
Structure en acier peint en blanc. Recouvrement en moelle. (Photo : T. Vack)

5. Chaise "Riga", 1997. De M. Marconato et T. Zappa pour Bernini

6. Chaise "Young Lady" de Paolo Rizzatto pour Alias
Structure en aluminium. Cadre du siège et dossier en cerisier, canné. Siège pivotant
80 59 59 48 cm

7. Chaise "Hop" de Lorenzo Merani pour Schmidinger
Réalisée en bois laminé verni
72,5 68,5 72 cm

PEAU AU-DELÀ DU TEMPS QUI PASSE...

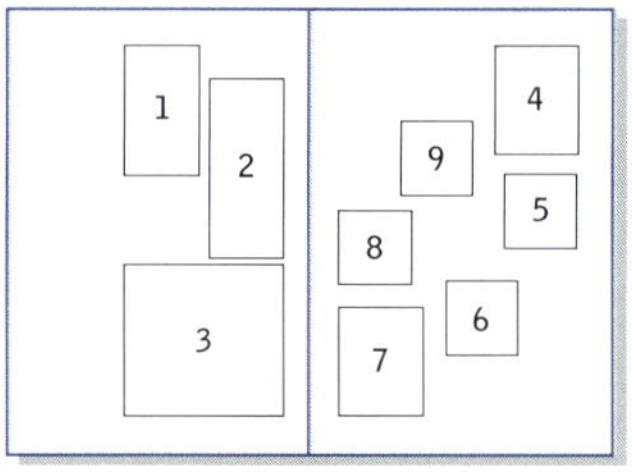

1. Chaise "Tecna" de Edy et Paolo Ciani pour Calligaris▪
⊟ 86 ⊟ 46,5 ⊟ 54,5 ⊟ 46 cm▪
2. Chaise "Elba" de Yoshiharu Hatano pour Frag▪
Structure en acier. Siège et dossier tapissés en peau▪
⊟ 81 ⊟ 40 ⊟ 46 ⊟ 45 cm▪
3. Fauteuil "Bancoquine" de Yamakado▪
⊟ 72 ⊟ 77 ⊟ 77 cm▪
4. Chaise "Circo" de Peter Maly pour Cor▪
Siège pivotant. Options de tapisseries multiples. Dossier avec bandes de peau tressées▪
⊟ 71 ⊟ 61 ⊟ 57 cm▪
5. Fauteuil "3244", 1998. De Peter Mogensen pour Fredericia Furniture▪
Structure en bois. Siège et dossier tapissés en peau ou en tissu▪
6. Fauteuil "Donna" de Gerard van den Berg pour Label▪
Structure en tube d'acier. Siège et dossier en tissu ou en peau▪
⊟ 98,5 ⊟ 62,5 ⊟ 62 ⊟ 49,5 cm▪
7. Fauteuil "Derby", 2000. De Eoos pour Matteograssi▪
Prix Good Design 2002, décerné par le Chicago Athenaeum Museum of Architecture and Design▪
8. Fauteuil "Bravo" de Sergi et Oscar Devesa pour Oken▪
Structure en tube d'acier et tapisserie en peau de vache. Technologie basée sur les classiques du Bauhaus▪
⊟ 71 ⊟ 64,6 ⊟ 64 cm▪
9. Fauteuil "Riri" de N. Gerosa et S. Vaio pour Dema▪
Structure en métal recouverte de bandes de peau entrecroisées. Siège avec coussin tapissé en peau▪

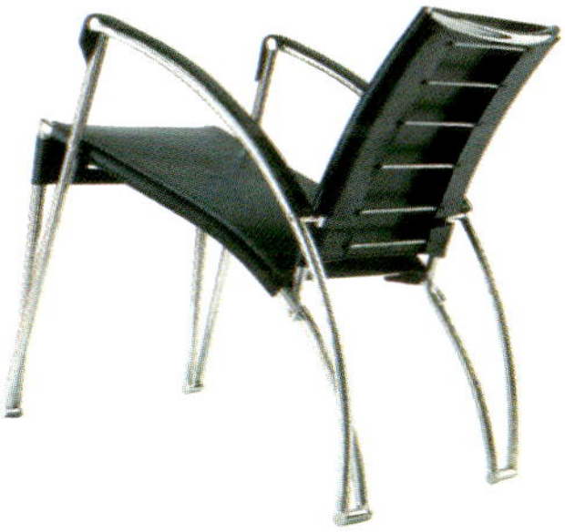

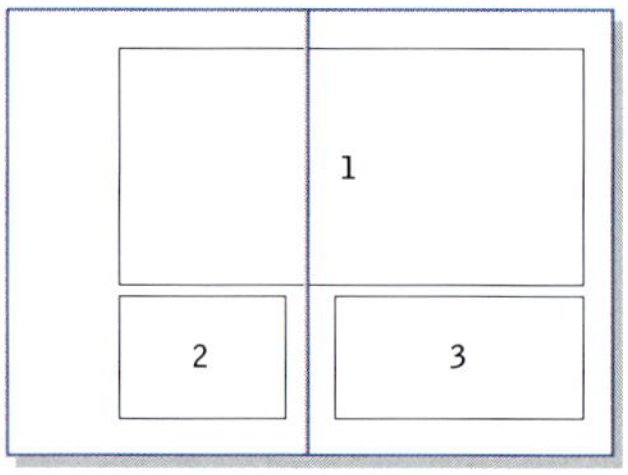

1. Fauteuil "Bloom", 2000. De Giorgio Cazzaniga pour Living Divani
Structure en acier inoxydable. Carcasse du siège réalisée en bois modelé de bouleau laminé, recouvert de peau
2. Fauteuil "Fun Bukko" de Natison Sedia
Base de type socle en acier. Siège tapissé en peau
3. Fauteuil "Poppea" de Enrico Tonucci pour Triangolo
Structure en acier inoxydable. Siège confectionné en cuir, modelé en forme de cône
66 80 80 42 cm

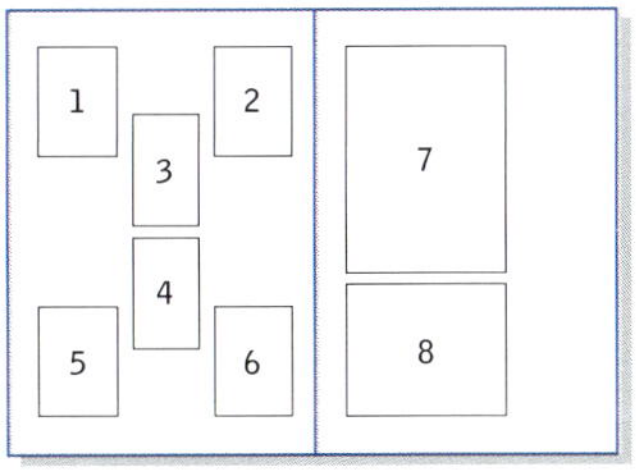

1. FAUTEUIL "CARMEN", 2000. De Miguel Milà pour CJC Concepta■
Structure en hêtre. Siège et dossier tapissés en peau ou en tissu■
⊟ 81 ⊟ 58 ⊟ 60 ⊟ 45 cm■

2. CHAISE "APRIL" de Carlo Bartoli pour Matteograssi■
Structure en acier, siège et dossier tapissés en peau■

3. CHAISE "SAMOA" de Titta Paoloni pour Frag■
Structure en tube d'acier. Dossier tapissé en peau. Siège modelé en hêtre contre-plaqué, tapissé en peau■
⊟ 90 ⊟ 50 ⊟ 50 ⊟ 45 cm■

4. CHAISE "KUMO", 1991. De Toshiyuki Kita pour Casas■
Structure en aluminium peint. Siège et dossier en cuir■
⊟ 80 ⊟ 56 ⊟ 55 ⊟ 46 cm■

5. CHAISE "CENTOCINQUE" de Galvano Tecnica■
Structure en acier totalement recouverte en peau■
⊟ 93 ⊟ 62 ⊟ 59 cm■

6. Chaise de Mario Botta pour Alias■
Structure en acier. Siège et dossier tapissés en peau naturelle■

7. FAUTEUIL "AGRA" de Enrico Franzolini pour Accademia■
Structure en tube d'acier. Siège et dossier tapissés en peau■
⊟ 75,5 ⊟ 69,5 ⊟ 77,5 ⊟ 37 cm■

8. FAUTEUIL "WIBBER", 1964/2002. De Friedrich Hill et Scooter & Partners pour Leolux■
⊟ 81 ⊟ 88 ⊟ 86 cm■

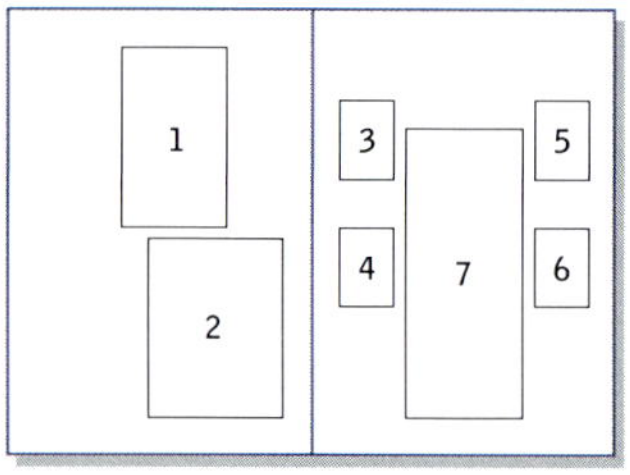

1. Chaise "St. Tropez", 2000. De Rossire et Salvi pour Bernini▪

2. Fauteuil "Saga" de Gioia Meller Marcovicz pour Classicon▪
Base en acier. Carcasse du siège en cerisier. Siège et dossier tapissés en peau▪

3. Chaise "Vittoria" de Sviluppo Frau et Centre de Rechercher de Poltrona Frau▪
⊟ 90 ⊟ 53 ⊟ 61 ⊟ 46 cm▪

4. Chaise "Evia" de Titta Paoloni pour Frag▪
Structure en tube d'acier, totalement tapissée en peau▪
⊟ 90 ⊟ 49 ⊟ 50 ⊟ 47 cm▪

5. Chaise "Liz" de Sviluppo Frau et Centre de Recherche de Poltrona Frau▪
⊟ 89 ⊟ 45 ⊟ 58 ⊟ 47 cm▪

6. Chaise "Trama" de Umberto Bertoni pour Calligaris▪
⊟ 83 ⊟ 46 ⊟ 49 ⊟ 45 cm▪

7. Chaise "Sumbawa" de Paolo Valcic pour Frag▪
Structure en tube d'acier elliptique. Siège et dossier tapissés en peau▪
⊟ 103 ⊟ 43 ⊟ 47 ⊟ 46 cm▪

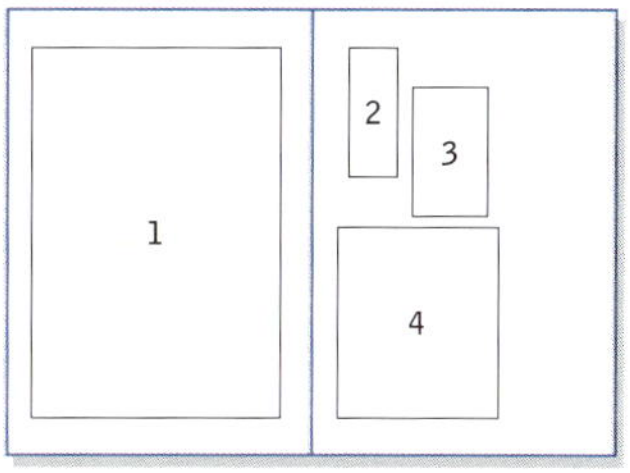

1. Tabouret "Way" de Francesco Ruffini et Margherita Quinto pour Calligaris

110 48 53,5 75 cm

2. Tabouret "Golia", 1993/2002. De Maurizio Peregalli pour Zeus Noto

Structure en acier. Siège en peau ou alcantara

80 35 35 cm

3. Tabouret "Manhattan", 2002. De Maurizio Peregalli pour Zeus Noto

Structure en acier. Siège tapissé en peau ou alacntara. Trois hauteurs possibles : 49, 67 et 82 cm

4. Tabouret "Urbe" de Nancy Robbins pour Andreu World

Structure en bois. Siège tapissé en peau et dossier en bandes de peau entrecroisées

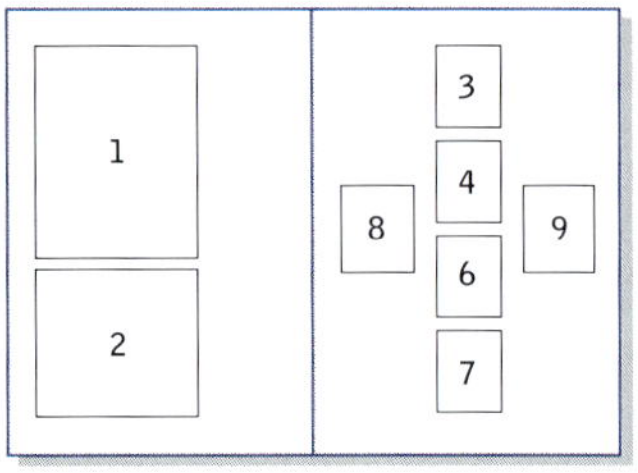

1. CHAISE "POLTRO" de Misura Emme■
Structure en acier. Siège et dossier tapissés en peau ou en toile■

2. FAUTEUIL "SPAGUETTI" de Giandomenico Belotti pour Alias■
Structure en tube d'acier. Siège, dossier et accoudoirs en peau■
⊟ 71 ⊟ 68 ⊟ 59 ⊟ 42 cm■

3. CHAISE "GOA" de Paolo Valcic pour Frag■
Structure en tube d'acier. Siège et dossier tapissés en peau■
⊟ 83 ⊟ 58 ⊟ 58 ⊟ 47 cm■

4. SIÈGE "MEDITATION POD", 2001. De Steven Blaess pour Edra■
Base en acier. Siège aux formes évoquant le mouvement Pop■
⊟ 90 ⊟ 150 ⊟ 145 cm■

5. FAUTEUIL "AM", 2002. De William Sawaya pour Swaya & Moroni■
Structure en métal chromé. Carcasse du siège en bois teint en couleur wengé. Siège et dossier tapissés en peau■
⊟ 80 ⊟ 60 ⊟ 59 ⊟ 45 cm■

6. CHAISE "EDITH", 1998. De Masafumi Katsukawa pour Zoltan■
Pieds en acier et siège tapissé en peau■
⊟ 85 ⊟ 30 ⊟ 49 cm■

7. CHAISE "HIMBA" de Gerard van den Berg pour Label■
⊟ 89 ⊟ 46 ⊟ 62 ⊟ 44,5 cm■

8. CHAISE "VERONICA", de Afra et Tobia Scarpa pour Casas■
Structure totalement recouverte en peau■
⊟ 72 ⊟ 51 ⊟ 59 ⊟ 45 cm■

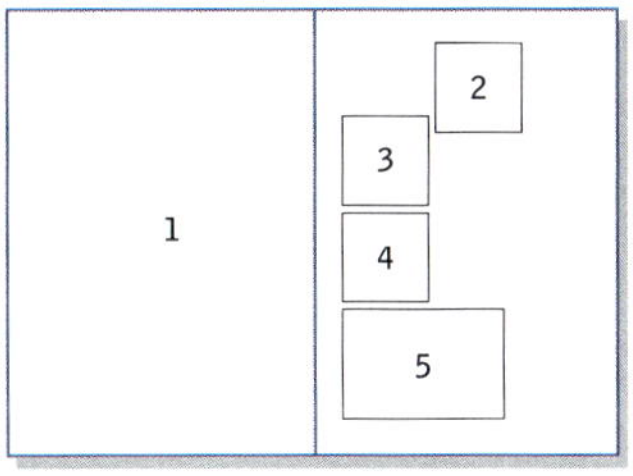

1. Chaise "Lara" de Giorgio Cattelan pour Cattelan Italia■
Structure totalement tapissée en peau■
⊟ 92 ⊟ 49 ⊟ 52 ⊟ 48 cm■

2. Chaise "Gallery", de Carlo Bartoli pour Segis■
Structure et accoudoirs en aluminium. Siège et dossier tapissés en peau ou en tissu. Peut être empilée■
⊟ 83,8 ⊟ 57 ⊟ 49 ⊟ 46 cm■

3. Chaise "Panarea" de Titta Paoloni pour Frag■
Structure totalement tapissé en peau. Disponible avec les pieds en acier■
⊟ 85 ⊟ 55 ⊟ 49 ⊟ 46 cm■

4. Fauteuil "Artemisia" de Yoshiharu Hatano pour Frag■
Structure en acier. Siège et dossier tapissés en peau■
⊟ 86 ⊟ 83 ⊟ 74 ⊟ 42 cm■

5. Fauteuil "Natrix" de Claudia et Mattia Frignani pour Wunderkammer Studio■
Structure en aluminium poli. Siège et dossier tapissés en peau, aux teintes végétales■

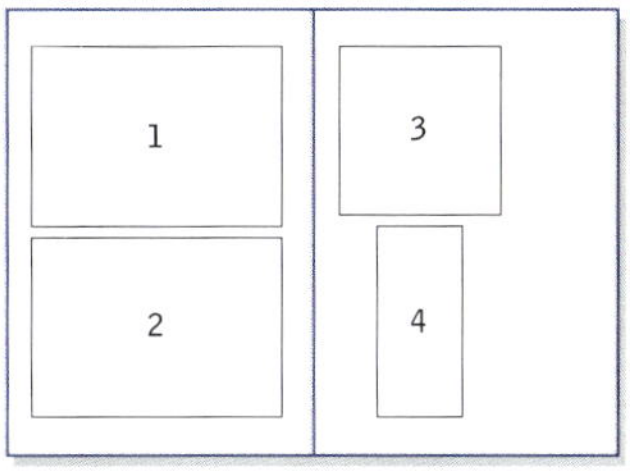

1. Fauteuil "Drop", 2001. De Emilio Nanni pour Zanotta■
Structure en acier chromé. Siège et dossier tapissés en peau ou en tissu■
⊟ 67 ⊟ 60 ⊟ 73 ⊟ 38 cm■
2. Fauteuil "Lucca", 2002. De Joan Casas Ortínez pour Indecasa■
Deux hauteurs possibles pour le siège : 37 cm, ou 45 cm dans la version salle à manger■
3. Fauteuil "Oto Croco", de Peter Karf pour Iform (Collection Voxia)■
Structure en bois laminé modelé d'une seule pièce et recouverte de peau■
⊟ 71 ⊟ 78 ⊟ 61 ⊟ 38 cm■
4. Fauteuil "Daphne", de Claudia et Mattia Frignani pour Wunderkammer Studio■
Structure en acier chromé. Siège et dossier tapissés en peau naturelle■
⊟ 117 ⊟ 42 cm■

ERGONOMIE ET TRAVAIL

FORMES AU SERVICE DE LA FONCTION

W+S

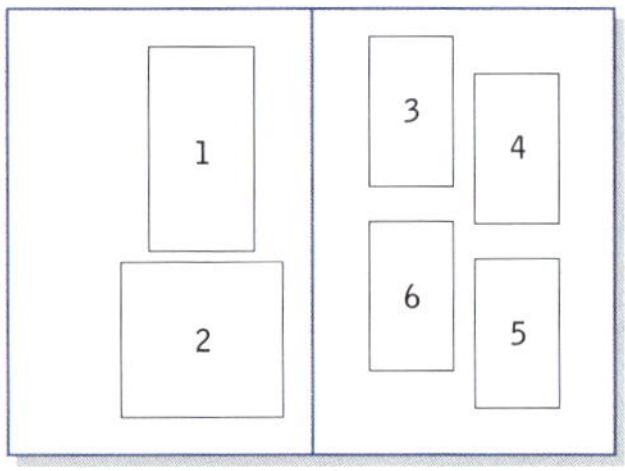

1. CHAISE "WEBB EXECUTIVE" de Burkhard Vogtherr pour Davis Furniture■
Structure en aluminium poli. Siège et repose-tête tapissés en peau. Dossier formé par des sangles entrecroisées fabriquées chez DuPont et s'adaptant à la posture de l'utilisateur■
2. CHAISE "VERSUS", 1999. De Miguel Ángel Ciganda pour Casas■
Base en aluminium injecté. Réalisée avec des matériaux recyclables. Adaptable en hauteur■
⊟ 97,5/108,5 ⊟ 69 cm■
⊟ 64,5 ⊟ 44,5/55,5 cm■
3. CHAISE "SOLIS", 2002. De Wiege pour Wilkhahn■
Chaise pivotante avec adaptation synchronisée. Structure en aluminium. Carcasse du siège en polypropylène, tapissé avec différentes finitions. Version avec dossier bas■
4. CHAISE "G15" de Offix Klass (Collection K&K Technogel®)■
Siège développé avec Technogel®, une substance de polyuréthanne provenant du domaine médical, s'adaptant à la forme du corps, distribuant le poids et diminuant la fatigue■
⊟ 96/109 ⊟ 44 ⊟ 49 ⊟ 46/59 cm■
5. CHAISE "MODUS", de Klaus Franck, Werner Sauer et Wiege pour Wilkhahn■
Chaise pivotante avec adaptation synchronisée automatique. Structure en aluminium. Dossier en maille semi-transparente élastique. Accoudoirs en polypropylène renforcé avec de la fibre de verre■
6. CHAISE "X-88", du Groupe de Design ITO et de l'équipe de design de Comforto pour Haworth■
Base disponible en acier ou en aluminium. Trois types d'accoudoirs possibles. S'adapte aux mouvement du corps. Zone lombaire et hauteur adaptable. Dossier en tissu de maille ou tapissé■

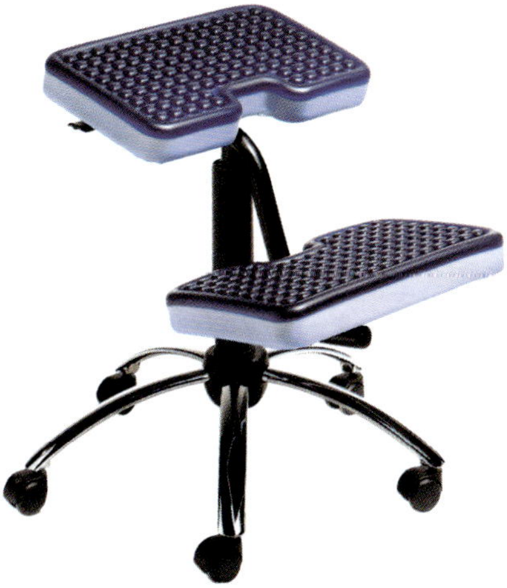

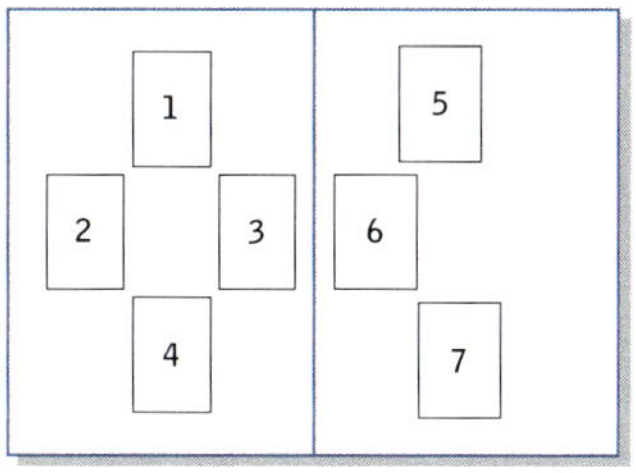

1. Chaise "Clia", 2002. De Bateman, Dillon et Grieves pour Casas■ Chaise pivotante avec dossier réalisé en maille Netware. Zone lombaire et hauteur adaptables■
⊟ 92/103 ⊟ 68 ⊟ 69 ⊟ 44/55 cm■

2. Chaise "FS Line", de Klaus Franck et Werner Sauer pour Wilkhahn■
Base en aluminium. Carcasse du siège et accoudoirs en polypropylène. Dossier extrêmement flexible s'adaptant automatiquement à la position de l'utilisateur■

3. Chaise "Inge Girevole", de Enrico Franzolini pour Sintesi■
Structure en tube d'acier. Siège et dossier en polypropylène. Comprend un mécanisme adaptable■
⊟ 76 ⊟ 49 ⊟ 47 cm■

4. Chaise "Vittoria" de Sviluppo Frau et Centre de Recherche de Poltrona Frau■
Base en acier. Siège et dossier tapissés en peau. Hauteur adaptable■

5. Chaise "G12" de Offix Klass (Collection K&K Technogel®)■
Siège développé avec Technogel®, un substance en polypropylène provenant du domaine médical, s'adaptant à la forme du corps, distribuant le poids et diminuant la fatigue■
⊟ 82/91 ⊟ 63 ⊟ 52 ⊟ 45/54 cm■

6. Chaise "Young Lady" de Paolo Rizzatto pour Alias■
Structure en aluminium. Siège pivotant avec cadre en cerisier, canné en osier■
⊟ 80 ⊟ 59 ⊟ 59 ⊟ 48 cm■

7. Tabouret de travail "G20" de Offix Klass (Collection K&K Technogel®)■
Tabouret développé avec Technogel®, une substance en polyuréthanne provenant du domaine médical et diminuant la fatigue■
⊟ 43/60 ⊟ 57 ⊟ 57 cm■

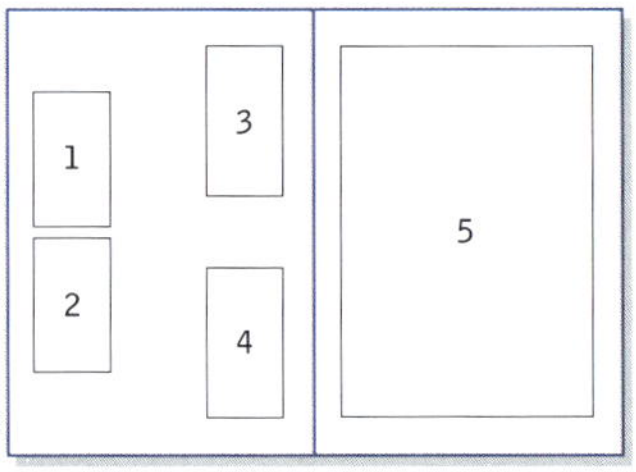

1. Chaise "N7", 2000. De Marcello Ziliani pour Zago■
Mécanisme d'adaptation synchronisé. Siège, accoudoirs, support lombaire et repose-tête adaptables■

2. Chaise "Talle", de P. King et S. Miranda pour Sellex■
Base en aluminium fondu. Carcasse du siège en hêtre contre-plaqué incurvé, totalement tapissé en peau■
⊟ 95,9 ⊟ 45,7 ⊟ 56,8 cm■

3. Chaise "Fluid", de Miles Keller pour Allseating■
Siège et dossier en tissu grille distribuant le poids du corps. Support lombaire et accoudoirs adaptables. Prix Good Design 2001 du Chicago Athenaeum■

4. "The Spin Chair", 1996. De Burkhard Vogtherr pour Fritz Hansen■
Base en aluminium. Carcasse du dossier en hêtre contre-plaqué tapissé. Existe avec quatre types d'accoudoirs et de nombreuses combinaisons de hauteurs et de finitions■

5. Chaise "Modus", de Klaus Franck, Werner Sauer et Wiege pour Wilkhahn■
Chaise pivotante avec adaptation synchronisée automatique. Structure en aluminium. Siège et dossier tapissés en peau. Accoudoirs en polyamide renforcée avec de la fibre de verre, tapissés en peau■

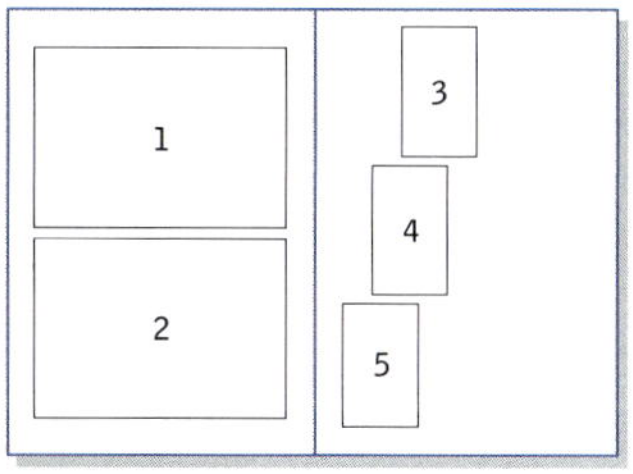

1. COLLECTION "ROOKIE" signature Röder pour Haworth
Multiples combinaisons de tissus et finitions

2. CHAISE "S-CON", 1998. Signature Lepper, Schmidt, and Sommerlade pour Haworth (Art Collection)
Surfaces métalliques avec finition en aluminium mat. Dossier en tissu de maille ou avec finition en peau

3. CHAISE "SOLIS F", 2002. De Wiege pour Wilkhahn
La construction du siège et du dossier est basée sur des recouvrements transparents tendus et très élastiques, encadrés par un contour en aluminium injecté. Système d'adaptation de synchronisation automatique

4. CHAISE "GOGO" de Marcello Ziliani pour Sintesi
Base en tube d'acier. Siège et dossier tapissés en peau
⊟ 84 ⊟ 59 ⊟ 59 cm

5. CHAISE "PILA", 1995. De Alfredo Arribas pour Casas
Base pivotante en tube d'acier. Accoudoirs en aluminium fondu
⊟ 109 ⊟ 65 ⊟ 65 ⊟ 44/57 cm

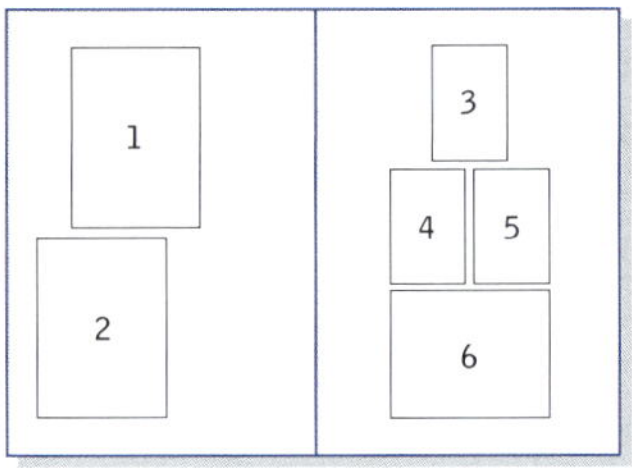

1. Chaise "Partner", de Johannes Foersom et Peter Hiort-Lorenzen pour Erik Jørgensen
Structure en acier chromé mat. Siège et dossier tapissés en tissu ou en peau
⊟ 91,5 ⊟ 69 ⊟ 76 ⊟ 43 cm

2. Chaise "Flow", 2000. De Burkhard Vogtherr pour Fritz Hansen
Base en aluminium. Dossier flexible. Soutenu en un point sur le rail arrière en aluminium. Options de combinaisons multiples pour les tailles et les finitions

3. Chaise "Bahia Girevole", de Galvano Tecnica
Base en nylon ou acier chromé. Structure du siège en tube d'acier avec recouvrement en peau
⊟ 90/104 ⊟ 56 ⊟ 60 cm

4. Tabouret de travail "SBG 43", design s'inspirant de l'original créé par Egon Eiermann en 1949/51. Produit par Wilde+Spieth
Comprend le type de pied Bruselas

5. Chaise "SBG 41", design original de 1949, de Egon Eiermann. Produite par Wilde+Spieth
Le modèle "SGB41" comprend le type de pied Bruselas. Siège et dossier en bois teint

6. Chaise-pupitre "Easy Rider". De Danny Venlet pour Bulo
Structure en EPS (Polystyrène Dilaté) modelé par injection. Les pieds se présentent avec ou sans roulettes

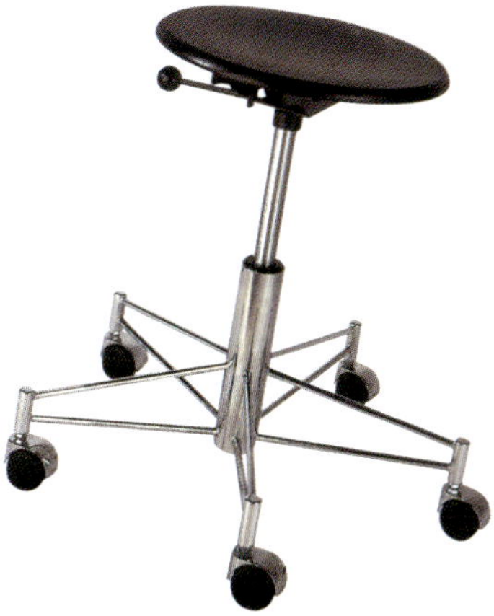

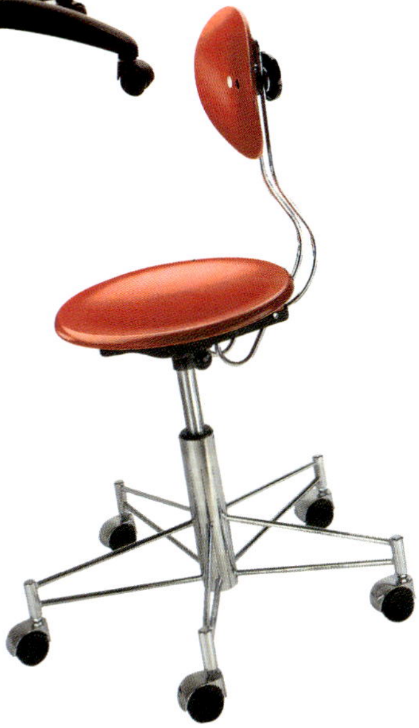

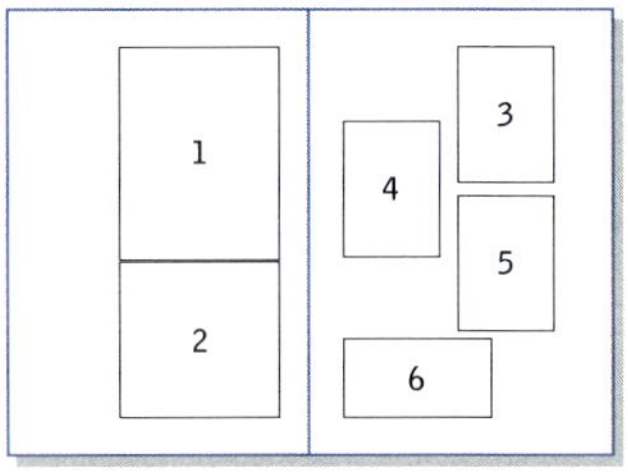

1. CHAISE "LILLY LIFT", de Sintesi
Structure en tube d'acier. Siège en bois contre-plaqué recouvert d'aluminium
83/95 63 63 44/56 cm

2. SÉRIE "BULLDOG", de Dale Fahnstrom et Michael McCoy pour Knoll
Multiples possibilités d'adaptation. Sept modèles différents

3. CHAISE "PUB & CLUB", de Bulo
Ces chaises associent l'utilisation des techniques les plus actuelles et les prestations ergonomiques à une esthétique contemporaine et ludique

4. CHAISE "D14", 1998. Produite par Tecta
Base métallique et carcasse du siège en osier naturel
82/95 56 58 44/57 cm

5. CHAISE "D49", de Tecta
Base en aluminium. Carcasse du siège en acrylique modelé
88/101 72 62 48/61 cm

6. CHAISE "EGOA", 1988. De Josep Mora pour Stua
Structure en acier chromé. Siège en hêtre, frêne, cerisier ou wengé. Le dossier s'adapte à la position du dos. Prix Innovative Design de Melbourne
80/93 59 59 40/53 cm

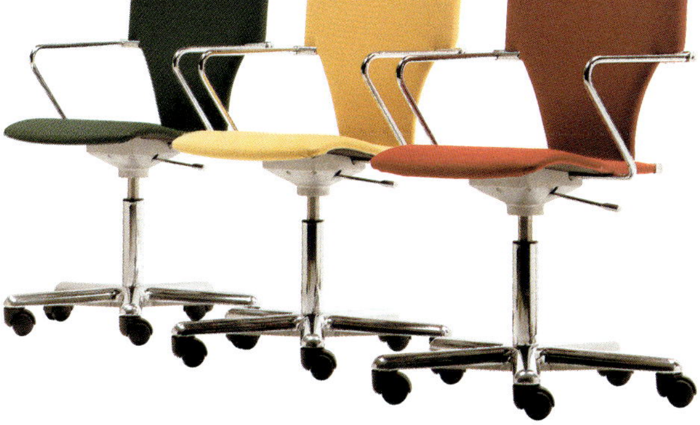

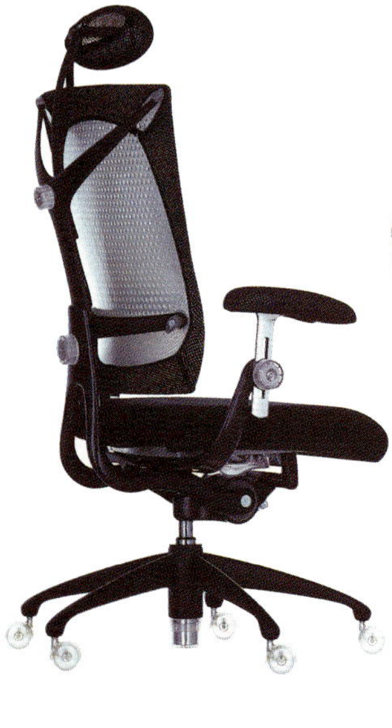

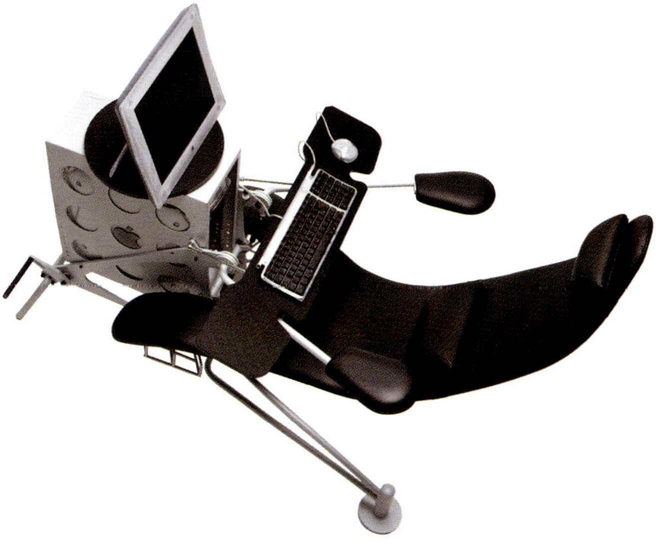

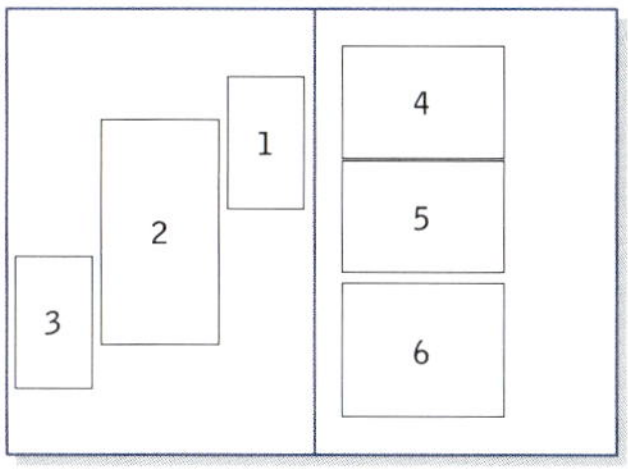

1. Chaise "Picto", de Roericht, Burkhard Schmitz et Franz Biggel pour Wilkhahn▪
Structure en aluminium. Siège et dossier perforé en polypropylène. Accoudoirs en hêtre naturel. Adaptation synchronisée automatique▪

2. Chaise "N5", 2000. De Marcello Ziliani pour Zago▪
Mécanisme d'adaptation synchronisé. Siège, accoudoirs, support lombaire et repose-tête adaptables▪

3. Chaise "Ypsilon" de Mario et Claudio Bellini pour Vitra▪
Dossier flexible et sans châssis s'adaptant à n'importe quelle position du corps et permettant la circulation de l'air. Tapissé en tissu de maille Mesh, ou en cuir. Prestations optionnelles multiples, comme le siège thermoactif Clima Seat®. (Photo : H. Hansen)▪

4. Collection "Life" développée par Knoll▪
Dossier et siège flexibles. Mouvements d'adaptation synchronisés et intuitifs. Support adaptable. Options de prestations et finitions multiples▪

5. Collection "Webb Meeting" de Burkhard Vogtherr et Jon Prestwich pour Davis Furniture▪
Structure en aluminium poli. Siège tapissé en peau. Dossier formé par des sangles entrecroisées fabriquées par DuPont et s'adaptant à la posture de l'utilisateur▪

6. Station de travail "Netsurfer", 1995. De Teppo Asikainen et Ilkka Terho pour Snowcrash▪
Structure en acier. Siège tapissé en peau▪
⊟ 98 ⊟ 78 ⊟ 161 cm▪
(Photo : Urban Hedlund)▪

PLASTIQUES ET NOUVEAUX MATÉRIAUX
TRIOMPHE DE LA TECHNOLOGIE

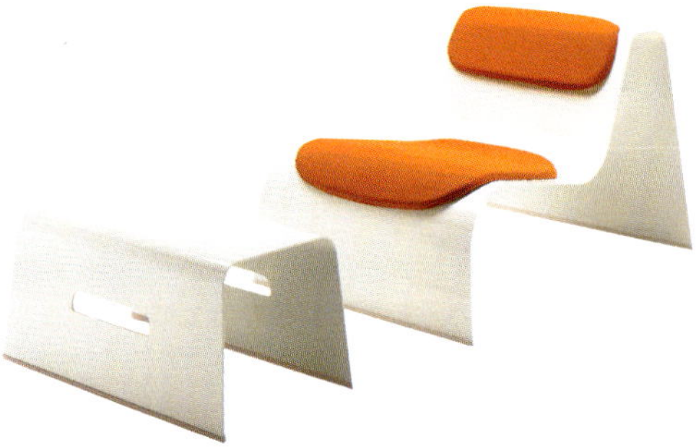

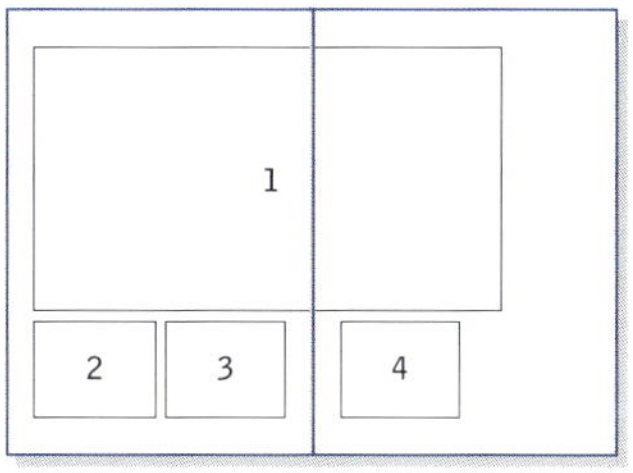

Page 247:
Chaise "Free", 2002. De Monica Graffeo pour Kristalia■
Structure en tube d'acier. Recouvrement en tissu ou en polyester, obtenu avec la même technologie que celle utilisée pour les chaussures de sport. Peut être empilée■

1. Chaise "Spice", 2002. De Jehs & Laub pour Ycami■
Structure en aluminium. Siège en fibre de verre, peint avec de la laque brillante■
⊟ 78 ⊟ 45 ⊟ 48 ⊟ 45 cm■
2. Chaise "Eva", 2002. De Marc Sadler pour Kartell■
Structure en acier chromé. Siège et dossier obtenus à partir d'un nouveau composé plastique, mou et confortable, suivant la technique d'injection■
3. Fauteuil avec repose-pied "Molly", 2001. De F. Bertero et A. Panto pour Zanotta■
Structure en alliage d'aluminium, avec émail blanc pour la version réservée à l'extérieur. Coussins en polyuréthanne. Mesures : fauteuil,
⊟ 66 ⊟ 73 ⊟ 105 cm■
repose-pied,
⊟ 35 ⊟ 73 ⊟ 41 cm■
4. Chaise "Zaia", de Galvano Tecnica■
Structure en acier. Carcasse du siège en polypropylène■
⊟ 81 ⊟ 51 ⊟ 58 cm■

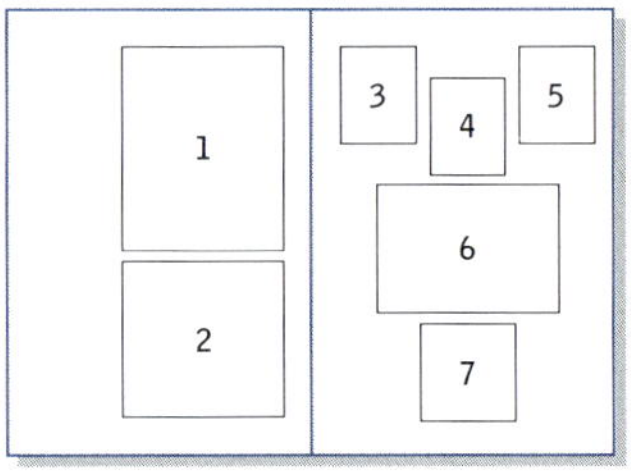

1. CHAISE "MARIPOSA", 2001. De Afra et Tobia Scarpa pour Casas■
Structure en tube d'acier ovale. Carcasse du siège en tereftalato de polyétilène (P.E.T) tapissé■
74 61 60 44 cm■

2. FAUTEUIL "HYDRA", de Roberto Semprini pour Sintesi■
Structure en tube d'acier. Siège et dossier recouverts avec des bandes de PVC■

3. CHAISE "NUVOLA", 1999. De Jutta et Herbert Ohl pour Wilkhahn■
Structure en acier poli. Siège et dossier en grille noire de polyester. Peut être empilée. Prix Good Design Award du Chicago Athenaeum 1999■
75 56 57 40 cm■

4. FAUTEUIL "GHOST", de Cini Boeri et Tomu Katatanagi pour Fiam Italia■
Réalisé d'une seule pièce en verre incurvé de 12mm■
68 95 75 cm■

5. CHAISE "BREEZE", 1997. De Carlo Bartoli pour Segis■
Structure en aluminium. Siège et dossier en polypropylène recycable. Peut être empilée. Apte pour un usage en extérieur. Prix ID Design Distinction 1997, USA. Prix Red Dot for High Quality Design. Prix IF Award for Excellent Design, 1998■
80 58 49 46 cm■

6. CHAISE "OUTLINE", 2001. De Jean Marie Massaud pour Cappellini■
Structure en acier. Carcasse du siège en fibre de verre, tapissé à l'intérieur avec du tissu ou en peau■

7. TABOURET CONVERTIBLE ET CHAISE À BASCULE "SUTRA", de Kundalini■
Réalisé en polyuréthanne. Mesures :
petit,
43 35 50 cm■
grand,
43 67 90 cm■

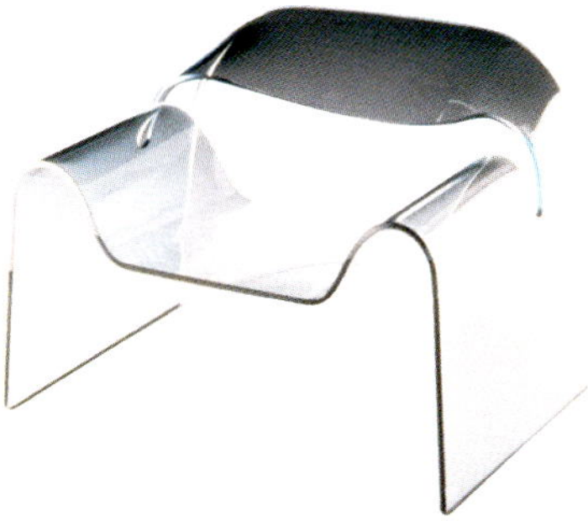

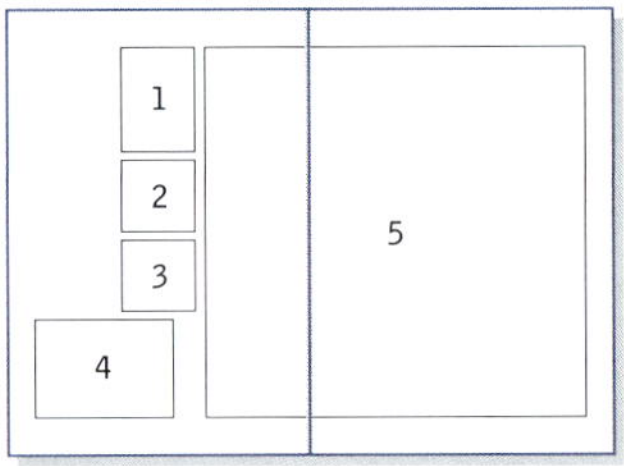

1. Chaise "Sonica", de Arkiline pour Calligaris
Structure en acier. Siège et dossier en technopolymère REK
80,5 46,5 52 44 cm
2. Siège convertible "Z-Play", 2002. De Zaha Hadid pour Sawaya & Moroni
Pièces réalisées en mousse de haute densité. Les différents blocs se présentent comme un puzzle et offrent plusieurs possibilités de siège
72 72 42 cm
3. Pouf "Globulo", 1999. De F. Bertero et A. Panto pour Zanotta
Réalisé en plastique de diverses couleurs. Apte pour un usage en extérieur
20 70 70 cm
4. Siège transformable "Pisoló", 1997. De Denis Santachiara pour Campeggi
Tabourets en plastique contenant un matelas gonflable, convertible en lit
82 67 cm
5. Chaise "Mar", 2001. De Joan Casas Ortínez pour Indecasa
Structure en aluminium. Siège et dossier en polypropylène. Peut être empilée. Apte à un usage en extérieur

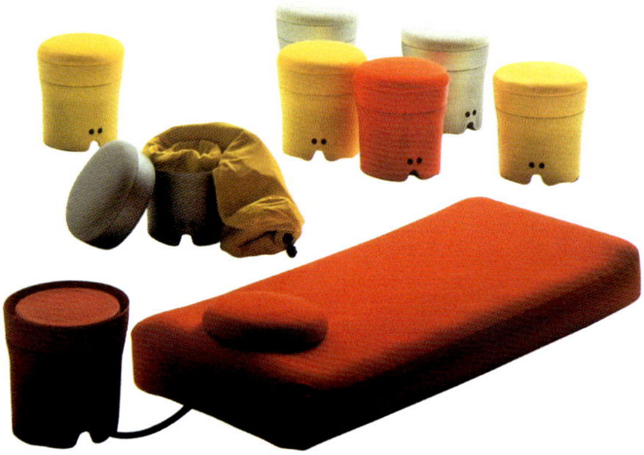

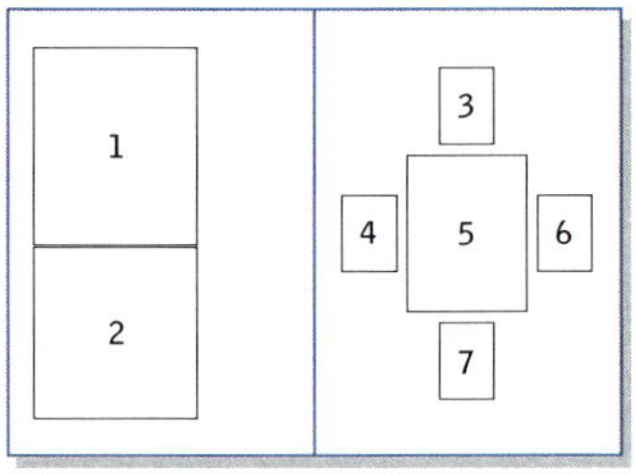

1. Chaise "Gali", 1992. De Carlo Bartoli pour Ycami■
Structure en aluminium poli. Siège et dossier en mousse de haute densité■
80 49 46 45 cm■

2. Chaise "Tempesta", de Album International■
Structure en acier tubulaire. Siège et dossier en résine transparente. Peut être empilée■
78 54 51 46 cm■

3. Chaise "Capsule", de Innovation■
Réalisée en plastique■
59 55 55 cm■

4. Chaise "Aida", 2000. De Richard Sapper pour Magis■
Structure en acier chromé ou inoxydable. Carcasse du siège en polypropylène modelé par injection■
85,5 57 54 44 cm■

5. Chaise "Lilly", de Sintesi■
Structure en tube d'acier. Carcasse du siège en composé de haute technologie Hirek®■
86 49,5 50 47 cm■

6. Chaise "Gigi" de Marco Maran pour Knoll■
Structure en acier inoxydable. Carcasse en polypropylène■

7. Chaise "Bahbar" de G. Bardet pour Liv' It (Grupo Fiam Italia)■

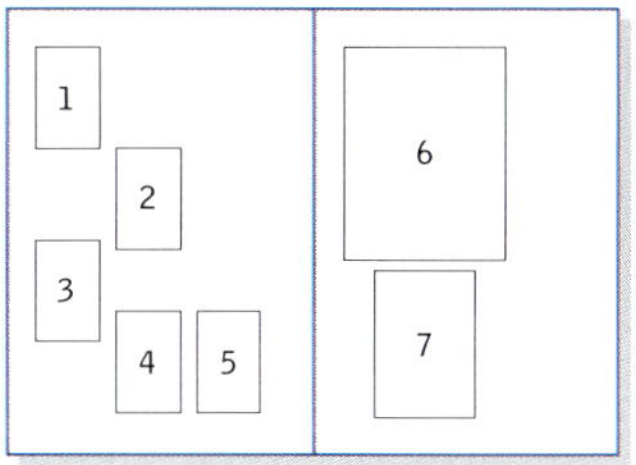

1. Chaise "Sand", 2002. De Pocci Dondoli pour Desalto■
Structure en aluminium, finition gris arctique ou aluminium brillant. Siège et dossier en polypropylène renforcé avec de la fibre de verre■
82 47 54 45 cm■

2. Chaise "Bellini", 2001. De Mario Bellini pour Heller■
Première chaise modelée par injection de gaz. Prix Compasso d'Oro 2001. Prix Good Design du Chicago Athenaeum■

3. Chaise "Carta", 1998. De Shigeru Ban pour Cappellini■
Structure en bouleau laminé. Siège et dossier réalisés avec de petits tubes de carton■

4. Chaise "Inge", de Enrico Franzolini pour Sintesi■
Structure en tube d'acier. Siège et dossier en polypropylène■
76 57 47 cm■

5. Chaise "Calla", 2002. De William Sawaya pour Heller■
Structure en polypropylène renforcé avec de la fibre de verre. Dossier flexible. Apte pour un usage en extérieur■

6. Chaise "Isis", 1997. De Olaf von Bohr pour Sintesi■
Structure en tube d'acier. Siège et dossier en polypropylène. Prix "Top Ten" et "Chaise de l'Année" 1997, au Salon International de la Chaise (Promosedia)■
77 42 50 cm■

7. Chaise "Waves", 2001. De Jens Ring Burshe pour Natison Sedia■
Réalisée en plastique. Pliable. Apte pour un usage en extérieur. Chaise de l'année 2001 au Salon International de la Chaise (Promosedia)■
80 48 57 45 cm■

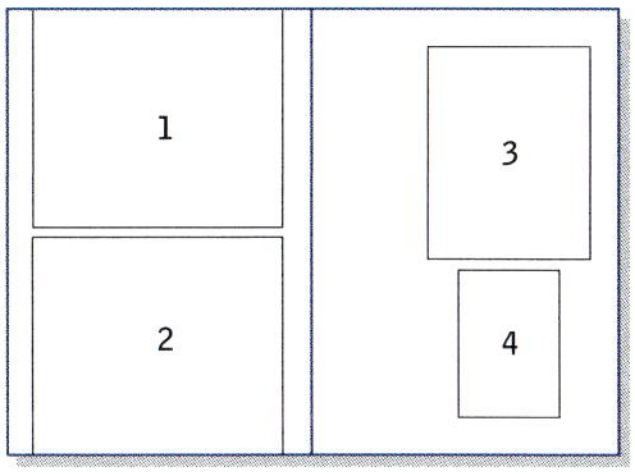

1. CHAISE "MARGHERITA", 1997. De Carlo Colombo pour Ycami■
Structure en aluminium. Siège et dossier en polycarbonate transparent coloré. Apte pour un usage en extérieur■
⊟ 82 ⊟ 42 ⊟ 54 ⊟ 45 cm■
2. CHAISE À BASCULE "CHIP", 1996. De Teppo Asikainen et Ilkka Terho pour Snowcrash■
Structure en bois contre-plaqué avec une base en polyuréthanne■
⊟ 37 ⊟ 60 ⊟ 140 cm■
(Photo : Bobo Olsson)■
3. SIÈGE "OM", de Maurizio Rusconi et Swami Anand pour Kundalini■
Structure en fibre de verre laquée. Le modèle de la table est "Hari"■
⊟ 80 ⊟ 60 ⊟ 50 cm■
4. CHAISE "GOGO", de Marcello Ziliani pour Sintesi■
Structure en tube d'acier laqué. Carcasse du siège en polypropylène coloré■
⊟ 84 ⊟ 59 ⊟ 59 cm■

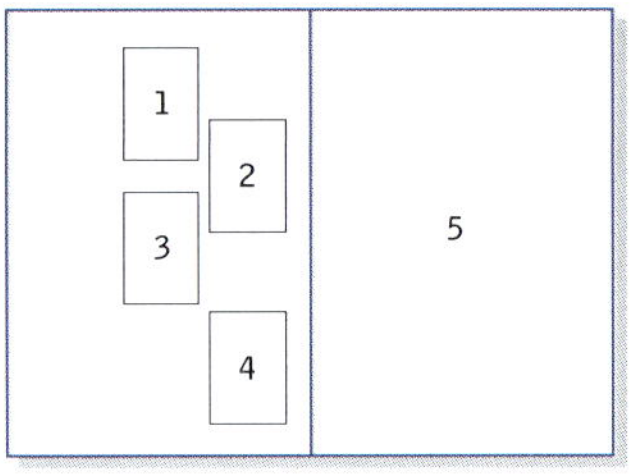

1. Chaise "Gas", 2002. De Jesús Gasca pour Stua▪
Structure en aluminium brillant. Siège et dossier en grille synthétique ou plastique. Prix IF Silver Design, 2002. Prix Red Dot, Essen▪
□ 78,5 □ 50 □ 48 □ 44 cm▪

2. Chaise "S360F", de Delphin Design pour Thonet▪
Structure en tube d'acier chromé. Siège et dossier en plastique. Peut être empilée. Peut être rattachée à d'autres pour un usage en salle de conférence▪
□ 80 □ 55 □ 53 cm▪

3. Chaise "Wing", 1998. De Sviluppo Frau et Centre de recherche de Poltrona Frau▪
Réalisée en fibre de carbone, un matériau utilisé dans la construction aéronautique et pour la Formule 1▪
□ 87 □ 44 □ 51,5 □ 44,5 cm▪

4. Fauteuil "Gravity", 2002. De William Sawaya pour Sawaya & Moroni▪
Produit en édition limitée, numérotée et signée▪
□ 75 □ 84 □ 74 □ 34,5 cm▪

5. Chaise "Net", de Daniele Molteni pour Bontempi▪
Structure en acier chromé. Siège et dossier en plastique. Peut être empilée▪
□ 81 □ 48 □ 59 □ 46 cm▪

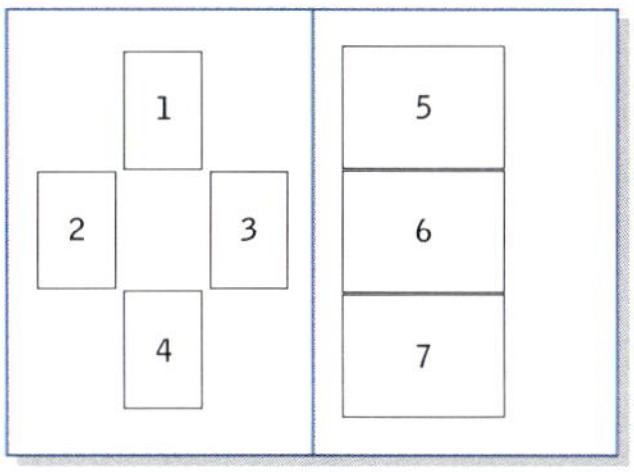

1. Chaise "Maxima", de William Sawaya pour Sawaya & Moroni■
Structure en acier inoxydable. Carcasse du siège en polyuréthanne compact de haute densité■
⊟ 80 ⊟ 45,5 ⊟ 56 ⊟ 45 cm■

2. Chaise "Orbit", de Robby e Francesca Cantarutti pour Sintesi■
Structure en acier et carcasse en composé de haute technologie Hirek®■
⊟ 81 ⊟ 56 ⊟ 47,5 cm■

3. Chaise "Boum", 2002. De Monica Graffeo et Ruggero Magrini pour Kristalia■
Structure en acier. Tapissé au moyen de la technologie utilisée pour le recouvrement intérieur des voitures■

4. Chaise "Ah Chair", de Tom Deacon pour Umbra■
Structure en acier. Carcasse du siège en polypropylène■

5. Fauteuil "Primary", de Quinze & Milan■
⊟ 47,5 ⊟ 44 ⊟ 44 cm■

6. Chaise "Carre", 2002. De Christophe Marchand pour Ycami■
Structure en aluminium. Carcasse du siège en mousse intégrale■
⊟ 76 ⊟ 52 ⊟ 54 ⊟ 46 cm■

7. Chaise "Dress", 1999. De Rane Vaskivuch et Timo Vierros pour Snowcrash■
Structure en acier laqué. Siège et dossier tapissés en nylon■
⊟ 82 ⊟ 63 ⊟ 75 cm■
(Photo : Bobo Olsson)■

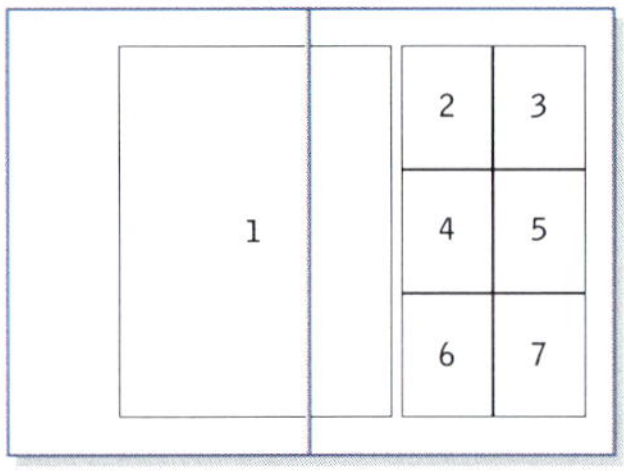

1. Fauteuil "Airbag", 1997. De Pasi Kolhonen et Ilkka Suppanen pour Snowcrash
Siège tapissé en nylon avec rembourrage de polystyrène. Comprend des bandes de polyester pour réguler l'angle entre le siège et le dossier. Convertible en matelas. Mesures : chaise,
80 85 90 cm
matelas,
25 85 155 cm
(Photo : Bobo Olsson)
2. Chaise "Flex", 2002. De Allseating
Siège flexible Flexion™ et dossier inclinable. Peut être empilée. Prix Good Design 2002, du Chicago Athenaeum
3. Chaise "Network", 2002. De Archirivolto Design pour Segis
Structure en fibre de verre renforcée en polyamide modelée par la technique d'injection d'aire. Siège en grille d'acier ou PVC
4. Chaise "K818", 2000. De Erik Magnussen pour Thonet
Pieds avants, siège et dossier en polyamide. Pieds arrières en acier. Peut être empilée. Apte pour un usage en extérieur
78 51 56 cm
(Photo : Michael Gerlach)
5. Siège "LCP" (Low Chair Plastic), de Marteen Van Severen pour Kartell
Structure réalisée d'une seule pièce en plastique PMMA modelé
70 48,5 80 31 cm
6. Chaise "Ice", de Kasper Salto pour Fritz Hansen
Structure en aluminium. Siège et dossier en plastique
79 50 48 45 cm
7. Chaise "Casablanca" de Christophe Pillet pour Artelano

3

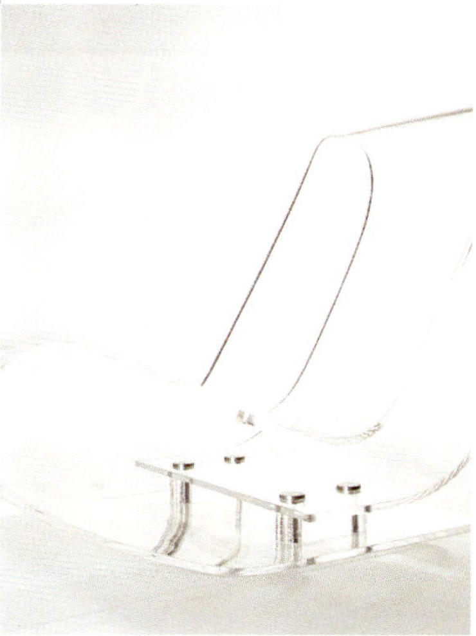

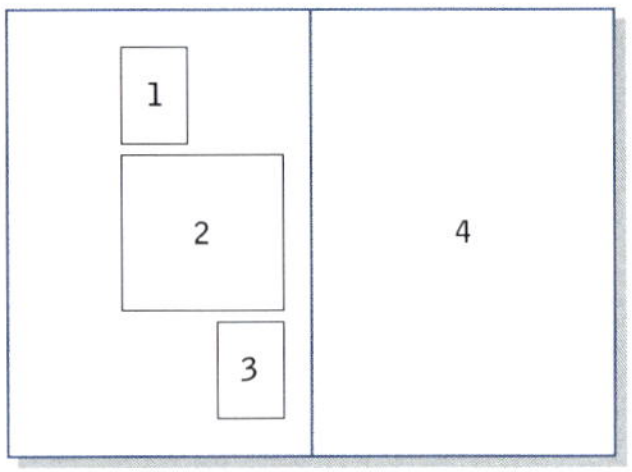

1 et 3. "Pink Barbie Chair" et "Tweetie Barbie Chair". De Hannah Mae ▪
Version rénovée de ce classique des années 60, créé à l'origine par Burke Maurice pour Arkana. La structure est réalisée en plastique renforcé avec du verre (GRP), poli et avec une finition brillant, disponible en sept couleurs. Apte pour un usage en extérieur ▪
75 50 50 cm ▪

2. Siège "Statuette", de 1995. De Lloyd Schwan pour Cappellini ▪
Base métallique vernie en couleur aluminium. Structure en fibre de verre ▪
106 103 60 40 cm ▪

4. Chaise "Ensemble", 1992. De Alfred Homman pour Fritz Hansen ▪
Structure en tube d'acier. Carcasse en matériau synthétique "Stapron N". Peut être empilée ▪
81,5 59 45 43 cm ▪

CHAISES
ET ART

"Une chaise conçue comme une œuvre d'art est-elle tragique ou comique ?"
James Joyce, *Portrait de l'Artiste Adolescent*, New York, 1916■

Une chaise sur laquelle personne ne s'est jamais assis peut-elle être considérée comme une chaise ?
Une chaise cassée que nous trouvons abandonnée dans un terrain vague garde-t-elle son intention première ?
Une chaise qui se trouve sur le premier plan d'une composition picturale, de quelle absence nous parle-t-elle ?
Une chaise placée au milieu d'une salle vide, est-ce le symbole d'une perte ?
Une chaise aux formes anthropomorphiques, est-elle capable de raconter une histoire ?
Une chaise à l'esthétique qui transgresse, est-ce un manifestant politique exprimant sa colère contre les normes établies ?
Une chaise qui contemple la mer, est-ce une poésie ?

Dans les mains d'un artiste, cet objet domestique dont la présence est obligatoire perd la définition que lui donne le dictionnaire et se remplit de nouvelles significations, aussi variées que la personnalité et l'état d'âme du créateur qui se trouve derrière chaque œuvre. La chaise se transforme ainsi en une métaphore de la vie, de la présence et de l'absence, de la solitude et de la compagnie. Comme l'écrivit Henry David Thoreau, un auteur américain du XIXe siècle, "moi, j'ai eu trois chaises chez moi. Une pour la solitude, deux pour l'amitié et trois pour la société"■
Ce n'est pas un hasard si la chaise a une relation aussi étroite avec l'art. C'est un objet avec plus de cinq mil ans d'histoire, chargé de symboles, de tensions de pouvoir, capable de refléter la personnalité, la culture et le niveau économique de son pro-

Image de la page 269: Création sur papier de Sergio Massetti (Gênes, 1962). Image fournie par Promosedia, de l'exposition "20 Artistes interprètent la Chaise"■ *Page précédente :* Shannon Landis Hansen signe la création de "The Chair and I", réalisée avec la technique de la mosaïque. De la collection de la Galerie d'Art Fonctionnel de Santa Mónica (Californie)■

priétaire, capable, également, de refléter le rythme d'une époque, brillant représentant des courants esthétiques et sociaux du moment.

Depuis la chaise de la chambre de Arles de Vincent Van Gogh, témoin déchirant de sa solitude et de son austérité, jusqu'à la chaise électrique de Sing Sing, sujet d'une sérigraphie aux couleurs intenses de Andy Warhol en 1971, protestation implicite contre la violence et la peine de mort, de nombreux artistes ont montré leur approche conceptuelle particulière de cette pièce de mobilier, devenue un moyen de communiquer les émotions et nous rappelant seulement de temps en temps qu'elle sert à nous y asseoir.

La relation entre la chaise et l'art peut être observée selon trois perspectives différentes : depuis une position contemplative ; en tant que partie intégrante de l'œuvre ; ou en tant qu'art fonctionnel. En ce qui concerne la relation de type "contemplatif", de nombreux artistes pensent qu'une chaise est le meilleur endroit pour contempler une œuvre d'art. Il s'agit du côté spirituel de la chaise, permettant de détendre le corps, d'adopter une posture confortable facilitant la concentration de l'esprit sans avoir à se préoccuper des autres nécessités corporelles. Dans ce sens, le fait de s'as-

Image de l'exposition "Bestseller", lors de la 26e édition du Salon International de la Chaise, Promosedia. Des entreprises comme Thonet et Poltrona Frau présentaient des pièces emblématiques dans l'histoire de la chaise.

seoir peut s'identifier à une activité intellectuelle, comme une posture intermédiaire entre le mouvement que suppose une station debout et l'abandon total permis par la station couché. Prendre place sur une chaise face à une œuvre d'art signifie adopter une attitude contemplative entre l'activité et la passivité, entre le jour et la nuit▪

En ce qui concerne la chaise dans l'art, c'est sa large gamme de significations métaphoriques qui font d'elle un objet de désir. Sa propre morphologie est une métaphore fascinante du corps humain ; ses bras, ses pieds, son dos et sa tête s'adaptent parfaitement à notre silhouette. Au-delà de cette symbiose, elle peut exprimer d'innombrables contradictions : une critique ironique de la société de consommation ; une réflexion sur l'aliénation et l'uniformité ; un cri de liberté et de libertinage ; une raison de force ou de faiblesse ; une explosion de joie ou de tristesse ; un symbole de pauvreté ou de richesse ou, au premier ou dernier plan, une apparition devant nos yeux pour saboter nos convictions les plus enracinées. Tout dépendra de l'endroit, du moment et de l'état d'âme de celui qui expose et de celui qui regarde▪

Timbre émis par le Service de Postes d'Italie en septembre 2001, dans la série "Design Italien". Il s'agit de l'image de la chaise "Free", de Monica Graffeo pour Kristalia▪

La dernière perspective est celle de la chaise en tant qu'art fonctionnel, à mi-chemin entre la créativité pure et les conditions de l'industrie. Dans ce sens, la chaise comprend la dualité de ces deux types d'œuvres : comme sujet d'admiration et comme objet utile. L'ambiguïté existante dans de nombreux cas dans la division entre l'art et la marchandise s'accentue dans cette supposition. De fait, les prototypes des grands maîtres du XXe siècle (ces merveilleuses créations de Breuer, Van der Rohe, Le Corbusier ou Eames, parmi tant d'autres), et de ceux qui continuent à travailler avec leurs mains en ce XXIe siècle, pourront apparaître dans ce texte. Il y a une raison au fait que les grands musées et galeries les exposent comme faisant une partie de l'héritage culturel d'une époque■

En fait, il s'agit de chaises créées comme une excuse pour construire des espaces, comme des représentations architectoniques à petite échelle. Créées pour avoir des visions et des représentations, avec des pleins et des vides, avec des matériaux et des techniques. Chacune d'elles suppose une capacité de voir de façon différente les choses avec lesquelles nous cohabitons chaque jour. En fin de compte, ne s'agit-il pas d'art ?

Comme aurait dit Joyce, bienvenus à la tragi-comédie de la chaise, aux contradictions de la vie■

De gauche à droite : "Lotus chair" de David Delthony ; "The Cat Bird Seat" de Shannon Landis Hansen ; chaise de Gordon Chandler ; chaise en forme de fleur de David Burry. Toutes les œuvres font partie de la collection de la Galerie de l'Art Fonctionnel de Santa Mónica (Californie)■ *Page de droite :* Chaise créée par Alessandro Mendini (Milan, 1933), pour l'exposition "20 Artistes interprètent la Chaise", organisée par Promosedia■

1985 - 1998

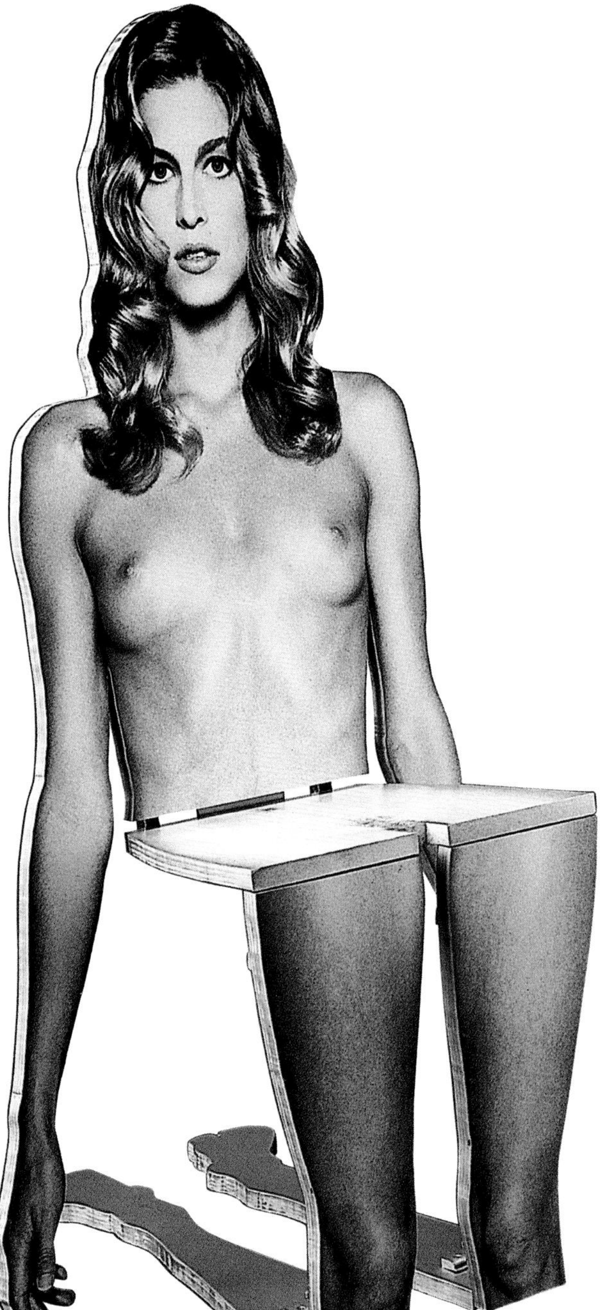

Pages précédentes : Image de l'exposition "100 Années-100 Chaises", organisée par le Vitra Design Museum de Weil am Rhein (Allemagne)■ *Image du haut :* Création de Piero Gemelli (Rome, 1952), faisant partie de l'exposition "20 Artistes interprètent la Chaise", organisée par Promosedia■

Chaise "Coveri" créée par l'architecte Raffaello Rossi pour la firme de mode italienne fondée par Enrico Coveri. Image fournie par Promosedia, de l'exposition "20 Artistes interprètent la Chaise"■

Sculpture en bois réalisée par Urano Palma (Varese, 1936), pour l'exposition "20 Artistes interprètent la Chaise", organisée par Promosedia■

Sculpture en fer de Shlomo Harush (Jérusalem, 1961). Fait partie de l'exposition "20 Artistes interprètent la Chaise", organisée par Promosedia■

Bancs réalisés par Gordon Chandler. De la collection de la Galerie de l'Art Fonctionnel de Santa Mónica (Californie)■

Photographie de Albano Guatti, évoquant l'arôme d'un passé simple et authentique à partir d'une vieille chaise. L'œuvre fait partie de l'exposition "20 Artistes interprètent la Chaise", organisée par Promosedia■

Création de l'artiste et designer Cesare Sartori (Vicenza, 1930) pour l'exposition "20 Artistes interprètent la Chaise", organisée par Promosedia■

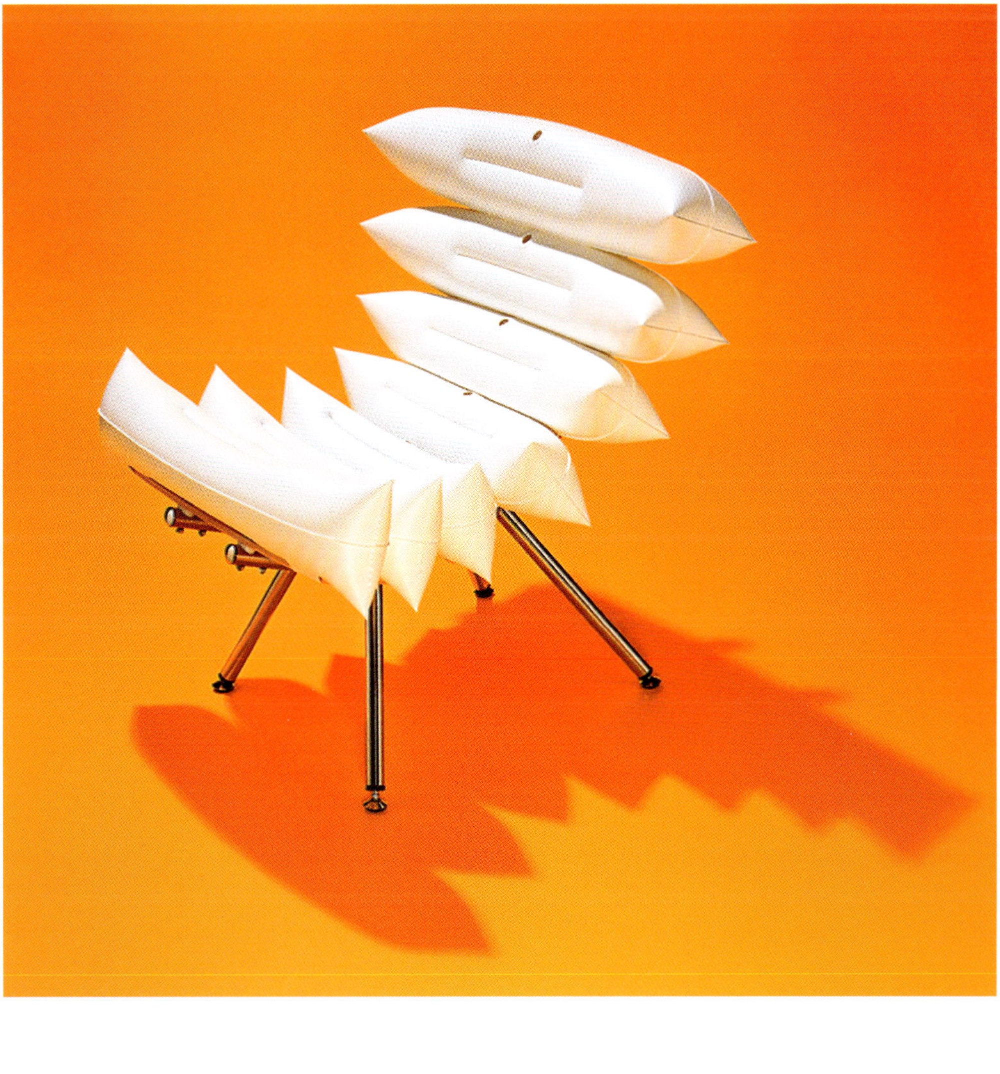

Fauteuil Gonflable "Lounge Chair Signal" créée par Nick Crosbie en 1997, fait partie de l'exposition itinérante "Blow Up-Shaped Air in Design, Architecture, Fashion and Art", organisée par le Vitra Design Museum de Berlin. (Photo : Jason Tozer/Inflate)■

À gauche : "Meteor Chair", une pièce d'art fonctionnel réalisée en acier■ *En haut :* "Chain Mail Chair", réalisée en acier inoxydable et côte de maille. Les deux pièces sont l'œuvre du sculpteur nord-américain Bruce Gray■

"Chopper" est une œuvre d'art fonctionnel de Bruce Gray, réalisée en acier peint■

Image en haut à gauche : CHAISE "ZIG-ZAG", réalisée en acier■ *En haut à droite :* "WEDGES CHAIR", réalisée en aluminium■ *Image d'en bas :* "E2 RIDER CHAIR", réalisée en acier et parties recyclées de motocyclette. Toutes les pièces sont l'œuvre de Bruce Gray■

"Triad Chair", réalisée en aluminium■ *À droite :* "Mehdown Chair", réalisée en acier. Les deux pièces sont l'œuvre de Bruce Gray■

Image d'en haut : Chaise "Scarlet", an 2000, réalisée en aluminium■ *En bas :* "Little Easy", an 2001, réalisée en aluminium. Les deux pièces sont l'œuvre de l'artiste nord-américain Christopher Poehlmann (Photo : Ed Chappell)■

CHAISE À BASCULE "RED ROCKER", 2002, de Christopher Poehlmann. Réalisée en aluminium (Photo : Ed Chappell)

Deux versions du modèle "CHUNKY CHAIR", créé par Christopher Poehlmann. Peut être fabriquée en acier ou en aluminium et avec diverses finitions■

La chaise "CHUNKY" avec une finition différente. Créée et réalisée par Christopher Poehlmann

L'artiste Kathryn Semolic récupère les anciennes pièces de mobilier pour leur donner une nouvelle vie grâce à la peinture et à la restauration■ *En haut :* CHAISE "GROWTH", décorée avec de la peinture acrylique■ *En bas :* CHAISE "GREAT BLUE HERONS"■

Chaise haute pour enfants "Apple of My Eye", peinte à la main avec les couleurs de l'arc-en-ciel. Selon sa créatrice, Kathryn Semolic, "chacune de mes pièces est une ode à la nature"■

Ron Arad est l'artifice de "AFTER SPRING", de 1992. C'est une chaise longue qui remplit également la fonction de chaise à bascule, réalisée en acier inoxydable poli■

"A.Y.O.R.", 1990, créée par Ron Arad pour la Galerie Mourmans. Lorsqu'on ne l'utilise pas, on peut incliner sa base arrondie et lui faire perdre son aspect de chaise■

Chaise "Well Tempered Chair" de Ron Arad. Design original de 1986, réalisée en acier trempé pour Vitra International■

Deux versions du fauteuil à bascule "Rolling Volume", créé en 1990 pour Ron Arad. Réalisé en acier satiné ou en acier inoxydable poli ; il n'existe que 20 pièces pour chaque finition■

Fauteuil en fibre de verre et polyester "New Orleans", 1999. Créé par Ron Arad pour la Galerie Mourmans, en une édition limitée à 18 pièces, toutes différentes

"NARROW PAPARDELLE", 1992, création de Ron Arad. Chaise au contour en acier, soudée à un tapis réalisé en acier inoxydable poli. La trame du tapis peut s'enrouler et faire office de repose-pied■

Deux perspectives différentes du tabouret en bronze poli "Fausto", créé par Novello Finotti pour Ultramobile

Deux perspectives du trône "MARGARITA", construit avec un tambour métallique recyclé et avec une structure en bronze. Créé par Sebastian Matta pour Ultramobile■

Pages 308 à 311 : Toutes les images font partie de l'exposition et du livre "150 articles, 150 œuvres d'art", dans lesquels, sur l'initiative de Kartell, 150 photographes et artistes contemporains donnent leur vision personnelle de diverses objets de design produits par cette firme italienne■
Image du haut : photographie de Bill Silano avec la chaise "FPE", créée par Ron Arad, comme protagoniste■

En haut : Bruce Weber est l'auteur de cette photographie où est exposée sa vision personnelle de la chaise "Eros", créée par Philippe Starck■ *En bas :* la même chaise fait l'objet d'une interprétation très différente aux yeux de Vanessa Beecroft■

Un jeu d'ombres est une proposition de Helmut Newton, dans lequel participe la chaise "La Marie", créée par Philippe Starck■

En haut : Luca Rabini est l'auteur de cette photographie où la chaise "Moorea" de Vico Magistretti est la protagoniste■
En bas : Enrique Badulescu propose ce portrait avec la chaise "La Marie", de Philippe Starck, en premier plan■

Posters de Knoll, contemporains aux créations présentées par Eero Saarinen. *En haut :* "DAD IN WOMB CHAIR", poster réalisé par Norman Rockwell■ *À gauche :* poster d'un ramoneur assis sur la chaise Womb■ *En bas :* poster présentant la collection "DIAMOND" de Bertoia■

À gauche, deux posters de Knoll : *En haut*, poster des chaises en plastique modelé de Saarinen▪ *En bas :* poster d'esthétique Pop, présentant la chaise TULIP▪ *À droite :* image de Tina Turner sur la chaise 3107 de Arne Jacobsen, produite par Fritz Hansen▪

RÉPERTOIRE

ACCADEMIA
Via Indipendenza, 4
33044 Manzano (Ud)
Italie
Tel. 39 0432 754439
Fax. 39 0432 751187
www.accademiaitaly.com

ACERBIS INTERNATIONAL SPA
Via Brusaporto 31
24068 Seriate (Bg)
Italie
Tel. 39 0352 94222
Fax. 39 0352 91454
www.acerbisinternational.com

AKABA
C/ Nagusia, 56
E-20160 Lasarte
Espagne
Tel. 34 943 372211
Fax. 34 943 371052
www.akaba.net

ALBUM S.R.L.
Via Cavallotti, 19
20046 Biassono (Milan)
Italie
Tel. 39 039 220041
Fax. 39 039 2200444
www.album.it

ALIAS SPA.
Via dei Videtti, 2
24064 Grumello del Monte (Bergamo)
Italie
Tel. 39 035 4422511
Fax. 39 035 4422590
www.aliasdesign.it

ALIVAR
Via B. Cellini, 190
50028 Tavernelle Val di Pesa
Italie
Tel. 39 055 8070115
Fax. 39 055 8070127
www.alivar.com

ALLSEATING
175, Britannia Rd. E. Unit 4
L4Z 4B8 Mississauga, Ontario
Canada
Tel. 1 800 5633502
Fax. 1 800 2729911
www.allseating.com

ANDREU WORLD, S.A.
Autovía A3 Madrid-Valence,
Km 323
46370 Chiva (Valence)
Espagne
Tel. 34 961 805 700
Fax. 34 961 805 701
www.andreuworld.com

ARCO MEUBELFABRIKEN B.V.
Parallelweg 2-III
7100 AA Winterswijk
Hollande
Tel. 31 543 51 25 04
Fax. 31 543 52 13 95
www.arcomeubel.nl

ARTEK
Eteläesplanadi, 18
00130 Helsinki
Finlande
Tel. 358 9 613 250
Fax. 358 9 6132 5260
www.artek.fi

ARTELANO
57 Rue Bourgogne
75007 Paris
France
Tel. 33 1 444 20161
Fax. 33 1 444 20160
www.artelano.com

B&B ITALIA SPA
Strada Provinciale 32
22060 Novedrate (Como)
Italie
Tel. 39 03179 5213
Fax. 39 03179 5224
www.bebitalia.it

BD EDICIONES DE DISEÑO
C/ Mallorca 291
08037 Barcelone
Espagne
Tel. 34 934 586909
Fax. 34 932 073679
www.bdbarcelona.com

BERNINI
Via Milano, 8
20020 Ceriano Laghetto (Mi)
Italie
Tel. 39 0296 469293
Fax. 39 0296 469646
www.bernini.it

BONALDO SPA
Via Straelle 3
35010 Villanova (Padova)
Italie
Tel. 39 049929 9011
Fax. 39 049929 9000
www.bonaldo.it

BONTEMPI FURNITURE
Via Direttissima del Conero, 71
60021 Camerano (An)
Italie
Tel. 39 071 7300032
Fax. 39 071 7300036
www.bontempifurniture.it

BULO
Industriezone Noord B6
B-2800 Mechelen
Belgique
Tel. 32 015 282828
Fax. 32 015 282829
www.bulo.be

CALLIGARIS SPA
Viale Trieste 12
33044 Manzano (Udine)
Italie
Tel. 39 043274 8211
Fax. 39 0432750104
www.calligaris.it

Campeggi srl
Via del Cavolto, 8
22040 Anzano del Parco (Co)
Italie
Tel. 39 031 630495
Fax. 39 031 632205
www.campeggisrl.it

Cappellini
Via Marconi, 35
22060 Arosio (CO)
Italie
Tel. 39 031 759111
Fax. 39 031 763322
www.cappellini.it

Carl Hansen & Søn
Kochsgade 97 -Postbox 225
DK 5100 Odense C.
Danemark
Tel. 45 6612 1404
Fax. 45 6591 6004
www.carlhansen.dk

Casas
Pol. Santa Rita; P.O. Box 1.333
08755 Castellbisbal (Barcelone)
Espagne
Tel. 34 93 7724600
Fax. 34 93 7722130
www.casas.net

Cassina
Via Busnelli, 1
I-20036 Meda (Mi)
Italie
Tel. 39 036 2372.1
Fax. 39 036 2342246
www.cassina.it

Cattelan Italia Spa
Via Pilastri 15
36010 Carre' (Vi)
Italie
Tel. 39 0445 318711
Fax. 390445 314289
www.cattelanitalia.it

CJC Concepta
Apdo. 243; Pol. Ind. "Els Xops";
Ctra. C-17, Km 17
08400 Granollers (Barcelone)
Espagne
Tel. 34 938 491377
Fax. 34 938 400060
www.cjconcepta.com

Classicon
Sigmund-Riefler-Bogen 3
81829 München
Allemagne
Tel. 49 089 748133-0
Fax. 49 089 7809996
www.classicon.com

Club 8 Company
Fabriksvej, 4 -P.O. Box 74
6870 Ogold
Danemark
Tel. 45 7013 1366
Fax. 45 7013 1367
www.club8company.com

Cor Sitzmöbel
Nonenstraße 12
D-33378 Rheda-Wiedenbrück
Allemagne
Tel. 49 0 5242 4102-0
www.cor.de

Crassevig
Via Ciampanutis, 2
33040 Como di Rosazzo (Ud)
Italie
Tel. 39 432 759043
www.crassevig.com

Davis Furniture Ind. Inc.
2401 South College Drive; P.O. Box 2065
NC 27261-2065 High Point
États-Unis
Tel. 336 8892009
Fax. 336 8890031
www.davisfurniture.com

Dema
Via della Città, 33
I-50052 Certaldo (Fi)
Italie
Tel. 39 0571 651232
Fax. 39 0571 651233
www.dema.it

Desalto
Via per Montesolaro
22063 Cantú (Como)
Italie
Tel. 39 031 7832211
Fax. 39 031 7832290
www.desalto.it

Do+Ce Muebles Doce,S.L.
Pol.Ind.Massanassa C/N.1 Nave 44
46470 Massanassa (Valence)
Espagne
Tel. 34 961 252 467
Fax. 34 961 252 554
www.do-ce.com

Domodinamica (Modular)
Via Molise, 23
40060 Osteria Grande (Bologne)
Italie
Tel. 39 51 845896
Fax. 39 51 945853
www.domodinamica.com

Driade
Via Padana Inferiore, 12
29012 Fossadello di Caorso (PC)
Italie
Tel. 39 0523 818618
Fax. 39 0523 822628
www.driade.com

E15 GmbH
Hospitalstraße 4
61440 Oberursel
Allemagne
Tel. 49 0 61 71 5 82 577
Fax. 49 0 61 71 582 578
www.e15.com

Edra spa
P.O. Box 29
56030 Perignano (Pisa)
Italie
Tel. 39 058761 6660
Fax. 39 058761 7500
www.edra.com

Emeco
805 Elm Avenue Hanover
17331 Pennsylvanie
États-Unis
Tel. 1 717 6375951
Fax. 1 717 6336018
www.emeco.net

Enea
Ola Auzea, 4

20250 Legorreta (Guipúzcoa)
Espagne
Tel. 34 943 806 275
Fax. 34 943 806 174

Erik Jørgensen
Industrivaenget, 1
DK-5700 Svendborg
Danemark
Tel. 45 6221 5300
Fax. 45 6222 9024
www.erik-joergensen.com

Fiam Italia
Via Ancona 1/b
61010 Tavullia (Pesaro)
Italie
Tel. 39 07212 0051
Fax. 39 072120 2432
www.fiamitalia.it

Fontana Arte spa
Alzaia Trieste, 49
20094 Corsico (Milano)
Italie
Tel. 39 0245121
Fax. 39 024512660
www.fontanaarte.it

Frag
Via dei Boschi, 2
33040 Pradamano
Italie
Tel. 39 0432 671375
Fax. 39 0432 670930
www.frag.it

Fredericia Furniture
Treldevej 183
7000 Fredericia
Danemark
Tel. 45 75 92 3344
Fax. 45 75 92 3876
www.fredericia.com

Fritz Hansen
Allerødvej, 8
DK-3450 Allerød
Danemark
Tel. 45 48172300
Fax. 45 48171948
www.fritzhansen.com

Galvano Tecnica
Zona Industriale Cosa
33097 Spilimbergo (Pordenone)
Italie
Tel. 39 042750150
Fax. 39 042750202
www.sintesi2.it

Halifax (Grupo Tisettanta)
Via Tofane, 37
20034 Giussano (Mi)
Italie
Tel. 39 0362 3191
Fax. 39 0362 319300
www.tisettanta.com

Hannah Mae Studios
2 East Workshop; Harley
Foundation
S80 3LW Werbeck-
Nottinghamshire
Angleterre
Tel. 44 7939 001903
Fax. 44 1909 506753
www.hannahmae.co.uk

Haworth
Von-Achenbach Strasse, 21-23
D-59229 Ahlen
Allemagne
Tel. 49 5042 501230
Fax. 49 5042 501190
www.haworth.de

Heller
41 Madison Avenue
10010 New York, NY
États-Unis
Tel. 212 685 4200
Fax. 212 685 4204
www.helleronline.com

Iform
Box 5055
SE 20071 Malmö
Suède
Tel. 46 040 303610
Fax. 46 040 302288
www.iform.net

Indecasa
C/ Manresa, 91-Apdo. Correos 20
08271 Artés (Barcelone)
Espagne
Tel. 34 938 305 225
Fax. 34 938 305 175
www.indecasa.com

Innovation Randers
Blommevej 38
8900 Randers
Danemark
Tel. 45 86 43 8211
Fax. 45 86 43 8488
www.inno.dk

Kagan New York Collection
P.O. Box 286434
10128 New York, NY
États-Unis
Tel. 212 2890031
Fax. 212 3607307
www.vladimirkagan.com

Kartell
Via delle Industrie, 1
20082 Noviglio (Mi)
Italie
Tel. 39 02 900121
Fax. 39 02 90091212
www.kartell.it

Knoll
105 Wooster Street
10012 New York, NY
États-Unis
Tel. 212 343 4158
Fax. 212 343 4194
www.knoll.com

Kristalia
Via Calderano, 5
33070 Brugnera (PN)
Italie
Tel. 39 0434 623678
Fax. 39 0434 624901
www.kristalia.it

Kundalini srl
Via de Sanctis 34
Milan
Italie
Tel. 39 02 84800088
Fax. 39 02 84800096
www.kundalini.it

Label Produkties B.V.
De Vliert 46
PB-4849 Dorst
Hollande
Tel. 31 0161 412642
Fax. 31 0161 412643
www.label.nl

Lago srl
Via Morosini 22/24
35010 San Giogio in Bosco (Padova)
Italie
Tel. 39 049599 4299
Fax. 39 049599 4199
www.lago.it

Lammhults
Box 26
SE-360 30 Lammhult
Suède
Tel. 46 472 269500
Fax. 46 472 260570
www.lammhults.se

Leolux
Kazernestraat 15
5928 Venlo
Hollande
Tel. 31 77 3 87 72 16
Fax. 31 77 3 87 72 88
www.leolux.nl

Liv' It (Grupo Fiam Italia)
Via Macerata, 9
61010 Tavulia (Ps)
Italie
Tel. 39 0721 202709
Fax. 39 0721 202711
www.livit.it

Living Divani
Strada del Cavolto
22040 Anzano del Parco (Co)
Italie
Tel. 39 031 630954
Fax. 39 031 632590
www.livingdivani.it

Magis
Via Magnadola 15
31045 Motta di Livenza (Treviso)
Italie
Tel. 39 04 22 76 87 42-3
Fax. 39 04 22 76 63 95
www.magisdesign.com

Magnus Olesen
Agertoft 2, Durup; Postbox 131
DK 7870 Roslev
Danemark
Tel. 45 97 592411
Fax. 45 97 592922
www.magnus-olesen.dk

Marcello Ziliani
Via Amba d'Oro, 68
25123 Brecia
Italie
Tel. 39 030 363758
Fax. 39 030 360430
www.marcelloziliani.com

Matteo Grassi
Via Padre Rovanati, 2
22066 Mariano Comense
Italie
Tel. 39 031 757 711
Fax. 39 031 748 388
www.matteograssi.it

Misura Emme
Via IV Novembre, 72
22066 Mariano Comense(Co)
Italie
Tel. 39 031 754111
Fax. 39 031 754111
www.misuraemme.it

Mobles 114,S.A.
Riera dels Frarers 24
08907 L'Hospitalet de
Llobregat (Barcelone)
Espagne
Tel. 34 932 600114
Fax. 34 932 600115
www.mobles114.com

Montina
Via Comunale del Rovere, 13-15
33048 S. Giovanni al Natisone (Ud)
Italie
Tel. 39 0432 747300
Fax. 39 0432 747377
www.montina.it

Montis
Steenstraat 2-postbus 153
5100 AD Dongen
Hollande
Tel. (01)162377777
www.montis.nl

Moooi
Minervum 7003
4817 ZL Breda
Hollande
Tel. 31 (0) 76 5722070
Fax. 31 (0) 76 5722069
www.moooi.com

Natison Sedia
XI° Zona Industriale Regionale
33040 Moimacco (Ud)
Italie
Tel. 39 0432 733431
Fax. 39 0432 733407
www.natison.it

Offix Klass
Via Casali, 52
33048 S.Giovanni al Natisone
(Udine)
Italie
Tel. 39 0432 744944
Fax. 39 0432 744955
klass@offix.it

Oken
Narváez s/n; Pol. Ind. "Can Jardí
08191 Rubí (Barcelona)
Espagne
Tel. 34 935 882568
Fax. 34 935 880345
www.oken.es

Perobell
Avda. Arraona 23
08205 Sabadell (Barcelone)
Espagne
Tel. 34 937 457 900
Fax. 34 937 271 500
www.perobell.com

Poltrona Frau
S.S. 77 Km. 74,500
I-62029 Tolentino
Italie
Tel. 39 0733 909.1
Fax. 39 0733 971600
www.poltronafrau.it

Promemoria
Via per Como 84/a
23868 Valmadrera (Lecco)
Italic
Tel. 39 0341 581021
Fax. 39 0341 210054

Pure Design
16646-111 Ave. Edmonton
T5M 2S5 Alberta
Canada
Tel. 780 4835644
Fax. 780 4835661
www.puredesignonline.com

Quinze & Milan Designers
Poortakkerstraat 17
9051 Gent
Belgique
Tel. 32 9 2459605
Fax. 32 9 2459606
www.quinzeandmilan.tv

Robots spa
Via Galvani 7
20082 Binasco (Milano)
Italie
Tel. 39 02 90 54 661
Fax. 39 02 90 54 664
www.robots.it

Ron Arad Associates
62 Chalk Farm Road
NW1 8AN Londres
Angleterre
Tel. 44 020 72844963
Fax. 44 020 73790499
www.ronarad.com

Santa & Cole
Stma. Trinidad del Monte, 10
08017 Barcelone
Espagne
Tel. 34 934 183 396
Fax. 34 934 183 812
www.santacole.com

Sawaya & Moroni
Via Andegari, 18
20121 Milan
Italie
Tel. 39 02 863951
Fax. 39 02 86464831
www.sawayamoroni.com

SCP
135-139 Curtain Road
EC2A 3BX Londres
Angleterre
Tel. 44 020 7739 1869
Fax. 44 020 7729 4224
www.scp.co.uk

Schmidinger Modul
Stangenach 146
a-6867 Schwarzenberg/Voralberg
Autriche
Tel. 43 5512 2782-14
Fax. 43 5512 2782-2
www.schmidingermodul.at

Segis
P.O. Box 279- Loc. Fosci;
Via Umbria, 14
53036 Poggibonsi (Si)
Italie
Tel. 39 0577 980333
Fax. 39 0577 938090
www.segis.it

Sellex
Donosti Ibilbidea, 84
20115 Astigarraga (Gipuzkoa)
Espagne
Tel. 34 943 557011
www.sellex.es

Sintesi 2 spa
Zona Industriale Cosa
33097 Spilimbergo (Pordenone)
Italie
Tel. 39 0427 3138
Fax. 39 04274 0077
www.sintesi2.it

Snowcrash
Textilwägen 1
SE-12030 Estocolmo
Suède
Tel. 46 8 4429810
Fax. 46 8 4429811
www.snowcrash.se

Stua
Poligono 26
20115 Astigarraga
Espagne
Tel. 34 943 330 188
Fax. 34 943 556 002
www.stua.com

Tecta
Sohnreystraße 10
37697 Lauenförde
Allemagne
Tel. 49 5273 37890
Fax. 49 5273 378933
www.tecta.de

Tonon & C spa
Via Diaz 22
33044 Manzano (Ud)
Italie
Tel. 39 0432 740740
Fax. 39 0432 740770
www.tononItalia.com

Triangolo (AC&T srl)
Via Icaro, 10
61100 Pesaro
Italie
Tel. 39 0721 425356
Fax. 39 0721 268614
e-mail: ac-t@ac-t.net

Ultramobile
Via della Resistenza
61030 Calcinelli di Sattara (PU)
Italie
Tel. 39 0721 878511
Fax. 39 0721 878545
www.ultramobile.it

Umbra
1705 Broadway
14212 Buffalo, New York
États-Unis
Tel. 800 387 5122
www.umbra.com

Vibiemme srl
Via Cividale 44
33044 Manzano (Udine)
Italie
Tel. 39 043275 0473
Fax. 39 043274 0050
www.vibiemme.it

Vitra Hispania
Pl. Marqués de Salamanca 10,
1° dcha
28006 Madrid
Espagne
Tel. 34 914 264 560
Fax. 34 915 783 217
www.vitra.com

Vitra International AG
Klünenfeldstrasse 22
CH-4127 Birsfelden
Suisse
Tel. 41 613 770 000
Fax. 41 613 771 510
www.vitra.com

Wilde + Spieth GmbH & Co.
Zeppelinstraße 126
D-73730 Esslingen
Allemagne
Tel. 49 0711 31971-0
Fax. 49 0711 31971-55
www.wilde-spieth.com

CHAISES ET ART

Wilkhahn
Fritz-Hahne Straße, 8
D-31848 Bad Münder
Allemagne
Tel. 49 5042 999-0
Fax. 49 5042 999-226
www.wilkhahn.com

Wunderkammer Studio
Via Lombardini, 24
Milan
Italie
Tel/Fax. 39 02 8372781
www.wunderkammerstudio.it

Yamakado
Viaduc des Arts- 65, Avenue
Daumesnil
75012 Paris
France
Tel. 33 0 1 43 40 79 79
Fax. 33 0 1 43 40 79 80

Ycami
Via Porvinciale 31-33
22060 Novedrate (Como)
Italie
Tel. 39 031 7897311
Fax. 39 031 789735
info@ycami.com

Zanotta spa
Via Vittorio Veneto 57
20054 Nova Milanese (Mi)
Italie
Tel. 39 0362 4981
Fax. 39 0362 451038
www.zanotta.it

Zeus Noto
Corso San Gottardo 21/9
20136 Milan
Italie
Tel. 39 0289 401198
Fax. 39 0289 401142
www.zeusnoto.com

Zoltan
Via Croce, 8
20090 Vimodrone
Italie
Tel. 39 0227 400160
Fax. 39 0227 400184
www.zoltan.it

Bruce Gray
688 South Avenue 21
90031 Los Angeles (CA)
États-Unis
Tel. (323) 223-4059
www.brucegray.com
Bgrayart@aol.com

Christopher Poehlmann
727, 102nd Avenue North
34108 Naples (FL)
États-Unis
Tel. (866) 597-4800
www.christopherpoehlmann.com
cpinfo@cplighting.com

Fritz Hansen
Allerødvej, 8
DK-3450 Allerød
Danemark
Tel. 45 48172300
Fax. 45 48171948
www.fritzhansen.com

Galerie de l'Art Fonctionnel de Santa Mónica
Bergamot Station, 2525
Michigan Ave. E3
90404 Santa Mónica (CA)
États-Unis
Tel. 1 (310) 829-6990
Fax. 1 (310) 829-5707
www.galleryoffunctionalart.com
gfa1@mindspring.com

Kartell
Via delle Industrie, 1
20082 Noviglio (Mi)
Italie
Tel. 39 02 900121
Fax. 39 02 90091212
www.kartell.it

Kathryn Semolic
(Spider Mountain Studio)
29 Nova Street
72632 Eureka Springs (AR)
États-Unis
Tel. 1 (479) 363-9682
www.spidermountainstudio.com
kathryn@spidermountainstudio.com

Knoll
105 Wooster Street
10012 New York, NY
États-Unis
Tel. 212 343 4158
Fax. 212 343 4194
www.knoll.com

Promosedia
(Salon International de la Chaise)
Via Trieste 9/6
33044 Manzano (Ud)
Italie
Tel. 39 0432 745611
Fax. 39 0432 755316
www.promosedia.it
promosedia@promosedia.it

Ron Arad Associates
62 Chalk Farm Road
NW1 8AN Londres
Angleterre
Tel. 44 020 72844963
Fax. 44 020 73790499
www.ronarad.com

Ultramobile
Via della Resistenza
61030 Calcinelli di Sattara (PU)
Italie
Tel. 39 0721 878511
Fax. 39 0721 878545
www.ultramobile.it

Vitra Design Museum
Charles Eames Str. 1
D-79576 Weil am Rhein
Allemagne
Tel. 49 (0) 7621/702 37 29
Fax. 49 (0) 7621/702 4729
www.design-museum.de
reiner.packeiser@design-museum.de